RUTHLESS HAWKE

A SECOND GENERATION HAWKE FAMILY NOVEL

BILLIONAIRES OF NEW ORLEANS: THE HAWKE
FAMILY SECOND GENERATION
BOOK 1

GWYN MCNAMEE

RUTHLESS HAWKE
© 2023 Gwyn McNamee

Cover Model: Andrew Biernat

Photographer: Wander Aguiar

Cover Design: Michelle Johnson at Bluesky Design

Editing: Stephie Walls at Wallflower Edits

To anyone who ever felt the weight of expectations and broke free of them...

HAWKE FAMILY TREE

THE HAWKE FAMILY
Antonia and Sam "The Savage" Hawke

SAVAGE COLLISION

Savage Hawke & Danika Eriksson
|
Kennedy Hawke

STONE COLD

Stone Hawke & Nora Eriksson
/ \
Isaac Hawke   Coen Hawke

TAINTED SAINT

Solomon "Saint" Clarke & Caroline Brooks
/ \
Pope Clarke   Bishop Clarke

TORTURED SKYE

Skye Hawke & Gabe Anderson
/ \
Atlas Anderson   Astrid Anderson

BUILDING STORM

Storm Hawke (Matthews) & Landon McCabe
/ \
Angelina Matthews   Alessandra McCabe

STEEL RESOLVE

Luca "Steele" Abello & Byron Harris
|
Jude Harris-Abello (ad)

1

ISAAC

Nothing better prepares me for doing battle against some asshole in the courtroom than having my dick sucked by the judge's clerk right before the hearing.

And Tina is a damn queen when it comes to working over my cock and relieving all my stress so I can go to counsel's table with a clear mind.

Sweet fucking hell, is she good...

Groaning, I drop my head back against the door of her office while she swirls her tongue around my length, one hand grasping the base, the other digging sharp nails into my bare thigh. My hips jerk, pushing me forward slightly, and she issues a little moan of approval and redoubles her efforts, sucking me deep into her throat.

"Fuck, Tina..."

I bury my fingers in her curly, blond hair, tugging on the strands and squeezing my eyes closed to rein in the need to drive harder into her mouth and fuck away the true frustration of having to be here today for this hearing has built up within me.

Bad fucking idea.

As soon as I lose sight of the woman on her knees in front of me, the face of another one flashes through my head.

The blond strands become red...

Blue eyes become amber...

Not fucking now.

I should have known it would happen today, should have anticipated *her* haunting me on the fifth anniversary of our spectacular weekend together in Chicago, but all I want is to enjoy the woman I'm *with* and forget about the one who inhabits my fantasies relentlessly.

As if that's ever worked.

Day after day. Week after week. Month after month. Year after year. Nothing changes. I still feel the gentle brush of her hand, the way her cunt encased me so perfectly. Her moans and gasps still ring in my ears like some ethereal call to find her when it's impossible.

God knows I've fucking tried...

I shake my head to try to clear the old memories and tighten my grip on Tina's blond tresses. She twists her hand up my shaft with each withdrawal of her mouth, dragging me even closer to release.

The alarm on my phone blares, warning us that court will start in a few minutes, but it doesn't even faze her. If anything, it only spurs her on, makes her more determined. She keeps going harder, working me over like a true master.

Shit.

Judge Cramer is nothing if not punctual, and he'll be walking into his chambers right next door to Tina's office any minute now.

Fuck.

There's one surefire way to make sure I come before he does. And it's the one thing I don't want to do. The thing I've been avoiding since the minute Tina dragged me back here and put her mouth on me, but I do it anyway.

I close my eyes and picture *her* on her knees, *her* lips wrapped around me, sucking me down. I hear *her* voice echoing in my ear, saying the name I gave her.

Nolan...

"Fuck!" I explode instantly, cum shooting out of my cock into Tina's eager mouth. "Fuck, fuck, fuck..."

She swallows it quickly, the rippling of her throat making my body spasm even more until I finally have nothing left but regret at having to use that memory when I'm with Tina.

I sag back against the door, relax my grip on her hair, and let my eyes drift open to meet her green ones staring up at me with amusement.

Tina climbs to her feet, straightens her skirt, and casually walks over to her desk to grab the files on it, as if she didn't just work me over like a fucking queen.

I suck in a heavy breath as I grab my boxer briefs and pants from around my knees and tug them back up, tucking in my still-hard cock and securing my belt in place. "That was incredible."

Truly.

And just what I needed this morning to break through the dark cloud of annoyance hanging over me at having to be back here to argue about the same thing again and again.

She grins at me over her shoulder, her pride making her practically glow in the harsh, artificial fluorescent light. "I know."

I bark out a laugh and run a hand through my hair. "Am I going to see you tonight?"

Files in hand, she approaches and shakes her head. "No. I have a date."

I raise a brow at her. "Really, who with?"

She leans in and smiles coyly. "Why? You *jealous*?"

With a smirk, I reach out and run my thumb under her lips to wipe away the smeared lipstick. Our little arrangement works so well for both of us precisely because there *is* no jealousy. We get our itches scratched when we need to, with no feelings involved.

If she really is dating someone now, I'd be happy for her and would back off so there weren't any potential problems. But the same protectiveness that always rises when any of the Hawke women go out with anyone swells in my chest.

"Not jealous. Curious." And concerned. "Who is he?"

She presses a quick kiss to my cheek before she reaches for the door handle at my side. "It's a blind date, actually. A friend set me up."

The words *"blind date"* flash through my head and tense my shoulders. I grab her arm, my humor deflating slightly. "Do you know anything about the guy? You need to be careful, Tina."

Her gaze softens. "He's an old friend of my *best* friend who just moved to town. I assure you, she's known him since they were like ten, and he's completely safe."

No man is completely safe. If I've learned anything during my time working on criminal cases with the Innocence Project in law school and doing the dirty work for the family since graduating, it's that very simple fact.

"Just be careful and let me know if I need to have a talk with the guy."

Her lips curl into a grin. "Thanks for watching out for me, Counselor."

My unease over the situation relaxes slightly. "You know I always will."

She nods and twists the doorknob, and I step away so she can tug open the door just as heavy footsteps echo down the hall, moving toward us.

Tina casts a quick peek at me before smiling at whoever approaches. "Good morning, Judge."

I give myself a once-over to ensure I'm presentable and grab my briefcase from the floor, where I tossed it when I came in so I can follow her out. "Good morning, Your Honor."

His old blue eyes widen, his bushy, white brows rising up his wrinkled forehead. "Mr. Hawke, you're here early."

Tina smiles and holds up the files in her hand. "He needed me to make some copies for today's hearing. I got it taken care of, Judge."

The old man bobs his head. "Oh, excellent. Excellent. So, we'll be ready for the hearing to proceed?"

I shrug. "As long as Attorney Whitaker shows up and is prepared to proceed, I'm ready to go."

Judge Cramer waves me off. "Yes, yes. You're always ready. I don't have to worry about you. It's the other one I worry about..." He mumbles the last few words under his breath. "I'm going to grab my coffee, then I'll be right out."

He trudges back to his chambers while I follow Tina into the main courtroom for what promises to be another contentious hearing if Whitaker continues his typical bullshit.

Which he will.

His clients show no intention of slowing down their campaign against the Hawkes, and he doesn't seem at all fazed by coming in here and defending their actions.

Bailiff Henry inclines his head toward us from his post next to the double doors of the courtroom, and the object of my disdain and the reason we're here today pushes through them from the main courthouse hallway and offers me a smug grin.

Douchebag.

Turning my back to him, I settle at the plaintiff's table, and he casually strolls through the swinging wooden gate that separates the spectator area and slides his briefcase onto the defense table next to mine.

He slowly lowers himself into his chair, apparently confident he's got this hearing in the bag, if his relaxed, nonchalant demeanor and smugness mean anything. Unless he knows something I don't, the man is delusional to believe he's going to win today.

I pull out my file and flip it open to the injunction I filed. "You ready to go, Cass?"

Asshole.

His lips twitch. "I'm always ready to go, Isaac. You know that."

"It would save both of us an awful lot of time and energy if you could get your client to just stop with this bullshit."

A slow grin pulls at his lips. "And miss all this fun?"

Arrogant fucker.

Almost two years of this, and they're still going at it with no end in sight. And Cassius Whitaker seems to enjoy it far more than he should, given the number of times I've wiped the floor with him.

His clients don't appear to have learned their lesson yet, but today, I will ensure they get the message—when you go up against the Hawkes, you're playing with fire and you're going to get burned.

Judge Cramer steps out from chambers, and Tina stands.

Bailiff Henry's deep voice rolls through the courtroom. "All rise."

Judge motions for us to be seated as he lowers himself into his. "Everyone sit."

Tina hands him the file, and he flips it open and takes a sip of his cup of coffee, examining the contents even though he clearly knows why we're here today based on our earlier interaction in chambers.

She peeks my way before she retakes her seat and calls the case. "The court calls Orleans Parish case number 2023-022323. Hawke Enterprises, Inc. versus Falco Enterprises, Inc."

Judge Cramer looks up from the file. "Good morning, Counselors."

I rise and incline my head toward him in acknowledgment. "Good morning, Your Honor. Isaac Hawke appears on behalf of Hawke Enterprises, Incorporated."

Whitaker does the same. "Good morning, Your Honor. Cassius Whitaker appears on behalf of Falco Enterprises, Incorporated."

And is a total dick.

We take our seats again as the judge continues to flip through the file. Finally, he eases back in his chair and darts his shrewd gaze between us. "We're here this morning for a decision on the injunction request of Hawke Enterprises. I've reviewed the submissions of both parties, and I'm ready to hear any oral arguments you've prepared."

Oh, I'm definitely prepared.

It's time to really let Whitaker and Falco Enterprises have it.

I push to my feet. "Your Honor, while our affidavits and attachments filed with the injunction clearly demonstrate the violation of Hawke Enterprises' trademarks by the defendants." I cast a pointed glare at opposing counsel. "*Again.* I would like to say a few additional things about this matter."

He nods. "Of course, Counsel."

"As Your Honor is well aware, this injunction request mirrors several others that this court has granted over the last few months." I look at Whitaker. "And frankly, the pattern that's emerged has gone from problematic and annoying to outright harassment. Hawke Enterprises has valid trademarks on dozens of business names and logos, and the Hawke family has been a pillar of this community for decades, operating numerous businesses, spanning from restaurants to coffee shops to bars and even adult entertainment establishments." I tighten my jaw. "But over the last few years, Falco Enterprises has decided to compete with Hawke Enterprises in these areas. Now, there's nothing illegal about some friendly competition in the business sector, but what is concerning to me and should be to this court is the apparent attempt by Falco Enterprises to violate those trademarks continually—"

Attorney Whitaker starts to get to his feet. "Your Honor, if I may interject—"

"No, you may not." The judge's glare cuts like a knife across the room. "You'll have your chance, and you're going to let Mr. Hawke finish."

I fight a smirk and catch Tina doing the same.

It's time to lay this out for Whitaker and hope he can get it back to his clients in a way they will understand.

"The first incident was the opening of 'The Hawk Club' adult entertainment establishment eighteen months ago, which was not only named very similarly but also included a business logo that bears a striking resemblance to that of 'The Hawk*eye* Club' owned by Hawke Enterprises. As the court and Mr. Whitaker are aware, you ruled in favor of Hawke Enterprises in their injunction based on the trademark of said name and logo due to the risk of confusion. Then, you ruled in favor of Hawke Enterprises again twelve months ago, nine months ago, and seven months ago when Falco Enterprises opened 'The Hawk Bar,' 'The Hawk Grill,' and 'The Hawk House Tavern.' Again, because all bore strikingly similar names and logos to existing Hawke Enterprises entities."

I shake my head and spread out my hands. "I'm not sure how much more direct I can be about this, Your Honor. After four decisions against Mr. Whitaker's client, they continue to pursue this avenue of business practice. Now, they've opened a restaurant with a similar name and logo to an existing Hawke Enterprises restaurant and expect there to be a different result."

Judge Cramer narrows his eyes on Whitaker. "Do you care to offer an explanation on behalf of your clients?"

Whitaker pushes to his feet, rebuttoning his suit coat. "I would, Your Honor. Falco Enterprises adamantly maintains that none of these businesses violate the trademarks of Hawke Enterprises. The Hawkes spell their name with an *E* at the end, and none of Falco Enterprises' businesses use that spelling. In addition, the Falco Enterprises' logos—with respect to all these entities—are distinct enough that there is no room for confusion in the marketplace."

The coolness in Judge Cramer's look could ice over the room. "My decisions have begged to differ, Attorney Whitaker."

"And the court is aware that those are under appeal. But appeals take time, Your Honor, and Falco Enterprises can't sit back and do nothing while it waits for your decisions to be overturned by the higher court."

Judge Cramer doesn't appear as amused by Whitaker's words as I am.

"If I may respond, Your Honor?"

"Yes, Mr. Hawke."

I climb to my feet and rebutton my suit coat, squaring my shoulders. "I'm not sure what Falco Enterprises has against the Hawkes, whether it's a personal issue or they just want to ride the coattails of someone who came before them to make some easy money, but I have confidence that the court's prior rulings on these issues are correct as a matter of law and will be upheld on any appeals. I would further ask Attorney Whitaker to inform his clients—as I've asked him *many* times before—to reconsider their business plan because if they want to continue to harass my family, they will be facing a lot worse than what's already been done in this courtroom."

Okay, that might have gone a bit too far.

Threatening the opposing party is generally frowned upon in the legal system, but the fact that these douchebags insist on repeatedly coming after us like this has pushed me to the point of no return. I won't stop at filing suits against them for tortuous interference, intentional infliction of emotional distress, and anything else I can come up with, either.

It's long past the time to play dirty and take care of things *outside* of court. Everyone loves the Hawkes, and there are plenty of people in New Orleans willing to help us fight our battles.

Whitaker shifts slightly on his feet, the only hint of unease at my words. "Your Honor—"

"No." Judge Cramer cuts him off, holding up a hand and

leaning forward. "I am again ruling in favor of Hawke Enterprises and granting the injunction. Falco Enterprises will change the name and the logo to avoid brand confusion with any Hawke Enterprises entities. And counsel...I'm going to warn you right now that this continued practice is likely to result in additional trouble for you, including lawsuits from the Hawkes that I'm frankly surprised they haven't filed already."

Only because we've been trying to dig through layers and layers of shell companies and trusts to determine who actually owns *Falco Enterprises...*

If we're going to an all-out war, we're dragging these people in personally and not just going after the corporate entity.

Judge shakes his head, seemingly as exasperated with the situation as I am. "Everyone in New Orleans knows the Hawkes and enjoys their establishments. Perhaps you should tell your clients to learn to do the same instead of copying them."

Tina hands a paper to Judge Cramer.

He scans it. "And I see Attorney Hawke has been kind enough to prepare the order for the court to sign. Thank you, Mr. Hawke."

"Of course, Your Honor."

Tina fights a smile as she types in the notes on her computer.

Judge scribbles his signature on the prepared order. "We're done, Counselors."

Thank fuck.

That wasn't nearly as bad as I had anticipated it would be. I thought I would have to bring out some of my boxing moves— throwing jabs and hooks at this fucker. But it seems Judge Cramer is at the end of his rope just as much as the family is with all this.

I slide my file back into my briefcase, incline my head to Tina and the judge, and make my way out of the courtroom and into the hallway. Whitaker follows behind me shortly and stops next to me, releasing a light sigh as he scans the corridor and examines the people hustling back and forth.

He casually checks his watch.

It takes every ounce of willpower I possess not to deck him right here. Remaining professional in the courtroom is one thing, but if I ever ran into this fucker on the street, it would be a different story. "You didn't think you were going to get a different result today, did you?"

Whitaker offers a slight shrug. "I get paid the same no matter what the result is. If my clients want to keep defending lawsuits, I'll keep showing up as long as they're still dropping $500 an hour for it." He smirks. "Judge Cramer won't be around forever, you know. Your dad and uncles may have him in their hip pocket, but eventually, we'll get a judge who understands the law and isn't blinded by their loyalty to your family."

I let out a mirthless laugh. "You really are an arrogant prick, aren't you?"

"You have no idea."

The fucker has the balls to wink at me before he saunters down the hall.

My phone vibrates in my inner coat pocket, and I pull it out to check the message—likely Dad or Kennedy checking in on what happened in the hearing.

UNCLE GABE

Get back to the office ASAP. Family emergency.

Shit. This can't be good.

MINA

THE CITY of New Orleans flies by outside the window of the SUV, foreboding storm clouds building in the sky above it. It mirrors the dark dread resting squarely on my chest and the unstable anger brewing inside me that's only grown since this awful day began.

"Mina, look at me, *tesoro.*"

I continue to stare out the window, refusing to give my attention to the man who has caused all this turmoil and ripped me from my life without any real explanation.

His hand curls around my forearm and tightens gently, the touch full of all the love and affection he's always given me, but also with the fear of how he anticipates I'll lash out at him. "Please, *tesoro...*"

Like using that nickname is somehow going to break the stony wall I've put up for very good reason. He knows the one surefire way to piss me off—and he's done *just* that.

Made decisions about *my* life for me while keeping me in the damn dark.

Once again, giving me no option.

Making demands.

Issuing orders.

Sometimes, it's hard to process how much I can love him and hate him at the same time, but maybe that's just the nature of family. They're the only ones capable of hurting you so much in the name of protecting you.

I finally glower at him in the driver's seat, trying to fight the desire to lash out in the confined space. "I don't have anything else to say to you."

The flight here from Chicago gave me plenty of time to let him know my thoughts on being woken at the asscrack of dawn, told to pack a single bag, and then being forced to board a plane without any idea what the hell was going on—without even an opportunity to say goodbye to Mom.

His jaw tightens while he maintains his focus on the road. "Look, I understand you're pissed at your mother and me, but this is the best thing. I promise—"

This is the best thing?

Insanity!

He's literally *insane* if he really believes that.

"How is it the best thing for me to be here and not with you and Mom? You've spent years preventing me from leaving Chicago, telling me I have to stay there and live with you because it's the only place that's safe. You kept me from going to art school in Paris. You kept me from going out on my own. But now, you're sending me away like you can't wait to get rid of me and acting like home is the most unsafe place on the planet."

His hand slips from my arm, and he pushes it back through his dishwater-blond hair that's finally starting to show signs of gray after all these years. "I won't involve you in this."

"Yeah, no shit." I cross my arms over my chest with a huff of annoyance. "You know, maybe if you *actually* told me everything instead of trying to hide the truth, it would make this a little easier on everyone."

A muscle in his jaw tics as he considers his response. "If you knew the truth of what your mother and I do...the threats I have to protect all of us from every day, you'd never leave the goddamn house."

I scowl at him. "I barely do *now*. You don't fucking *let* me."

"That's for good reason, Mina. More than one." He glances at me before returning his attention to the road. His hands tighten on the wheel until his knuckles whiten. "This isn't some fucking game. The people we're dealing with mean business. They're going to make a point, and they're going to do it by coming after the people your mother and I care about. You're at the top of that fucking list."

"Then why can't I go wherever you and Mom are headed?"

"Because having all of us in one place is a recipe for disaster. Your mother is safe. By bringing you here, someplace they can never find you, then I can be confident *you're* safe and I can concentrate on doing what *I* have to do. The Hawkes *will* keep you safe."

The confidence in his voice should give me some, but without knowing what's happening, all I can feel in the moment is anger and unease. I don't know these people, never met a single one of them, yet I'm being asked to just *accept* that he's dumping me here and not offering any sort of explanation.

"How do you know that?"

All I've heard about the Hawkes over the years is that they are some sort of pussy peddlers in New Orleans. People Dad knows going way back. It doesn't exactly instill a lot of confidence in using them as a hideout from whatever threat Mom has brought on us today.

"There are very few people in this world I trust more than Gabe Anderson. He saved my life more times than I can count. If anyone is going to be able to keep you hidden and safe, it's going to be him and his family. He knows how to deal with these situations, and nobody will ever link us to them."

"You hope."

He slams his hand against the steering wheel, the tension of the day finally boiling over. "Why can't you just trust me, Mina?"

"Because you don't trust *me!* Every time I find something that makes me happy, something I want, you destroy it."

A flash of another car ride where I felt the exact same way hits me so hard it steals my breath. All the anguish of that morning, of the ones that followed, slam into me and make my eyes burn with unshed tears.

Oh, my God...

I check the radio clock display in the SUV and zero in on the date.

Of all the days...

No wonder the memory feels so fresh, so painful.

Things are so different from five years ago, yet so much has stayed the same. Mother and Father controlling me.

Commanding my life like I'm some sort of marionette on strings. Telling me what's good for me. Dictating what I have to do. Demanding what's *required* of me.

How can everything have changed, yet nothing has changed in five damn years?

I release a heavy sigh and rest my temple against the cool glass as Dad takes a left turn and pulls to a stop in front of an old, painted brick building that reminds me of every photograph I've ever seen of historic NOLA.

If I weren't so annoyed at the moment, I might be able to actually appreciate the beauty of it all.

"Look, Mina..." Dad throws the SUV into park, turns to me, and pulls off his sunglasses. He must mean business if he's doing that. "There's only one thing that's important to me, one thing that matters in this fucking world—my family. I will protect each and every one of you with my last fucking breath. Do you understand me? Even if it means you hate me for it."

A knife twists in my chest at the pain in his statement. "I don't hate you, Dad."

He barks out a mirthless laugh. "Really? Because you're fucking acting like it now."

"I hate *this*." I spread out my hands. "I hate the *situation*. I hate the fact that you're always trying to decide my life and what's best for me. I'm twenty-six years old. I can make decisions for myself."

"We're not going to discuss the consequences of your decisions right now, Mina, because we're here." He points toward the building. "We'll go in, talk to Gabe and the Hawkes, figure out a plan, and then, I have to take care of business."

"You're really not going to tell me everything?"

He releases a little sigh, the same one he has always given me when I push him to tell me something he can't or won't. "You know I can't. It would only put you in more danger. And you know what could happen if you're under too much stress."

Like dragging me from my bed without explanation isn't stressful?

"I'm not dumb, Dad. I understand the kind of shit that goes on behind closed doors with yours and Mom's 'business associates' or whatever you want to call them—"

"There are things that could put you in even more danger if you knew them, and you have to trust me, Mina. Your life depends on it."

It isn't the first time I've heard this speech from him, but it is the first time I've seen this look in his eyes.

He's *scared.*

Dad doesn't *get* scared.

Not ever.

Until this very moment, I didn't even realize it was possible, but there it is, staring back at me in white and blue.

I push open my door. "It's not like I have a choice, anyway."

All I can do is go along with whatever he has planned.

I can't run.

I can't hide.

There *is* no hiding from who I am, and there never will be.

I learned that the hard way a long time ago and have had to deal with the very real fallout of that. Today is no exception. No one can control who shares their blood, and what runs through my veins is precisely what makes me a target.

Dad steps out onto the street, sliding the shades back into place and scanning around us, ever vigilant, the skills drilled into him in the military always present. He looks over the hood at me. "Grab Vivi, and let's go."

A bird flies overhead, swooping and swirling in the ocean-scented air blowing in with the storm. I inhale deeply what might be my last breath of fresh air for a long time. Something tells me that what is going on isn't going to resolve easily or quickly, and Dad doesn't have any intention of allowing me anywhere someone might get to me. That means keeping me under lock and key.

Apparently controlled by the Hawkes.

I open the back door of the SUV and carefully unstrap Viviana from her booster seat, trying not to wake her. It's been a long, eventful day already, and the last thing I need is her melting down because she's exhausted and confused about what's happening. It's hard enough keeping myself together through this; it might not be possible with a tired and cranky four-year-old.

As far as she knows, this is a "vacation" with her grandfather, and we've done our best to hide our concern over the rushed flight out of Chicago from her. Relatively easily done so far, but once she's more alert, she'll be asking questions that will be hard to answer.

Especially when I don't even know anything.

Her eyes flutter slightly, and I gather her in my arms. She wraps hers around my neck and clings to me, burying her face against my shoulder with a little groan before she settles back down.

Hopefully, back to sleep.

Dad monitors the area, his body tense, sunglasses-covered eyes zeroing in on the movements of every person walking down the sidewalk and every vehicle passing by on the street.

He approaches the building, pulls open the door, and I follow him into *Hawke Law.*

A middle-aged woman sits at a desk in the center of an opulent yet tastefully elegant waiting area. She looks up at us from her computer with a quick jerk of her strawberry-blond head. "Oh, hello, can I help you?"

Dad approaches her but doesn't remove the glasses when she stares at him like he's crazy for wearing them indoors. "I'm here to see Gabe Anderson."

"Oh..." Her eyes widen slightly. "Of course. He said he was expecting you. Hold on one moment." She slides from her chair and hustles to a door on the left while I scan the framed newspaper articles on the walls. The receptionist cracks the door, sticks her head in, and steps back out. "You can come in." The woman's gaze zeroes in on Vivi's sleeping in my arms. "If you want, you can let her sleep on the couch in the other office while you guys talk."

Dad glances at Vivi. "It's probably a good idea."

Whatever is going on has him rattled, and he doesn't want any chance of Vivi overhearing anything that might scare her. As much as I don't want her out of my sight right now, I don't want to risk that, either.

I nod and follow the woman to a door on the right of the waiting room area.

She pushes it open and ushers me in. "This is Isaac's office. He isn't back from court yet." She motions to a large, plush leather couch along one wall. "You can leave her there. I'll listen for her and peek my head in. If she wakes up, I'll let you know right away." Turning back to me, she offers a wide smile. "I'm Evelyn, by the way."

I force a tight smile I don't feel and lower Vivi to the couch with her head on one of the pillows. She protests and squirms for a second, but once I grab the blanket off the back and drape it over her, she settles back to sleep. "She's a pretty heavy sleeper, so she should be okay."

Evelyn offers me another kind smile and follows me back into the waiting area, then across the hall to the other office, where the door stands open and voices carry out.

"I appreciate you sending the plane, Gabe. Valentina and I didn't want to risk using ours and having anyone track us."

"Of course. Anything we can do—"

I step in, and Evelyn closes the door behind me, sealing me in the room for what feels like a meeting of monumental importance.

Dad stands to my right, in front of a man with sandy-blond hair sprinkled with gray and a muscular build who must be Gabe. I let my gaze drift toward the desk and the man sitting behind it, who climbs to his feet and adjusts his perfectly tailored suit coat, locking his cool Caribbean-blue gaze on me.

He extends a hand. "I'm Stone Hawke."

My breath catches in my throat.

No.

It can't be...

His eyes...

The familiarity of them staring at me from under thick, dark hair with gray at the temples makes goosebumps erupt across my skin.

"Tesoro?"

Dad's voice snaps me from my daze, and I slide my hand into Stone's and shake weakly, unable to tear my focus from the familiar lines of his face. The set of his jaw. His broad, strong shoulders encased in the immaculate suit. I've seen them in my mind too many times to count, drawn them from memory easily, as if it were my hands touching him again instead of merely holding the charcoal pencil and putting it on paper...

Even five years later, the striking similarities he bears to the man who rocked my world and changed my entire life are impossible to ignore.

"Mina?"

Shit.

I've been staring at him, and I gladly take the invitation to look away from the man who's unnerved me so much.

Dad waves me over. "Come meet Gabe."

The blond man with haunting green eyes extends a hand toward me. "It's nice to meet you after all these years. I'm sorry it's under these circumstances."

I accept his proffered hand and shake it. All the things Dad told me about what Gabe did with these hands when they were deployed together rush through my head. If Mom and Dad believe this threat is real, then bringing me to the sniper who saved Dad's life and hundreds of others makes sense.

"Yeah, me too."

He motions toward the man behind the desk. "This is my brother-in-law."

Dad approaches the desk and offers his hand to the man whose hard, lean body looks more like that of a thirty-year-old than the mid-fifties he must be.

Stone gives Dad a lopsided smile. "It's great to meet you finally, Cutter. Gabe's told us an awful lot about you over the years."

Eyes still hidden behind his ever-present shades, Dad casts a glance over his shoulder at Gabe. "I sure as hell hope not."

Gabe offers a knowing grin and motions for us to take a seat in two chairs facing the desk. "Why don't you fill us in on the situation?"

At least I'm not the only one in the dark.

All I got was a rude awakening before the asscrack of dawn and the order that we had to leave. Maybe now, I'll finally get some answers.

Dad and I both lower ourselves into the chairs, and I wait for him to start. Instead, he scrubs a hand across his jaw—a sure sign he's on edge. That doesn't bode well and makes acid rise in my throat.

Cutter Jackson isn't just my father; he's a stone-cold killer—if anything I've ever heard about him from the men who work for him is true. He would never let me see that side of him, but I know enough to understand that people fear him for a reason.

And that he fears *nothing.*

His unease means something is very, very wrong.

"Well"—he glances my way—"without going into too much detail, a threat has been made by one of Valentina's business associates."

Gabe leans his hip against the side of the desk and crosses his arms over his large chest. "What kind of threat?"

Stone reclines slightly in his big leather chair, listening to every word, shrewd blue gaze assessing Dad in a way that makes me squirm in my seat. I've seen that look before...just from a different man who looked like a younger version of this one.

Dad pulls off his shades, showing in full detail the destruction to his face and dead eye, and looks directly at Stone. "One that's real enough that I need you to protect my family."

His words send a rush of cold dread through my veins.

Fuck. This is bad.

Maybe dragging us here isn't an overreaction...

The door opens behind us, and Dad twists toward it, reaching for the weapon he always has ready at his hip.

Gabe lashes out and presses a hand against his shoulder, stopping him before he can unload into whoever is entering. "It's okay. That's just Isaac."

Isaac?

Instantly, the energy shifts in the room.

A slight crackle of electricity sizzles across my exposed skin, tightening it like it's too small for my body.

My mouth goes dry.

The skin on every inch of my body heats.

And even though I continue to face the older man across from me at the desk, my gut tells me the truth of who's standing behind me before I can even turn around.

2

ISAAC

The moment I step into the room, the conversation ends abruptly, and Uncle Gabe snaps his hand to the wide shoulder of the man in the chair in front of him, who turns toward the door. He glares at me with one blue eye and one dead white one that's surrounded by gnarly red scars crawling up the right side of his face and down his neck.

It can only be one person—Cutter Jackson.

And if Cutter Jackson is here, it means the shit has *really* hit the fan.

Family emergency.

I can't even count the number of times I've received a text saying that from *someone*. It's my job, after all, to *fix* things for the family. That's what Dad and I do, but if they've called in Cutter to assist, it must be deadly serious.

His reputation precedes him and has only grown over the years from all the stories Uncle Gabe has told us. I can only imagine the things he *hasn't*. This isn't a man you fuck with, and you don't bring him in unless it's a last resort.

Hell...

Here I thought my showdown with Whitaker was going to be the roughest part of my day. Seems I may have underestimated how much shit the family can get into.

I close the door behind me and briefly scan the tense room. Dad offers me a nod of recognition from behind his desk, and my eyes drift to a long tangle of thick, brunette hair cascading down the back of a woman in the chair next to Cutter.

My entire body heats and tenses, my mind racing back to another waterfall of hair spilling over slender shoulders...

They were exposed that night in the dress that left very little to the imagination, and the tresses were red—definitely not this dark brunette that shimmers under the lights in the office. But something clicks in my head, traveling straight to my heart and seizing it up in my chest.

No.

It can't be...

Cutter pushes to his feet, and the woman next to him slowly moves to hers. She still faces Dad at his desk, but I don't have to see her face.

I know that body.

I know those curves.

I know that electric charge I've only ever felt with her that now fills the room.

Even though the hair color is different...

I know *her.*

Jack?

Cutter turns to me and offers a hand. "Isaac, nice to meet you. I'm Cutter."

Somehow, I manage to move my arm enough to slip my palm again his and accept his tight grip, but I can't look away from the woman who refuses to turn in my direction.

"And this is my daughter, Giacomina, but you can call her—"

"Jack..." The name tumbles from my lips before I can bite it back and hangs in the thick air between us.

She slowly turns toward me, and the same amber eyes that have haunted my dreams for five years meet mine.

Cutter releases my hand. "No...she actually goes by Mina."

Fuck.

I clear my throat, trying to swallow through the lump suddenly clogging it. "Sorry. I, uh, know Jack is a common nickname for Giacomina. I just assumed..."

Christ, I sound like a fucking idiot.

Her eyes widen slightly as her panicked gaze darts between her father and me. She takes a step forward and offers me the hand that so thoroughly explored my body that epic weekend. "It's nice to meet you, Isaac."

Nice to meet me?

I spent thirty-six hours fucking this woman on every surface available in that hotel room. The rush of release when she came down my throat in that hallway still fills my mouth. I haven't been able to stop thinking about her for five damn years, and she apparently doesn't want anyone in this room to know we've "met" before.

Gathering myself as much as I can, I close the distance between us and slip my hand into hers, instantly regretting it when the same electric sizzle that danced between us that weekend in Chicago radiates through my skin, up my arm, and between my legs.

I grit my teeth. "Yes, nice to meet you, *Mina.*"

Gabe returns to his position perched on the edge of the desk, and Jack jerks her hand from mine, wiping it on her dark jeans frantically before she retakes her seat.

What the fuck is going on?

My legs shake as I walk to the other side of the desk, opposite Gabe, and I take up post there and cross my arms over my chest to keep anyone from seeing the way my entire body is vibrating.

Jack is Valentina Marconi and Cutter Jackson's daughter...

The reality sends my head spinning so badly that I stumble a half-step back slightly before I catch myself.

Dad tosses me a concerned look. "You okay?"

"I'm fine."

Fuck.

I'm not fine.

I'm anything but fine.

Jack is Giacomina fucking Jackson-Marconi...

And now, it all makes sense.

It explains so much about what she said that weekend. About why she acted like she was running from parents who kept her locked away like fucking Rapunzel, who controlled her life and suffocated her desire to be free.

When your mother runs the Italian mob in Chicago and your father is a ruthless killer who sits at her right hand and does her dirty work, it certainly complicates life.

I can see now why they would keep her on a short leash. One she must have slipped that weekend...

Uncle Gabe looks around the room at everyone, narrowing his eyes on me in a way that tells me I'm not doing a very good job concealing how shaken I am. Hopefully, he'll believe it's because of our unexpected visitors and not because I know the woman sitting with us in the Biblical sense.

Dad relaxes back in his chair slightly, casting one quick look my way before concentrating on our guests. "Now that everyone's here, Cutter, why don't you fill us in?"

Someone fucking better.

I keep my eyes locked on Jack, who averts her gaze, looking at her father, then her hands on her lap, *anywhere* but at me.

Cutter's already-terrifying face gets even harder. "There's been a threat made, one that I deem quite credible, and there's every reason to believe they may come after members of our family."

So, this isn't about the Hawkes at all.

It should be a massive relief to know the family is safe and there isn't another fire I need to put out, but instead, my chest tightens at the thought of a threat against the Marconis. Because that means a threat against the woman who has suddenly rematerialized after five fucking years.

Dad leans forward and rests his elbows on the edge of his desk. "Who made the threat?"

Cutter regards Jack for a second before he answers. "One of the families in Italy that Valentina and the Marconis have had long-term dealings with. There have been some disagreements as of late, and they've apparently decided that nothing and no one is off limits."

Uncle Gabe raises an eyebrow. "She's safe?"

Cutter nods. "I have her in a safe location, but I can't risk all of us being in the same place."

Because Jack is a target, too.

Acid climbs my throat, threatening to make me retch, and I swallow it back as Gabe exchanges a pointed look with Dad. They've known each other for so long they don't even need to speak sometimes.

But I fucking do.

I have about a thousand questions, starting with why this woman ran from me that morning and shattered my fucking heart, but as soon as I open my mouth, Dad cuts me off.

"What do you need from us?"

"I need you to protect my family"—Cutter slips his glasses back into place, like having them off for a few minutes is too much exposure—"as if they were your own."

Dad looks to Gabe. "No one will ever look here."

Gabe slowly bobs his head in agreement. "There's nothing that ties us together. Even if anyone went digging into old military records, they wouldn't be able to get to any files on any of the missions we were on together. They either don't exist or are so highly classified, they might as well not exist."

Given what I have heard about Gabe's time in the Rangers and Cutter's in Delta Force, the kinds of missions they went on aren't the ones the government ever wants to be made public. Anyone trying to locate old connections would need serious sources deep in the Pentagon, or higher, to get to anything of use.

Cutter turns to Jack, who finally lifts her head and looks at her father. "That's why I came here and moved so quickly."

Gabe looks to Dad. "We can put her up at the house in Metairie. Have Saint and Bishop arrange to keep an eye on her twenty-four-seven. Between the two of them and their guys—"

"No." The word comes out of my mouth before I can stop it.

It seems to echo around the room, far louder and more intense than I had intended.

Everyone freezes and turns their attention toward me.

Gabe raises an eyebrow. "What?"

Shit.

I didn't think this through before I spoke, and now I need to cover my outburst with something that sounds rational when nothing I've ever felt has been close to rational when it comes to Jack.

"No to the house in Metairie. Mina should stay with me."

Calling her anything but Jack feels wrong, but if there's some reason she doesn't want her father knowing we're "acquainted," I'll do my best to cover it until we're alone and I can get some fucking answers.

Dad whips his head to the side to examine me like I'm something foreign he's never seen before. "What?"

I lock eyes with the woman who twisted me up so badly five years ago and has managed to again in five short fucking minutes. "She should stay at my place. The house in Metairie is too exposed. Close neighbors. Prying eyes. The condo is secure. Lobby guards are the first line of defense. Then anyone trying to get in would need the elevator code to even get to our floor."

There.

That sounded rational.

Sort of.

Gabe and Dad exchange a look, and Cutter raises a brow over his glasses.

It's a stupid idea, having this woman in my home, in my personal space, within reach of the hands that have itched to touch her for so long, but the thought of her being anywhere else won't settle right in my head.

Gabe rubs his jaw. "You're right. It probably is the most secure place, and we can have Saint and Bishop provide additional security."

I refocus on Jack, who stares back at me, amber eyes wide, hands clenched together on her lap, her mouth twisted together like she's trying to prevent herself from saying something.

She knows what being alone with me will mean. She can see the storm brewing in me, just like the one outside.

Cutter turns to Gabe. "Additional security might draw more attention, though."

Shit.

I hadn't thought of that, and he could be right. If we keep things business as usual, it will be less likely that anyone will notice the new brunette at my place. Anyone who *does* see her will just assume she's one of my "friends" and will have no idea the danger she brings with her.

Gabe offers a half-shrug. "It could, but I'd feel a lot better with some extra personnel there. We'll have someone in the condo at all times—whether that be Isaac, Saint, his daughter, Bishop, my son, Atlas, or someone else. We can maintain the regular security downstairs. They're well trained, and I trust them, or we wouldn't have hired them in the first place."

He's right about that. Anyone the Hawkes employ is held to a rigorous standard most can't live up to. It's why when we find someone good at their job, we keep them around and make them family.

Cutter reaches out to rest a hand on Jack's arm. "You're going to stay at Isaac's." He quickly glances up at me. "As long as you're sure you're okay with Mina and Viviana being there."

Viviana?

I look to Dad and Gabe in question, but neither offers an answer.

Dad raises a brow. "Who is Viviana?"

Do Cutter and Valentina have another daughter?

Jack gulps in a breath and shifts uneasily in her chair, focusing on her hands again. "My daughter..."

JACK

A SECOND PASSES where I stare at my hands, allowing my words to register, but the moment I dare lift my eyes and meet Isaac's gaze, I see the question swimming in the Caribbean blues.

And the accusation.

It sets his lightly stubbled jaw hard as granite.

He looks every bit the powerful, successful, unflappable attorney I knew he would become when I left him sleeping in that bed that morning. One who would destroy a witness on the stand to get to the truth. But with all that scrutiny now directed at me, a cold sweat breaks out across my skin.

Stone glances at Gabe. "I wasn't aware you had a child. That makes this even more concerning. Is the father going to be a problem?"

Oh, God...

I cringe and shake my head, avoiding looking at Isaac. "No."

Dad's hands tighten on the armrests of his chair. "The father was never in the picture and won't be an issue. I need you to protect *both* of my girls as if they were your own."

"How old is your daughter?" The strain in Isaac's voice makes me wince.

It's the obvious question. The one that had to come the moment he found out about Viviana. But actually *hearing* it makes the room spin around me, and I grip the arms of the wooden chair and squeeze my eyes closed against the feeling like I'm going to pass out.

"Mina?" Dad's voice tries to cut through the fog of fear enveloping my head. "Mina, are you okay?"

"I-I..." My chest constricts, making it nearly impossible to take a breath.

"Shit!" Dad's strong hands grip my shoulders, and I manage to open my eyes enough to find him squatting in front of me, his sunglasses off again as he examines my face. "Mina, are you all right? Is it—"

"No!" I cut him off before he can say anything else. The last thing I need is everyone in this room worrying about me even more when this is nothing more than a panic attack brought on by the fact that I'm finally staring my past in the face. "I'm okay, just a little dizzy and tired from the rush to get out of Chicago and down here. All the excitement just finally got to me."

I peek over Dad's shoulder to Isaac, concern now creasing his brow, his arms still crossed defensively over his chest.

Dad squeezes my shoulders gently. "Let's get you somewhere you can lie down." He pushes to his feet and turns back to the men now charged with keeping Vivi and me safe, focusing on Isaac. "As long as you're okay with having Mina and a four-year-old at your place."

A muscle tics in Isaac's jaw as he struggles to conceal his reaction to Dad's simple words that revealed far too much.

She's four years old...

He knows exactly what that means. "It's fine." An icy, fake smile curls his lips. "I'm sure *Mina* and I can find a lot to talk about."

Oh, God.

The room spins again, and I grip the chair to steady myself.

Deep breaths.

Calm.

It's easy to tell myself those mantras I've repeated so many times in my life, but now, they seem useless in Isaac's presence.

Gabe shoves off the desk. "We should get going."

"I'll go get Viviana." I push to my feet and stumble slightly, but Dad places a strong hand on my arm to steady me. "I got it."

"Are you sure you're all right?"

I know what he's asking, why he's so worried, but I refuse to expose that weakness right now, especially given the circumstances. There are too many other fires to put out to worry about something that likely won't even be a factor while we're here.

Isaac steps around the desk and toward me. "It looks like you could use some help."

Blood rushes in my ears, and my legs shake so badly that they feel like they might collapse, but I force myself to meet his gaze.

"She's asleep in your office."

Her father's office...

Images of the weekend we spent together flash through my head, including that final moment when I looked out the car door and saw him rush out of the hotel and onto the street, barefoot, disheveled, frantic, calling for me to stop.

The one that has broken me over and over again for years.

How can this be happening now? Here?

I take a few unsteady steps and suck in a deep breath, forcing myself to find some semblance of control. As if this situation isn't bad enough—fleeing Chicago, leaving Mom, being forced here against my will, a threat hanging over my head. And now, after all this time, I find *him*.

Fate is playing some wicked trick, trying to drown me in the tsunami of uncertainty crashing down around me right now. And there's no way to escape the heat of his presence close behind me as we step through the waiting area and across the hall to his office.

Evelyn barely acknowledges us, phone held to her ear, typing away at her computer. I push open the door and step in, but before I can move any closer to Viviana's sleeping form on the couch, a strong arm wraps around my waist and drags me back against a familiar hard, lean body.

Lips that gave me so much pleasure that weekend, that did things I still dream about, brush against my ear. Warm breath flutters through my hair. My body sags against his, craving that touch as much as I fear what's coming from him.

"Is she mine?"

The question steals any remaining air from my lungs, and I struggle with a way to answer him, a way to tell him what I've wanted to for five years if I'd been able to find him.

Vivi stirs on the couch and sits up, rubbing at her eyes, blinking rapidly, and taking in the unfamiliar space around her. She looks our way, and the same Caribbean-blue eyes that Isaac and his father share stare at us, dark eyebrows furrowing. "Mommy?"

Isaac's entire body tenses against me. "Fuck..."

He barely breathes the word so softly that there's no way Viviana could have heard him, but it rings in my ears like a bomb exploding.

There isn't any question now.

There can't be.

Not now that he's seen her.

His arms start to fall away, and I slip away from him and make my way to her. "Hi, *bambina*."

She scans the room again, searching for anything familiar. "Where are we?"

"Visiting some friends in New Orleans."

As soon as I say it, the name Isaac gave me that weekend finally clicks in my head.

Nolan...

He's from NOLA...

Vivi ducks her head and peeks around me toward Isaac, who stands frozen just inside the door, eyes locked on his daughter. "Is this your friend?"

Jesus Christ...how do I even begin to answer that question?

At the beginning, when I thought there was still some hope of finding him, I had played through telling him, but when it became clear it was futile, I gave up on ever having to explain this to Vivi.

Now, I'm staring the truth right in the face and have to deal with the fallout.

I plaster on a smile and pull her into my arms. "One of them."

It's all I can come up with in the moment, the only thing that seems appropriate to say.

But it's also a lie.

Isaac—the man I knew as Nolan—isn't a *friend*. For that weekend, and in my memories, he was so much more. And he gave me the best time and the greatest gift in my life. He gave me *her* without even knowing it.

Now, the truth could shatter her entire world the same way it has his in the last few minutes.

How do I tell Vivi he's her father in a way she can understand?

Should I even tell her?

What if he doesn't want *to be a father?*

Doesn't want to be involved in her life?

The questions won't stop rushing through my head as I lift her and slowly approach Isaac, who hasn't moved an inch, his face a hard, impassive mask. Though he might try to hide behind it, his eyes can't conceal the turmoil brewing in him. It churns the typically warm, inviting blue into a twisting, violent hurricane of emotion that makes me stop short.

I shift Vivi to face him. "This is Isaac. Isaac, this is Viviana."

His Adam's apple bobs as he swallows, his gaze locked on hers like he's physically unable to look away. A muscle tics in his clenched jaw, his hands fisted at his sides.

This isn't how I wanted any of this to go. In a million years, I never could have anticipated *this* would be how he finds out he has a daughter.

"Oh, good. You're awake." Dad enters the office behind Isaac, completely oblivious to the tension between us. He pulls Vivi from my arms and glances toward Isaac. "Did you meet Isaac?"

She nods her little head, her soft, dark hair floating around her face making her appear even younger.

Dad bounces her on his hip and smiles, the move causing the scars along the side of his face to twist along his lip. "You're going to go stay with him for a little bit. Isn't that fun?"

Vivi casts a suspicious look at Isaac, who still stands frozen, unable to respond. "I guess so. What about all my toys?"

Priorities.

What else would a four-year-old care about?

Dad kisses her on the cheek. "Don't worry, *bambolotta*. We won't be here long."

He glances toward me, and the word "hopefully" goes unspoken.

Whatever this threat is, it's scary serious, so no one can say how long it will take to resolve. Meanwhile, I'm going to be stuck here...with Isaac Hawke. The man who stole my heart in two days and has the power and money to destroy me now that he knows I gave birth to his child.

Gabe appears in the door jamb. "Isaac, I'll ride with them. You can meet us there."

Isaac finally seems to snap out of his shock and turns to nod at his uncle. "Yeah. Okay."

Stone steps out of his office and watches all of us. "Son, a word before you leave?"

His words hold no warmth or humor, the deathly serious tenor of his voice sending a shiver through me.

What does he need to talk to him about?

Isaac gives me a final look, then disappears into his father's office, closing the door behind him.

Dad leans toward me. "Are you sure you're okay? Do we need to—"

"I'm fine." I peek at Gabe speaking with Evelyn to ensure he isn't listening to our conversation. "I told you, I'm just tired."

Even though I can't see the look he gives me behind the reflective sunglasses, I can feel the question in it. It isn't like me to be so passive in a meeting like that, to sit there and let them discuss mine and my daughter's life and what is going to happen with it without voicing my opinion—and likely displeasure—with at least some part of the plan.

It's what I've always done to him and Mom when they issue their edicts and control our lives, but this is different, so much different. He has no idea what he's done by bringing us to the Hawkes. He has no concept of the hornet's nest he's cracked opened and is going to drop Vivi and me into.

Still, I can't tell him the truth. Not now. Not when I know how he's going to react and that he has more important things to deal with. He needs to be concentrating on eliminating whatever this threat is, so everyone can go home, not focusing his wrath on the man who knocked me up.

I force a smile, reach up, and brush a strand of Vivi's hair behind her ear, then watch her sleepily lower her head to Dad's shoulder again. He glances toward Gabe, who now has his phone to his ear, not paying any attention to us, completely engrossed in his conversation.

"I need you to *behave* while you're here, Mina. I need you to do whatever Gabe and the Hawkes tell you to do. I need you to follow the rules and listen to what they say."

"But—"

"No buts, Mina. This is serious. Probably the most serious threat your mother has ever received. I just gave them some more details while you were getting Viviana so they'll really under-stand what's happening and why I can't worry about you when I have to protect your mom. Until we figure out a way to end this, I need you to promise me you're not going to cause any trouble."

Too late for that...

The door to Stone's office opens, and Isaac steps out, his jaw locked so hard it looks like he might crack his teeth.

Gabe ends his call and raises a brow. "We ready?"

Isaac gives a sharp nod. "Dad filled me in."

"Good." Gabe lifts his phone. "I filled in Savage. He and Coen are going to be gone a few more days on their trip, but he's in agreement on the condo. I just talked to Saint, and he's sending a team to your place to double-check all the security measures and ensure it's locked down tight."

Stone leans against the wall next to his office door, arms crossed over his chest. "What about Atlas?"

Gabe scowls. "I just texted him at the gym to let him know what's going on. He'll be home later, but I explained enough." He turns his attention to Dad and me. "Between the security measures and having my son, Atlas, right across the hall, the girls will be safe."

At least from whatever threat Mom has stirred up this time, but the look in Isaac's eyes tells me I'm far from safe from what-ever he's going to do to me.

3

JACK

The condo building towers above those surrounding it. A tall, gleaming, modern-looking building that somehow screams danger to me as we pull up and park at the curb. It's supposed to be the safest place, but it doesn't feel that way—not knowing Isaac is going to be waiting for me. Waiting for answers.

Gabe turns back to me from the passenger seat. "Isaac will meet us inside and bring you up while I talk to security and the rest of my guys."

All I manage is a nod because I'm afraid of what will happen if I open my mouth to speak. In a few minutes, I will be alone with Isaac, and I'm going to have to answer a lot of questions I'm not fully prepared for.

So much happened that weekend.

So much has happened in the last five years since I pulled away from that curb outside the Palmer House.

I'd given up hope that I would ever find "Nolan," that Viviana would ever meet her father, and now that it's staring me in the face, now that he's right here, all I want to do is hide from the explosive reality of it.

But hiding isn't an option.

At least, not from Isaac Hawke.

I unstrap Viviana—who seems content to watch some sing-songy children's video on her tablet for the moment—and help her from the SUV. Dad scoops her up, and Gabe scans the sidewalk outside the building, vigilant for any threats even when the entire reason we are here is that it *should* be the safest place for us.

Gabe opens one of the glass double doors. We step into the elegant lobby and move past the security desk toward the bank of elevators across gleaming Italian marble tile.

Isaac stands just outside them, shoulder leaned against the wall, body tense, waiting for us. His eyes zero in on Viviana and me, then flick to Cutter.

Dad motions behind us. "Gabe is talking to security."

About keeping us *safe.*

Who is going to keep me safe from that look in Isaac's eyes?

Isaac gives a stiff nod. "I'll bring you up and get you settled. He'll join us when he's done."

He motions for us to enter the elevator car, and I step in and move to the side, instinctively giving him as much room as possible in the tight space.

It doesn't matter, though.

An entire continent wouldn't be far enough away to lessen the effect Isaac Hawke has on me.

Even after all these years, it's still there.

That *something* buzzing through my veins.

Heating my body.

Igniting something deep inside me that hasn't been alive since that weekend.

Something that makes *me* feel alive despite the fear also coursing through me.

He follows us in, punches in a code on a keypad, and the doors slide closed, sealing me in with Viviana, her father, and mine. Isaac steps to my left and slightly behind me, and I squeeze my eyes closed and my legs together against the memory of the last time we were in an elevator together.

Damn!

Heat floods my body, starting in my core and spreading out through my limbs, infiltrating every fiber of my being. I shake my head to try to clear it. I can't allow myself to relive those memories the way I have over the years. I can't permit myself to get lost in them when he's so close. If I do, there's no way I'll be able to defend myself against what's about to come.

And it *is* coming.

The way the heat of his stare bores into me, rippling over my skin and making me hyper-aware of just how close he is, promises a cataclysmic confrontation to come.

Dad whispers something to Viviana, who nods and clings to him, unsure of the situation. I can't blame her at all. She's always been incredibly observant and very attuned to what's happening around her.

She knows something's up. The rush of packing this morning. The race to the airport. Her grandmother not being here with us. Now, this. She may only be four, but she's wise for her age, and there are so many things I'm not ready to explain to her yet.

The elevator rises slowly. If I thought that ride up at the Palmer House with "Nolan" was tense, then this takes the meaning of the word to a whole new level. He isn't toying with me now the way he did that night; this is actual torture. Like waiting at the guillotine for the blade to fall.

Every second agonizing.

Every breath labored.

A ding finally sounds, signaling our arrival, and the elevator opens to a single hallway with two doors facing each other—one on either side of it. Isaac brushes past me, his shoulder bumping against mine in what I'm sure is an intentional move, and heads to the one on the left. He enters a code on the keypad and pushes it open to a beautiful penthouse.

The soaring two-story ceiling in the living and dining area and floor-to-ceiling windows that overlook the water invite us farther in. Dad steps inside first, and I follow cautiously, moving past Isaac, who is waiting and holding open the door. His large, warm hand hits my lower back and ushers me forward, forcing me to enter his domain instead of running from it like a huge part of me wants to.

The heat of his palm radiates through my thin shirt, seeping into my skin and sending me back to entering another room with him—one that changed my life forever.

God!

I shouldn't love the feel of his hand on me. Not like this, not now.

Dad scans the place, shifting Viviana from one hip to the other. "Nice place."

Isaac finally allows his hand to slip from my back and takes a few steps farther in. "Thanks. My Uncle Savage and Aunt Danika used to live here. They renovated it, then rented it out for a while after they moved into their house, but I bought it from them almost five years ago and renovated it again, added a second floor."

I examine the vast, open space and the modern glass and metal stairwell leading up along one wall to a second floor. So different from the lush, rich, warm woods and carpets back at home but no less elegant.

"It used to be two bedrooms on a single floor with a theater room, but I made the original master a guest suite, converted the other bedroom to a large home office, and the entire upstairs is now the master suite."

I swallow through my dry throat. "Where do you want us?"

Isaac slowly turns to face me, his eyes hard.

That wasn't the right question to ask.

His answer would likely differ greatly were Dad not standing a few feet from us.

"Why don't you put your daughter in the guest room at the end of the hallway down here. You can take the master suite, and I'll sleep in my office. It has a pullout couch."

"What?" I shake my head. "No, I can't take your bed. Viviana and I can share the guest room down here."

He looks ready to argue, but Dad starts to walk down the hallway, still holding Vivi, who examines everything with wide, interested eyes.

"Back this way?"

Isaac nods. "Yes, sir."

I start to follow them, but Isaac's strong hand grabs my bicep before I can move. That same firm grasp he kept on my hip while he thrust into me...

No.

I clench my eyes closed against the feel of his warm skin, of his strength holding me in place again. I've been given a brief reprieve, but it's going to end soon. I'll have to face the past.

"I have a lot of questions, Jack. Ones you are going to answer."

I whip my head toward him. "Are you insane? If we say anything in front of my dad, he's going to fucking kill you."

Before he can reply, Vivi's sweet voice comes from down the hall. "Mommy..."

He relaxes his fingers on my arm, and I slowly slip from his hold and move down the hallway past two closed doors and to what used to be the master suite that Isaac indicated he converted.

The massive room fits him to a T. Dark-gray walls set the mood, with lighter-gray linens softening the hard, masculine look. Vivi jumps up and down on the bed, her dark hair flying around her as her giggle fills the high ceiling.

I step into the room and move toward them. "Be careful."

Dad sighs where he sits on the edge of the bed. "Like I'd let anything happen to her. It's the whole reason you're here—to protect you two."

"I just don't understand why you couldn't do that somewhere else. Why you couldn't have used this as an opportunity to do what I've always wanted to."

Break free...

It's all I ever wanted, what I was trying to accomplish that weekend with Isaac, but instead, it turned my entire world inside out and only made it even more impossible to escape from the clutches Mother and Father have on my life. Suddenly, I was pregnant—and terrified.

He glances at Viviana, pushes off the bed, and approaches me so she won't hear what he says. "You know why, and I'm not going to explain it again."

"Everything okay?" Isaac's voice from the doorway stops my retort.

I stare down Dad. "Yes, fine."

Isaac motions toward an open door on the other side of the room. "There are clean towels and bathroom necessities in the bathroom. We'll have any luggage brought up from your car."

Not that there's much—two small bags.

Only the absolute necessities I could throw together in five minutes.

A few clothes, my sketchbook, everything I needed from the bathroom medicine cabinet...

Almost as if he can sense it, Isaac shifts uncomfortably and zeroes in on Vivi bouncing on the bed. "If there's anything else you need—clothes, toys, anything, we'll get it."

Dad approaches him. "Thank you, Isaac, for your hospitality and for keeping the girls safe."

At least from the threat out there against the Marconis...

I turn toward them in time to see Isaac give him a hard smile. "My pleasure. I'm sure you'd do the same if it were one of the Hawkes."

Dad claps him on the shoulder. "Your Uncle Gabe is like a brother to me. There's no one else I would trust with my girls."

Isaac's eyes darken to almost black, and he squares his shoulders, never looking away from me. "I'll make sure they're safe, sir. I promise. They're my responsibility."

Something about the way he says the words sends a chill through me.

His responsibility.

Everything I've always heard about the Hawkes leads me to believe that he means it in every sense of the word, and now, he knows Viviana is his.

A child he never wanted or expected dropped into his life in the most abrupt way...

ISAAC

I WALK Cutter and Uncle Gabe to the door and open it for them, pausing just inside the threshold as Cutter jabs the elevator button. "You talked to Atlas?"

Gabe nods. "He'll be over later." He narrows his green eyes on me. "Are you okay?"

Fuck.

He knows me too well not to have noticed my odd behavior at the office. No matter how good I am at maintaining my cool, calm demeanor in court, seeing Jack and learning Viviana is mine has thrown any ability for me to remain in control out the damn window.

Still, I don't know what the fuck is going on, and I'm not about to open up and let the truth rush out. Especially not with Cutter standing two feet away and a major threat to the lives of the woman I've scoured the damn planet for and my damn child.

"Yeah." I force a half-smile. "Why wouldn't I be?"

"Well"—Gabe casts a quick peek over his shoulder at Cutter, who has pulled out his phone—"I have to say, I was a bit surprised you offered to let them stay here."

Me fucking too.

"It's the safest place for them, given everything we know."

Gabe gives a sharp nod. "Agreed."

I check over my shoulder toward the hallway that leads back to the guest bedroom to ensure Jack isn't within earshot. "Does Mina really not know everything?"

Cutter slides his phone into his pocket and shakes his head. "No, and I don't want her to. If she knew how bad this was..." He sucks in a deep breath. "I want her scared, but not any more than she needs to be. Stress...isn't good for her. She only needs to know enough to comply and not fight me on dragging her down here."

What Jack told me about her parents that weekend comes flashing back. The way they controlled her and prevented her from living the way she wanted to.

"So, you want her to stay in the dark?"

Exactly how I've been the last five years.

"Not *in the dark*"—Cutter shakes his head—"just not fully in the light."

That light came to me the moment that little girl opened her eyes.

I fucking *knew.*

Felt it somewhere deep in my soul.

There wasn't a doubt in my mind that she was mine, that our weekend together did more than just fuck me up for any future relationships. It did more than just cement Jack in my memory as the perfect woman who got away.

We made a baby that weekend.

We have a daughter who has no idea who I am and whose grandmother and grandfather will fucking kill me if they find out

I'm the one who knocked up their daughter five years ago, then fucking disappeared.

I manage a smile at Cutter and Gabe. "I'll talk with you guys again tomorrow."

Cutter runs a hand over the scars on his right cheek. "I'll keep you updated on anything you need to know in the meantime. I took Mina's phone before we left Chicago. It's best I don't speak with her, and she doesn't contact anyone back home."

Gabe inclines his head toward me. "Make sure she understands that."

The elevator arrives, and they step in, both offering a slight nod by way of goodbye before the doors close, leaving me alone with Jack, Viviana, and my thoughts for the first time.

I close the door and lean against it, dropping my head back and letting my eyes drift closed.

Was it really only this morning that Tina was on her knees while I was in this position?

I wince and try to shake off that memory. "Fuck."

How the fuck did this happen?

I drag my hands across my face.

The entire world I thought I knew, that I believed I was completely in control of, flipped upside down the moment that little girl's blue eyes met mine.

What the fuck do I do?

My hands shake, and I shove them back through my hair to try to stop it. I need answers, an explanation. I need to know why Jack left me that morning after everything we had together. Why she never tried to find me to tell me about Viviana.

Why?

Just fucking why?

But first, I need a fucking drink.

Or five.

I push off the door and stalk across the room to the full bar set up next to the fireplace. This calls for the good stuff, and I grab a bottle of Blanton's Takara Gold and pour myself two fingers, slamming it back in one gulp.

The liquid burns down my throat and in my gut, and I let my head drop on my neck as I stare into the empty glass. The same way my soul has felt empty since I stood barefoot on that fucking street in Chicago all those years ago, watching her drive away.

How could she just leave?

My fingers tighten on the glass, and I grab the bottle and pour myself another.

"I could use one of those."

Jack's voice freezes my hand with the glass halfway to my lips, and I slowly turn to face her, where she stands in front of the fireplace, looking every bit as beautiful as she did the first time I saw her. Only instead of the blazing-red hair, long chestnut tresses cascade down her back and over her shoulders. Her full breasts peek out of the V-neck T-shirt, and dark jeans hug her shapely thighs and the ass I couldn't get enough of then.

"I bet you could." I toss it back and slam down the glass harder than I intended. The clank makes her wince. "But I think I should be the one drinking here, don't you?"

"I'm so sorry, Nolan."

I wince at the fake name I gave her that night. The one I thought was so damn clever after she had used "Jack," what I had assumed was a reference to the Jack and Coke she was drinking. "You have a lot of explaining to do."

She takes a tentative step toward me. "I thought I was prepared for this moment. I've gone over this conversation and how I would tell you—if I could find you—a thousand different times in a million different ways. But standing here, it suddenly seems impossible to form words that—"

"Fucking *try*." My words come out more of a growl than actually spoken, making her flinch. "Fucking. Try."

Jack sucks in a long breath. "I tried to find you."

"Bullshit." I release the glass and take a step toward her, anger flaring to life in my blood. "If you had really tried, you could have found me."

It likely isn't true, but my anger is making me far from rational in this moment.

"I *did* try, Isaac." Tears shimmer in her eyes, but she swipes at the corners to keep them from falling. "When I realized I was pregnant, I knew I had to find you. I contacted every law school in Chicago to try to find a 'Nolan,' but of course, there wasn't one. I even went on all their websites and scanned through pictures, hoping to see you in one of them so I could get them to give me your fucking name." She scoffs and issues a mirthless laugh. "But do you have any idea how many law school graduates there were in Chicago that year? Almost two thousand between the six law schools. And I couldn't even do it with any of my parents' resources because I knew as soon as they found out I was pregnant, they would put me on fucking lockdown even *more* and try to kill whoever knocked me up."

"I thought you were on birth control." Her confirmation that there wasn't any reason not to fuck her bareback echoes through my head, followed rapidly by the memory of how hot and slick her cunt was when I shoved into her bent over the bathroom counter and fully *felt* her for the first time. "How did this even happen?"

Jack squeezes her eyes closed and pushes the hair back from her face. "I had been on a certain medication for years, but I started a new one two weeks before that weekend. It never occurred to me that it could mess with my birth control, that it could make it less effective. I didn't know until it was too fucking late and I Googled it to try to determine how it was possible."

"Jesus Christ..." I drop my face into my hands and shove them back through my hair, pacing in front of the fireplace, trying to stop myself from punching my fist into the marble that would surely break it.

"I tried to find you, Isaac. I fucking *tried*."

Her voice breaks on a sob, and I allow my eyes to meet hers again.

The pain they hold matches my own, and my stomach clenches tightly. The bourbon sloshes inside it, threatening to come back up.

I take a step toward her, then another, until I'm close enough to reach out and touch her if I wanted to. And God knows, if she were here under any other circumstances, I would already have her up against the damn wall and be buried inside her.

"Why did you leave, Jack? You wouldn't have had to search for me if you had just stayed that morning. You saw me on the street before the door closed. I know you did. Why didn't you stay?"

It's the question I've been asking endlessly for five years that's made me second-guess everything I felt that weekend.

Tears well in her eyes. "Because I didn't have a fucking choice."

"Bullshit!" The word booms around the room, making her flinch again. "You *always* have a choice, Jack. You *chose* to leave me that fucking note and sneak out while I was asleep rather than stay and face the fact that there was something there between us. You *chose* to get in that fucking car. You *chose* to let it pull away from the curb when you saw me run out of that damn hotel like a fucking lunatic after you. But *you* didn't *stop* it." I step forward and grip her chin, jerking her head up in a way that might be painful. "You didn't even stop it when I was running down the damn street barefoot, screaming for you."

She closes her eyes, unable or unwilling to look me in mine anymore, her entire body trembling. "I didn't have a choice, Isaac."

"Fucking *bullshit*." I drop her chin, stalk back to the bar, and pour myself another drink, tossing it back like it's fucking water.

Jack approaches me cautiously like one would a wounded animal ready to lash out at anyone who tries to help it. "Do you remember what I told you that weekend about my family? Now that you know who I am, do you fucking understand?"

I turn my head and glare at her over my shoulder. "I don't give a fuck who your parents are. That's irrelevant."

"It sure as fuck isn't, Isaac. Do you know what I did that weekend? I ditched my bodyguards, the men my mother and father had tasked with protecting me. I just needed some time away from them, from all of it, from being watched every fucking minute. I was so afraid of being caught, my best friend and I dyed my hair red so no one would recognize me." She shakes her head, a wistful look in her eyes. "I needed a weekend away. I needed..." She swallows thickly. "I needed *you*. And I got everything I wanted that weekend until I woke up Sunday morning with a call on my burner phone, the one I had used all weekend to avoid my parents being able to track my real one. It was my father saying he knew I was at the Palmer House and that he was going to be there in five minutes and would be coming in for me."

I wince.

"Do you have any idea what would've happened if I had allowed my father and his men to come up to our suite that morning? Do you have any idea what they would've done to you?" The true worry in her voice over events that *didn't* occur five years ago hangs heavy. "I couldn't let that happen. I couldn't let you get dragged into my mess when you were about to leave to come back here and deal with your own family bullshit. Which, fuck, I understand now. I didn't have a choice, Isaac. I mean that. Just like you had none but to come home and do *this*."

I try to figure out a way to describe how I felt that morning, waking alone, finding that note, standing there on that damn street, watching her speed away when I *knew* there was something there worth fighting for.

A tear slides down her cheek. "I was scared, Isaac, of what they would do to you. So, yes, I left you a note. And maybe that was a chickenshit way out. But I didn't know what else to do. I ran downstairs and out onto the street just as they pulled up, just in time to stop them from coming in, looking for me. And even then, my father seemed intent on going in to find out who I'd been with. The only thing that stopped him from doing it was my promising it would never happen again. And when you came out, I almost caved. I almost jumped out of the fucking SUV and raced into your arms. But there were three armed men in that SUV, one of which was my fucking father, and you have no idea what he's capable of."

I whirl to face her, anger tightening the muscles in my neck and shoulders, and stalk toward her until my chest brushes hers. "You have no idea what *I'm* capable of, Jack. No fucking idea."

"Mommy?" Viviana's voice comes down the hallway.

I jerk back from her. Her wide, frantic eyes dart to the hall, and she uses the opportunity to make her escape. She slowly backs away from me, then dashes around the corner and out of sight.

But this conversation is far from over.

4

ISAAC

My fist connects squarely, rocking the heavy bag to the side so I can attack it with my jab and level three more sharp hooks. Each snap of my glove against the leather echoes in my ears, but the sound can't drown out the anguish in Jack's voice last night or alleviate any of my own.

Nothing has since she fled down the hallway.

Not even drinking myself blind.

Atlas approaches from the left and steps behind the bag, holding it steady as I continue to pummel it. "What'd the bag ever do to you?"

I scowl at him and keep hitting it, over and over again, my shoulder muscles burning, my hands stinging, but I don't even care. "Fuck off, Atlas."

He chuckles, offering a smug grin. "I'm good. Just got laid this morning before I came in."

Asshole.

"Good for you." I throw another shot, this one hard enough to rock him back on his feet slightly. "Glad someone can tolerate you long enough to let you come."

His eyes widen. "Jesus. I was just kidding before, but seriously, what the hell is going on?"

Okay, that comment may have gone a bit too far.

"Don't worry about it."

I throw a few more jabs and a hook, the smash of my fist into the hard leather sending a satisfying jolt through my arm. He watches me for a while, holding the bag steady and letting me pummel it and work out some of my frustration. The muscles under his heavily tattooed arms bunch and flex, trying to hold the bag against my assault.

Then he gives me a smug smile. "This have anything to do with your unexpected visitors?"

I flinch and step back, my chest heaving. My breaths come out in hard pants, and I shake my head, unable to fill my lungs enough to speak right away. "I don't know what the fuck you're talking about."

He smirks. "My dad filled me in. I was going to come over last night and introduce myself, but it was pretty late by the time I got done—"

"Fuck. Yeah, I know."

Atlas flashes me a grin. "Already annoyed at having a woman and a child at your place?"

I clench my jaw to bite back the truth sitting on the tip of my tongue, the truth I still can't wrap my head around—I'm a father. I have a goddamn kid who's almost five years old, and she doesn't know who the fuck I am.

How would I even tell her?

How would I explain why I've been absent from her life?

I launch forward and throw a few more shots, trying to beat out my frustration so I don't take it out on the very person who has me so pent up. No matter how much anger I have at Jack and what's happened, how her choices led us here, if I rage at her, I'll only make things worse.

Atlas watches me intently. "Well, something's definitely up because I haven't seen you worked up like this in a long time."

"It's none of your fucking business, Atlas."

"Well, I'm making it my business." He pulls the bag away from me, stopping my punches. "What's going on? If it isn't about the woman and kid, did something happen in court?"

I step forward so I can reach the bag and throw another jab. "Just the usual asshole, doing his usual things."

"Whitaker again?"

I scowl. "I don't know why Dad insists on holding off on our lawsuits against them to end this shit."

Atlas shrugs, his muscular bare shoulders flexing. "Not sure, but knowing your father, there's a good reason."

I land another blow. "Not good enough in my book. He said he wants to include the owners personally, and since we can't find them, we have to hold up. If it were up to me, I'd walk over there and land a few of these punches on Whitaker to get that information."

"So, it is about that?"

"Sure."

Let him think that because I don't know what to do with the real reason I'm so pent up. Jack doesn't want anyone to know. Maybe because she doesn't want me involved in Viviana's life.

"So, what's she like?"

I pause and narrow my eyes on him. "What's who like?"

"Cutter's daughter. After all the stories we've heard about him and Valentina, I have to say, I'm a bit curious."

"You know what they say about curiosity?" I land another shot that rocks him back on his feet. "It killed the fucking cat."

He steps back and holds up his hands. "Jesus, man. Maybe you're the one who needs to get laid."

I clench my teeth. There's only one woman I want to be inside of, and instead of pounding into her, I'm pounding this bag into oblivion. "What I need is a good sparring session. I need to hit something real, not this fucking bag." I had hoped Uncle Savage would be here this morning, but he and Coen aren't back from their recon trip yet, which only leaves one other option. I tip my head back toward the ring, set up in the middle of the gym. "Let's go."

His dark-blond eyebrows rise. "I don't think that's a good idea."

I take a step toward him. "You fucking scared, asshole?"

"Whoa..." He holds up a hand. "Okay. You know I'm not scared of anything. I was thinking more about the fact that you would have to appear in court with a black eye or worse. But if you really want to go, let's go."

"Good." I bounce up and down on my feet, shaking out my arms to try to work out the fatigue I'm already feeling from beating away at the bag for the last half hour. "Let's do this."

Getting into the ring with Atlas isn't smart.

Anyone would know that—especially me after watching him train since we were toddlers and seeing how he decimates his opponents during every fight.

But I need to *hit*.

I need to *be* hit.

I need it to *hurt* so it might take away the agony I feel everywhere else that's utterly consuming me.

Atlas makes his way to the bench along this side of the ring and starts wrapping his hands. "You really don't want to talk about what's going on?"

I shake my head and crack my neck from side to side. "I really don't."

He slips on his gloves, and he uses his teeth to secure the Velcro. "Okay. Rules?"

I slide under the ropes and move to the center of the ring. "Since when have we ever had rules?"

A grin spreads across his face. "It's your funeral, Isaac. As everyone loves to keep reminding me, I don't have a real job and don't have to maintain any sort of appearance."

I snort as my gaze sweeps over the tattoos covering his arms, chest, and neck. "You certainly don't."

Of all the cousins, Atlas has always had a way of bucking what all our parents expect of us and doing his own thing. He could have any job he wants in any of our dozens of businesses, but instead, he chooses to get his face bashed in as a profession.

Boxing may be in the Hawke blood, but it certainly isn't on the top of the list of choice professions for the Hawke kids.

We dance around each other, each of us looking for an opening to start the brawl. We've sparred enough in our lifetimes to know each other and our moves well, to anticipate what's coming. But like he said, he's never seen me like this, ready to go to war with anyone and anything at the moment.

Even though my anger doesn't have a direction, it's all-consuming, racing through my blood, coiling deep in my chest, and tightening around my heart, every time I think about that little girl.

And with that distraction, it allows Atlas to strike first, his right hook connecting with my cheek and sending my head snapping backward, but I recover quickly, swinging back at him and maintaining my feet.

That blow likely would've knocked out someone who wasn't used to it, but I've been taking hits from Atlas since we were kids, and he's holding back. That wasn't even close to his full force, and we both know it.

He moves in for another shot, and I duck and weave, laying a body shot to his kidney that makes his abdomen fold slightly before he retaliates. This may be a fun sparring session for him, but it's a necessity for me. If I don't do something, hit something, hit someone, I'm going to go insane.

"Don't hold back on me now, Atlas."

"You don't want me at full force, dude."

"Fucking try me."

I advance on him, jabbing with my left and swinging with my right. The final shot connects with his cheek, snaps his head back, and he stumbles slightly.

He regains his footing and wipes his mouth across his forearm. "Okay, fucker. You asked for it."

In less than a split second, he comes at me, fists blazing with a speed he rarely uses on anyone who isn't a professional fighter. He lands a blow above my left eye that makes me see stars and lose my footing for a second, but I stagger back up and swing a return, a blow that barely grazes across him and gives him the opening for a jab to my gut.

It knocks the wind completely out of me, the same way seeing Jack did, and the next blow sends an agonizing slice of pain through my head before the world goes dark.

JACK

OUR CURRENT "BABYSITTER," whose sheer size should be intimidating if it weren't for his quick smile and soft, teddy bear vibe comes out of the kitchen with two plates stacked high with pancakes and hash browns and sets them in front of Viviana and me on the table. "You guys need anything else?"

I look up at the older man and smile. "No, thanks, Saint. This looks great."

He inclines his head, then leans against the counter next to the stools while I cut up the pancakes for Viviana.

"Here you go, kiddo."

Vivi grins at me. "Yum. I love pancakes."

I ruffle her hair. "I know you do. I do, too."

Saint's assessing gaze tickles the hair at the back of my neck, and I peek over at him. Ever since I woke and found him in the living room instead of Isaac, he's been quiet, stoic almost. Other than telling me who he is and that Isaac had called him because he had to go out this morning, I know very little about the man apparently charged with keeping us safe at the moment.

"So, you do security for the Hawkes?"

The corners of his lips twitch. "I do a lot for the Hawkes. I've been working for them for over thirty years now. They're more like family than employers, though."

I take a bite of my pancakes, my mouth watering at the sweet flavors on my tongue. "These are incredible. I never would have thought to put bananas *in* pancakes."

"Thank you. My grandmother's recipe."

"Did you grow up here in New Orleans?"

He shakes his head. "No. Jamaica."

I pause with my fork halfway up to my mouth, and he chuckles, a low, deep sound that seems to vibrate from him.

One of his dark brows wings up. "But I don't have any accent?"

Heat rushes to my cheeks. "Uh, yeah."

He shrugs slightly. "I came here as a teenager and realized pretty quickly I was never going to fit in, which I so desperately wanted to at that age. High school is hard enough without standing out the way I did, so I trained it out of myself. Learned to talk like the other kids around me. Looking back, it's something I regret because it's my culture, part of who I was, part of who I *am*."

His words draw me back to watching Vivi dig into her plate.

Vivi doesn't know.

She doesn't have a clue who she is, who her father is, that these people she will be seeing while we're here are family the same way her grandpa and grandma are, and there isn't any delicate way to address it.

I take another bite and chew slowly. "Are you staying all day?"

It isn't really the question I want to ask, and he knows it, given the way his chocolate-brown eyes light with slight humor.

He examines his watch. "I'm sure Isaac will be back soon since he and his dad have an important meeting today."

My back stiffens, and I glance at Viviana, who happily shovels the food into her mouth. "About me? About the situation?"

What if Isaac told his dad about Viviana?

The food that was so delicious only a second ago sours in my stomach, and I set down my fork as I wait for him to answer.

"I'm sure that will be discussed in length today by everyone so we can ensure your safety, but no, they have a meeting with the zoning administrator for the city to discuss the plans for the hotel."

"They're building a hotel?"

He nods. "The first of what will hopefully be several over the next couple of years."

"Wow. I didn't realize the Hawkes had their hands in so many different things."

He barks out a laugh and pushes off the counter to walk into the kitchen and pour himself a cup of coffee. "The Hawkes enjoy diversity in their businesses. As you know, some are rather"—he clears his throat and glances at Viviana—"adult in nature. Others are family-friendly restaurants. They even have an indoor go-kart track."

I raise an eyebrow at him. "Really?"

Saint chuckles and takes a sip of his coffee. "Yep. Savage and Gabe pretty much buy up or build anything they're interested in."

"And they run everything by themselves?"

"Yep. More or less. Savage's daughter, Kennedy, has taken on a lot more over the last few years working with her dad and her uncle, but pretty much everyone in the family works for us in some capacity except Gabe and Skye's son, Atlas, and Byron and Luca's son, Jude—" Saint's phone buzzes on the counter, and he picks it up and checks it. "Isaac is back."

My entire body heats with that knowledge, and almost instinctually, I reach out and rub Vivi's back. I peek down at her half-eaten plate. "You doing okay, kiddo?"

"So good."

"Yeah, they are."

Too bad I completely lost my appetite.

I should be worrying about this *threat* that brought me here, but instead, my focus is on the threat Isaac poses to the life Viviana and I know.

Saint narrows his eyes on me. "Are you all right?"

"Hmm?" I nod. "Oh, yeah, sorry, I was just wondering why Atlas doesn't work for the family?"

Nice cover.

Saint returns to lean against the counter with his cup of coffee in hand. "Atlas has had a bit of a rebellious streak that's lasted the last twenty-eight years."

The humor in his words finally brings a genuine smile to my face. "What does he do for a living?"

"He's a professional boxer."

"Really? Is he any good?"

The door handle turns, and Saint focuses on it before he takes a sip of his coffee. "You're about to find out."

Huh?

The door swings open, and Isaac steps in, a sweat-soaked T-shirt clinging to his rock-hard chest and muscled arms, athletic shorts covering his lower half, but my eyes immediately dart to the giant gash over his left brow and the trickle of blood down his cheek.

"Oh, my God." I push up from my chair and rush over toward him. "Are you okay? What happened?"

His eyes connect with mine and spell a warning he doesn't have to say, stopping me in my tracks a few feet from him. "I'm fine." His gaze immediately darts to Viviana, and he swallows thickly before turning his attention to Saint. "Any problems?"

Saint shakes his head. "Nope. Got the girls fed. Now that you're back, I'm going to head into the office."

Isaac's focus bounces from Saint to me to Vivi, who continues to eat, blissfully oblivious to what's happening around her. "But you'll have someone here all day?"

"Bishop is coming in about twenty minutes so you can head to your meeting."

"Good." Isaac gives Saint a stern look. "They're not to be left alone."

Saint nods. "Gabe made that very clear."

Isaac doesn't acknowledge me. He just moves past where I stand in the middle of the living room, bumping me with the athletic bag slung over his shoulder as he makes his way toward the stairwell that leads up to his room.

I follow him closely, keeping an eye on Viviana. "You're bleeding."

He glances at me out of the corner of his eye. "You think I don't fucking know that."

"That looks bad. You might need stitches."

He stops at the bottom of the glass steps and turns to me, leaning in slightly so Saint and Vivi won't hear him. "I'm a big boy, Jack. I can take care of it."

His words hit me like a blow to the chest.

Maybe it's the mothering instinct in me to try to fix it and heal something when it's hurt...

Maybe it's his rejection of my attempt to do just that...

It just feels like a personal attack.

He turns away from me and starts up the stairs.

"Mommy, why is he bleeding?" Vivi's sweet voice rings out through the room.

Isaac freezes, his entire body going rigid, and he slowly twists his head and peers over his shoulder at Viviana. It takes a moment before he fully turns around and comes back down the steps.

He squats next to her chair as her big blue eyes that match his stare at him and the wound over his brow. Isaac offers her a half-smile that makes my breath stop and lets his bag slide from his shoulder to the polished wood floors. "I'm okay. Do you know what boxing is?"

She shakes her head. "No."

He regards me for a second before he continues. "That's when two people try to hit each other."

Her little brow creases in confusion. "Why would they want to do that?"

A grin spreads across Isaac's lips. "For fun."

Her mouth droops into a frown. "Doesn't sound fun to me."

That draws a light chuckle from Isaac as he pushes to his feet. "You'll understand when you're older, kiddo. Sometimes, you just need to fight."

He locks his gaze with mine when he says those words, and a chill rolls down my spine. Our conversation may have ended abruptly last night, but it's going to continue—that much is certain.

I am not ready for this.

"I'm okay, though, Viviana. Don't worry about me." He grabs his bag again and hustles up the steps, not looking back even once.

I can't tear my eyes away from his retreating form until the door at the landing on top of the stairs clicks closed, locking him away with his anger.

Saint clears his throat behind me, and I jump slightly and turn back to him.

"Well"—Saint offers an amused grin—"that was tense."

I force a smile. "Sorry. He doesn't seem to be too comfortable having us here."

It's the only thing I can think to say, and Saint's eyes dart to Viviana.

"I wouldn't think so. Isaac isn't exactly known for his fondness for children."

I wince and retake my seat so I won't have to look Saint in the eyes anymore. The man seems to see right through me the same way Isaac does, and there's far too much that he could see that I need to keep hidden.

5

ISAAC

"You can't be serious." I glare at Matthew Broussard, the chief of the zoning division, as he leans back casually at his desk like he didn't just pull the rug out from under us.

He shrugs nonchalantly. "I don't know what to tell you, Isaac. The division has some concerns about your plans."

I glance at Dad, who looks just as tense next to me. "What sort of concerns? No one said anything at the last meeting when we presented the plans."

Broussard leans forward slightly at his desk and rests his hands on top of each other. "As you're both well aware, the city has been most generous to Hawke Enterprises with all of your endeavors. We haven't blocked any of your strip clubs or other establishments, even when there was some community concern over what was going to be happening within their walls. But a hotel is a different beast. This is a massive undertaking. And the neighborhood surrounding it has to be considered, what effect it will have on them."

"What effect could it have other than raising their property values? This is only going to benefit them." Dad shifts forward in his seat and slides a piece of paper across to Broussard. "The area is zoned for a hotel. We've already presented a community impact assessment with the original plans, and we haven't heard any concern from any of the neighbors in the community meetings."

"Some citizens feel"—Broussard examines the ceiling like it holds some answer—"what's the word? *Concerned* about voicing their opinions publicly."

What the fuck is even happening right now?

Today's meeting was supposed to just be to touch base on scheduling the groundbreaking and the timeline for the project once we had approvals. We never anticipated any sort of issue coming out of the blue like this.

I lean forward slightly toward him, ensuring my eyes are relaying my annoyance. "Why?"

He raises a brow at me. "Really, Mr. Hawke? Your family may be well-respected, but let's make no mistake about it and stop beating around the bush. There have been some tactics used in the past that raise concern for people opposing you."

Fucking hell.

I don't look at Dad because I know what I'll see—the accusatory stare he always gives me just because I'm willing to go beyond what others may deem as appropriate to get the job done and ensure our businesses in the family are protected. He wants things done but loves to question the way I do them.

Dad clears his throat, likely biting back what he really wants to say. "Are you suggesting we somehow pose a threat to members of the community should they oppose the hotel?"

"That's exactly what I am suggesting, Mr. Hawke. Having Luca Abello as one of your partners doesn't help that situation."

I clench my jaw, but that move only puts more tension on the wound near my eye that I barely managed to keep shut with butterfly bandages this morning. "Luca Abello is a fine, upstanding member of this community, Mr. Broussard, with no criminal record and a pristine reputation."

He barks out a laugh. "Just because Abello isn't sitting at the head of the mob now and handed things off to the Rosellis doesn't mean you can simply brush who he is or what he's done in the past under the rug and expect everyone else to forget it, Mr. Hawke. He's a major member of the Hawke Enterprises partners. I don't think people are ready for the former head of the mob to be opening a hotel when God only knows what might be happening inside it."

My fingers tighten on the armrests. "You can't block us from doing this, Broussard."

"You're right. I can't. If I deny the plans, you'll have to go to the Board of Zoning Adjustments to appeal, and ultimately, they'll have to vote. But I can tell you right now, I have to ensure this doesn't get off the ground until any and all concerns are resolved. It just doesn't seem right."

I lurch to my feet and lean across the desk, my palms flat on the smooth, hard wood surface. "You need to remember who you're dealing with, Broussard. If I find out you have ulterior motives or have been putting any undue pressure on any members of the board or in any way interfering with this vote, you'll have to answer to me."

He raises an eyebrow. "That might sound like less of a threat if it didn't appear you've already been in one fight recently, Mr. Hawke."

Dad places a strong hand on my shoulder and tugs me back. "It isn't a threat, Broussard. It's a promise. The Hawkes will use any legal means necessary to ensure this approval goes through with the board so we can break ground."

I force myself to step back from the desk and follow Dad out of the office, barely containing my rage.

Legal means and then some.

The staggering number of ways I have to get to Broussard and ensure he acts in our interests will make sure this doesn't go any further.

Who the fuck does Broussard think he is?

This was a done deal.

We already have everything lined up to break ground in mere months, and he wants to try this shit now.

The man must have a death wish.

He should know better than to cross us. Broussard has been around long enough to see what we can accomplish when we set our sights on something, the lengths we're willing to go to in order to ensure we get it. Times may have changed from the days when Luca ran this city and wasn't afraid to spill rivers of blood to maintain his stranglehold, but I have ways to accomplish the same outcome without having to actually pull a trigger.

Broussard just made an enemy he doesn't have a chance in hell of beating.

We stalk down the tile floor of City Hall in absolute silence, the tension radiating off Dad matching my own. Shoving open the doors, the crisp fall air hits me, but it does nothing to cool the heated anger boiling in my veins.

I descend the steps just in front of Dad, and when I reach the sidewalk, he grabs my arm and jerks me back, spinning me around to face him.

"What the fuck was that in there?" Fury flashes in his gaze. "You're threatening the head of the zoning division after he just accused you of using illegal tactics?"

"I didn't threaten him."

"Bullshit. We all know what that was." He motions to my head. "And what the hell is this? Had I known you would come in here looking like you just got out of a bar fight, I would've handled the meeting myself this morning."

Which is exactly why I texted Dad to tell him that I would meet him here instead of at the office.

"Just a little boxing mishap with Atlas."

"You got in the ring with Atlas?" He throws up his hands. "Fucking idiot. I can't have you going around looking like a common fucking criminal representing this family. What if you had to be in court today?"

I meet his icy-blue glare. "Then I would've explained the same thing to the judge—that I got a little overzealous during a boxing workout."

Dad clenches his jaw and shakes his head. "What the hell has gotten into you the last couple of days?"

"Nothing."

He scowls at me. "I'm calling Gabe and Saint and telling them we're moving Giacomina and her daughter to my house."

"What?"

"Whatever the fuck is going on with you, the last thing you need is to have a vulnerable woman and a damn child in your condo. I don't even understand why you volunteered to let them stay there in the first place."

Because Jack and I have some unfinished business.

"Because it's the safest place, and you know it."

"That might be true, but it's not safe when you're like this. I've seen you worked up before, Isaac, and I've seen you make bad fucking decisions when you are. This hotel project is too important to get fucked up because you're in a shit mood about something. Having a stranger and a kid at your place is only going to make things worse. I'll have them come stay with your mother and me."

"No."

His dark brow wings up. "*Excuse* me?"

Fuck.

He has that look in his eyes, the one that says I'm dancing on the thin line that will take me somewhere I don't want to be with him.

"You aren't ever there, Dad. You're in the office or meetings all day, and Mom is gone at the hospital. When you're both there, you don't want anyone else around interrupting your time together. Plus, your place would be too hard for Saint and Bishop to watch with nosy neighbors. They'll be fine with me."

If anyone has the incentive to protect them, it's me—even if I can't reveal the real reason I need them there.

Dad shoves a finger into my chest. "You listen to me, Isaac. Whatever's going on in your fucking head, get your shit together. And if I hear from anyone that you are in any way upsetting Cutter's daughter or granddaughter, you're going to have to answer to me...and you're going to end up looking a lot worse than what Atlas did to you."

He storms toward his car down the street, and I release a heavy breath, trying to gather some control over my racing heart. Because Dad isn't wrong—I have to get a hold of myself, or things are going to slip more than they already have.

No one knows how long this threat against the Marconis is going to last or how it's going to end, and I have bigger things to worry about.

JACK

THE DOOR to Isaac's guest bedroom makes a little click that causes me to cringe and pause to listen if the noise woke Viviana, but there isn't any sound from the other door. I release a little breath of relief and make my way down the hall toward the living room, where Bishop sits on the couch, book in her hand.

She glances up at me, her dark brows rising. "Where's Viviana?"

I motion backward. "She fell asleep watching *Frozen*."

Bishop checks her watch. "You're okay with her taking a nap this late in the day?"

Hell, yes.

I chuckle and lower myself into the leather chair facing her. "Yeah, she's exhausted after everything that happened yesterday, plus being in a new bed last night. She's a good sleeper, anyway, so I'll still be able to get her down tonight."

Saint's daughter tucks a bookmark between the pages of her novel and sets it on the coffee table next to her. "I'm glad she's sleeping. My Uncle Gabe is across the hall at Atlas' and wanted to talk to you but didn't want to do it with little ears around."

My stomach tightens. "Um...okay."

She pulls out her phone, fires off a text message, and a minute later, the condo door opens and Gabe steps in...with Isaac directly behind him. Our eyes meet across the open space, and Isaac sets his briefcase on the floor next to the door, his body tense.

Bishop starts to get up from the couch, but Gabe holds out a hand.

"No, you should stay for this, so you can fill in your dad."

"Okay." She returns to her seat and darts her gaze between Gabe, Isaac, and me. "What's going on?"

It's the same question I've been asking since the minute Dad woke me and said we had to leave Chicago. He's kept me in the dark, ostensibly to protect me, but all it has done is make me more nervous and angry about the entire situation.

Less stress? Bullshit.

Gabe takes a seat in the matching chair across from me while Isaac stands behind the couch, his jaw clenched. "I just talked to your dad, and I have a lot more information than we had yesterday."

"Why didn't he call me?"

Gabe glances at Isaac and Bishop. "He thinks it's best if he doesn't have direct communication with you, and he warned me he will likely be going dark for a while."

"Shit, that bad, huh?"

I haven't been away from him or Mom for more than a few days my entire life, and that was only when they had business they had to take care of and couldn't drag me along. But even then, they called. We talked. I got to hear her voice assuring me things were going to be okay.

Not having that, not even getting to say goodbye to her, has left me more rattled than I care to admit.

Gabe runs a hand back through his hair. "Apparently, your mother has made a very serious enemy with someone who used to be an ally—the Satriano family."

Ice floods my veins as I shift in my seat. "That's who this is about?"

One of Gabe's blond brows rises. "Do you know them?"

I nod. "My parents tried to keep me insulated from the business...but I heard things." Listening at the door while they had meetings and eavesdropping on their men who didn't know better than to keep their mouths shut when I was around yielded far more information than they ever thought I had. "The Satrianos run all of Calabria and control what gets in and out, and back to Chicago to my mom."

"Yes." Gabe bobs his head. "The Marconis' relationship with them has existed for a long time, going back to your grandfather, but your mother was asked to do something she wasn't comfortable with."

"Shit. And she isn't afraid to say no. Is she?"

That draws a slow half-smile from Gabe, and he shakes his head. "From what your father's told me, she doesn't back down from anyone or what she thinks is right. So, the Satrianos have made it clear they want her gone since she won't comply. And if they can't get to her, they'll get to anyone else they can to force her out."

They're damn monsters.

Isaac issues a low growl that draws my attention away from his uncle. His grip on the back of the couch tightens, his fingers digging into the leather hard enough for his knuckles to whiten. "Whatever happened to women and children being off fucking limits to these people?"

Gabe shakes his head. "Those sort of ethics died a long time ago. Those kind of rules don't seem to apply anymore, at least not to the Satrianos."

It's been an issue for Mom since the day she took over the family business—the unwillingness to cross certain lines others easily ignore. Given the viciousness of the Calabria 'Ndrangheta, it may be the very reason they're after her now. If they asked her to do something that crossed *her* ethical line and she said no, it could have started this war. And now Viviana and I are caught in the crossfire Dad has always tried to protect us from.

"So, what? I hide out here in this condo for the rest of my fucking life?" I shake my head, trying to get control of my growing anger—not at them but at the entire situation. "I had to pull Viviana out of preschool. All we have are two small bags with a few things in them. I can't stay here indefinitely. Not like this."

Not with *him*.

Not having to see the hatred in his eyes every time he looks at me.

The disdain every time he looks at his daughter.

Isaac tenses again, his eyes hardening to ice.

Gabe offers a sympathetic look. "I understand your distress, but this is the best place for you right now. I know you met Saint this morning and Bishop"—he inclines his head her way—"and there are a few other people who will take turns to ensure you're never here alone." He inspects his nephew and smirks. "And believe me, Isaac can handle himself despite what his current appearance may suggest."

Several stitches now hold the cut above his eye closed, indicating he finally got some sort of medical care.

Isaac glares at his uncle. "Yeah. Tell Atlas it won't happen again."

Gabe grins at him. "Plus, Atlas is across the hall, and you can see his handy work. Nobody's getting up here without us knowing about it and approving it."

"So, I'm a prisoner in an ivory tower."

First, I was one in Mom and Dad's house; now, I'm one here.

It never fucking ends.

"This is for your own safety. Yours and Viviana's. My daughter, Astrid, has a teaching degree. She said she'll come work with your daughter daily for a few hours. And Isaac or anyone else can ensure you two have whatever you need."

What we need is a fucking life.

A life not looking over our shoulders. A life where we're not being watched and followed. A life not being locked away. A life where I'm more than just the daughter of Valentina Marconi and Cutter Jackson. A life where I can just *be* with Viviana and live like we aren't constantly under threat.

That's what I wanted in Paris.

A fresh start with Vivi. New names. New city. A whole new world opened to us and the ability to finally pursue the only thing that ever made me happy beyond Isaac—my art.

Isaac shifts uncomfortably behind the couch. "It's for your own good."

I turn my head toward him fully. "And how would you know what's good for me?"

An icy chill falls over the room, and Bishop slaps her palms against her thighs loudly and pushes to her feet—offering a much-needed break from the atmosphere.

"I know this is a tense situation, but I assure you we're all just looking out for you and your daughter." She offers a warm smile. "I'll be seeing a lot of you in the next couple of days."

Hell.

I don't want to sound ungrateful and come across like some spoiled brat. It's impossible to explain to them what it's been like my entire life, especially since Viviana's birth. How rarely I've been able to do anything for myself, anything I enjoy other than what I can do at the house.

That weekend with Isaac was the last time I remember having true freedom to just *live*...and now, the consequences of that are sleeping down the hall and her father is staring at me with so much hatred that it sends a chill through me.

I push to my feet and offer Bishop a quick hug. "I know. I'm not mad at you. Just the situation..." *And maybe Isaac at his comment.* "Thank you for babysitting us today."

"No problem." Her lips quirk into a smile. "Next time, I'll bring some stuff to help keep us entertained. I play a mean game of Scrabble."

She heads out of the condo, leaving me in the room with Gabe and Isaac, the remaining tension so thick you could cut it with a knife.

Gabe glances between the two of us. "Did something happen between the two of you that makes you feel unsafe to stay here, Mina?"

Fucking hell.

The last thing I want to do is cause problems for Isaac with his family.

I shake my head. "No, just the entire situation is a little difficult to manage right now."

Gabe rises and lays a strong hand on my shoulder, squeezing it gently. "I'm sorry you're stuck in the middle of this, Mina, but I promise you, your dad is working on it. He's doing everything he can to make sure you get home."

Where I'll just be locked away forever in that house the same way I am here.

Even if everything with the Satrianos gets resolved, after this, there's no way Mom and Dad are ever going to let Viviana or me out of their sight again.

6

JACK

The quiet stillness of the condo belies the turmoil raging through me and the cold sense of dread that has sat in the pit of my stomach since Isaac came home. Knowing what's coming is almost worse than being completely in the dark. At least then, there's hope, an ability to see a positive outcome, one where people aren't hurt and lives aren't torn apart.

But that isn't going to happen here.

It can't.

I've waited for hours, sat and ate with Gabe, Atlas, and Viviana while Isaac excused himself to work in his office on something he described as "pressing." Though the look he gave me before he disappeared down the hallway and slammed the door suggested it had everything to do with me and the shitstorm I've brought to him rather than anything work-related.

A showdown is inevitable.

Both of us waited until everyone else left and Viviana was deep asleep before we finally faced each other. And I can't avoid it anymore. I can't avoid him or the fear of what's coming.

My bare feet don't make any noise as I pad down the hallway toward the living room. A warm glow emanates in front of me, and I step out from the brief protection the dark passageway grants me, holding my breath.

Isaac sits in one of the large leather chairs facing the fireplace, a crystal tumbler of amber liquid in his hand. Rather than acknowledge me, he takes a sip and continues to stare at the fire roaring in front of him, the flames leaping and jumping and twisting the same way my gut is.

"Finally decided to come out of hiding?" His gravelly voice floats to me, laden with despair and barely contained anger.

It stops me in my tracks. "I...I wasn't hiding."

If anything, he has been, locked away in his office all night. Though, I did take Viviana back to the bedroom almost immediately after we finished eating to have a bath and try to calm down before bed. I don't have a clue when he actually came out here or how long he's been waiting for me.

Something tells me it's been a while, though, given the level of liquid in the decanter compared to earlier today. I can't blame him for drinking like this—if the roles were reversed, I might be doing the same.

It isn't every day a woman from your past shows up not only with your child but also one of the most powerful mob families in the world after them. It would be a lot for anyone—even someone as strong as Isaac Hawke.

He finally turns his head to look at me, his normally bright-blue eyes dark with an emotion I can't quite place. The stitched cut above his brow makes him look dangerous, deadly, like he could lash out and strike at any time. And that's exactly what he plans to do.

I move toward the fireplace and stop in front of him, my hands shaking as he takes another drink from his glass and sets it on the table beside his chair.

Forcing myself to take long, deep breaths can't slow my racing heart or quell my shaking body. I have to say something, *anything* to him, to try to assure him I'm not going to ask anything of him, to let him know I won't force him to be a father when he doesn't want kids.

"I never asked for any of this, Isaac. God, I wish I could go back...I never wanted to get pregnant. I never wanted to hide her from you. I know you're angry about everything, that you're mad at me, that you blame me and hate me for saddling you with a child and that responsibility, that I..."

He's up and out of his chair so fast that I jerk away from his advance, but he backs me toward the fireplace until I can't retreat anymore without physically stepping into the flames. Yet, somehow, the heat of the inferno behind me is nothing compared to that blazing in his eyes right now.

"That's what you think? That I'm *mad* at having to deal with the *responsibility* of having a child?"

"I...Yes. I mean..." I swing out a hand and point back toward the room. "Other than this morning, you haven't said two words to her. You won't even look at her, or me, for more than five seconds without your jaw tightening." My words rush out with the release of all the emotions I've pent up over the last two days. "You think I don't see that? You think I can't feel how angry you are?"

"Jesus, Jack." His lips curl into a snarl, and he shakes his head, his thick, unruly, dark hair falling over his forehead. "I'm not mad that you got pregnant. I'm not mad that I have a daughter. I'm fucking *furious* because I missed *all of it.*"

It takes a moment for his words to break through emotional fog and register in my head. "What?"

He takes another step closer, until his heaving chest brushes against mine, and braces one hand on the mantle behind me. "I'm fucking *livid* that I missed out on everything. That I wasn't there when you found out you were having my baby, when you had to tell your parents. That I wasn't there when you got morning sickness. That I wasn't there to get you all the crazy things you craved while you were pregnant."

His free hand slides down and across my stomach almost reverently, flattening over the place that held our child.

"I'm *shattered* that I didn't get to see your belly grow with my baby inside of it, that I didn't get to feel her kick. That I missed going to the goddamn ultrasound appointments with you and never got to see that grainy picture or hear her heartbeat. I'm fucking *pissed* that I didn't get to hold your hand while you were giving birth, that I didn't get to try to help ease that pain for you, that I didn't get to witness my daughter being born, didn't get to hold her in my arms and tell her I'm her father. That I didn't get to hear her first laugh or see her crawl and her first fucking steps. I missed all of it, Jack. Fucking *all of it*."

Barely contained tears well in his eyes as the flames dance across them, and I can't stop my own from finally falling.

"I'm fucking *destroyed* because Viviana doesn't know who the fuck I am. I'm just some stranger whose house she's staying in for reasons she doesn't understand. I'm *no one* to her. *That's* why I'm mad, Jack." A single tear trickles out of the corner of his eye. "And I haven't said anything to her because I don't know *what* to say to a little girl who doesn't know me and because every fucking time she looks at me with *my* eyes, I can barely breathe, let alone form words."

He pulls his hand from my body to swipe away his tears, then pushes off the mantle and stalks to his chair to grab his drink and toss it back.

My entire body shakes so violently I can barely keep my feet under me. Each of his words slammed into me the same way I imagined Atlas' fist did him this morning to cause the damage to his face, leaving me battered and weak and on the verge of total collapse.

I open and close my mouth a few times, unable to speak.

Nothing I can say will make any of this better.

Nothing can ease the pain he's in.

How could I have misjudged him so badly?

I immediately thought the worst, that he didn't want Viviana, didn't want to be saddled with a child and responsibilities and ramifications of what was supposed to be one incredible, carefree weekend. And I couldn't have been more wrong.

"Forgive me...I'm so sorry, so, so sorry. I don't know what to say, Isaac, except I'm so fucking sorry."

Tears stream down my face.

It isn't the first time I've cried over this man, and it certainly won't be the last. Years of wondering, of hoping, of wanting have all come to a head. There isn't running from the hard reality we now face. The one that *I* caused. "This is all my fault. If I hadn't left that morning..."

But I stop that train of thought because any excuse I make would sound hollow compared to how much he's suffering in this moment, how much he has been since the second he saw Viviana.

I saw him in her every single day over the last five years.

In each laugh.

Each smile.

In her kindness and intensity and wicked intelligence.

I saw it so clearly, and he did, too, in the instant their eyes met.

She may have come from my womb, but she is so much of her father. She is so much Hawke.

It shouldn't surprise me that he'd react this way, that learning he has a child would be torture for him, not when I know how important family is to the Hawkes. These people have taken us in without a second thought, brought potential danger to themselves in order to ensure our safety when we're nothing to them but relatives of an old military friend.

They're selfless and giving, just like he was the two nights we spent together.

And now I'm being selfish by asking him to keep this a secret. That little girl back there is his flesh and blood, and no one but us knows it. *She* doesn't know it. He has to look at her every day and know she's completely oblivious to the reality staring back at her, that she got her wavy, dark hair and beautiful blue eyes from him. That she's so damn much his daughter.

He keeps his back to me, spine ramrod straight, shoulders locked solid like fucking granite. All the emotions I thought I'd worked through years ago now overwhelm me, forcing me to choke back a sob and fist my shaking hands at my sides to try to gain control over a body that's always warring with me.

I take a tentative step toward him, wanting to reach out, wanting to wrap my arms around him and comfort him in his moment of turmoil. "Please, Isaac. Turn around and look at me."

ISAAC

Turn around...

Like I can just do that so easily.

I can't look her in the eye again. Have her see the tears I'm desperately trying to keep back, the way I'm on the fucking edge and barely stopping myself from completely falling apart.

Even having two days to process this hasn't been enough.

A lifetime wouldn't be.

How the fuck am I supposed to react to finding out I have a daughter and that I've missed four years of her life?

That the woman I've been dreaming about for five damn years had my baby and I had no fucking idea?

Soft footsteps approach, and Jack's warm arms wrap around me from behind and tighten on my waist. She presses her face against my back, and I squeeze my eyes closed, warring against the desire to turn around, take her in my arms, kiss the everloving hell out of her, and drag her up to my room to do to her what I've wanted to since the moment I saw her in Dad's office.

But I can't do that.

And not just because it would complicate the hell out of an already-complicated situation, but because I still don't know how the fuck I feel about her, about this.

Because she's *right*—if she hadn't left that morning, if she hadn't run, none of this would've happened.

I would've told her my real name the second we woke up, and I would've begged for hers, would've made her give it to me, would've done everything in my power to ensure that when I got on that plane to head back here, I knew how to find her, knew a way to ensure I would see her again.

Instead, I woke up to an empty bed and a shattered fucking heart.

So, as much as I'd love to stay enveloped in her hold, the arms I've been dreaming about, the hands I've been fantasizing about touching me for years, I can't.

You can't, Isaac.

You fucking can't.

I reach down and push her hands off my stomach, stepping forward and out of her reach before I finally turn to face her to ask the ultimate question and confront the elephant in the room. "Why did you leave?"

She squeezes her eyes closed, almost as if she's in physical pain, and inhales a deep breath. "I told you last night, my dad found me. He was going to come in. He was—"

"I could have handled your father, Jack. I *would* have handled your goddamn father. And deep down, I think you know that. So, tell me why you *really* ran. Tell me why that little girl doesn't know me. Tell me why I'm a stranger to my own goddamn daughter."

She winces, but I can't let myself feel bad about it, about questioning her, not when *that* decision created *this* situation.

Her bottom lip trembles, and I have to fight every desire in me to step forward and envelope her, comfort her, bury my face in her hair and inhale that scent that has haunted every breath I've taken since she left me that morning.

Even though I'm the one upsetting her so much, I can't risk being that close to her.

Not now.

Maybe not ever.

"There are things you don't know, Isaac. Things you don't understand. My father, my parents, they never would've let me leave. Even if my dad didn't kill you on the fucking spot, you were leaving in just hours. You told me you were coming back here. And God"—she throws up her hands—"everything you said makes so much sense now that I know you're a Hawke. How your family expected you to be *this*, to do this for them. How you felt like you didn't have a choice. I get it now. And back then, I thought there was no chance of you staying, of us ever seeing each other again." She snorts incredulously. "I mean, for Christ's sake, Isaac, what would we have done? Seen each other a few times a year, flown back and forth for visits? We both know that never would've worked. *This* never would've worked. I was saving both of us a lot of heartache and you a lot of physical pain by leaving, by ensuring my father never knew who you were. I protected *you* as much as I protected *myself*."

"Bullshit!" I sneer at her, taking a step closer when everything in me screams to stay away. "You fucking *ran* because you were *scared*, and *not* of your father, but because you felt the same thing I did, and it terrified you. You *ran* because you were too chicken to fucking stay."

My words make her flinch, as if I've physically struck her, and regret instantly settles on my chest at seeing her distress. Yet, now that I've started, I don't know if I can stop. Railing at her like I do a witness on the stand, firing off all the rage I have built inside of me over the last two days, over the last five years, over how she left me, what she did to my heart, feels like releasing an avalanche.

"We both know what happened that weekend was more than just two strangers trying to fuck away their problems. We both felt something, and you didn't know what to do with it. So, you fucking ran. Rather than standing up to your father, standing up to your mother, standing up for what you wanted, you ran, and look at the damn consequences." I clench my fists at my sides, letting my nails dig into my palms until it stings, trying to draw the pain somewhere else and away from my heart. "Do you know what I did after you left?"

She shakes her head and wipes away a tear. "I assume you got on the plane."

I bark out a mirthless laugh and shove my hands through my hair as I pace. "No, I went back into that fucking hotel, barefoot, disheveled, after I just chased you down the damn street like a lunatic, and I begged the manager to let me see the surveillance video so I could try to find you by getting the license plate of the car."

Her eyes widen slightly. "You did?"

"Of course, I did, Jack. I would have done anything to find you. But one thing I'll give the Palmer House credit for: they respect the confidentiality of their clients. He wouldn't let me see shit. I even asked my friend who worked there to try to get it for me, but he said he would've lost his job if he got caught."

"So, then, you got on the plane?"

I shake my head. "No. I went back up to the room, went over every fucking inch of it for anything you might have left, any way I could find you. And when I came up empty-handed, I booked the room for another night, hoping you'd come back."

Her shoulders slump slightly. "Oh, my God, you did?"

"I fucking *did*. Then I called my brother, who was waiting at my place, and told him to leave without me. Told him to tell the family I'd be a few days late. And when you didn't come back that night or the next morning, I went back to the bar, but the bartender assured me that was the first time you had been in there and that he hadn't seen you since. I even tried looking for your friend, but no one seemed to know her, either. It was dead end after fucking dead end." I lock my gaze with hers. "I spent three days in Chicago trying to find you before I finally realized the truth."

"What truth?"

"That you didn't *want* to be found. That if you felt even half of what I did, you would've come back."

She averts her gaze and swallows thickly. "I'm so sorry. I thought I was doing the right thing. I thought it was for the best for both of us."

"Yeah. Well, you thought wrong."

Her actions destroyed me then, and learning the truth is breaking me down even more now, like digging a shoe heel into already-broken glass and pulverizing it into vicious shards designed the inflict the most pain.

Jack takes a little half-step toward me. "What are we going to do now?"

I run my hands back through my hair again and tug at the ends, the sharp pain on my scalp somehow welcome. "I don't know, Jack. You fucking tell me."

She opens and closes her mouth a few times, those soft, pink lips of hers calling out to me despite all my anger. Before she can answer, I advance on her and drag her into my arms, pushing her back to the fireplace again until her shoulders press against the mantle and my hard body aligns with hers.

A tiny moan falls from her mouth, and I slide my hands into her hair, tilting her head up and capturing the kiss I've been dying for. Her body molds to mine, her hips grinding against my growing cock, and I slip my tongue between her lips, tangling with hers, taking everything I've ever needed. That familiar, sweet taste that's all Jack, the one I've somehow remembered vividly despite the lapse in time since I last kissed her, fills my mouth and makes me groan in appreciation.

But before I let this go too far, I jerk my head back and force her head up even more.

"You think about your answer, Jack. But don't take too long because I'll tell you this right now—there's only one thing I've ever wanted in my life, *truly* wanted, that wasn't forced upon me or expected of me, and that was *you*. And now that I have you back, now that I have my *daughter* here, I won't let anything or anyone ever touch you or her. I'll die before I let anything even close to a threat get anywhere *near* you. I always protect what's mine. *Always*."

I release my grip on her hair and step back, leaving her panting and her wide eyes struggling to focus on me. Slowly, I reach into my pocket and pull out my wallet, then remove the folded piece of paper that's remained there for five years and push it against her chest.

She grabs it before it can fall, but she doesn't look at it.

Both of us know what it is and what it says.

That was fun!
- Jack

It was the only thing I ever had of her, and I carried it with me every single day since she left it for me.

Before I can regret it, I move to the stairs and ascend them quickly, not looking down again.

God knows if I do, I won't stop.

7

ISAAC

A sharp knock sounds before the door to my office opens and Dad steps in. He shuts it behind him without even asking if now is a good time to talk, then settles into the chair facing my desk and crosses one ankle over his knee casually, even though his body language is anything but. "What are you doing?"

The same thing I did all day yesterday after Mom stitched me up... researching and finding every damn thing I can about the Satrianos.

I quickly close the web browser screen and turn to face him fully. "Just some research for a motion."

That's what I *should* be doing—my job.

But I can't stop thinking about what happened between Jack and me last night—the flood of emotions threatening to drown me in the moment I finally unleashed on her about how I felt. And I can't concentrate on anything else when there's a very dangerous someone out there willing to do anything to get to her and my daughter.

Dad rests his elbows on the arms of the chair and steeples his hands in front of his mouth, watching me carefully, letting the silence drag out between us the same way he does witnesses when he wants to make them uncomfortable and get them off their game.

It's a tactic he's *tried* to use on me my entire life. It may work on Coen—and likely Mom—but it never does on me, and he knows that. If he's attempting it, it must mean he thinks there's something I need to tell him that I'm withholding.

And there are at least a half dozen things he could be waiting for a confession on.

My hooking up with Tina in her office just outside Judge Cramer's chambers as the judge arrived.

My threat to Whitaker outside the courtroom.

My threat to Broussard that he already reamed me out for.

The fact that even after he did that, I still called our PI and asked him to follow Broussard and get any blackmail material he could find on him that we didn't already know about.

That I wasn't actually researching for a motion and was instead tracking down any information I could locate about the Satrianos so I can protect my *family*.

But it's the possibility that he knows the truth about Jack and Viviana that makes my chest tighten uncomfortably and causes me to shift under his hard stare.

Every once in a while, I catch glimpses of why there are so many people who are afraid of him. A brilliant lawyer, he's a tough man who has the determination and strength of a bull, and he hides his ability to decimate anyone and anything that stands in our way behind a five-thousand-dollar suit, thousand-dollar loafers, and his smile.

I learned everything I know from him—about this business, about actually practicing law, about what it takes to protect an empire like the ones we have created here, and about lying and getting others to admit when they are.

We could sit here forever doing this—staring each other

down until someone or something comes in and breaks the stalemate.

"I didn't know you were back from court yet." I finally end the uncomfortable silence, not because his ploy is working, but rather because I want to get back to what I was doing, learning everything I can about my adversary.

Dad shifts slightly in the chair, reclining to appear almost relaxed in an effort to get me to let down my guard. "Oh, that was a quick hearing. I was done almost two hours ago."

"Where were you, then?"

Any other day, I might have noticed he hadn't popped in with an update on the case like we always try to do after a court appearance, but I've been neck-deep in the single thing that has occupied my mind since the moment I learned Jack was in danger—figuring out a way to end it.

He scrutinizes his cuticles, pretending to appear disinterested, but I know him too well to believe that. "I stopped by your place."

I barely bite back a litany of curses I want to spew at him. If he went there, especially without telling me, he did it with purpose, one he didn't want me to be aware of so I couldn't stop him. But instead of tearing into him, which would only escalate into an argument that would bring Evelyn in here to check to ensure we aren't tearing each other's throats out, I try to remain casual and rest back in my chair, mirroring his position.

"Yeah? Why'd you do that?"

"I wanted to make sure Cutter's daughter and granddaughter were okay. After the way you behaved yesterday, I needed to ensure you weren't going to say or do something that would make it any more uncomfortable for them than this situation must already be."

"And?" I wait for him to get to the point he's intentionally dancing around.

He finally shifts forward, locking his gaze with mine. "And...I finally met Viviana."

She had her face buried in Cutter's neck at the office when we all left for my place two days ago; he wouldn't have seen her.

"Oh?" My heart thunders against my ribcage as he stares me down again.

"Quite a beautiful child, isn't she?"

I nod. "Yes."

"Is there something you want to tell me, son, because things would be a lot easier if we stopped lying to each other, don't you think?"

Fuck.

I should have known the moment he laid eyes on her that he would know. Dad always seems to know every answer without even asking the question—and that answer is spelled out in Caribbean blue.

"You can't say anything to anyone else."

"Jesus, Isaac, how the fuck did this happen?"

I scrub my hands over my face. "The weekend of my law school graduation. We met at a bar and..." I end my explanation there because Dad sure as shit doesn't want to hear about my weekend in bed with that woman.

"And what, she never told you she was pregnant? Please tell me she never told you she was pregnant and I don't need to come over there and smack you myself for saying you didn't want to be involved."

"Fuck you for even saying that. Of course, I didn't know she was pregnant. She didn't know my real name, and I didn't know hers. I only knew her as Jack."

"It certainly explains your odd behavior in my office when you two 'met.' I knew something was up; I just never thought..." He trails off and inhales a deep breath. "So, Cutter and Valentina don't know?"

I shake my head. "No one does except us."

"Don't be so sure about that."

"What do you mean?"

"You're blind, Isaac, if you can't see that little girl is your spitting image. I knew it the moment she looked up and smiled at me. If Gabe, Atlas, Saint, and Bishop haven't already figured it out, they will soon. Anyone who sees the two of you together has to notice it."

Shit.

Shaking my head, I say the words that burn like acid in my mouth. "It's better if people don't know, safer. At least until all of this is resolved with the Satrianos."

As soon as Nana finds out she has a great-grandchild, she'll blab it all over New Orleans, and if it gets to certain ears, it will bring the threat straight to them here.

"I have to tell your mother."

"No, you can't."

"I have to." He offers a mirthless chuckle. "We promised a long time ago that we would never keep things from each other, and I'm not about to start now. I value my life far too much."

Fucking hell.

"Well, make sure she understands she can't say anything to anyone and that Vivi doesn't know. Is she going to be able to see her and not go all grandma on her?"

"I'll make sure she understands." Dad's brows draw together. "But what's going to happen after all this with Satriano gets resolved?"

I slam my fists against my desk. "Don't you think I wish I fucking knew that? Don't you think I want to know exactly what to do and how to do it? Fuck." I shove out of my chair, unable to sit still anymore, and walk to the window overlooking the street. "I don't have a fucking clue how to tell her I'm her father or what it means for...any of us."

Dad remains silent for a moment, giving me time to cool down before he launches into whatever he has to say next. "I've been looking into these people, the Satrianos."

"So have I." I glance over my shoulder at him. "That's what I was just doing."

His lips press into a firm line. "It isn't good."

"No, it isn't." The words I've been reading, the images I've seen splashed across the screen of what they've done, make acid crawl up my throat. I swallow it down and watch a car drive past on the road, trying to concentrate on the way the damp street sprays water up behind each tire instead of on the rage racing through me. "Rumor is Satriano killed his older brother to take over as head of the family." I shake my head. "And they've slaughtered entire families to get what they want. They aren't afraid to pull a trigger without regret, and we all know what people like that are capable of."

I don't have to expand for him to know what I'm talking about. What happened with Dominic Abello all those years ago destroyed so many people, changed so many lives in this family. Even now, Luca can't escape what his father did or what he did with his name after. It still follows us now that he is part of our business empire—and family.

When you're part of that life, it has consequences, real, agonizing ones Dad has to continue to live with every day.

His eyes soften slightly, but his body remains tense in his determination. "I don't want you getting involved, Isaac."

I whirl back to face him fully. "Getting involved? What the fuck do you mean?"

He pushes to his feet. "You leave this to Cutter and his men. I don't want you poking around or doing anything that might draw unwanted attention here."

"Do you think I'm some sort of fucking idiot? Do you really think I would do anything that's going to endanger my child or the woman who gave birth to her?"

"I know you, Isaac. For as good of an attorney as you are, you very often act with your heart before you think with your head. Is she why you didn't come home as planned that weekend?"

Fuck.

I grip the back of my chair. "Yes."

There isn't any point in lying; he knows me too well.

The tiniest of grins pulls at the corner of his lips. "Coen told us you had a few things to finish up before you could come back. I should have known it was a girl."

"Not just *any* girl." I stop short of expanding on my complicated feelings for the woman currently living in my condo who has occupied my heart and thoughts for years. "I'm going to do whatever it takes to make sure she and Viviana are safe."

Dad's jaw hardens, and he points a finger at me. "You listen to me, Isaac. I'm sorry you had to find out about her this way and that it's complicated this situation, but I'm telling you right now, stay the fuck out of Cutter's way and let him handle this.

"The last thing we need is to bring the wrath of the Satrianos to New Orleans. We're already walking a fine line with the Rosellis. We've managed to maintain a peace after they took over from Luca. They've left him alone and allowed him to go legit. They might not be so kind if you do something that brings a man like Satriano into their territory. You're going to stay the fuck out of it, right?"

I give him a sharp nod.

Fuck no, I'm not.

Cutter may be Jack's father. He may be the one trained in all the ways necessary to end this, but I'm not going to sit back and wait for God knows what and who to come after her, after them.

I'll protect them at any cost.

JACK

THE SOOTHING NATURE of Saint's deep voice floats through the living room as I work in my sketchbook, and even though it's a children's story I've heard a thousand times, the words somehow relax a bit of the tension I've been carrying around all day.

My hand moves almost of its own accord, the drawing on the page coming to life easily from memory, as they almost always do.

Of all the things I've spent years drawing, only one subject flows like this, natural, vivid, like something is literally working itself out of my body and onto the page.

Familiar pain in the eyes reflects back at me from the page, and I look at Viviana sitting on Saint's lap, enjoying his recitation of *The Mischief Kittens*.

His dark eyes dart up to me, and he offers a grin, then returns his focus to the page, doing different voices for the various kitty characters that make Vivi giggle.

The door opens behind me, and I close my sketchbook and slide it between the cushion and the side of the chair as Isaac comes in, juggling several bags in his hands.

Isaac's gaze darts immediately to Viviana snuggled in and completely content to listen to the big man read to her. "Looks like I missed a party."

Saint smiles at him. "Miss Viviana here wanted me to read to her, and I thought it might give Mom a little break."

A very welcome one.

It's only been a few days, but already, her energy is hard to keep contained in this place. She needs to run and play, and that's hard to do, even with the toys the Hawkes have brought over for her.

Isaac makes his way across the living room toward the kitchen, drops the bags on the counter, and returns. "About that. I was thinking it would probably be okay if we took the girls out, as long as someone was with them."

Saint considers Isaac's statement. "I remember what Bishop and Pope were like at this age. It's hard to keep kids inside for too long. I'll discuss it with Gabe. Give me a list of everywhere you were thinking about potentially going, and we'll go over it."

Viviana bounces on his lap. "Keep reading, keep reading."

He ruffles her hair with his free hand and dives back into the book as I approach Isaac.

"Thank you for that."

He raises a brow, the move pulling at the stitches over his eye. "For what?"

"For making the suggestion about getting out of here. We're both going a little stir-crazy."

His blue eyes focus on Viviana for a minute. "I figured as much. At her age, it can't be easy to be away from school and toys and everything she knows and have to stay here with very little to entertain her. It isn't exactly the most kid-friendly place." He locks his gaze with mine, a determination deep in it. "But it *is* safe. And if Gabe and Saint don't think taking you out of here would be, then it's off the table."

There isn't any room for question in his statement, and as much as I hate being cooped up in here, if it isn't safe, I would never take Vivi out.

"I know. I understand that. I would never put her in any unnecessary danger. You have to know that."

Isaac offers me a little half-smile, some of his seriousness and animosity melting away. "I do. You're a great mom. I can already see that."

He doesn't elaborate, but I can almost feel what he wants to say, that he missed a chance to be a great father, to be there for her over the last couple of years and have the kind of relationship I do with her.

I take a half-step closer and peek at Saint to make sure he's not paying attention, but he's completely wrapped up in the little girl on his lap.

"You can be a great dad, too, Isaac. It isn't too late for that."

He slowly peeks at me out of the corner of his eye but doesn't respond, just continues to watch them, the pain still etched on his face.

Finally, Saint announces, "The end," and closes the book, then easily lifts Viviana and settles her on the couch next to him while he climbs to his feet. "Well, I'm going to take off since you're here. You guys need anything?"

Isaac shakes his head. "No, go home to Caroline. I picked up dinner on the way here. I hope everybody loves hamburgers and french fries as much as I do."

Viviana's eyes fly wide, and she bounces up and down, clapping her hands with sheer glee. "I *love* french fries."

I move over to the couch and squat in front of her. "But you're not going to have any until you finish at least half your hamburger, right?"

She pouts and crosses her arms over her chest defiantly. *So damn much like her father.* "Fine, but only half."

Getting a four-year-old to eat sometimes feels like an uphill battle, but bribery with fries always works. I ruffle her hair and walk back toward the kitchen, her father's roving gaze following my every move.

Isaac leans into me as I approach. "I wonder where she gets that attitude from."

I gape at him as Saint makes his way to the door.

"You two have a good night." He returns his gaze to Viviana. "Next time I come, we can do the next book in the series."

She claps excitedly. "Yay! Thank you, Mr. Saint."

He grins at her. "Just Saint."

The door clicks shut, and Isaac goes over and flips the latch into place. "There shouldn't be anyone else coming tonight. Why don't we eat?"

Viviana rushes from the couch into the kitchen and reaches up to the bags, but Isaac slips in front of her and shakes his head as she grabs a fry.

"Your mom said no fries until you had half your hamburger."

She pouts at him, her bottom lip falling out impossibly far, her big blue eyes staring up like a lost puppy. "Aw, just one?"

He looks to me as if asking for permission, and as much as I want to stick to my guns, the little bit of real sadness on her face is too damn hard to ignore when I know she's had a hard time being here the last few days.

I nod. "Just one."

She shoves it into her mouth as I usher her away from the counter and over to the table. Isaac unpacks everything, occasionally peeking up at us, but mostly quiet. The sharp contrast between the man I met five years ago, how open he was, how easily we talked as if we'd known each other forever, and the tension with this one now makes my stomach flip-flop.

We have to figure out what we're going to do about Viviana, when we're going to tell her and how, and what that means for the future once this is all over. That's another conversation I'm not sure I'm prepared to have with him, given the way it ended last night.

Definitely not ready.

My lips still tingle at the memory of Isaac crushing his into them.

I'm not sure I slept at all last night, tossing and turning, the vivid images of our time spent together haunting me relentlessly.

He settles the food in front of each of us and takes a seat across from us. "So, Viviana, you like kittens?"

She takes a bite of her hamburger and nods, mumbling around her food, "I wuv kittens. They're so cwute and fwuffy."

He chuckles and shoves a french fry into his mouth. My eyes immediately following the motion to watch his lips close around it.

God, that shouldn't be so hot.

But I know what that mouth can do...

It makes me shift on my seat to press my thighs together tighter.

Isaac takes a bite of his burger and chews, watching her do the same. "Do you have a cat back home?"

Viviana frowns and shakes her head. "No. Grandpa's awergic."

Isaac grins and shakes his head. "That's too bad. I am, too."

I swallow my bite of hamburger and take a sip from my glass of water. "I don't know that Viviana is prepared for the responsibility of taking care of a pet anyway, right, Viv? You have to feed it, make sure it has water, and take it to the vet if it's sick. It's a lot of work."

Leaning back slightly in his chair, Isaac gives Vivi a sad grin. "My mom and dad wouldn't let me get a dog, and I really wanted one. I've been thinking about getting one now that I have my own place here."

I freeze with my hamburger halfway up to my mouth.

He points to her. "We may have to take a little trip to the animal rescue to see who's there. What do you think?"

Viviana bounces in her seat and claps her hands. "Yes. Yes. Can we, Mommy?"

"Maybe." I point to her plate to refocus her attention. "*Mangia!*"

I'll have to have a little talk with Isaac about mentioning things to her that might not happen. Getting her hopes up only to dash them is worse than her never getting what she wants. If she helps him pick out a dog, then we leave both him and it, she'll be crushed.

And enough major things are going to be hitting her hard soon.

We all tuck into our food, and somehow, I manage to get Viviana to eat half of her hamburger before she plows through the entire bag of fries.

I shove another one into my mouth. "This is really good. Where is it from?"

Isaac motions back toward the now-empty bags in the kitchen. "Lee's. It's one of my favorites. We get it delivered for lunch a lot at the office."

"Are you guys busy?"

He freezes and glances toward Viviana again. "You could say that."

"I heard you're opening a hotel."

His jaw hardens, and his hand tightens on his burger slightly. "Trying to."

"Problem?"

Isaac shakes his head, trying to dismiss my concern, but the way his eyes darken gives away that there clearly is one. "Nothing I can't handle."

For some reason, his words send a shiver through me. The way he described his family and the way Mom and Dad have talked about the Hawkes over the years tells me they aren't the type who would let anything interfere with a plan like that. But he clearly doesn't want to discuss it with me in front of Viviana, or maybe not at all, so I don't press him, just help him clear the table as she grabs her iPad from the couch and pulls up a video.

I dump our trash into the can, and the warm wall of Isaac's body covers my back. He doesn't say anything, just pulls my hair over one shoulder and feathers his lips slowly across my nape.

Another shiver rolls through me, this one causing me to press against him even more, instinctually seeking his warmth and strength.

"I want to know everything, Jack, what she loves, what she hates. I saw the look you gave me when I was talking about the dog. If she wants a damn cat or a dog or a hamster or a fucking pig for that matter, I'm going to make sure she has it."

I turn my head sideways toward him, his warm breath mingling with mine. "You can't buy her affection or just give her whatever she wants all the time, Isaac."

"We'll see." He trails his fingertips down my arm, raising goosebumps across my sensitive skin. "I want to give both of you everything you want, Jack. All you have to do is ask…"

He moves away from me, leaving me speechless and my skin

on fire. How that man can do it to me with one simple brush of his lips makes me feel weaker than I ever have in my entire life.

I follow him out of the kitchen and find him leaning against the wall, watching her.

What he said last night trickles through my head.

I haven't said anything to her because I don't know what to say to a little girl who doesn't know me and because every fucking time she looks at me with my eyes, I can barely breathe, let alone form words.

The pain of seeing him watch his daughter almost makes me want to tell her right now, but it's better if she doesn't know, not until all of this shit with the Satrianos is resolved...and definitely not until Isaac and I have some sort of understanding about what we're doing when it is over.

Though that somehow feels harder than eliminating a damn mob boss.

ISAAC

A cold breeze whips off the Mississippi and swirls around me where I stand on the balcony, staring out at the vast blackness of the water juxtaposed with the glittering city lights all along the banks.

I take another sip of my bourbon and let the liquid's burn warm me from the inside out, but it doesn't do anything to calm the turmoil raging inside me.

Sitting across from Viviana at the dinner table, realizing I know nothing about her, only drove home how badly I want to, how much I want to be a father to her, to give her everything she ever wanted, to be there for her no matter what.

I've been robbed of that, and despite what Jack assured me, it feels like it's too late, like I've missed the parts that really counted, that I've had no role in shaping her and the type of person she's going to be.

At her age, I was sitting on Dad's knee in this office while Mom worked at the hospital. I was forming a bond with him that turned me into the man I am today. All those years, I had them both. I had it all—everything I could ever want or need. Knowing what I do about Cutter, Valentina, and Jack, they would never allow Vivi to want for anything they could give her, but they could never give her a father.

I tighten my hand around the railing until it hurts, fighting the desire to want to blame Jack for all of this, but even though she's the one who left, the one who *ran,* my own role in all this is what keeps making rage flood my veins.

That night in the bar, I was perfectly happy to give Jack a fake name and spend an anonymous weekend with a beautiful woman. I was the idiot who didn't tell her who I really was the second I realized how different things were with her.

If I hadn't waited, if I hadn't so easily tumbled back into bed with her and sought our pleasure instead of coming clean, we wouldn't be in this situation.

And isn't that a hard fucking pill to swallow?

I down the rest of my drink, take one last look at the water, and make my way back inside. The entire condo has somehow felt different the last few days since they arrived.

Full.

More alive.

Like something that was missing has finally been found.

But there are people who want to rip it apart again.

The Satrianos won't get anywhere near them, but the truth of who Viviana is might be enough to ruin everything. Jack's parents aren't going to let them go easily, and Jack doesn't seem to want to stay.

I set my empty glass on the bar, but instead of refilling it and sitting in front of the fireplace or pacing the way I have been for the last two days, I'm drawn toward the hallway to the guest bedroom.

My eye catches something tucked into the chair, and I grab what appears to be a notebook of some sort and flip it open.

Sketches of the river and the buildings visible from the

balcony fill the pages—stunningly beautiful and perfect renditions that could appear on any postcard for the city. Page after page, I flip through, knowing exactly whose deft hand did this.

Jack...

She never mentioned being an artist before, but this is her hand. I know it deep in my soul, and I flip to the next page and stop, my assumption confirmed by my own face on the page.

Only it isn't me now, with this cut over my eye.

It's me. Sleeping in that bed in Chicago the way she left me that morning.

She must have drawn it from memory, and seeing the way she saw me simultaneously heats my blood and draws my ire.

Jack saw this and left.

I close the book and put it back, then make my way down the hall to the guestroom.

It feels wrong to open the door, to want to see my daughter and check in on her, to want to see Jack after seeing that, but knowing they've been here the last two nights has made it impossible for me to sleep, and I know I won't again tonight until I ensure they're comfortable and see them one last time.

It's been hours since they came back here to go to bed, and there's no way Viviana is still awake, but still, I turn the handle slowly and ease the door open as quietly as I can so I don't accidentally wake them.

Darkness envelops the room.

Light streams from under the bathroom door, and the sound of rushing water in the shower slips out.

A small nightlight I had Bishop bring with her to keep in here for Viviana so she wouldn't wake up in a strange place and be scared in the dark glows next to the nightstand.

It casts a faint glow across the massive bed where Viviana lies facing me, snuggled deep in the thick comforter, her lips parted slightly, soft little pants of breath slipping from them.

My heart clenches in my chest, and I have to force myself to take another step and not remain frozen in place, watching her. Other than her steady breathing, she doesn't move.

Completely at peace in her sleep...like I have never been.

I wish I could sleep like the weight of the world wasn't on my shoulders, like the future of this family and our businesses doesn't rely on my being perfect at my job.

But it does.

Everyone relies on Dad and me to hold the businesses together, to ensure any threats are removed, and to use anything and everything at our disposal to ensure we succeed.

If I fuck up, it isn't just about me.

And staring down at Viviana, that reality slams into me like a freight train.

I have a daughter now.

This little girl is my flesh and blood. Everything I do, each choice I make, will ultimately affect her and her future.

I reach out and brush a soft strand of Viviana's dark hair from her face, letting my fingertips linger on her soft cheek. What I wouldn't give to have been able to be there all this time to tuck her in, read her a story before bed, have her throw her arms around me and say, "I love you, Daddy."

Fuck.

Somehow, I manage to choke back the strangled sound that tries to escape my throat. Then I quickly move away from her before I lose control over my emotions completely and wake her. The last thing she needs is to find me in tears, wondering what the hell is going on.

A sharp thud followed by a crashing sound comes from the bathroom.

Jack!

I rush across the room and push open the door. She freezes where she stands in the shower, steam filling the room, the water cascading over her with her hand between her legs.

Sweet fuck.

My eyes immediately roam over the body I explored so thoroughly over those two days, one that has changed since the last time I saw her this way. She's even more stunning. Her hips slightly wider and thicker, begging for me to dig my fingers into them. Her breasts higher and fuller, making my mouth water to taste them again.

Her wide eyes find mine through the fogged glass.

Turn around.

Walk away.

It would be so easy to listen to that little voice inside my head, to give her space and time to figure out how we're going to handle this situation like rational adults.

But there's nothing rational when it comes to how I feel about Jack.

I push the door closed behind me and approach her slowly. She remains frozen, watching my every move, her hand still buried between her thighs. It's the worst temptation. An invitation to the greatest kind of sin.

And I don't have the power to walk away right now.

Not after everything that's happened in the last few days, not after years of dreaming about this, about *her.*

I slide open the shower door and step in, still fully clothed and not giving a single fuck that I am. Things are so uncertain between us, so tense, but I warned her last night, told her she wasn't going to have much time before I came for her, before she would have to face whatever this is between us.

Seeing her like this, her cheeks pink, and not just from the heat of the water, her lush body dripping wet, nipples high and pointed, her hand still frozen at her core, I don't think it's possible for me to walk away, even if I tried.

I move toward her, kicking the shampoo and conditioner bottles that must have caused the noise from around her feet so I can get close until the length of my entire body is pressed against her, pinning her to the wall of the shower.

Hot water beats down on us from the left, soaking my clothes and warming my skin that's still chilled from standing outside. Her chest heaves against mine, her hand pinned between our bodies, lips parted, and eyes wide in anticipation.

I drag my hand up the side of her right thigh and stop at her hip, squeezing there, letting my fingers dig into her heated flesh. "Have you thought about what I said last night?"

She gives a sharp nod, and her body trembles against mine.

"You are my family, Jack, you and our daughter, and as soon as you're both safe, I'm going to claim what's mine."

Jack issues a little low mewl at my statement, staring up at me with thick, dark, wet lashes and burning amber orbs. I slide my hand slowly across her stomach, giving her every chance to tell me no or to push me away. Her eyes squeeze closed, and her flesh under my palm trembles.

"What were you doing when I came in here, Jack?"

Slowly, I wrap my hand over hers, burying it between her legs where she still has one finger inside her cunt. She opens her eyes to meet mine, the same lust I saw there years ago flaring.

"Were you touching yourself, thinking about me?"

A strangled groan sounds deep in her throat like she's caught between answering my question and pushing me away. "*Yes...*"

Her admission comes breathy and barely audible, and I fight the grin of satisfaction that threatens to appear.

"Do you do that a lot, Jack?" I lean in and flutter my lips against her ear, the sound of the rushing water and her soft pants echoing in mine. "Do you touch yourself and think about that weekend, about the time we spent together?"

She groans and nods again, and I nip at her earlobe, grinding my pelvis against our hands caught between our bodies.

"I do, too. I've thought about it every day for the last five years." I press my hard cock against her thigh tightly. "I haven't come in half a decade without picturing you, without wishing I was with you again."

She finally lifts her other hand to grab my waist, then slip it up under my wet shirt, gripping me there, her touch igniting a fire within me the same way it did all those years ago.

"So, tell me, Jack." I pull my head back and hover my lips over hers. "Tell me what you want..."

JACK

There's no easy answer to that...

There never really was, and recent events have made it even more impossible to give him one. So much has changed in the last few days; I can't tell what's right or wrong anymore. Before my life was uprooted, before I had to rip apart *his* and change it forever, all I wanted was freedom from the things that kept me chained in place and unmoving.

I wanted Mom and Dad to allow me to live my life away from everything being their daughter means, to treat me like the adult I am who can take care of myself and doesn't need to be monitored like a damn child.

It's the same thing I was searching for that weekend I spent with Nolan. When I was just "Jack," the redhead he met at the bar, and not Giacomina, the daughter of a mob boss who ditched her guards and sent her parents tearing across Chicago, looking for her.

For those two days, I could pretend who I *wasn't* and that my body didn't betray me. That weekend was the first time I could just feel and absorb everything he did to me so damn well. The only time I've ever just *enjoyed* being without needing to question motives.

Those two nights ignited my body.

Just like he is now...

Flashbacks to that elevator and the way he made me come

harder than I ever have in my life in that hallway have kept me going for years, have given me a glimpse of what I could have, what's *out* there, in the place I could never go because I would never be allowed to leave.

All I want is *freedom.*

To be anyone else. To go to school and learn from people who can make me better, who can teach me to become a better artist. To give Vivi a different kind of life than the one I've had.

One where her future isn't determined by what flows through her veins but rather by what she chooses for herself.

That's what I wanted then.

It's still what I want—to be free of all of *this.*

I want a life where I can walk on the street with Viviana without bodyguards at the ready, where I don't have to look over my shoulder and be ready to shield her from bullets. I want a life where no one tells me how to live or tries to control me. I want to go back to that weekend and be Jack again, to allow Isaac to do to me now what he did to me then.

It was the first and last time I ever *truly* felt free, and being here, with him pressed against me, his hard, solid body pinning me to the slick shower wall, I'm starting to feel that way again, starting to believe there *might* be hope somewhere for something even remotely like the life I could have had with "Nolan" if I hadn't left that morning...

"*Non avrei mai dovuto andarmene...*" The words tumble from my lips like a confession, done in a language he won't understand to keep him from knowing the truth of how much I truly regret it, of how much it tears me apart inside.

I roll my hips as much as I can in his hold, desperate for it, for him, for that feeling *one more time.*

Isaac adjusts his hand over mine between us so he can force my finger deeper inside me. I bite back a moan, his lips just in front of mine, the warm, sweet bourbon on his breath, and my pussy clasps, wanting more. So much more.

"Go ahead, Jack." He uses his hand to control mine, grinding my palm against my clit and thrusting my finger inside me, his joining in. The addition stretches me wider, but he doesn't give me any room to move and get the friction I really need. "Tell me what you want from me."

I toss my head side to side, the barely there movements between my legs not enough to give me release, just enough to leave me hanging in that place that's so exquisitely painful. It's the same game he played that night in the elevator that was equal parts pleasure and agony.

Until he finally brought me somewhere I had never been before, somewhere I want to be again—completely *free*.

Not this.

Pinned to a wall by the man who controls so much of my past and future.

Stuck between two worlds.

Forced to endure uprooting my life and my child only to be thrown in with the man who wants it all and isn't afraid to go after it.

The man who is making a point right now—one that is crystal clear.

He *is* the one in control here.

I'm helpless putty in his hands, just like I was back then.

This is torture...

He knows what he can do to my body. How he can completely unravel me. He did things to me I didn't even know were possible.

And he knows it.

Isaac's confidence and outright arrogance should enrage me. It should make me shove him away and rail at him for coming in and interrupting my very private moment. It should fuel my desire to get far away from him. It should make me want to fight my traitorous body for reacting this way to him.

It should...

But the way his blue eyes burn with barely restrained desire make it impossible for me to, and his admission that he thinks about me, that he's *been* thinking about me for five years the same way I have him, makes me finally open my mouth with the answer to his question.

"I want to go back to that day and not get out of bed. Not get in that car." I take a shaky breath. "I want to go back and do it all over again."

His body stiffens, and his hand stops moving against mine. A tiny bit of the anguish he's been carrying around in his gaze seeps away, replaced by a softness and light that existed that weekend when he looked at me. "I want that, too, Jack. More than I can possibly ever put into words, but that's impossible." That pain returns to his gaze, along with resolve. "Tell me something that *is* possible."

That's easy.

In this moment, there's only *one* thing I want.

"I want to come."

He presses a soft kiss to the corner of my lips. "I bet you do."

His hand molded over mine begins to move again, harder and faster, guiding me to fuck myself with his finger and mine while my palm rubs against my clit almost violently.

It doesn't take long for that, plus the heat of the water cascading around us and radiating from his body against mine to set me on fire. A flame deep within me flickers, my release on the horizon, so close my body begins to shake in anticipation of it finally hitting.

My mind goes back to Isaac on his knees in that hotel hallway, his tongue thrusting into me, his fingers working me over, the way I came like a fucking waterfall rushing out of me and down his throat.

Oh, God...

The same image has been the only thing that allowed me to reach climax since, and *never* like that. I'm so damn close now, with the water pounding down around us and Isaac's familiar scent invading every breath I take.

I can almost imagine being there again, in that hotel, as Jack and Nolan, the way we let ourselves go completely...

So. Damn. Close.

Every fiber of my being reaches for it, strains to find that pinnacle of ecstasy I'm seeking, to release everything that's built up for so long.

But Isaac stills his hand. My eyes fly open to meet his, now icy cold and sharp enough to slice me wide open. His lean, hard muscles ripple under the fingertips of my hand at his side, and his cock pushes against my leg, straining against the soaked fabric of his pants, seeking the same thing I am.

God, yes.

I want *all* of him right now, not just to come on my hand.

Only instead of freeing himself, instead of giving us what we both want, he feathers a kiss to my forehead, then backs away under the water, pulling his hand from between my legs.

I stumble forward slightly, but his steady grip on my hip keeps me from falling completely.

Somehow, I manage to form words through the haze fogging my head. "Wh-what are you doing?"

"What do you *really* want from me, Jack? I'm going to ask you that question again. Very soon. And you're going to have to give me an answer that isn't just about getting off."

With that, he slides open the shower door, steps out soaking wet, and stalks from the bathroom—a trail of hot water, frustration, and heartache in his wake.

Everything I did to him then, all the consequences of my actions, of *our* actions, have come crumbling down around us. I ran from who I was that weekend and straight into his arms. And now, because of who I am, I've been put back in them.

But somehow, it feels like moving from one prison to another.

Now that I'm here, now that he knows Viviana is his daughter,

Isaac isn't going to let us leave. Even if Mom and Dad manage to resolve this threat, I can't go back to Chicago with Viviana. Isaac isn't going to let me walk away that easily again, especially not with her.

Despite his asking, what I want doesn't really matter.

Isaac is going to take what he wants and ensure it doesn't disappear again. The moment his eyes met mine in his father's office, I knew it was over.

I can never escape.

Everything I was always told about the Hawkes has proven true. They're powerful and hard businessmen who control their empires carefully, callously, and heartlessly.

But it's more than that.

Isaac isn't heartless; he's proven that over and over again—in what he said and did that weekend and in his reaction to finding out about Viviana. Heartless men don't care about anything or anyone but themselves. Isaac Hawke isn't that.

He's worse than heartless...he's ruthless.

9

ISAAC

Broussard answers his phone with as much friendliness as I would expect, given how we last left things. "Isaac, I wasn't expecting to hear from you. I figured you'd save anything you have to say for the zoning board meeting."

I lean back in my chair and grin, anticipating what I'm about to do to Broussard with the information in the file folder on my desk. How quickly one's skeletons are easily discovered... "I thought it was best we talk privately before the meeting."

"Why? You going to threaten me some more?"

Issuing a low chuckle, I kick my feet up onto the desk and swivel my chair slightly so I can see out the window. "Like my father said, we don't issue threats. We just make things happen."

"I don't care what you call it, Hawke. You and your father have no problem getting your hands dirty, and to suggest otherwise is ludicrous. I have been around long enough to see your handiwork."

"You *have* been around a long time, Mr. Broussard, and that's why I'm so shocked that you would make a move like this against us."

"It isn't a move against you, Isaac. I'm going to lose my position if I don't support the people of the community and acknowledge their concerns."

"Bullshit. You bought and paid for your position, and everyone knows it. I'm more shocked that you would choose to stand against us, knowing the skeletons you have hiding in your own closet and how easily they could be found."

Silence lingers for a second before Broussard makes an uncomfortable coughing sound. "I-I don't know what you're talking about."

I lean forward to shuffle through the papers to get to the back and all the photos my PI brought me. "Let me give you a little piece of unsolicited legal advice, Mr. Broussard. If you want to take payoffs, it's best that you don't meet with those *paying* you somewhere a camera can get a good angle."

The images of him and Cassius Whitaker make my jaw tighten and are clear enough to show some form of exchange and relationship. That alone would be enough to raise with the board and get him removed from office, and he knows it.

"I have a lot of friends, Mr. Hawke." Broussard's anger raises his tone. "It's not a crime to talk to them."

"You're right, it's not, but it *is* a crime for a government official to accept a bribe. And I have photographic evidence that shows you have."

"Photos don't show shit. Just me having coffee with a friend."

"Gosh, Broussard, you're right." I flip through a couple more pages. "But what's really interesting are the bank records that show a $20,000 check deposit on the same day as that meeting. And based on the timestamps of these photographs and the information provided to me by a friend at the bank, it seems that little deposit was made just after your meeting. That's what we call strong circumstantial evidence in court."

And with that, I can rake him across the coals...if he doesn't cooperate.

"You-you-you can't do this. You can't blackmail me like this."

"I'm not blackmailing you. I'm a concerned citizen raising my concerns. Isn't that what you just said your job is? To address the *concerns* of citizens?"

"You better—"

"Ah, ah, ah, before you continue that statement, you might want to hear what else I have *concerns* about." My smile falters at even having to bring this up, at knowing what Broussard's been doing. If we had any idea any of this was going on before, we would have ensured he was dealt with properly a long time ago. "This is where things get even dicier. Do you have any idea what the penalties are for sex with someone under the age of sixteen in Louisiana?"

"Wh-what?" He blubbers some unintelligible words and jostles the phone like he's trying to get somewhere more private. "I don't know what the hell you're talking about."

"Oh, you don't?" I finger the edge of one of the photos. "That's funny, because again, these photos are pretty suggestive of something inappropriate going on, showing you entering a hotel with her and kissing before the door even closes. The girl you're with wasn't hard to find. You need to learn to cover your tracks better, Broussard."

This time, he doesn't respond, so I continue.

"Here's what's going to happen—"

"You don't get to tell me what to do, Hawke. I'm the one holding all the cards here."

The man is delusional. Well and truly insane to believe he has any way out of this. He dug himself his own grave when he decided to fuck with our plans, and now, he's scrambling for a way up and out of it with bravado he doesn't have.

"If you don't want to go to prison for the rest of your fucking life, Broussard, then you need to shut up and listen to me. The night before the zoning meeting, you are going to announce that due to a family emergency, you will be stepping down from your position on the board and from your formal office. You will announce that the deputy director will be stepping up in your place until a proper appointment can be made to refill the position. You will be retiring from political life, and you will never be alone with *any* juvenile again. If I find out that you are, and believe me, I *will* be watching and I have ways of knowing, then going to prison is going to be the least of your worries. Do you understand?"

It's an easy question to answer, one he should be able to quickly, but the man is clearly not in his right mind.

"You can't threaten me like this. I'll..."

"You'll what? Call the police? I'm sure they'd be very interested in all the information I have on you. This isn't a request, Broussard. This is what is going to happen. I expect to see your press conference the night before the board meeting. Keep yourself clean until then. I'll know if you don't."

I end the call and slam the folder shut, the contents sending a mix of rage and pleasure through me. It always feels so good to take down someone like Broussard, but knowing I can't risk doing what I *want* to that slimy fucker makes it impossible to truly be content or enjoy this victory.

This isn't the time to risk that sort of move. If I made it and anyone got wind or we got caught, it would complicate the hotel deal more than Broussard already has. Still, the thought of him walking the streets free after what he did makes my hand tighten into a fist on the top of my desk.

Saint checked on the girl who apparently met Broussard at a youth leadership conference where he was an invited speaker. The fucker took advantage of his position with a young, impressionable student. He deserves to be shot in the gut, dropped out of a boat in the middle of the fucking Gulf, and left to the sharks, which would've been my preferred route.

But one thing Dad said the other day is true—the last thing we want to do is draw any attention to ourselves or do anything that might hold up this deal.

Now that Broussard's out of the way, the meeting with the board is going to go a lot smoother. All we have to do now is get everyone to sign on the dotted line, and we'll be able to break ground on The Hawke Hotel and finally advance what will be our future.

A future that felt so certain only a few days ago before I got that text from Gabe.

Before I saw Jack.

Before I saw Viviana.

Now, everything I once thought was so clear is shrouded in uncertainty. All I can see when I try to look past today is that little girl's blue eyes and the way Jack looked at me in the shower last night.

I check the clock hanging on the wall above the door and wince. It's only 10:30 AM, but it already seems like five. It feels like I've been away from Jack and Viviana for days, even though I only left two hours ago.

While they're in good hands with Bishop—that girl rivals Saint in what she's capable of at a third his size—I still want to grab my keys, jump in the car, and race back home to them.

My home.

When this is all over, they'll want to go back to theirs. The thought of that happening makes my stomach crawl into my throat. Keeping them cooped up there won't do anything to make them want to stay, but there may be something I can do about that.

I grab my phone and dial Saint.

"Isaac. What's going on?"

"I want to take the girls out to lunch today, get them out of the condo."

"Gabe and I discussed it, and as long you let us know

where you're going to be and you, Bishop, me, or one of the guys are with them, then we think it's okay for you to go to a few places. No one here should recognize them, but just be aware of what you're talking about, and don't say anything anyone could overhear."

"Of course not. I'm not an idiot, Saint."

"I know. I know, but I have to do my due diligence, too."

I bark out a laugh. "Due diligence? Look at you, using legal terms."

"Shut up, kid. I've been around you and your father long enough to have picked up a few things."

Chuckling, I lean back in my chair again and run a hand through my hair. "I'm going to take them to The Hawkeye Grill. We control it, and I know every inch of it by heart, but I need to go talk to Savage first now that he's back in town."

If anyone will understand my situation with Viviana and Jack, it will be him. The patriarch of the Hawke family has always had his door open to all of us when we need help, and I definitely need help—from someone who *isn't* Dad.

He can't remain neutral when we're talking about his own granddaughter. At least Savage will *pretend* to be and let me vent my frustrations over the situation to a friendly ear.

A bit of static comes through the line. "I just left the club. He's in his office."

"Great. I'll have Bishop bring the girls to meet me there, and we can head to the grill."

"Just be careful, Isaac. You have precious cargo with you."

"I know."

Saint doesn't expand on his statement, but what Dad said the other day rings in my ears. If he so easily recognized my connection to Viviana, then Saint likely has, too.

It's going to be the worst-kept secret in New Orleans, but as long as the Satrianos don't find out who they are or where they are, my girls will stay safe.

And I'll do anything to ensure that.

Even if it means tracking down Satriano myself and putting an end to him.

Until then, I'll be ready.

I pull open my top center drawer and grab my Glock.

JACK

I STARE at the Scrabble board and back at my letters, frowning.

This fucking sucks.

Losing might be the thing I hate the most—except maybe being told what to do or having Isaac almost jerk me off in the shower last night, then walk away, leaving me hanging.

Fucking asshole.

I shift in my seat, my body still feeling the lingering effects of what that man did—and didn't—do to me. By the time I processed what had happened, I was too angry to even finish myself. My ire didn't dissipate drying off or climbing from the shower and back into bed with Viviana, who remained blissfully unaware of what just had happened in the bathroom.

After I cleaned up all the goddamn water he trailed across the wood floors.

The letters in front of me finally coalesce into a word that could not be more on-point, and I grin.

Bishop shakes her head. "I don't like you looking that happy."

I offer a little half-shrug as I pull the required letters and drop them onto the board, crossing her word "baby" at the *A.* "Asshole. A-S-S-H-O-L-E."

She barks out a laugh and glances over to the couch where Astrid sits with Viviana, trying to get her to work on some alphabet games and reading projects since it seems like we may be here for a while and she won't be heading back to school in Chicago.

I wave a hand at Bishop. "Don't worry about that. Growing up in my parents' house, that kid has already heard far more than she should. She can curse in two languages. We very rarely succeed at censoring ourselves much in front of her."

Bishop chuckles as I draw my replacement tiles. "That's the way it was around my house, too. My mom curses like a sailor."

"And your dad?"

She shrugs almost nonchalantly. "He does. He was an athlete, so he definitely has a bit of that in him just from being around jocks all the time. However, he was also raised in a very religious family, and that reins him in when he's in public most of the time. Private's a different story. My brother, Pope, and I both got an awful earful from them and the Hawkes."

Why does that not surprise me?

Isaac certainly has a way with words, and he doesn't have any problem telling it exactly like it is.

"What does your brother do?"

She looks at her letters, pulls them, and plays *SOAP* for a triple-word score.

"Nice one."

"Pope is a doctor."

"Really? I would have expected he would work with you and your dad or do something else for the Hawkes."

"He just graduated medical school and started as an intern."

"Is he here in town?"

"Yep. He went to Tulane for medical school but got really lucky to end up here for his residency placement. He works at UMC, which is the only level-one trauma center in New Orleans. The same place Isaac's mom works."

"She's a doctor, too?"

"Yep, chief of the emergency department, actually." She grins. "Stripper turned doctor."

"Excuse me?"

Bishop laughs. "That's a funny story. Well, maybe not so funny, depending on how you look at it. But yeah. Anyway, she used to strip at the Hawkeye Club, and her sister is married to Savage."

"I don't know if I'm going to remember all of this. My dad used to talk about the Hawkes a lot, but it was more vague references to people's names in passing and a lot of talk about Gabe."

And I never really paid attention.

There wasn't any reason to. I certainly never imagined I would be hiding out with them—or have a child with one of them.

The strange twist of fate that brought us together in Chicago that night only to bring us back together now keeps giving me whiplash. So does that dark-haired man with the striking blue eyes that first met mine across that bar and lured me in with his witty banter and weak pool skills.

Push and pull.

Hot and cold.

Anger and lust.

Everything twisted up between us so much it's impossible to untangle it.

Bishop writes down her score. "Yeah, they were really close when they served together. Anyway, don't worry too much about the names and who is who. I'm sure you'll meet everybody and get to know them soon enough."

"I don't know how long we'll be staying."

She tenses and peeks at Viviana and Astrid again before she leans across the table slightly. "Look, I wasn't going to say anything, but..."

"But what?"

"I got the feeling you and Isaac might have known each other prior to your dad bringing you down here. You don't interact like two people who were strangers only a few days ago."

Shit!

Apparently, I really suck at hiding my emotions around that man. Everything has been coming at me so hard and fast; it's a wonder my body hasn't revolted under the stress and pressure.

I play *SPARKLE* for a double-word score, mulling over her observation. "If you're asking what I think you're asking"—I glance at Viviana—"then...yes."

Regret settles on my chest almost immediately.

I shouldn't have admitted it to her.

It's better if people don't know—safer—but I don't have anyone here I can talk to. No confidant, no one who can understand what I'm going through and give me any advice. No one who knows Isaac Hawke better than she does.

Her eyes widen slightly. "Holy shit. I mean, looking at her, I can see it, but wow. Did he know?"

I shake my head. "No."

"Shit. So, the first time he found out was..."

Pressing my lips together, I offer a sharp nod. "Yep. When he walked into his dad's office and saw me there with my dad and then met Viviana."

"I bet that didn't go over very well."

Understatement of the year.

That look on Isaac's face when he saw her was enough to crumble even the stoniest of hearts.

"No, it did not." Far from it. The last several days have been like walking a tightrope with no net beneath me and a hungry lion waiting for me to fall into his open jaws. "Things are complicated...intense."

"I would think so."

I check on Viviana again before I shift forward and lower my voice. "Look, you know him better than anybody, right?"

She sighs. "As well as anyone can really know Isaac, I guess. All of us grew up like cousins, you know. We're family. We've been together our whole lives."

"Then maybe you can offer me some insight."

Her dark eyebrows rise slowly. "Insight into *that* man?" She scoffs and offers me a half grin. "Trust me, Mina. Nobody knows Isaac, not really. Even as a child, he spent so much time with his dad at the office. His mom was in medical school, then her internship and residency, followed by various shifts working her way up to the badass she is now. A lot of Stone rubbed off on him, and that might not necessarily be a good thing."

"What do you mean?"

Stone Hawke seems like an incredible man and father, and although Isaac feels pressure from him to fix everything for the family, there's love and support there. At least from what I can see. Even when Isaac talked about him five years ago, it was never anything *negative,* really. More like he had a lot to live up to, and his father's expectations might have been too much for him to handle.

The way Bishop says it makes it sound like there's something sinister underneath the polished surface of Stone Hawke.

"Stone has a complicated history." She chances a glance at the girls again to ensure they're busy. "Do you know who the Abellos are?"

The familiar name I haven't heard in years makes me freeze. "The mob family here?"

With quite the reputation for violence and cold, calculating maneuvers to keep their iron grip on the Gulf Coast for decades.

"Well, they *were* the family in control here. Dominic Abello grew up kind of like an uncle to Savage, Storm, Skye, Star, and Stone. And since Stone was the baby and their father passed away when he was really young, he needed a father figure. Dom stepped in."

"Shit."

Talk about choosing the wrong role model.

I don't wear rose-colored glasses when it comes to what the Marconis do or have done, but I know enough. My grandfather had values. A system of checks and balances to ensure no lines he drew were crossed. And Mom does her best to ensure that continues.

It's likely what started this damn war with Satriano in the first place.

But the Abellos? They had a reputation for not caring about any fallout.

Damn the consequences.

"Anyway"—she flits a hand—"Stone ended up in some pretty dark situations because of it. He eventually went to work for Abello after law school, and let's just say there were some unintended consequences."

"Well, what the hell happened?"

She freezes. "I probably shouldn't be telling you all this."

"Well, now, I have to know."

Leaving me hanging seems to be a real Hawke trait.

"I think you should ask Isaac. Really, Mina, I shouldn't be airing the Hawkes' dirty laundry. Even if you are one now."

Even if I am one now?

I chuckle. "I am *not* a Hawke."

Her gaze locks on Viviana, then returns to me. "Honey, you have Isaac Hawke's child, and I've seen the way he looks at you. I don't care what you say. You're a fucking Hawke whether you like it or not." Her phone buzzes on the table, and she checks it. "Speak of the devil. He wants me to bring you and Viviana to the club."

"The club? As in one of the strip clubs?"

She smirks. "Yeah, but don't worry, it doesn't open 'til noon. He wants to go to lunch. We'll meet him there before it opens, and you'll get to see where it all started, then grab something from the grill."

"Where all what started?"

Her muscular shoulders rise and fall. "The Hawke Empire. Savage opened a bar when he graduated from college, but things really took off when he and Gabe started the strip clubs. Savage's office is in the original one."

"Aren't they like bazillionaires now?"

A grin splits her lips. "Yeah."

"Then why is he still working out of a strip club? Shouldn't he have some sort of fancy office like Stone and Isaac?"

"You'll understand once you meet Savage. He's very sentimental about certain things. That was the office he always used, so he is going to keep using it, despite pretty much everyone, including his wife Dani, telling him he needs an upgrade."

I huff and fold my arms over my chest. "Sounds like all the Hawke men are a bit stubborn."

She pushes to her feet, all humor draining from her face. "You have no fucking idea."

10

ISAAC

It's always weird coming into the club this time of day without the lights and the dancers and the music, but it always feels like coming home. That might be strange to some people, considering what goes on here, but sometimes, it seemed like I spent more time at The Hawkeye Club growing up than I did in my own house.

Sitting on Uncle Savage's lap up in his office, getting a soda from Byron at the bar, sneaking back to the girls' changing rooms and having them fawn all over me.

It may not be the ideal place to raise kids, but I turned out okay...*ish*.

I let the door close behind me and head toward the elevator that will take me to the offices on the second floor, but movement behind the bar draws my attention that way.

Coen looks up from something he's doing and raises an eyebrow. "What are you doing here?"

I divert toward the bar and slide onto a stool. "I could ask you the same question. I thought you'd be at home relaxing after the trip with Uncle Savage."

He shakes his head and inclines it toward the dressing rooms. "I wish. As soon as we got back, Byron said there was a lighting issue in here that needed to be addressed and that no one seems to be able to figure it out. He asked if I would see if I could help today."

"So, what are you doing behind the bar?"

A lazy smile tilts his lips. "Having a drink." He lifts a glass of what looks like bourbon.

"Hitting the hard stuff already?" I check my watch. "It's only 11:30."

He shrugs. "It's five o'clock somewhere."

"Well, in that case." I smack my hand on the bar. "Pour me one, too."

My conversation with Savage can wait. I honestly don't even know what I was going to say to him. Maybe having some time to think about it will help me organize my thoughts more.

Coen grabs a glass for me. "No court today?"

I shake my head. "Thankfully, no, and I'm celebrating."

"Celebrating what?"

"Let's just say I resolved a nagging issue."

He pours me a glass of Makers and clinks his against mine. "The zoning thing?"

I pick up my glass and swirl the amber liquid inside it. "How'd you know about that?"

Coen and Savage were already out of town when we had our meeting with Broussard, and before they left, everything was on track.

"Dad called Savage when we were on the road."

"I'm sure glad he did. I hate having to deliver bad news."

Since I always seem to be the one who gets blamed for it in the end.

Coen chuckles and takes a sip of his drink. "You and me both."

"How was the trip?"

He offers a nonchalant shrug but averts his gaze.

"Oh no. What happened?"

"Nothing. Really." He waves a hand off dismissively. "We met with a few people, got a tour of the place. Uncle Savage pissed off some people."

"Yeah. What's new about that?"

"Exactly."

"You learn anything useful?"

Coen rests his elbows on the bar and looks almost wistful. "I guess. That place has over five hundred rooms, and they sell out every fucking night, so they're doing something right."

Sure fucking seems so.

We've been researching our competing boutique hotels along the coast for years, but somehow, Savage finally managed to get what will be one of our biggest rivals to let us in the door.

"Anything we didn't know already?"

He swirls his drink and looks down into it. "I think the fact that they have a casino attached makes a huge difference. Our inability to do that could be a real hindrance."

"No shit, but that location is too good to pass up, even if we can't get a casino approved by zoning."

That is beyond even our reach.

"Uncle Savage says he's going to talk to you and Dad about another campaign on that front soon."

With Broussard gone, there may be a real shot at getting some of the zoning changed that has been so problematic. While I can appreciate the city's desire to keep certain aesthetics and feels to neighborhoods by limiting where gaming is allowed, it limits where we can set up shop, too, if we hope to have that to draw in customers.

"Great." I raise my glass to take a sip of my bourbon. "Let's hope we can make some changes."

Coen takes a drink and leans against the bar. "Speaking of

changes, I hear we had some unexpected visitors while I was gone."

I almost choke on my sip and cough to clear the burning liquid from my throat.

Shit.

I've been so wrapped up in having Jack here and finding out about Viviana that I didn't even tell Coen—the one person who would actually fucking know the truth the instant he sees her.

Unless Dad already said something to him...

"Yeah, about that. Did Dad say anything to you?"

His brows draw down low. "Just that Cutter dropped off his daughter and granddaughter and went off to try to take out some Calabrian mafioso."

"Well"—I rub the back of my neck—"remember when you came up to Chicago for my graduation?"

He smirks and takes another sip. "Yeah, and you ditched me for that hot redhead at the bar."

I nod slowly. "Turns out that hot redhead at the bar was Cutter Jackson and Valentina Marconi's daughter."

His hand freezes with this glass halfway to his mouth. "What?"

"Yeah."

"But...how?"

I offer a half-shrug. "She ditched her bodyguards that night and decided to have a fun weekend with her friend, which turned into a fun weekend with me."

"And you never figured it out?"

"No. We kept things casual while we were together."

Or at least tried to.

Nothing about that weekend felt casual.

Coen finally picks up his jaw off the bar. "Fuck. I bet that was a real surprise seeing her sitting in Dad's office."

"You could say that."

More like my heart actually stopped and my lungs seized.

His brows rise. "So?"

"So, what?"

"What happened when you saw her?"

"I about lost my shit in front of everyone, but she made it clear that she didn't want them to know we knew each other, so we pretended we didn't, which was pretty difficult once I saw Viviana."

"Oh, yeah. I heard she has a daughter. But..." His eyes widen again. "You're not saying..."

"Yeah." I down half my drink and set down the glass slowly. "I knew as soon as I saw her. When you see her, you'll know why."

"Holy shit. You have a daughter?"

"I do."

"With Giacomina Jackson-Marconi?"

"Yep."

"Holy shit. Who the fuck knows?"

"Dad, for sure, and I know he told Mom, but I've managed to avoid her calls since he confronted me about it. I'm frankly surprised she hasn't shown up at my place, looking for Vivi yet. And I'm pretty confident Saint, Gabe, probably Bishop and Atlas know, too. But honestly, we're trying to keep it quiet."

Coen shrugs. "Why?"

"Why do you think they're here hiding out? We're trying to protect them from a family with a bad reputation. What the hell do you think would happen if Nana found out she has a great-grandchild? She'd probably tell the whole fucking world and put a spotlight on her."

The thought of that happening and how it could lead the Satrianos straight to the girls makes my hand tighten around the glass until my knuckles whiten.

He snorts a laugh. "You're right. Nana can't keep her mouth shut if she's happy *or* pissed about something."

"Besides, her parents don't know."

"Oh, my God, what the hell is going to happen when *they* find out?"

I down the rest of my drink. "I don't even want to think about that right now. My focus is on making sure they stay safe. Everything else, we'll figure out later."

Even though I can't stop thinking about it, every single second of every single day.

What happens when this threat is gone? When Cutter shows up to bring Jack and Vivi back to Chicago?

Coen throws up his hands. "So, in the meantime, we all pretend we don't know she's your daughter?"

"Basically."

He snorts. "What are you going to do when you have to bring her to Sunday dinner?"

I freeze. "Fuck, I hadn't even thought about that. I'll make an excuse. Say I can't go and then I don't have to bring them."

"You can try, but expect a call from a very unhappy Nana."

"I know." I glance at my watch again. "They're going to be here any minute."

"Who will be?"

"Jack and Viviana. Bishop is bringing them over so I can take them to lunch."

"You're letting them out of the condo?"

"I spoke with Saint and Uncle Gabe about it, and we're all in agreement that as long as we're careful about where we're seen and who we talk to and we make sure their identities aren't revealed, that it's okay. Besides, I'm packing." The weight of my gun at my hip provides a modicum of comfort, but I still shift uneasily on the stool. "I can't keep them locked up at my place. We have no idea how long this will drag on, and Viviana is only four. We're being careful. I'm not going to let anything happen to them—ever."

Footsteps sound from near the dressing rooms. "Hey, Coen, can you come up here, man?"

I peer over to the hallway that runs along the side of the club and where the stairwell leads up to the lighting rigs and wave at Logan.

Coen acknowledges him with a nod. "Yeah, coming." He downs the rest of his drink, takes our glasses, and sets them in the sink. "Hey, congratulations, brother."

"On what?"

His dark brows wing up. "Being a father."

"Oh, thanks."

That reality hasn't really sunk in yet, maybe because Vivi doesn't know.

I know it's true, but hearing it from Coen somehow makes it feel *real* for the first time.

He pauses for a second. "I can't begin to understand how complicated this must be for you, but have faith that it'll work out."

I snort. "Easy for you to say. You just go with the flow and let life take you wherever it leads."

"I feel like we've had this conversation a thousand times, brother. Having no focus and purpose in life isn't exactly a good thing."

"It might be from where I'm sitting."

"We'll have to continue this conversation later." He raps his knuckles on the bar and hustles out toward the stairs to the lighting rig.

I turn around to face the stages and the glimmering silver poles on them.

The eerie quiet settles around me and sends a shiver down my spine.

That's fucking weird.

Nothing looks out of place. Nothing off. Yet tension builds between my temples like something is coming that none of us will be prepared for.

The Hawkeye Club has always been a safe place for everyone.

Where Mom and Dad met and fell in love. Where Uncle Savage and Uncle Gabe built this empire that now rests so heavily on my shoulders.

Don't fuck it up, Isaac.

Those words ring in my ears on a constant loop, the never-ending reminder from Dad that we are the ones who ensure the family legacy. We protect everyone against all threats, and the older Dad gets, the more things fall to me to handle. This is what I was groomed for, what I was *born* to do. It's in my blood and has been engrained in me since the first time Dad brought me to the office with him as a baby.

Be strong. Be confident. No weakness.

That was never a problem because I never had one.

I don't show emotion.

I don't bend and certainly don't break.

I definitely don't get rattled.

Until Jack walked back into my life...

Now I don't know what's wrong or right, up or down, real or imagined anymore, and it's thrown me off my normal game.

And fuck if I know how to get back in it.

The door to the club pushes open, and Jack and Viviana step in, followed closely by a watchful Bishop.

Jack's eyes meet mine, and she scowls at me, clearly still pissed off about what happened last night.

Good, she should be.

It'll give her reason to think. Really fucking think about what we're doing and what the fuck we're going to do when all this is over.

"Hi, Isaac." Viviana runs up and stops in front of me. The delight of finally being out of the condo lights a grin on her cherub face. "This place is cool."

I can't say I blame her.

It's the last place I would want to be cooped up at her age, and The Hawkeye Club is a pretty "cool" place.

"Hey, Vivi…"

Jack watches us carefully, and I glance over and catch Bishop smirk where she stands near the door.

She fucking knows.

Bishop points at me. "Since you're in safe hands, I'm going to take off. Just text me when you guys are done with lunch if you need me to come back to the condo."

"Thanks, Bishop. Will do."

Though something tells me I won't be making it back to the office today. It was hard enough being away from them for a few hours this morning, and this uneasiness I couldn't shake before seemed to melt away the instant they arrived—even with the cold shoulder Jack is giving me.

Bishop disappears back outside, and I turn my attention to the woman who has twisted me up and battered me worse than the last fucking hurricane did the city.

She watches Vivi examining my watch and comparing it to the pink one on her arm with some sort of cartoon character on it.

"How does lunch sound?" I glance between them. "You guys hungry?"

Jack glowers at me. "I'm definitely hungry for something."

Ouch.

Maybe it wasn't playing fair doing that to her last night, but she didn't play fair when she left me standing on that street five years ago, either.

"Okay, well, let's get going." I slide off the stool. "I'll see if my brother wants to come, too. If you don't mind? Let me go ask him."

Viviana steps back from me as the club lights come on and start swirling, flashing strobes of white and the entire rainbow of colors.

"Oh"—I scan the club—"looks like they fixed the lights."

Jack stiffens, her eyes wide and unfocused.

GWYN MCNAMEE

I take a step toward her. "Jack?"

"Oh no." Viviana scrambles away from me and reaches for her watch, pressing a button on the side of it. "Grab her!"

"What?"

Vivi rushes toward her. "Get her on the floor."

Jack's eyes close, and her entire body jerks violently. I lurch forward and manage to get my arms around her before she drops. My breath catches in my chest as she convulses, her limbs twisting and straining.

What the fuck is happening?

Lowering her to the floor, I glance up at Vivi, who drops to her knees next to us, her focus on the watch and Jack, like she knows exactly what to do.

"Turn her on her side. Keep her head from hitting the floor with your hands."

Jack's body continues to shake, her limbs twitching and thrashing while she takes uneven, choppy breaths like she's having trouble filling her lungs.

It reminds me to force myself to take one, and I suck in some air, but with my heart racing and blood rushing in my ears, I'm having trouble speaking. "Wh-what's happening? Jack? Jack!"

Vivi keeps her eyes on her mother. "A seizure." She looks at her watch. "I'm timing it."

She's timing it?

"If it goes five minutes, call an ambulance." Her blue eyes sweep up to the lights. "Turn those off."

JACK

"I spoke with neuro, and they said all your scans looked good. Hopefully, we'll have you out of here tomorrow. Just try to get some rest." The stunningly beautiful Dr. Nora Hawke pats me on the arm, peeks over her shoulder at Isaac, and leans in closer. "And don't let him scare you. He's a real puppy dog underneath all that macho bullshit, just like his father."

I laugh and shake my head at his mother's fearlessness when it comes to the Hawke men. "Okay, I won't."

"Good." She pats my hands and gives me a long look that tells me she can sense something more is going on between Isaac and me, even if she isn't saying anything. "I'll check on you again before I head home."

Nora pushes up from the bed and makes her way over to where Isaac has stood in the corner of my room for the last three hours, leaning against the wall, staring at me like I'm some sort of porcelain doll that's shattered and can't be put back together.

Exactly what I didn't want.

She gives him a hug and says something that has his stare hardening slightly before he gives a harsh nod. Pulling back, she narrows her eyes on him. "I mean it, Isaac."

He doesn't respond to her this time, just watches her walk out the door and into the hallway, closing it behind her. My entire body tenses the moment it clicks shut.

Alone with Isaac—the place that always seems to get me in so much trouble.

And it's the first time we have had the room to ourselves since they brought me in here after a brief stay in the ER. Between his mom and various nurses coming in and out and the heavy fog still enveloping my brain, I haven't even had a chance to figure out what to say to him about all hell breaking loose.

He hasn't taken his eyes off me and keeps examining me like I'm something he doesn't quite understand. Yet even that confusion can't hide the anger underneath it all. "Why didn't you tell me?"

And there it is.

I push myself up into a more seated position and adjust the pillow behind my head, even though I know it never gets any more comfortable in a hospital bed. "There wasn't anything to tell."

His brows rise slowly, the move almost threatening in some way. "You didn't think you should tell me you have epilepsy?"

"There was no reason to. I've had it my whole life, Isaac. It's just something I live with, and seizures happen. I deal with them, then move on."

He slowly approaches the bed, stopping a foot away from me, his jaw tight, arms still crossed over his chest defensively. "That was the worst fucking five minutes of my life, Jack. At least if you had told me, I could have been prepared. I would've known what to do."

"Vivi knows what to do."

"Jesus..." He shoves his hands back through his hair, the unruly waves going off in a thousand different directions now. "I saw that. It was pretty fucking impressive, to be honest."

I can't stop from grinning, the pride swelling in my chest. "I hate that she has to know all that. But she's really smart and understands how important it is."

"She sure as hell is, and I didn't have a fucking clue what was happening or what I was supposed to be doing." He releases a heavy sigh and drops down into the chair at the side of the bed. "Fuck, Jack..."

It would be easy to leave it at that—that the reason I didn't tell him was that it doesn't define my life or who I am and it's not something I need to make a huge deal about with every person I come into contact with. But there's more to it than that, and seeing how distraught he is right now, I owe him an explanation that he can hopefully understand.

"My parents' protectiveness over me has always been about more than just who they are. After I had my first seizure at age four, they kept me on a very tight leash, never wanted me out of their sight for even a minute. I only had one friend—Felicity, who I was with at the bar that night. And I only knew her because her dad worked for my parents, and they allowed him to bring her along. It felt like growing up in a cage—always watched and monitored by *someone*. And I *hated* it. Resented it and them the older I got." I issue a little half-shrug. "But now that I'm a parent, I have a different understanding of why they did that. I can't imagine how I would feel if it were Viviana."

"So"—his Adam's apple bobs with this thick swallow —"she's...okay? I mean, she doesn't have seizures?"

I shake my head. "She hasn't so far, but she's still young. We'll know more in a couple years, but I think we would've seen something by now. My grandmother had it on my mom's side. It's one of those things that can skip a generation." I shrug, "Some people get it; some people don't."

He leans back slightly in the chair, the sound of all the machines in the room around us filling my ears over the uncomfortable silence.

"I thought..." He swallows thickly again, his eyes flooding with tears, and he glances up at the ceiling for a second, idly toying with a button on his jacket, before he finally refocuses his gaze on me. "I thought you were dying."

His words make a vise tighten around my chest, and I offer him the best smile I can muster. "Not dying, just a little fucked up in the head."

A half grin tilts his lips.

"But you're right, Isaac. I probably should have warned you so you could be prepared if I had one while I was here. It's been over four months since my last one, and I typically only have a few a year, so I didn't *think* it would happen, but I should have let you know."

"I never would've brought you to the club if I had known about the lights."

I nod slowly. "They can be a trigger, but I wasn't worried because Bishop said the club wasn't open yet. Viviana's usually pretty good at scoping things out for me for anything that might be a trigger. But triggers are tricky. Simple things like stress can be one, and this situation is certainly stressful. I might have had one even without the damn lights. And sometimes, I just have seizures without any triggers or warning at all."

"Are they always this bad?"

I drop my head back on the pillow and sigh. This one lasted just over five minutes, but anything over five can be dangerous. There have been a few that really knocked me out of commission for a while. I don't want to scare him or give him any reason to change how he sees me, but I have to be honest with him.

"Not always. Sometimes I get what are called partial seizures or focal seizures. My body gets really hot all over, and then, I'll start seeing auras. Weird spots of color. I can usually walk and talk during them, though what I say may be garbled or not make a lot of sense, and they don't last more than a minute or two. I usually feel completely normal within a few hours. Those are often brought on by a lot of stress, and they really don't affect me too much." I suck in a deep breath. "But the seizures *can* also be worse. They can go for longer than the one today, and sometimes, things happen to my body...it's not pretty to watch."

He leans forward and tugs my hand over with his, his large palm settling over mine. "I don't give a fuck what you looked like having a seizure, Jack. I was just fucking terrified, the most scared I've ever been in my life."

"I'm sorry, Isaac. I should have prepared you."

He squeezes my hand. "Don't apologize. You don't have any control over it. It's my fault for bringing you there in the first place."

"No, it isn't. That's my whole point, what I was trying to explain to you five years ago when we met. I hated how my parents treated me like I was something fragile that could break so easily. They tried to insulate me from everything that could potentially be a trigger because there are so many. They're so different for everybody, and we never knew what might potentially set me off. But all they ended up doing was insulating me from life."

Everyone sees me as this mafia princess who always had everything she wanted, living at the massive estate with endless resources. But it was a prison created by the people who love me the most and thought they were doing what was best for me.

"I was homeschooled by tutors and never got to have the type of experiences you do in a real school. I wasn't allowed to have any close friends besides Felicity because my parents thought someone might be able to use this 'weakness' against them somehow, as a way to hurt them. That weekend…"

He glances up at me, the heat that's always there when we talk about it returning to his eyes.

"I had a seizure about a month before that, and I had one three months before that and a month before that. It was the most frequent series I've ever had since I had been on that particular medication. So—"

He nods slowly. "So, they switched your medication?"

"Yes, and after a month, I felt really good. My body had adjusted to it, and I was doing well, but after being cooped up in my parents' house and them fawning all over me and treating me like I was made of glass, I had to get the fuck out of there. I couldn't stand having everyone walk around on eggshells like they were around me, like they were waiting for the other shoe to drop or something."

"Shit." He pulls his hand back and scrubs at his jaw.

"And that's how we ended up with Viviana."

"What about when you were pregnant?" His brow furrows. "Isn't being pregnant dangerous when you're epileptic?"

"It *can* be, but everyone is different. Some people end up having more seizures; others might have none the entire pregnancy when they normally would expect to. Hormones do unpredictable things to your body—that's what my neurologist and OBGYN told me."

"But...you were okay?"

That anguish in his voice tells me exactly what he's thinking —that he should have been there. It's like a knife slicing through my heart again, just like when he said it the other night.

"I was, thankfully. My parents waited on me hand and foot. They did everything they could to make sure I was well fed, well monitored—probably overly so—and that they removed any potential stressors from around me that might trigger anything."

"They put you right back in the cage you escaped."

I offer him a sad smile. "It was necessary. And thankfully, there weren't any of the potential birth defect issues because the medication I was already on is relatively safe for a growing baby. So, I may have been locked away and miserable, but in the end, I got a perfect baby girl."

"I'm so sorry I wasn't there."

"Don't apologize again. We both know you would have been and never would have missed a second with Viviana."

That proud smile returns to his face even through his pain. "She really was pretty fucking incredible today."

"I know."

"Do you want to call her?"

I already spoke to her once to assure her I was okay once the brain fog had cleared enough for me to. "No, I don't want to interrupt her if she's doing something fun with Bishop and Astrid back at the condo."

"I didn't know if I should let her stay here or not." He shrugs. "I didn't know what you'd want."

That vise returns to tighten around my chest. "It's okay. She could have stayed here with us, but it's better that she's somewhere else doing something she enjoys and not thinking about it and constantly seeing me hooked up to all this shit." I wave my hand around toward the IV stand and all the monitors. "She'll be fine with the girls."

"My mom said you'll be getting out of here tomorrow morning, but shouldn't they be running more tests and stuff?"

I shake my head. "There isn't anything else for them to do. My body just has to recover. My brain has to reset."

"How long does that take?"

"I'm usually really foggy for a couple days, sometimes a week after one this bad."

He twists his lips together. "Do you remember it?"

"I usually don't. The last thing I remember was walking in with Bishop and Viviana and seeing Viviana looking at your watch."

He smirks. "She can have it if she likes it."

I examine it. "You're going to give her a Panerai?"

Isaac grins. "She should have one of the best timepieces in the world if she needs it to help keep you safe."

The sentiment in his words melts some of the ice still lingering from what he did last night. "I think that's excessive. Her *PAW Patrol* watch works just fine."

He lifts a brow. "Paw patrol?"

"That's what her watch is, Skye from *PAW Patrol*."

"Shit." He pushes to his feet and shakes his head. "I'm really behind on the kid stuff."

"We'll catch you up."

The same agony I've seen in his eyes every moment since he first saw her returns, and he rubs his jaw again. "Do you think that's really possible?"

He's missed so much of her life and now has been thrown head-first into an open ocean on being a father, and we can't even tell her yet. But Isaac Hawke is the kind of man who is good at everything he does, and seeing how loving the members of his family have been since we arrived, I have no doubt he will be a great dad, too.

"I don't know, Isaac, but we can try."

11

JACK

I finally give up trying to ignore Isaac's heated stare and peek at him, where he leans against the elevator wall. "Stop that."

His brow crinkles. "Stop what?"

Like he doesn't fucking know...

"Looking at me like *that*."

That slight tilt of his lips gives him away. He knows exactly what he's doing, and there isn't any way to conceal the fire burning across his blue eyes. The tension continues to rise along with the elevator toward his condo, and he casually offers a little half-shrug.

"I'm not looking at you like anything."

"Yes, you *are*. You're looking at me like you're thinking about the first time we were in an elevator together."

The corner of his mouth twitches. "Are you telling me you aren't?"

I scowl at him, but he just offers a satisfied grin as the ding indicates we've reached the top floor. The doors open to the hallway—and freedom. A means to escape being in such tight quarters with him.

Thank God.

Trapped in any confined space with Isaac Hawke might be harder than with the devil himself. Even with my body weak and my mind still covered in the familiar post-seizure haze, it still remembers what that night was like. What *both* nights were like. It would be impossible to forget. I couldn't after years of trying, and being in his orbit again has brought the memories crashing back like a tsunami I can't flee from.

Definitely can't now.

No running for me.

I'm too exhausted to do anything but sleep.

I step from the elevator, and almost instantly, the door to Atlas' condo opens.

Astrid pops her blond head out, her blue eyes zeroing in on me. "Oh, you're back. How are you feeling?"

I force a smile. "Okay."

That's a lie.

My entire body feels like it wants to give out. Just the act of walking from Isaac's car in the parking garage to the lobby elevator and standing for the ride up has taken any energy I did have and drained it completely.

Nothing sounds better than crawling into bed to sleep for the next few days.

Almost as if she can sense it, Astrid frowns slightly. "You look like you should get to bed." She tips her head back toward Atlas' condo. "I have Viviana over here. We did some coloring, and we're all eating lunch. Do you want to join us before you lie down?"

I shake my head, my stomach turning slightly at the thought of eating. "I'm okay right now."

"Okay." She glances at Isaac. "I'll bring her back over when we're done."

Isaac approaches his cousin and kisses her on the cheek. "Thanks so much for your help, Astrid."

"No problem." She gives him a pointed look. "Anything for *family*, right?"

Oh, hell.

Astrid closes the door, and I turn to him.

"Does she know?"

He scowls and shakes his head as he opens the door to his place. "If she does, I didn't tell her. But…"

"But what?"

The door closes behind us with a click. "But my dad and mom know, and so does my brother, Coen."

"What? I haven't even met Coen. How could he—"

He holds up a hand to stop me. "I had to tell him. He was with me that night in Chicago. He would've known the moment he saw you and Viviana."

"And your parents?"

A heavy sigh slips from his lips. "One good look was all it took for my dad, and he was never going to keep that from my mom."

"So, what do we do? Do we tell everybody?"

He rubs at the back of his neck and shakes his head. "I'm pretty sure anyone who has met Vivi has figured it out. Saint, Bishop, Atlas, and Astrid…and I don't know what to do." He steps forward and brushes the hair back from my face. "You don't need to worry about that right now. My mom said you should get as much sleep as you can and just relax. So, that's what you're going to do."

I can't fight the smile at the mention of his mother. "You two are cute together."

"Excuse me?" His damaged brow wings up. "Did you just say I'm *cute*?"

I laugh. "With your mom. She's very…" I try to put my finger on the word. "Very…"

He groans. "Direct? Pushy?"

"I was going to say *direct*. Yes, that's the right word."

"She wasn't always like that. I think so many years with my dad rubbed off on her."

"Really? She seems so confident and, well, kind of badass. She sure handled you."

He simpers at my observation. "If anything I've heard about the time before I was born is true, then she's definitely changed. My parents have a very long and complicated history that I would love to fill you in on later. But now...to bed."

There isn't any point in arguing about it because if I don't get horizontal soon, I'll end up doing it on the floor. I start to walk toward the guest room down the hall where Viviana and I have been staying, but he steps in front of me, blocking my path.

"No." The single word comes from somewhere deep in his chest, full of resolve. "Definitely not."

"No, what?"

He plants his hands on his hips, still dressed in the suit he wore to work yesterday since he refused to come home last night, even though I *tried* to insist. "No, you're not going to sleep in the guest room."

"Excuse me?"

He points upstairs. "My room."

I open my mouth to argue with him, but he cuts me off.

"You need to sleep and to rest, and if you're in a bed with a four-year-old, that is not going to happen."

"But—"

"No buts."

Isaac lowers his shoulder and scoops me up into his strong arms before I can offer any protest except a sharp yelp of surprise that echoes around the condo. He easily carries me toward the stairs, his lean muscles rippling against me.

"So, that's it? You're just going to scoop me up like a caveman and take me to your cave?"

That smirk of his that equally makes me want to slap him and kiss him appears as we start up the glass staircase. "If that's how you want to put it."

"And what are we going to say to Viviana?"

While I've been far from a saint since giving birth, I've never brought a man home or spent the night in any other bed in that house—even if I might have spent some *time* in one with one of the guards who was more than a friend for a while.

He pauses his ascent and looks down at me. "That her mommy needs rest and can do it much better in my big bed up here?"

I scowl at him and cross my arms over my chest, but there's no point in arguing until he puts me down and I can get away from him. We reach the top of the stairs, and he shifts my weight to twist the doorknob to his bedroom and push it open.

He flips on the light, and I bite back my gasp of surprise, but he must see it anyway.

"Not what you expected?"

"Actually, it's exactly what I expected. You just did it very tastefully."

Unlike the downstairs guest room with all the heavy dark grays and blacks, up here, warmer tones of red offset the neutral colors, and a massive California king occupies the center of the room with a lush, soft-looking, pale-gray comforter on top of it.

Isaac heads straight toward it and carefully lowers me with my head on the pillow.

"You know I was perfectly capable of walking, right?"

He stays leaned over me, his hands braced on either side of my pillow. "Oh, I know you're capable of a lot of things, Jack, but it doesn't mean I'm going to let you do them yourself when I can do them better."

Fuck.

My entire body heats, including my traitorous cheeks, at the clear reference to what I was doing to myself in the shower. I squirm under his lust-filled assessment, watching the way his eyes burn as they rake over me appreciatively, even though I must look like absolute hell right now.

He shifts even closer until his lips are almost touching mine. "Did you get to finish what you started in the shower the other night?"

I dart my tongue out to wet my lips and shake my head.

"No?" The low rumble of the word in his chest vibrates to me across the short distance between us. "That's unfortunate. I came right back up here and stroked my cock, thinking about what you were doing down there."

Vivid images of him doing just that flash through my head, and I squeeze my eyes closed, trying to ignore the involuntary Kegel my pussy does in response.

"Just think, Jack. You could have been up here in this bed with me instead of down there, frustrated."

I inhale a deep breath, trying to formulate a retort with a brain that won't quite cooperate yet as I reopen my eyes.

"But that's okay"—he levels his heated gaze on me—"because you're here now, and it's time for you to rest." He presses a kiss to my forehead, then shifts away, the very evident bulge at the front of his pants making me squirm. "I'm going to go check on Viviana and bring her back if she's done. Then I'm going to figure out what we're doing for dinner and make sure you have everything you need."

"You don't have to take care of me like I'm a child, Isaac."

"No, I don't *have* to, and you're certainly not a child. But I *want* to, and I'm going to make sure you do exactly what my mother said—relax."

"That's easy for you to say." I sigh, thinking about all that's going on around us. Our secret from Viviana. This threat from Satriano. "Not so easy to do."

He frowns slightly. "Are you worried about your parents?"

"I wish I could say no, but I am. I haven't heard from my dad since he left, and he says he's not going to contact me directly. I haven't even spoken to my mother at all since Dad dragged Viviana and me away from the house that morning. I know it's probably safer that I don't talk to them..."

He lowers himself to the side of the bed, runs his hand up my leg, and squeezes my thigh. "I don't know your dad personally, or your mom for that matter, but everything my uncle has told me about him makes me confident in saying that if anybody on this fucking planet can fix this, it's your father."

I nod. "I know. It's just hard being here, you know?" I let out a mirthless laugh and shake my head. "I always felt like that house was a prison. That they were like my wardens, you know? Controlling everything I did, always watching me or having someone else do it. And then they dropped me here, and I feel like it's the same thing, yet all I want is to go back there and be somewhere familiar..."

Isaac stiffens slightly, pulling his hand away and pushing off the bed abruptly. "I'm sure they're fine, Jack. You'll be able to go home soon." He grits out the words angrily before he stalks out the door without a look back at me.

It takes a second for me to process what I said and his response.

Shit.

ISAAC

I CLOSE the book and set it on the nightstand as I try to process what I just read. "So, this kid, Ryder, runs around with a bunch of dogs and helps people around town by solving problems and stopping crime?"

Viviana looks up at me from where she's snuggled down under the covers and nods with a big smile on her face. "Yeah, they always save the day."

I grin at her. "That sounds pretty cool, but I need to introduce you to some superheroes who are even cooler."

"Really?"

"Uh-huh. Have you ever heard of the Teenage Mutant Ninja Turtles?"

Her little brows draw together, and she shakes her head. "No."

Of course not.

"I'll have to see if I can find the old cartoons or comic books for you, but right now, it's time to go to sleep. You need anything?"

She shakes her head again.

"Okay. You know where your mom and I are if you need something, right?"

She nods.

"You'll be okay down here by yourself?"

She offers me an annoyed look. "Yep. I'm not a baby."

Her words tug at something in my chest, and I reach up and rub at the spot. I never got to see her as a baby. Never got to experience her first smile, her first laugh, her first word, and now she's already this mini person with so much confidence and intelligence.

I ruffle her hair. "You're pretty adult for your age. Does anybody ever tell you that?"

A tiny grin spreads her lips, and she nods. "My *nonna.*"

Who's in hiding right now so she doesn't get murdered by a rival mob family...

How fucked up is that?

Viviana remains blissfully unaware of her family connections and what they could do to her—or that one even exists to me. It hasn't even been a full week and already it feels like I've had to sit with this secret weighing on my heart for an eternity.

I rise from the side of the bed before that line of thinking makes me tear up like a total fucking pussy again.

"Isaac?"

Stopping a few steps away, I glance back at her. "Yeah?"

"How do you know my mommy?"

Fucking hell.

I turn back to face her. "She and I knew each other back in Chicago. That's where I went to law school."

"How come I never met you before we came here?"

I approach the bed again, kneel on the floor, and rest my elbows on the edge of the mattress, staring into the eyes of the little girl who changed my entire world in an instant. "She and I lost touch for a while. Do you know what that means?"

She shakes her head.

"We couldn't find each other."

"Now you did?"

I nod. "Now...we did..."

Not that it changes anything, really, since apparently, she wants to go running right back to Chicago as soon as this is all over. The words she said earlier still ring in my ears, like an ominous bell tolling. The thought of her leaving, of her taking Viviana, makes me swallow back the bile that rises in my throat, and I climb to my feet.

"I miss my *nonna* and *nonno*."

"I know you do, kiddo, but you'll see them soon, I promise." Maybe I shouldn't, but my confidence in what Cutter can do overpowers my reservations about making a promise I might not be able to keep. "Goodnight."

"Goodnight, Isaac."

Isaac...

I flip off the light at the door, leaving only the small nightlight illuminating the room, and watch her roll onto her side and snuggle even deeper in the middle of the large bed.

Fuck.

I don't know if I thought this was ever going to get any easier, but all it's done has gotten so much harder. Not being able to tell her who I am, not being able to explain the situation, is making every moment with her feel like a knife being stabbed into my chest.

And Jack keeps pouring acid into the wound by saying she wants to leave.

I pull the door closed behind me softly and make my way to the bar in the living room, where I have been spending way too much of my time. The situation is beginning to weigh on me far more than I even knew was possible. I thought the stress of keeping Hawke Enterprises going was bad, but knowing that little girl is mine and having no fucking clue what to do about it is a thousand times worse.

So, even though I probably shouldn't, I pour myself a drink from the bottle that's starting to look far too empty after the last couple of days and throw one back as I stare up at the closed door to the bedroom where Jack has been sleeping on and off all day.

She was out cold when I checked on her at dinner time, and I haven't heard a peep from her since. Other than peeking my head in to make sure she doesn't need anything and that she's doing okay, I've avoided her like the plague since we got back.

After what she said, looking into her eyes is too painful, but I have to consider what she just went through, the trauma her body just endured, and stop thinking about my own pain.

"Stop being a selfish fucking prick, Isaac."

I down another quick shot, then make my way upstairs to ease open the door.

Jack rolls from her side to look up at me. "Hi."

"You're awake."

She stretches, yawning slightly. "Somewhat. What time is it?"

"After seven." I make my way over to her. "I just put Viviana to bed."

Her eyes widen, and she jerks up. "You did? I should go down and say goodnight to her."

I press a hand against her shoulder gently. "No, she's fine. I told her you were asleep and needed to rest and that you'd see her in the morning."

"She's okay?"

"She had a great time with Bishop and Astrid today, and we just read a *PAW Patrol* book, so I kind of understand who Skye is now."

She grins at me. "Good. Progress, then."

Progress.

Somehow, that word doesn't feel right, not after what she said earlier, and I shift my hand down to pull back the comforter.

She narrows her eyes on me. "What are you doing?"

"You're coming with me."

"What?" Her brow creases. "Where?"

I incline my head to the bathroom. "Time for a bath."

Her eyes widen slightly. "Isaac. No. We can't—"

The last time we climbed into a tub together, we ended up with that little girl downstairs. And as much as I'd love to sink into the hot water with her and hold her in my arms, that isn't what she needs right now.

"*You* are taking a bath, and I'm running it for you. You were in the hospital, and now you've been in bed all day. A nice hot bath will probably feel really fucking good right now."

She releases a heavy sigh. "You aren't wrong about that."

I hold out my hand, and she slides hers into mine and allows me to pull her to a seated position and help her off the edge of the bed. She stumbles slightly on unsteady legs, and I wrap an arm around her to keep her upright.

"You okay?"

She nods. "Yeah. Just still a little off."

After seeing the way her body betrayed her yesterday, that has to be the understatement of the year.

I help her to the bathroom and gently lift her up and settle her on the counter while I plug the tub and crank on the water. The rushing sound of it filling the room brings back the memory of the last bath we had together. The one that secured in my mind so solidly that Jack was everything I ever wanted and then some.

Christ, things have changed so much, yet not at all.

The woman sitting there, watching me, has just as much of a chokehold on me now as she did those two nights. Maybe even more so.

I pull open one of the drawers under the sink and grab a box of random bath stuff Mom left over here. Jack watches me rummage around in it until I find what I'm looking for and hold up a small bottle.

"Bubble bath?"

She giggles. "Wow. Trying to recreate a moment, Mr. Hawke?"

"Maybe."

I pour the bubbles in and watch them begin to build, then reach my hand in and swirl it around, considering the conversation I just had with Vivi. Jack needs to know, even if talking about it will only make me hurt more. "Viviana asked me how we knew each other."

Jack pulls her bottom lip between her teeth. "What did you say?"

"I told her we knew each other in Chicago years ago but that we lost touch." I rest my elbow on the edge of the tub and watch the water filling, unable to look at her. "I don't know how much longer I can do this, Jack. How much longer I can go on pretending she isn't mine."

Her feet create a soft padding sound as she makes her way to me. She sits on the tub edge and runs her fingers through my hair.

I close my eyes and lean into the touch, wishing things weren't so fucking complicated.

"I know, and I'm sorry, Isaac. Maybe we can tell her. What does it hurt if she knows?"

I glance up at her. "If she knows, my whole family will know."

"It seems like your whole family *does* know. It's kind of hard to hide the family resemblance."

Despite how utterly not funny the situation is, I can't help but smirk at her. "The Hawkes have strong genes."

Aside from Kennedy, Atlas, and Astrid, who all came out blond, the rest of us all have the dark hair and blue eyes people seem to associate with the Hawkes.

Jack grins. "Apparently."

"What do we tell her?"

She releases a heavy sigh and watches the water. "The truth, I guess. That you didn't know about her and that if you had, you would have been there her whole life. All I ever told her if she ever asked about her father in the past was that he loved her but couldn't be there."

"She'll want to know why I didn't know, why I wasn't there."

Jack sucks in a heavy, deep breath and lets it out slowly. "I'll take the blame for that. I'll tell her that there were reasons she'll understand when she's older, and I'll let her hate me in her four-year-old way until she's old enough to hate me in an adult way when she understands what really happened."

"Is that really the best thing to do?"

Her slender shoulders rise and fall. "I can't keep watching how painful this is for you. I think we should just tell her."

What about when she asks about going home to Chicago?

It's the question I want to ask her, but I bite it back. She's been through enough the last couple of days, hell, the last week. I don't need to force that agonizing question on her.

One traumatic conversation at a time, and hopefully, Viviana won't ask the question we're both dreading.

What happens when all this is over?

"Let's get you into the tub."

I turn off the water, climb to my feet, and step in front of her to help her stand. She stares up at me with the same eyes that offered me so much in Chicago and now seem to offer it and equally threaten to take it all away with one look.

That desire still lingers.

The same one I felt then that's only grown stronger the longer she's here.

My hand shakes as I skim it along the waistband of her pajama pants slowly, giving her every opportunity to push me away and tell me she can undress herself, but she just watches me with her lips parted slightly. Her breaths come out low and even, and she presses her hands to my chest.

Heat radiates from where her palms rest, and I slowly lift the hem of her shirt up until it forces her to remove them from me. She raises her arms to let me tug it over her head, and I let it fall to the floor next to us.

It takes every ounce of willpower in my body not to drop to my knees immediately and worship her perfect breasts hanging in front of me and lower my head between her legs to taste her cunt again. But what she needs right now is to get into that tub, not for me to be trying to get into her.

I move to the waistband of her pants and slowly nudge them down, along with the black underwear beneath them, and she kicks them off to the side, leaving her completely exposed.

Even though I saw her in the shower the other night, getting the full view of her beautiful, lush body again makes my cock harden instantly despite my best efforts. I run a hand along her hip and squeeze there, then slowly urge her to turn around and face the water because if she doesn't get under it quickly, she might not end up in there alone.

A man can only have so much willpower, and Jack is doing nothing to help me in the battle raging inside me right now. She leans back against me slightly, the warmth of her bare skin practically searing mine everywhere we touch.

I help her step over and into the tub, and she sinks under the water with a low groan of appreciation that makes my cock fucking weep.

Jack lets her eyes drift closed, her dark hair floating with the bubbles.

"This is incredible, Isaac. Thank you."

I lean a hip to the counter. "You're welcome."

One of her eyes pops open. "Are you staying?"

"Do you want me to?"

She considers my question for a split second before giving me a sharp nod, and I lift myself up onto the counter and lean against the mirror.

This is going to be the longest bath in eternity.

12

ISAAC

"You're sure you're ready for this?" I throw the car into park and glance over at Jack in the passenger seat. "We can just go back to the condo..."

She looks out the window at Hawke's Daily Grind. "I am. It's just coffee and pastries, right?"

I snort and shake my head. "You have no idea what you're getting yourself into with my cousins, Angelina and Alessandra, here."

"Oh, come on." She turns back to me with her eyebrow raised. "It surely can't be that bad."

Fighting a grin, I push open my door. "Just wait and see."

Allie and Angelina are going to be all over them with a million questions and likely inappropriate comments that will make me cringe and wish we never left our little cocoon in the condo.

I jog around to the front of the car to open Jack's door for her. She steps out onto the sidewalk and inhales a deep breath of her first fresh air in five days that wasn't from out on the condo balcony. Viviana bangs on the window in the back, eager to get out, and I pop open her door as she struggles to unbuckle herself from her car seat. She manages to get free before I can help and climbs out after her mother.

Vivi stares up at the sign. "Is this where we're going?"

Jack looks down at her and takes her hand, nodding. "Yeah. The Hawkes own it."

"Cool."

Though she still has no idea who the Hawkes are or who *I* am.

With Jack recovering and all of us still waiting on information about what's happening with her dad, plus the upcoming meeting with the zoning board to prepare for, there just hasn't been what felt like an appropriate time to have that type of conversation.

But we won't put it off much longer.

My sanity won't allow that.

I scan the street up and down as we make our way inside. The hairs on the back of my neck stand on end just being out here, though there isn't any reason to believe things are any more dangerous than they were when Jack and Viviana first arrived in New Orleans.

Ten days...

Over a damn week of waiting, and so far, the only update Gabe has gotten from Cutter is that he's in Italy trying to "resolve the issue" as quickly as possible and that Valentina is safe. And while that's certainly good news, considering the other possibilities, it doesn't do much to calm my concern over the girls.

And tracking down Satriano myself has proven far more difficult than I anticipated.

The man is well protected in his estate high up on a hill in Calabria with a damn wall around it and dozens of armed guards monitoring the perimeter. Even if I hopped on a flight today, there isn't any way I could get to him before I ended up with a damn bullet in my head.

But I try to shake off that thought.

Today is about good things—like Jack finally feeling better and well enough to come out and meet Storm's daughters.

I pull open the door and usher them inside. The bell jingles above us, and the familiar scents of coffee and baked goods fill my nose and make my mouth water.

Angelina looks over from her place behind the counter near the register with a grin. "I was wondering if I was ever going to see you again, cousin."

"Haha." I roll my eyes. "Very funny."

My daily stops here for coffee on the way to the courthouse have certainly trailed off since Jack and Vivi arrived, and Angelina knows precisely why I haven't been around.

Smartass.

Viviana races up to the pastry display case and sticks her nose against it, her eyes and mouth wide, examining all the confections.

Angelina's gaze darts from her to me, then to Jack. "Um, so you must be Mina."

Jack nods and steps forward, extending a hand, which Angelina accepts, shaking slowly. "And you seem to know an awful lot already."

With a smirk, Angelina shrugs and checks out Vivi again. "Things get around pretty quickly in the Hawke gossip chain, if you catch my drift."

She inclines her head toward Viviana, and I close my eyes and release a heavy sigh.

Worst-kept secret in the world, apparently.

Jack winces slightly. "And who are your parents again? I'm sorry. I'm just still trying to follow the whole Hawke family tree."

Angelina chuckles. "Let me get you a drink and something to eat first. Then we can talk."

I scan the café. "Where's Allie?"

Shit, wrong question.

Angelina tosses me an annoyed look. "I wish I knew."

"What do you mean? I thought she was supposed to be here."

"She *is* supposed to be here."

I watch out the picture windows at the front and across the street to the windows on the second floor there. "Did you check with Jude?"

Angelina nods. "I texted him. He hasn't seen her since yesterday after her shift."

My spine stiffens. "So, she just didn't show up for work? Should we be worried?"

She shakes her head. "No. She texted and said she'll be in 'later,' but it's now"—she glances at her watch—"10:30 in the morning, and still no sign of her. It's becoming kind of a habit for her lately."

"Lovely. Well, since she's not here to make it, give me a double espresso and a croissant."

Angelina turns to Jack. "What would you like?"

Jack examines the menu on the wall behind the counter. "I'll have chamomile tea and one of those paninis that look amazing." She leans down to Viviana. "What do you want, sweetheart?"

Vivi points through the glass to the stack of huge chocolate chunk cookies. "A cookie."

Almost immediately, Jack glances at me. "Maybe you should have something else..."

I lean down next to Vivi. "A cookie sounds great."

Jack glares at me, and I shrug and mouth, *"What?"* to her.

Angelina chuckles. "One cookie coming up. And how about a hot chocolate with that?"

Viviana's eyes grow even wider. "Yay."

She claps and bounces up and down.

Jack leans toward me, tilting her head away from Angelina and Viviana. "Someone's going to have to deal with the sugar rush after this."

I press my hand against her lower back. "Maybe we can see if Astrid's around to give her some lessons this afternoon."

She grins at me. "You're evil."

"I know."

I direct them over to an open table as Angelina works on preparing the drinks. Jack examines the café space from the floor-to-ceiling bookshelves along one wall to the small stage in the far corner.

"This place is really neat. Angelina owns it?"

I nod as she pulls out Viviana's tablet to entertain her. "Yeah, she opened it about six years ago after working for our uncles in various capacities for a while. Wanted something of her own, but it's still under the Hawke Enterprises umbrella. Her little sister, Alessandra, helps her run it as kind of assistant manager, I guess, when she's here, which apparently is an issue today."

Jack gives me a look.

"What?"

"Nothing. It's just you seem super close with all your cousins, more like brothers and sisters."

I chuckle. "We kind of are. Angelina's the oldest, and there's a six-year age gap between her and me. Kennedy is a year older than me, and then everyone else is kind of clumped together, going down younger. But we're all within about twelve years of each other, so we all kind of grew up together."

"Along with Saint's kids?"

"Yep, and Jude."

"Yeah, you mentioned him." She glances toward the front windows. "He lives across the street?"

I nod and clear my throat as I scan to see who's around. "He was adopted when he was about ten...by Luca Abello and his husband, Byron."

"Oh." Jack's eyes widen slightly. "Where are his parents?"

"That's a long, presumably painful story that he never really gets into, and I don't ask."

Not that he would tell me if I did.

For as brilliant as he apparently is, the man sure lacks basic social skills.

Angelina joins the table with four mugs and a few plates balanced on a tray and sets them in front of us, then pulls out a chair and settles into it.

Jack peeks back behind the counter. "You don't have to work at the counter?"

She shrugs and scans the café. A few customers occupy various tables, and a couple sit out at the tables on the front sidewalk, but they all seem engrossed in books or their phones or each other.

Waving a hand absently, she takes a drink of her coffee. "This is kind of a dead time. We'll pick up again closer to lunch. This is my mini break unless someone needs something. I'd much rather sit here with you guys." Her laser focus zeros in on Viviana. "Hey, Viviana."

Viviana glances up. "Hi."

"Here's your hot chocolate."

Viviana grabs it and sticks her face right into it, the marshmallow on top leaving sticky residue all around her mouth. "Yum."

"And here's your cookie."

Angelina slides the plate her way, and Viviana takes a giant bite, smearing chocolate and sticky crumbs all over her face.

I can't fight my grin watching her. "I think somebody might need a bath when we get back."

Jack points to me. "You mean after we hand her to Astrid?"

Angelina chuckles and elbows me playfully. "Already pawning off the kid?"

I scowl at her and mouth, "Knock it off," and she holds up her hands defensively.

Sipping at her coffee, Angelina examines Jack carefully. "So, Mina, how are you liking New Orleans?"

Jack releases a sardonic laugh and then takes a sip of her tea. "I would like to say it's been great, but the only things I've seen are Isaac's condo and the hospital, so..."

Angelina winces. "Yeah, my Aunt Nora told me. I hope you're feeling better."

She nods. "I am. Thank you." Jack nudges me. "So, how are you related to this one?"

Angelina smirks over her coffee cup. "Sometimes I wish I could claim I wasn't related to him."

I scowl at her. "Bullshit."

She chuckles. "My mom and his dad are brother and sister."

"Cool. So, she's Storm, right?"

Angelina nods. "Yeah. And you'll eventually meet her and my stepdad, Landon. And Alessandra, if we can ever find her. Allie tends to be a little spacey at times, but this is off, even for her."

"And Jude really has no idea where she is?"

Angelina shakes her head. "He's been deep in his writing cave lately and barely comes up for air, according to her. Other than when she brings him his morning coffee, he doesn't see or talk to anyone for days on end. Sometimes weeks."

I snort and take a sip of my espresso. "That's healthy."

"Cut him some slack, Isaac."

"Okay, okay."

Angelina and Allie have always been so protective of Jude. There isn't any point debating anything involving him with them.

I peek out toward the windows across the street again, and a man with dark hair and sunglasses walks by slowly on the sidewalk, glancing into the café.

Though he appears completely casual, something about him sends a shiver down my spine, and I stiffen.

Angelina glances toward the window. "Is something wrong?"

I clear my throat. "No. Just thought I saw someone I knew."

The girls keep gabbing, but I've zoned out the conversation, instead focused on where he just disappeared out of sight on the far window. I wait for him to reappear. Something tells me he will. But he doesn't.

Still, I can't shake the feeling and suddenly lose my appetite for the warm croissant sitting in front of me. My phone buzzes in my pocket. I pull it out and see a text from an unknown number.

UNKNOWN NUMBER

THEY KNOW.

JACK

"BYE, BABY. YOU HAVE FUN." I plaster on a fake smile and wave as Viviana heads into Atlas' condo with Astrid, but as soon as the door closes, I wheel toward Isaac, where he stands in the open door of his place, arms crossed over his chest, jaw locked tight. "What the hell is wrong with you?"

His eyes widen. "What's wrong with *me*?"

"Yes." I hiss at him as I storm past him into the condo. "You're a damn lunatic."

He lets the door slam closed behind him and follows me into the living room.

I wheel to face him. "Why did you drag us out of there like that? You scared the crap out of Viviana *and* me."

"With good fucking reason, Jack." He jerks his phone from his pocket, opens a message, and turns it toward me. "I got this."

I close the distance between us and pull the phone from his

hand so I can read it. "*They know*? Who the hell sent this? What does it mean?"

"I don't fucking know, Jack. But I wasn't going to take the chance that this was some sort of warning, especially when there was a guy outside the café who just gave me the creeps."

"A guy?"

"Yes."

"Where was he?"

"I saw him walk past on the sidewalk, and when I brought you guys out to the car after I got the text message, I thought I saw him down the street watching us."

I shove the phone back into his chest. "You're being paranoid."

He lashes out and grabs my wrist, tightening his fingers around it and jerking me backward toward him. "Am I? You, of all people, know what the Satrianos are capable of. If they somehow found you, if this message is a warning from your dad or your mom or someone else who knows what the fuck is going on, then don't you think we need to take it seriously?"

"I'm not saying we shouldn't take it seriously, Isaac. What I am saying is that you have to think about how what you do affects your daughter. You snatched her up and ran out of there like the whole place was on fucking fire. You scared her."

He clenches his teeth. "She's *fine*."

"She's fine *now* because I told her everything was okay and tried to play it off, but you can't do things like that in front of her. You can't let her see you've been shaken."

"I wasn't shaken."

"Bullshit. I know you well enough to know you don't act like that unless you are."

He tightens his grip on me. "The only thing that's ever shaken me in my life is *you*, Jack. You did it five years ago, and now, you're here doing it again."

"Yeah. Well, hopefully, it won't be for long."

I manage to pull out of his hold and stalk toward the stairs, but I only get up three before his arm wraps around me from behind and he spins me to face him a few steps below me.

"Won't be for long?" He practically spits the words back at me. "What the fuck does that mean?"

I shove my hands back through my hair, my head racing with a thousand thoughts at the same time. "It means...it means I'm going back. When all this is over, I'm going back to Chicago with Viviana. I always wanted to get away, to go to art school and be my own person, but it's the only home she's ever known, the only place she's ever known, and I can't take her away from my parents—"

"But you can take her away from *me*?"

His anguished words make me cringe and take a step back from him. "I won't keep her from you, but we can't stay here. All of this—it's too much."

"Bullshit."

"What?"

"You're running again."

I square my shoulders and grip the handrails on either side of me. "I am not."

He takes a step up and then another. "Yes, you are. You're doing exactly what you did that morning. You're making excuses for why you can't stay when, really, it's all in your fucking head. It's all because you don't want to acknowledge what's happening between you and me, and you're fucking scared to admit it to yourself."

I shake my head. "That isn't true."

Another step up brings him face-to-face with me, even though his feet are two steps below mine.

"It's not?" He lowers his hand to my hip and drags me up against him. "Then tell me, again, what you thought about every time you touched yourself and got yourself off since the night we met."

I squeeze my eyes closed and turn my head away from his.

"Tell me I didn't walk in on you with your hand between your fucking legs, saying my name the other night while you thought about my cock inside you."

I flinch.

"Tell me you didn't want me to kiss you that night I brought you back from the hospital. Hell, tell me you didn't want me to do more." He issues a low growl. "Tell me you don't want me to right now, that you don't want my mouth all over you and my cock buried deep in your cunt." His warm breath flutters against my cheek and moves closer to my ear. "Tell me you don't want me to do to you right now what I did to you in that fucking hallway."

A shudder rolls through me, but it isn't out of any sort of fear of Isaac harming me physically. He'll never let anything hurt Viviana or me. The only thing that hurts is his words, the truth in them.

The truth I'm not ready to face or accept.

"Tell me that if I slide my hand up your dress in between your legs right now, I'm not going to find you soaking fucking wet for me, ready and weeping for my fucking cock."

I clench my legs together against the throb there. The one I don't want to admit I get every time he's near. His hand slowly makes its way across my thigh to the hem of my dress and inches it up, gliding to the apex of my thighs. He runs a finger along the thin strip of fabric covering me there.

"Fucking soaked, Jack, just like I knew you would be." He flutters his lips against my ear, the heat sending another shiver through me as I grip the railings to keep myself upright. "Fucking tell me, Jack, who else has ever done this to you?"

I grit my teeth to keep from telling him the truth.

No one.

And just as quickly as he caught up with me, he's dropping to his knees on the glass stairs and shoving up my dress as he yanks down my thong hard enough to make the fabric rip.

His mouth is on me in a split second, and I gasp at the wet heat enveloping my entire core.

"Oh, God..."

It's the first thing I've managed to say and the only thing that'll come out as he thrusts his tongue inside me the same way he did that night.

Without hesitation.

Aggressive.

Demanding.

My legs begin to shake almost instantly, my arousal already nearing its peak before he even touched me. He glides his hand between my thighs and slips two fingers inside me, spreading me wider and laving his tongue over my clit at an almost frantic rate.

"Isaac, please..."

But he doesn't relent, and I tighten my grip even more on the railings, my body shuddering as violently as it did a few days ago. Only this time, it isn't another seizure threatening. It's the tension building to a force I've only ever experienced one other time.

With this man.

The kind that surprised me so much, I didn't know what to do with it.

I know what's coming, and I want to fight it as much as I want it to happen. The rush of truth that's about to explode from inside me. I try to close my legs, but he pushes them farther apart, spreading me wide open for him and giving him full access as he sucks and licks and devours me until I feel that low, dull ache that turns into a sudden rush of heat and warmth and wetness pouring from between my legs and down over his mouth.

It drips onto the stairs, but he just keeps going, thrusting his fingers into me and curling them, continuing to drag out the orgasm that has my body practically snapping in half right here on the fucking steps.

He's relentless, forcing a second wave I didn't know was possible until I finally shudder and gasp and sag forward against his drenched face. He pulls back slowly and looks up at me, his jaw wet with my release. With one arm wrapped around me, keeping me up, he reaches out and pulls my hands away from the banisters, then lowers me to the steps. The sharp bite of the glass treads on my back barely registers as he drops his head and slowly licks my release from where it's dripped down to my knees all the way up each thigh.

My body spasms and quivers, goosebumps breaking out across my heated flesh until he reaches my core again and flicks his tongue over my engorged clit. The zing of pleasure combined with pain shoots through me.

"No, I can't, not again." I push at his head, digging my fingers into his hair, trying to drag him away.

He presses a kiss over my mound, then shifts up until his body covers mine. Hard muscles at my front, hard glass at my back. Stuck between two immovable objects—the same way I've always felt stuck in this life.

And Isaac isn't going to move.

He isn't going to bend.

He will make me break.

Just like he did in that hotel room, he will keep finding a way to keep me needing more, believing I can have it when it really isn't possible.

What he just did was nothing compared to what this man has in store for me. I've known it since the moment I saw him in his dad's office.

All that passion and power have a single focus now.

Me.

And I don't know if I can survive it.

His arm braces on the step next to my head, keeping him hovering over me, and he stares down at me, his eyes darkening with determination. This is ruthless Isaac. This is the man I fear because I have no defenses against him.

"I'm going to take you to bed now, Jack." He captures my face in his hand and brushes a thumb across my cheek, almost reverently. "And I'm not going to let you leave until you admit that you don't really want to go back to Chicago."

13

ISAAC

Maybe I should have been gentler with her, considering it's been less than a week since she got out of the hospital. A better man wouldn't have touched her, would have given her more time, would have let her have her space.

But I just couldn't help myself.

This woman drives me utterly mad and washes away any ability to remain calm or rational, and her passion as she just railed at me when we came in felt like all the tension that's built up between us since she arrived finally exploding in a way that can't be contained anymore.

When she said she would go back to Chicago...that was the final straw.

I'm not losing her again, and I'm definitely not letting her walk out of here with Viviana.

I shift onto my knees, lower my shoulder, and tip her up onto it. She lets out a yelp as I make my way up the stairs, her beautiful ass bouncing right next to my face and the smell of her epic release filling my lungs.

"What the hell are you doing, Isaac?"

Here I thought I had made myself very clear. "I told you. I'm taking you to bed until you say you're going to stay."

"It-it's not that simple, Isaac."

"Yes, it is. Two words. *I'm. Staying.*" I smack her ass hard enough to make my hand sting. "You're not getting out of that bed until those two words come out of your fucking mouth."

Jack issues a low growl that just makes me grin wider as I nudge open the door to the bedroom, stalk across it, and toss her onto the bed. She releases another little yelp and bounces on the mattress, but any concern I may have hurt her, that what I just did to her on that step was going too far, vanishes the instant her eyes dip to the raging erection pushing against the front of my pants.

Her tongue darts out to wet her lips, and she visibly presses her legs together.

"You know how many nights I dreamed about you squirting down my throat like that, Jack?" I lean forward until I can feel her body vibrating. "*Every. Single. One.* And the taste is just as exquisite as I remembered."

I unbuckle my belt, yank it off, and snap it between my hands, making her jump slightly. But the heat in her eyes tells me she'd be game for that. And Christ, how I'd love to use it to tie her to the goddamn bed so she couldn't run away again, so she couldn't keep denying that whatever this is between us is something more than just a passing lust.

And I would...but I need her hands free.

Even years later, I can still feel her dragging her nails over my skin while I pounded into her in that hotel room, and I need to feel it again. Need to be cemented in the reality of her being here with me. Finally.

I toss the belt onto the floor with a clank, and she shifts back on the bed slightly until her back hits the headboard. The remnants of her release that I somehow missed despite my best effort still glisten on her inner thighs, and I unbutton my shirt as her gaze, heated with both lust and anger, devours every movement of my hands.

"You know you can't control everything like this, Isaac." She squares her narrow shoulders. "You can't control me."

I raise an eyebrow at her as I unhook my cufflinks, tug off my shirt, and toss it onto the floor, too. "Can't I?"

"If I tell Gabe or your father what you're—"

I drop my knee on the bed and lean into her until my lips are a mere hair's breadth from hers. "What would you tell them? That I'm begging for the woman I'm utterly obsessed with to stay because I want to keep her and my child here with me? You really think my father and Gabe are going to have a problem with that?"

She scowls and presses her lips into a thin line. "You can't keep me here against my will. You really think my father is going to allow that? The situation isn't forever. He *will* be back for me."

I run my thumb across her quivering lips. "And when he shows up, I'm going to explain to him that you and Viviana are mine and that you're not going anywhere."

She barks out a humorless laugh. "And how do you think that's going to go for you?"

So confident.

Well, her confidence in her father's ability to scare the everloving shit out of me is misplaced.

I press the pad of my thumb over her lips, silencing her. "Do you really think for one second that I'm afraid of your father, Jack? I've been up against men a lot more dangerous than him, and my family has fought things you can't even fathom. I've never feared anything in my entire life until I stood on that street in Chicago and watched you drive away. The only fear I've *ever* had was that I would never find you, and it's one I've lived with for five fucking years. So now that you're here, I'm not letting you go. Not for my dad, not for yours. Not for all the fucking money in the world."

I press my lips to hers before she can retort, and she groans and kisses me back, her hands tangling in the hair at my nape as she drags me against her, crushing the full length of my body to hers.

My cock settles against the apex of her thighs, the heat radiating there practically searing me through my pants. Her body, still ignited from the way she came down my throat on the steps, practically begs for me.

"Fucking Christ, Jack. You know how long I've waited to do this to you again? How much I've dreamed about it?"

"Probably not half as much as I've dreamed about this." She snakes a hand down my bare chest, leaving goosebumps skittering in its wake, and grasps my cock, stroking it through the pants I haven't managed to get off yet. "Why the fuck do you still have these on?"

Fuck if I know.

I've lost track of whether we're even arguing or not.

The only thing that matters is getting rid of any barriers between us. Anything that will interfere with me getting inside her and staying there for as long as humanly fucking possible.

I shift back, unbutton and unzip my pants, and free my cock, then work them down and kick them off as she reaches for the hem of her dress and pulls it up and over her head.

The lacy purple bra encasing her perfect breasts makes her tan skin practically glow in the faint light coming from the hallway, and I reach behind her and quickly unclasp it to free them.

Her nipples pebble in the cool air, and I lower my head and suck one between my lips as my hand finds that perfect spot between her thighs again.

"Oh, God." She drops her head back against the headboard, her neck arching and elongated, exposed in the most beautiful way. "*Mi dispiace quando fai questo.*"

Her mumbled words in Italian make me grin and nip at the taut peak, causing her to bow up and jerk under me, before I move to the other one as my fingers glide easily inside her again.

She shakes her head. "No." Her pussy clamps around my fingers. "Not this way. I need…"

Christ. I need the same thing.

I nudge open her legs farther, pull my hand away, and grip my aching cock with it. Her eyes flutter open to meet mine, then dip to watch me stroke myself a few times before I align the head at her slick opening and drive home.

"Fuck." I grit my teeth against the desire to blow my load instantly inside her, the familiar, welcoming heat, warmer and tighter than I ever remembered, even in the best of my fantasies. "Fucking hell do you feel good, Jack."

Her hands loop around my neck, and her nails score the skin there as she arches her hips to push me even deeper. "God, Isaac, please."

She doesn't have to beg.

Not this time.

I don't have the willpower to toy with her.

We've played games long enough.

I drag my hips back and plunge into her again, ripping a strangled cry from her that echoes around the room and in my ears. It's the most beautiful sound I've ever heard, and I want to hear it until the day I die.

All her pleasure belongs to me now. I don't want to miss a single gasp or moan. I want to see her face every time she comes and hear my name falling from her lips when she does.

I roll my hips with each drive, grinding my pelvis against the hypersensitive spot on her body I have already worked over twice, and she gasps and claws at me, then wraps her legs around my back, her feet digging against my ass and urging me to move harder and faster.

Pressing my mouth to hers, I tangle our tongues, the flavor of her release still lingering there like I wish it would forever.

Jack gasps slightly and pulls away. "I'm not on birth control anymore."

I grip her face and drag it to mine. "You think I fucking care? All I've thought about since the moment I knew you had my child was how fucking beautiful you must have been when you were pregnant." I pull my hips back and thrust into her again, making her eyes roll up into her head slightly. "And if I can put another baby inside you, good. As long as it's safe for you to be pregnant, I'd keep you knocked up for the rest of our fucking lives if I can. Just knowing my baby would be inside you, that I could watch and feel it growing. It's the biggest fucking turn-on in the world."

She releases a tiny little mewl as I shift my hips slightly, creating a new angle that drags the head of my cock against her G-spot.

Her gasp fills my chest with a swell of pride. "Oh, fuck, yeah, right there."

I tangle my hands in her hair and brace myself on my elbow as I pound into her relentlessly, chasing something we both want so badly. Not just the orgasm, but to go back to that night, to go back and undo everything that's happened since then. All the ways we've both been hurt. Go back to just being Nolan and Jack and start from scratch.

She comes suddenly, a wave rippling through her pussy and along my cock, like a tight vise clamping down around my dick. Her body undulates under mine, her eyes roll into the back of her head, her mouth falling open on a silent gasp.

"Nolan!"

It tumbles from her mouth, and just hearing her use that name, the one I did that weekend, is enough for my orgasm to race out of me. I come in hot spurts deep inside her, trying to drive myself even deeper with each thrust, closer to where I need to be. Every fucking ounce of me hopes I can get now what I missed out on then with this woman because, like I said, she's not leaving.

Not ever.

JACK

I CAN'T MOVE...

And it isn't just the weight of Isaac's body on top of me, pinning me to the bed and cocooning me in his warmth. It's the way this man has somehow managed to break his way into my heart and cement himself there, despite my best efforts to keep him out.

All these years, all the times I imagined what it would be like to find him, to be able to tell him about Viviana, it never occurred to me that I might see him and still have the same rush, the same feelings I did that weekend.

I tried to convince myself that it was all just lust. That my fun few days away I needed so badly back then had been conflated in my head and turned into something it never was.

Because how could that have been real?

How could a man like that be real?

But the moment Isaac walked into that office, the second I saw the same blue eyes Viviana has staring back at me, it was like I was back in that bar again, seeing him for the first time.

The more time we spend together, the clearer it becomes that he *is* that man I met five years ago. A man so loyal to his family that he was willing to bear the weight of their expectations in order to protect them. A man who loves completely. A man who beats himself up over his perceived failures even when things are completely out of his control.

Now, our hearts pound against each other, our hot breath mingling as we try to regain control of our bodies, and it might as well be *that morning*. When I woke and saw the message from Dad that he was coming for me. When I wrote that damn note and then stared at "Nolan" for what felt like an hour, memorizing every feature while he slept peacefully, expecting me to be there when he woke.

All the regrets I had that morning come rushing back, and tears begin to pool in my eyes. Isaac nuzzles the side of my neck and presses a soft kiss there, sagging even farther onto me, like he's trying to melt there until we're so entwined it will be impossible to separate us.

Maybe it's working because even with all the turmoil swirling around us, a sense of peace finally settles over me. I have no right to be feeling it, not with so much uncertainty, with so many conflicting desires warring within me.

Wanting to have my own life, to go to school and be anyone else.

Wanting to let Vivi have her grandparents and the life she's used to.

Wanting her to have her father every day.

Wanting to have him myself...

Finally, Isaac rolls to the side, bringing me with him, and wraps his arms around me with his right hand nestled under my cheek. He brushes his fingers over my temple, and I open my eyes and meet his heavy-lidded ones.

"You're not leaving."

I release a heavy breath. "I don't *want* to leave. Is that what you wanted to hear?"

The tiniest grin twitches the corner of his mouth. "God, no. I want so much more than that, Jack. I want everything." He tugs me even closer. "I want you and Viviana to be here, for us to be a family." He drags his left hand over my hip and presses it against my stomach. "I want to get you pregnant. I want you to have my baby again, and I want to be there for *all* of it. I want to see your breasts grow bigger and your belly expand. I want to see your skin glowing and wait on you hand and foot—"

"You want to see me puking all morning?" I raise an eyebrow at him. "Because my morning sickness with her was pretty fucking bad."

"Of course, I don't want you to suffer"—he locks his gaze with mine—"but I'll be there with you this time. You don't have to do it alone."

Sincerity rings in every word.

He means all of it.

And his continued guilt still lingers there.

"I wasn't alone." I run my fingers through the stubble on his jaw. "I had my mom."

"It's not the same thing." His words carry the heavy weight of regret. "You know I'd give anything to go back and be there." He lowers his forehead against mine. "Anything."

"I know you would. So would I."

I squeeze around his semi-hard cock still embedded inside me, and he groans and rolls onto his back, taking me with him to lie across his chest.

Propping myself up on my elbows, I stare down at the man who worked his way into my heart, despite the arrogance and the bullshit and every reason he shouldn't have. "Can I ask you a question?"

"You can. I don't know that I'll answer it."

I swat at his shoulder. "Asshole."

"You knew that."

"Yeah, I did. I just didn't realize how true it was until today."

One of his dark brows rises. "What did I do today?"

"Scared the shit out of our daughter."

His gaze softens. "I'm sorry about that. You're right. I should have figured out a way to get us out of there calmly so it didn't freak her out."

"I'm pretty sure you scared the shit out of Angelina, too."

"I texted Gabe on our way out to tell him what was going on. He will have let her know we're all okay. For now..."

For now.

The ominous words occupy the tiny space between us, and suddenly, he looks a million miles away instead of in this bed with me.

"Hey, Isaac, where'd you go?"

He returns his focus to me and shakes his head. "I'm here."

I'm not so sure.

He runs his hands down my bare arms, sending a shiver through me, making me squirm on his cock. It hardens fully inside me again, and he groans. "You move like that, we're going to have round two right now."

"You say that like it's a bad thing."

"Fucking hell, woman." He drags my face down and kisses me as he thrusts his hips up and pushes himself deeper. "Two rounds won't be nearly enough."

I groan into his mouth, then push back and begin to move slowly on him. He splays one hand across my stomach and the other on my right hip as I ride him slowly, lifting myself so I can feel every inch of him on the way up and the way down and relish the drag of the head of his cock in exactly the right spot.

Fuck.

My head spins, my body aching for another release, despite the fact that he just blew my mind three times. "Isaac, I don't know if I can—"

I shake my head and squeeze my eyes together against the growing pressure building inside me and zinging out from my overly sensitive clit.

"You can come again."

His words hold such confidence and pride that they make me move faster. I roll my hips, grinding down, rubbing myself in just the right spot against his warm skin.

He braces his feet on the bed and pushes up into me, finding a rhythm that makes my entire body tense in anticipation. "Relax, Jack. Look at me. I want you to look at me when you come this time."

I force open my eyes to meet his and see nothing but feral obsession in them. I was right about Isaac Hawke. He's far from heartless, but he is ruthless. He'll use anything at his disposal to get what he wants and what he loves.

He thrusts up into me again, and I grind down on him until that low, slow burn starts at my core and works its way out through my limbs in a glittering orgasm that steals my breath on a gasp.

With me still on top of him, he grits his teeth and thrusts up into me, squeezing my hips and maintaining the rhythm I've lost until he finally groans and empties himself inside me again.

I collapse on top of him, so exhausted I can't open my eyes again. Isaac wraps his arms around me and buries his face in my hair.

A perfect, comfortable silence fills the room around us. The first time I've been alone with him that the tension hasn't made me want to scream. It's a perfect moment, one I know can't last very long, but while I have it, I want to relish it. Relish this feeling of rightness with him I've never had before...except that one weekend five years ago.

The fogginess of sleep starts to settle in, but a door slams downstairs.

We both jerk up, and Isaac pushes himself to a seated position with me on his lap.

"Mommy?"

"Shit." I scramble off him and try to search the floor for my clothes. "I didn't realize they were going to bring her back so soon."

It seems like we just stumbled into the condo, arguing, but it could have been hours since I lost all sense of time the moment Isaac put his hands and mouth on me.

Isaac jumps from the bed. "No, go take a shower. I'll deal with her."

"You sure?"

He nods and grabs his pants from the floor.

I laugh and make my way toward the bathroom. "I'm pretty sure having sex interrupted by your kid is a rite of passage. Welcome to parenthood."

He freezes and looks at me as I stand at the door. "We still need to tell her."

We do.

"Tomorrow."

We can't put it off any longer.

It isn't fair to either of them.

Isaac's lips press into a firm line, the lightness of the moment we just shared long gone. "Yeah, after I meet with my uncles and dad about this text situation."

He jerks on his pants then buttons them as he grabs a T-shirt from the dresser and heads for the door. He pauses just outside it and turns back to me.

The look he gives me says everything he didn't in words before he disappears down the stairs to deal with our daughter and try to figure out what the mysterious text really means.

Thinking of those two words sends a chill through me as I close the bathroom door and lean back against it.

They know...

If it was Dad, why didn't he just call?

Unless he couldn't...

And that possibility makes the tears finally fall.

14

ISAAC

The grim set of Uncle Savage's shoulders aligns perfectly with the mood for the entire meeting before we even start, and I settle in the chair facing his desk, my gut already churning at the topic of conversation.

Uncle Gabe settles into the matching chair next to me, and Dad leans against the wall to our right. Given the way everyone's looking at me, it doesn't bode well for them having found anything since I told them about the text yesterday.

"Were you able to find out anything about who sent me the text message?"

Gabe leans back in his chair, his look grim. "I don't have a fucking clue. Whoever did it used an untraceable burner phone, but my bet is on Cutter."

It would seem like the obvious answer, but something doesn't add up. "Wouldn't he have just called *you* or texted *you*?" It's the question that's been rattling around in my head since those two words popped up on my screen. "You still haven't heard from him directly?"

Gabe shakes his head. "No."

Shit.

That little bit of news makes me shift in my seat. "It's been what? Almost two weeks. Shouldn't we have heard something more by now? From Cutter or Valentina? Hell, anyone?"

Gabe nods. "I would've thought so."

I shove out of the chair and pace behind them, rubbing at the tension at the back of my neck. Even a night in bed, wrapped up in Jack, wasn't enough to alleviate any of it.

Uncle Savage finally leans forward and rests his elbows on the desk. "I know this is stressful, Isaac—"

I whirl to face him. "Stressful? There's someone after the mother of my child and my goddamn daughter. Stressful doesn't begin to describe what this is."

He nods slowly, his strong jaw set hard. "I do understand. Believe me. I know what it's like to have someone you love in danger like that and how it feels to be completely and utterly useless in the situation."

Gabe tosses him a look. "That's not fair. You weren't useless."

Savage snorts and offers his best friend and brother-in-law a half grin. "Maybe not, but it sure fucking felt that way. All we can do is our best to keep them safe and hope our confidence in Cutter is well-placed."

"Yeah?" Somehow, that seems woefully inadequate. "And what the hell if it's not? What if the Satrianos get to them?"

Dad pushes off the wall and approaches, resting his hand on my shoulder. "We're not going to let that happen. You know Saint and Bishop are constantly monitoring things, and the girls are never alone. Even if someone knows they're here, which is still a big *if*, they're not getting to them, not on our watch."

I shove my hands back through my hair and jerk away from him. "I don't want your placations. I want a fucking *plan* here other than sitting around and waiting for something to happen.

Someone sent us that warning for a reason, and if it was Cutter and it's true, then it has to mean the Satrianos know they're here."

Dad exchanges a look with Uncle Savage. "What if it's not from Cutter?"

Savage twists his lips. "What do you mean?"

He scrubs a hand over his stubbled jaw. "What if it's not about the Satrianos at all? What if it's about something else altogether?"

I grab his shoulder and turn him toward me. "What the fuck do you mean?"

His dark brows rise. "Could anyone have found out what went down between you and Broussard?"

"Broussard?"

Fuck.

It feels like that was so long ago already, but I replay our telephone conversation in my head. "No. Definitely not."

Gabe looks from me to Dad. "But he could have told someone..."

"Who the fuck is he going to tell that someone is blackmailing him with evidence that he not only is taking bribes but is also having sex with people he shouldn't be touching?"

Gabe shrugs. "He could have friends we don't know about. People who have power here. Enough power to come after us."

I slam my palm on the back of the chair at the suggestion. "Who the fuck has enough power to come after us?"

Savage stiffens. "The Rosellis."

Just hearing the name from his lips makes me shudder.

I shake my head. "No, we're cool with them."

He holds up his hands and leans back in his chair slightly. "I don't know that *cool* is the way I would describe our relationship with them. Tenuous peace at best. They don't like that Luca is still walking around, breathing. Even thirty years after stepping down, you would think they would just accept that he's out." He levels his hard blue gaze on me. "But that's the problem with these people, isn't it? They don't accept anything at face value, and you can't believe anything they say, either."

"But why now? Why would they cause us an issue now?" None of this makes any sense to me. "If Broussard went to them for help and something to blackmail them with to try to secure their cooperation, they would've just killed him."

Gabe nods. "True. Unless they need him for something."

"What could they possibly need him for?"

Dad begins to pace. "Maybe they're trying to get something zoned, too, and us removing him from the board and his position will interfere with their plans."

That thought hadn't even crossed my mind, but it brings up an intriguing new possibility when it comes to what the text might have been about.

"If we're talking about who has something to lose if Broussard leaves the board, then the top of that list is Falco Enterprises."

The photograph of Broussard meeting with Whitaker and accepting the bribe flashes through my head.

Savage scowls at the mention of his faceless nemesis. "They sure have been pushing the boundaries lately, haven't they?"

I snort and shake my head. "To say the least. You should have seen how fucking pompous Cass Whitaker was at the last court appearance. Judge Cramer handed him his ass and basically told him he needed to tell his clients to stop this bullshit campaign against us. But he just laughed it off and said, as long as he gets paid, he doesn't care."

Savage looks to Dad and Gabe. "And we're no closer to finding out who the owners of Falco Enterprises are?"

Gabe shakes his head. "I've had people digging ever since they showed up, but they're well buried behind layers and layers and layers of offshore accounts and LLCs. They know what they're doing to hide themselves well."

"Shit." Savage shakes his head, his annoyance tightening his jaw. "So, where does that leave us?"

Dad finally stops pacing behind Gabe. "This could be a warning about the girls or a threat to us. Or hell, even a warning to us from somebody who knows something we don't."

I throw up my hands. "What the fuck do we do?"

Savage straightens his shoulders. "What we always do, we band together. We tighten the ranks. We make sure nobody says anything outside the family. Contact all our sources to find out what they've heard, if anything, about the Satrianos or the Rosellis. And what anybody's heard about Broussard. When's he set to give his resignation speech?"

I check my watch. The days are all starting to run together. "Fuck. Tomorrow night. And the zoning meeting is the day after that. That means his assistant director will step up and run the vote and coordinate any discussion and vote on the hotel zoning issue."

"And what about him?" Savage looks to Dad. "Anything to worry about there?"

Dad shakes his head. "No. You handled that, didn't you?"

I nod. "He's not going to be a problem. I met with him last year when he took the assistant director position, and I made it clear that we were willing to make it very lucrative for him to smooth things out for us when he can."

Savage narrows his eyes. "What's he going to want now that he's at the head of the board?"

"I don't fucking care." I look to Dad. "We pay it."

The man who has sat at the head of this family and built this empire from the ground up cuts right to the chase. "Does this guy have any skeletons in his closet?"

I step behind the chair and grip it tightly. "A few, but nothing like Broussard. Gambling debts, a mistress, the usual. We'll keep an eye on everything in case we need to use it, but I anticipate smooth sailing at the meeting."

Savage looks at each of us. "Until then, we keep a watchful

eye on the girls, find out what we can from everyone else, and go on with our lives as if nothing has changed."

"It has changed, though." I shove a hand through my hair. "Everything has changed."

He grins at me. "By the way, congratulations, *Dad*."

That word makes my chest tighten. "Thank you. But we haven't even told her yet."

His brow knits. "Why not? I thought pretty much everyone knew."

"It's complicated."

Gabe snorts. "You're afraid of what Cutter's going to do to you."

"Fuck, no. I'm not afraid of Cutter."

He smirks. "You should be."

I hold out a hand. "I can handle Cutter. What I'm not sure I can handle is a four-year-old finding out that I'm her father and haven't been there the whole time."

Dad releases a heavy sigh, walks over, and claps me on the shoulder. "Children are resilient, son. It's one thing we've all learned from experience. All the shit you and your cousins went through over the years, you've all turned out okay, relatively speaking."

I let out a sardonic laugh and shake my head. "Yeah, I guess."

Gabe looks up at me. "You're bringing them to Sunday dinner tomorrow?"

I clench my eyes closed and suck in a deep breath. I've been looking for ways to avoid it. Something I can tell Nana as an excuse for why I can't come. Last Sunday, I managed to hide the fact that Jack and Vivi were at my place by telling her I wasn't feeling well, but since everybody in the fucking family knows except her, there really isn't any point in keeping it secret anymore.

As long as she knows how important it is to keep who they

are quiet, I don't want to keep her from her great-granddaughter any longer.

"I'm coming, and I'll bring the girls. Jack and I are going to tell Vivi tonight."

Savage looks at Gabe and Dad. "Should I tell Mom?"

I look up at Dad. "Which way do you think is less likely to cause her a heart attack? Seeing me with Viviana and knowing it immediately, or having one of you tell her and have her call me to ream me out for having to wait for me to bring over her first great-grandchild?"

He smirks. "I think option A is your safest bet."

Uncle Savage clasps his hands together and chuckles. "Looks like we're going to have some fireworks tomorrow. I'll spread the word so I can make sure everyone's there."

Oh, great.

A full fucking house at Casa de Hawke.

Lovely.

But first, I need to have a very uncomfortable conversation with a four-year-old.

JACK

YOU'VE GOT to be fucking kidding me.

I look over the table at Isaac, where he jiggles his single card back and forth playfully. "Uno."

Vivi huffs next to me, her hand stuffed with cards. "No fair."

Isaac grins at her. "Sometimes you win, and sometimes you lose, Vivi."

"But you just won the last game. And the one before that."

Nora watches us with a grin, at least six cards still in her hand. "He always was a shark."

You're a shark…

The words "Nolan" said to me that night after I ran the pool table repeat in my head, and I smile at his mom as I lean over to Vivi and nudge her with my elbow. "I only have two cards. I can still beat him. We can be a team."

"Okay." She perks up and plays a green three, which allows me to play my green five on top of it.

"Uno." I mimic Isaac's little card action and mouth, "*Now, who is the shark?*"

He smirks at me across the table, then lays down his final card —a green nine. "I win." He offers a shrug. "Again. Three times in a row. Undisputed champion."

Viviana blows out a long sigh in a way that no four-year-old has a right to and tosses her cards onto the table before she crosses her arms over her chest. "No fair."

Nora throws her cards onto the pile and sighs. "I'm with her." She grins at her granddaughter, who still has absolutely no idea of her connection to the woman. "No fair."

I wrap my arm around Vivi. "We've talked about being a good sport even when we lose, right?"

She scowls but nods.

"So, you can't win every game. And tonight, Isaac was just better at Uno than we were."

Nora snorts a laugh and pushes up from the table. "I think that's my cue to leave. I don't want to get my butt kicked by my kid again. It's embarrassing."

Isaac laughs and climbs to his feet, approaching his mom with a grin and open arms. "Oh, come on, Ma. I let you beat me sometimes."

She rolls her eyes at him and smacks his shoulder. "*Let* me?"

He wraps his arm around her and squeezes. "Come on, be a good sport."

Nora casts a glance at Vivi and me and sighs. "Okay, congratulations on your feats of grandeur. Don't let it go to that already big head of yours." She slips from his hold and approaches Vivi, squatting next to her chair. "We'll get him next time, Vi. He can't win *all* the time."

He sure likes to think he can...

And he's been on a mission since the day I arrived to ensure he "wins" whatever game it is he thinks we're playing at any given time.

Only the time for games has come to an end. It's finally time to face the music. I lock gazes with him and raise an eyebrow, and he knows exactly what I'm asking. We've been dancing around it ever since he got home from meeting with his uncles and dad, but we have to do it tonight.

We have to sit her down and tell her.

Somehow, I thought this would be easier. I thought that once the moment came, I would know exactly what to say and how to say it. But acid churns in my stomach, threatening to make the dinner we ate make a reappearance.

He walks his mom to the door, and she hugs him and whispers something that makes him peek our way before he releases her and lets her out.

"Come on, Vivi." I motion to the living room, where a fire roars in the fireplace. "Come sit on the couch. We want to talk to you."

She happily slips from her chair, rushes over to the big leather couch, and jumps onto it, bouncing up and down like she's about to get some amazing gift.

I hope she still feels that way after this conversation.

This could go either way. With a four-year-old, it's so hard to tell.

I take the seat next to her while Isaac turns one of the chairs to face her and settles into it, too. He clears his throat, suddenly looking ten years younger and like he's about to throw up, too.

A man I have never seen nervous for one fucking moment, who is always self-assured and perfectly in control, suddenly looks like he's about to vomit all over his immaculate floors. "So, Viviana. Do you remember when you asked me how I knew your mom?"

She nods.

"Well..." He clears his throat again and shifts uncomfortably in his chair, looking to me for guidance. "Uh..."

I look at Vivi and smile. "And he told you that we lost touch for a while, and we didn't talk for a long time, right?"

She nods, her brow furrowed as she glances between us, trying to determine where we're going with this.

"Well, I had been looking for him to tell him something really important."

Viviana stares up at me so innocently, completely oblivious to the turmoil we're both feeling right now. "What?"

Isaac takes a deep inhale and lets it out in a rush. "Viviana, I'm your daddy."

She looks at him, her eyes wide for a second before she narrows them on him. "You're my daddy?"

He nods. "I am."

The moment of silence that follows leaves us both frozen, waiting for her to say something.

It drags on. And on. And on.

Finally, she twists her mouth. "Then how come I never met you before?"

Hell.

Her words cut like a knife to my chest, but it's probably nothing in comparison to how they hit Isaac.

Pain flashes in his eyes, and he reaches out and rests his hand on her leg. "Because I didn't know your mommy was pregnant with you or that you were alive. If I had known about you, I would've been there every day."

His gaze flicks over to meet mine, and my stomach flip-flops at the heat and truth in the way he looks at me.

"But"—tears start to form in her eyes—"but why didn't you just call each other? Then you would've known."

I wince because I should have known she'd be too smart not to ask that question. And just like I told him the other night, I'm willing to be the fall guy here because when it comes down to it, it was my fault. I'm the one who ran that morning. Ran from what I was feeling about him. Ran because I was afraid of what Dad would do if he found him. Ran because it's what I loved to do.

"I couldn't call him, honey, because—"

"It's my fault."

His words stop me in my tracks, and I open my eyes wide at him and mouth, "*What are you doing?*"

A muscle in his jaw tics, and he shifts to the edge of his chair, closer to Viviana. "Honey, you'll understand when you're older. But sometimes, people meet each other, and someone maybe does something that makes the other person think they don't care. And that's the furthest thing from the truth. But it's my fault your mom couldn't get in touch with me, that she couldn't tell me. I'm the only one to blame here."

What the hell is he doing?

Why is he taking the blame for this?

Viviana swipes at her eyes, preventing the tears from falling, and stares at Isaac like she's seeing him for the first time. Maybe she's seeing what I do. The same thick, dark, wavy hair. The same Caribbean-blue eyes. The same mouth and chin. She's a Hawke if there ever was one. And the more of the cousins I meet, the more I see it.

"Vivi"—I wrap my arm around her and rub her back—"do you have any other questions?"

She thinks about it for a second and smiles up at me. "Can I have ice cream before bed?"

Christ, the innocence of children...

I smile at her and catch Isaac's smirk out of the corner of my eye.

"Sure, honey." I swipe away a tear that tries to sneak out. "You can have some ice cream."

Isaac pushes up from his chair and scoops her from the couch up into his arms. "How about if we make sundaes? I got everything we need."

"What's a sundae?"

He gapes at me. "She's never had a sundae?"

I shrug. "Most of what we ate in my parents' house was gelato."

His laugh echoes around the room, and he shakes his head. "Why does that not surprise me?" He returns his attention to Vivi. "So, you've never had a banana split?"

She shakes her head.

The dirty look he tosses me is mixed with the humor of the situation. "Well, you're going to tonight."

She smiles at him and presses her hands on his face. "Thanks, Daddy."

He freezes, his eyes locked on our little girl, and my heart climbs into my throat. She said the word so easily, like it didn't mean anything different than calling him Isaac. But he's about to lose his shit completely. And I might, too.

I watch his Adam's apple bob as he swallows, then ruffles her hair.

"Of course, kiddo. I'd do anything for you. Anything."

And that's what terrifies me about him as much as it gives me confidence that we'll be safe here.

He *will* do anything for us, including crossing lines I undoubtedly wouldn't want him to.

I've lived in the shadow of what the Marconis do my entire life. Now, I've become enshrouded in the one Isaac Hawke casts, and there isn't any way out.

He carries her into the kitchen, and I follow and watch him set her down and gather all the ingredients he needs for the sundae.

His smile comes quick and easy, as if finally telling her has taken the weight of the world off his shoulders.

Maybe it has.

It definitely feels like something heavy has been pulled from my chest, but the reason we're here still hangs over us.

One that has no end in sight.

15

ISAAC

The door to Nana's house opens before I even make it halfway up the walkway, and Storm leans against the doorjamb, shrewd blue eyes locked on me as I carry Viviana toward her with Jack trailing closely behind.

"You're really just going to spring this on Nana?" She raises an eyebrow, giving me an *are you kidding me* look. "Are you trying to kill the poor old woman?"

Exaggerate much?

Nana may be almost ninety, but no one would ever suspect it from knowing the woman. Most of us have started to think she's going to live forever. She sure doesn't show any signs of slowing down anytime soon.

I scowl at Aunt Storm and set down Viviana. "No one offered me a better solution here."

It isn't something you tell someone over the phone, and we only just told Vivi herself last night.

Storm squats and smiles at Viviana. "Hi, Viviana. I'm your

Great-aunt Storm. I think you met my daughter, Angelina, the other day."

Viviana nods and smiles. "She gave me a cookie and hot chocolate."

Thank God that's what she remembers and not that I dragged her out of there like a psycho...

I release a heavy sigh of relief at that, even though not having any explanation for the text message continues to keep us all on edge.

Storm grabs Viviana's hand to lead her in. "She's really good at making both of those things. Nana taught her." She glances over her shoulder at Jack and me. "You coming?"

As if I have a choice.

Missing Sunday dinner at Nana's might as well be a cardinal sin that will send you straight to Hell. Jude is the only one who regularly gets away with it. I never could and never will be able to miss it unless I'm lying dead in a ditch somewhere. Skipping last week because I was "sick" will likely earn me a tongue-lashing and maybe a swat with the wooden spoon when I get into Nana's kitchen.

I take Jack's hand and follow Storm toward the door. "Is everyone here?"

"Everyone...but Allie and Jude. She is supposed to be coming, but I wouldn't hold my breath for him. I value my life too much." Storm holds out her free hand and takes Jack's. "It's nice to finally meet you, Mina. I hope you're feeling better."

Jack blushes slightly, clearly uncomfortable with the fact that the entire family knows about her medical condition now—but there isn't any keeping secrets in this family. At least, not for long.

She finally forces a smile at Storm. "I am. Thank you."

Jack moves to step into the house behind Storm, but I hold her back with a hand on her shoulder.

"You sure you're up for this, meeting the entire family? It's a little overwhelming at best. And once my grandmother sees Vivi..."

All hell might break loose.

On top of that, Mom will finally be able to explain that she's Viviana's grandmother, and I have a feeling that little girl will end up smothered by the Hawke women quite quickly.

Jack gives me a sharp nod. "We have to do it, right? No matter how uncomfortable it might be?"

Shit, truer words have never been spoken.

So much of life just seems to be about doing things you don't want to but you have to. It's what brought me back to New Orleans after law school when working for the Midwest Innocence Project was what really got to the heart of everything I loved about the law. It's what made me leave Chicago when all I wanted to do was stay so I could search for Jack indefinitely.

Loyalty is everything.

I lean in and press a kiss to her temple. "Then let's do it."

We step in, and I close the door behind me and turn to find Storm leading Viviana deeper into the house and closer to what's bound to be an "entertaining" meeting with Nana.

Let's hope her heart can keep up with the surprise.

Mine barely did...

I hustle to catch up with her and scoop Viviana back up into my arms. "Remember how I told you that you were going to meet some more family?"

She nods and examines the photos on the wall as we make our way to the galley kitchen.

"You want to meet my nana, your great-grandmother?"

A tiny smile plays at her lips, and she nods again. I glance over my shoulder at Jack, who looks as nervous as I feel.

I move toward the kitchen while almost two dozen sets of eyes follow me through the house. Most of the girls sit in the living room and all crane their necks as I walk past.

Dani climbs from her chair and moves in behind us, not

wanting to miss a minute of the fireworks, and others line up along the entry points to various other rooms of Nana's house, trying to get a better view.

I incline my head toward the kitchen. "She in there?"

Storm bobs her head. "Skye's with her."

"Okay..." I take a deep breath and step into the kitchen with Jack at my side, her fingers entwined with mine.

Nana stands at the oven with her back to me, a tray of what looks like lasagna in her hands, talking to Skye. Skye's eyes meet mine over Nana's shoulder, and they widen slightly before she reaches out and takes the pan from her.

"Let me take that, Mom."

"What?" Nana reaches for the tray. "Why?"

Skye inclines her head toward me. "You have a visitor."

Nana starts to turn. "Oh, is Isaac finally here with Cutter's daughter and granddaughter?"

Jack squeezes my hand, and I force myself to swallow through the lump in my throat.

"No, Nana. I'm here with your great-granddaughter."

She finally makes it all the way around to face me. Her old eyes widen as she takes in the little girl in my arms, her gaze darting between her face and mine, then over to Jack's, who stands beside me.

"Oh, my God." She presses a hand over her chest. "What..."

Skye sets the lasagna on the counter and moves to wrap her arm around Nana. "Mom, are you okay?"

Nana's mouth opens and closes a few times. "But how...why didn't you..." She rushes forward and slaps me on the shoulder with a stern look full of questions, then she scoops Viviana from my arms without hesitation.

At least it wasn't a wooden spoon this time.

"Hello, my darling." She smiles at Viviana, who gazes at her with the kind of awe only a four-year-old can. Nana's eyes dart to me. "I'm a great-grandmother."

I nod and rub at the back of my neck. "Yep."

"How old are you, sweetheart?"

Viviana grins at her and holds up her tiny fingers. "Four."

"When's your birthday?"

"February eleventh."

Nana narrows her angry eyes on me. "Four years and you didn't—"

I hold up a hand to stop her. "I'll explain everything later. I promise. I don't want to disrupt Sunday dinner."

The matriarch of the Hawke family snorts and shakes her head, her gray hair barely moving in the tight bun she always wears when she cooks. "I think it's a little late for that."

For an almost ninety-year-old woman, she sure hasn't slowed down or backed down even a little bit. She moves toward me and stops to plant a kiss on my cheek. "We're talking later, Isaac."

"Yes, ma'am."

Jack smirks at me until Nana stops next to her and narrows her scrutiny her way.

"You, too, dear." She pushes out from the kitchen and into the living room, where the remainder of the family has gathered. "Everyone, have you met my great-granddaughter, Viviana?"

A chorus of shouts and rushed conversation hits my ears, and I release a long, slow breath. Jack leans against me, wrapping her arm around mine.

Skye approaches and pats me on the shoulder. "I'm just glad it was you and not me."

"Gee, thanks, Aunt Skye."

She grins at me, then pulls Jack away from me to wrap her arms around her. "Welcome to the Hawkes. Today is going to be very interesting."

Jack swallows thickly. "I bet."

"*Interesting* is putting it mildly. I'm going to need a beer."

Gabe appears at the other end of the kitchen through the doors that lead out to the patio and chuckles. "I can help you there." He grabs a beer from the fridge, pops the cap, and hands it to me. "Can I get you anything, Mina?"

She shakes her head. "I'm good. Thank you."

"Well, just let someone know if you need something." He turns to me. "Your dad, Savage, and I are out here. Why don't you step out and join us?"

I glance at Jack. "Should she come?"

He offers me a grim look. "Probably a good idea."

Jack takes a step back and peeks into the living room. "Is she okay out there?"

I grin at her. "That depends on your definition of *okay*."

Likely being smothered—Hawke style.

She offers a half-shrug and turns back to me. "She's talking to a beautiful blonde I haven't met before."

"Kennedy, that's Savage and Danika's daughter. She's the one who helps Savage and Gabe run the whole show."

Jack nods slowly. "I'm really going to need a family tree or something."

I release a little laugh and take a sip of my beer. "Sometimes I feel the same way. Let's go."

If Gabe wants her out there, it means they're discussing the Satriano situation, and if it were anything good, he'd just say it right here.

I urge Jack forward with a hand at her lower back, and we make our way out onto the patio where Savage and Gabe sit with beers in their hand. Dad has his typical seltzer water and lime in front of him.

Savage inclines his head toward us. "Mina, it's nice to see you again."

Her brow furrows as she takes a seat at the large, round outdoor table. "Again? I don't think we've..."

He offers her a kind smile. "I was at the club and came down to help the other day."

"Oh, I'm sorry." She shakes her head, her dark hair fluttering in the cool breeze. "I don't really remember much. That usually happens after a seizure."

"It's quite all right. You don't have anything to apologize for."

The door slides open again, and Landon steps out to join us. I nod at him. "Landon..."

He inclines his head toward us and takes a seat next to Jack, offering her his hand. "I'm Landon, Storm's husband."

Jack smiles. "Nice to meet you. So, you're Angelina's dad?"

Everyone around the table fidgets slightly, and Landon gives her a sad smile. "Stepfather. Her father passed away when she was young."

"Oh, crap." Jack presses a hand over her mouth. "I'm so sorry. I didn't know."

I reach under the table and squeeze the top of her leg. "It's okay. There's a whole lot of family history to catch you up on."

She leans into me. "No, shit. And I somehow feel like I'm saying the wrong thing, no matter what comes out of my mouth."

"Don't worry about it. Everyone will just give you shit." *Lots of it.* "That's how we Hawkes show we love each other."

Dad glances back toward the door to ensure it's closed. "I'm glad you're all here. I wanted to update everyone."

I lean forward in my chair, my attention focused completely on him now. "On what? Have you found out anything since yesterday?"

He gets a slightly pained expression. "Sort of. The Satrianos have an estate in Italy they operate out of. There was an explosion there last night."

Jack's entire body stiffens, her thigh tensing under my palm. All the color drains from her face.

I slide my hand over and grab hers to squeeze it. "Cutter?"

Dad shrugs. "Could be."

Gabe twists his beer bottle in his hands. "I think it's safe to assume it was him."

"Do we know what happened? Was anyone killed, hurt? Where the fuck do we stand?"

Jack sucks in a nervous breath. "Is my dad..." She twists her hand in mine to interlock our fingers, the tension radiating from her. "Okay?"

Gabe shakes his head. "I don't know, Mina. I don't have any way to get ahold of him if he doesn't want to be found."

"What about my mom?"

"Your dad is the only one who knows how to get in touch with her, too. I don't know where she is."

"Shit." Jack clamps her eyes closed and inhales a sharp breath. Her body starts to tremble.

All this stress can't be good for her. She said it can be a trigger for her seizures. Her distress makes the beer sour in my stomach.

I squeeze her hand as hard as I can, trying to bring her attention to something else and away from the tension of the situation. "It'll be okay, Jack."

"How can you say that when we don't know what the hell is going on?" She looks at each of the men around the table. "We never found out who sent the text message, did we?"

Everyone exchanges hard looks, all of us bearing the same annoyance and frustration.

Savage shakes his head. "We haven't, but it could be completely unrelated to what's going on with the Satrianos. Saint and Gabe and their men are looking into it. We're doing everything we can to try to keep you safe and figure out what's happening with your parents."

Jack releases a mirthless laugh. "All of this because my mom didn't want to help them with something they probably shouldn't have been doing in the fucking first place." She jerks her hand from mine and shoves her chair back, the metal scraping on the cement. "Fucking great."

She storms away from the table and back into the house without looking back.

"Fuck." I run a hand along my jaw. "That went well."

Dad tilts his drink toward the door. "You should probably go after her, son."

I glare at him. "You think?"

Savage surveys through the open door, then looks to me. "What's going on with you two? Are you..."

"Fuck if I know."

I push back my chair and reenter the house after her. Her reaction isn't unwarranted, given what she just learned, but the last thing I wanted was to upset her today. Meeting the family is hard enough without throwing in the Marconi/Satriano drama.

Voices carry from all over the house as I move through the empty kitchen and out into the living room, where all the girls sit around, fawning over Viviana, but there isn't any sign of Jack.

I stalk past them to the massive dining room addition Uncle Savage put on the house years ago and find Coen, Pope, and Atlas with a deck of cards spread out across the table and a bunch of money in what looks like a makeshift poker game.

Scowling, I point at the pile in the center between them. "Nana better not catch you guys playing for real money."

Pope chuckles and flashes a grin. "Don't worry. I know how to handle Nana."

"Oh, I bet."

Teacher's pet...

Nana's favorite grandchild—even though there isn't an ounce of Hawke blood in him. Saint's son is her pride and joy—the *doctor*, following in Mom's footsteps and saving lives when all Dad and I do is save *our* world without any appreciation.

Coen's eye catches mine, and he raises a brow at me. "Everything okay?"

"I'm looking for Mina."

Atlas shakes his head. "She didn't come in this way. I said hi to Viviana and introduced her to Coen and Pope, but I never saw Mina."

"She was outside with me and came back in."

He shrugs. "Check the bedrooms, maybe, or the bathroom?"

"Yeah, maybe." I point at the game again and then the stack of dishes and silverware at the other end. "You guys better get this cleaned up before Nana wants the table set, or she's going to hand you your asses."

Coen waves me off. "Yeah, yeah, yeah."

I hustle back to the living room, unable to fight my smile at Viviana chatting with the girls, examining Kennedy's nails and Angelina's earrings.

She's in good hands and hasn't even noticed what's going on with her mother and me, which is good because I don't have a fucking clue, either.

JACK

An explosion...

There was a damn explosion, and no one has heard from Dad.

How the hell am I supposed to react to that information?

Probably not hysterical tears like the ones streaming down my face now or blowing up at the Hawkes when they are only trying to help me.

It's not their fault Mom got herself into some untenable situation and put Viviana and me in the crossfire. It's not their fault I'm a blubbering mess of uncontrolled emotions.

I swipe at the newest tears and try to inhale a few slow, calming breaths.

No stress.

Getting worked up like this isn't good, especially after having a seizure so recently. If I don't calm down and take care of myself,

I'll end up back in the hospital and knocked out of commission again.

That won't do anyone any good.

I just have to believe Dad is okay. That whatever the explosion was, it served its purpose and took care of anyone who posed a threat. That he will get back in touch with us as soon as he can. That Mom is safe. That I'll see them both again soon.

Keep telling yourself that.

This isn't just about me.

There are more important things.

I can't let Viviana see any of my fear. She's been so strong through all this because I've been able to keep what's really happening from her. Insulating her is the top priority.

And now I can understand why they did it to me, why they tried to keep me protected from all the bad things that exist in their world.

Whatever Mom did to draw Satriano's ire, it also brought us here, to Isaac. Almost like fate was playing some strange game and toying with my heart.

The door to the bedroom pushes open, and Isaac's concerned gaze instantly lands on me where I sit on the bed in the dark room.

I look down at my hands on my lap and shake my head, trying to keep the tears from falling, "I'm sorry, I didn't mean—"

"Don't apologize." He slips into the room and shuts the door behind him, then looks around with a wistful tilt to his lips. "This was my dad's room."

"Really?" I turn on the bed and scrutinize the room I hadn't taken the time to examine when I came in. Plaques hang on the wall—*Stone Hawke, first place, debate team.* "I didn't even look. I just needed somewhere quiet, away from..."

He motions over his shoulder. "Away from all that?"

"Yeah."

Isaac walks toward me slowly, then squats and takes my hands in his. "I know you're worried about your parents."

I shake my head and swipe away a tear. "It's not just that. It's all this. Everything changed so fucking fast, and I haven't been able to catch up with it. It feels like I'm spiraling out of control."

He offers a sad smile. "I know how you feel."

"Shit." I pinch the bridge of my nose and shake my head. "I'm sorry. I wasn't even thinking about how this must be affecting you."

The sheer amount of change and drama I've brought into Isaac's world would make most men run in the other direction, but he's still here, still staring at me like I'm the only thing that matters.

"It's okay." He offers a slight shrug. "I'm stronger than I look."

I smirk at him. "Shit, then you must be the Hulk."

He grins. "I prefer Superman. Mild-mannered attorney by day, crime fighter by night."

My laugh fills the room, cracking some of the tension. "First, you are far from mild-mannered. Second, I don't exactly think you're out there fighting crime, more like probably committing it."

His jaw drops open in mock offense. "You think I'm out committing crimes?"

I narrow my eyes on him. "My father told me some things. And I wouldn't put it past you or your father, your uncles, or anyone in this family to do whatever they felt was necessary, including things that may not be completely legal."

He slides his hands up my thighs and squeezes gently. "If you're referring to what I would do to protect you, to protect any of *them*, then you're right. I'll slit the throat of anyone who gets fucking close to you, then burn them and dance in the flames before I throw anything that's left into the fucking ocean."

"Well, that was a little aggressive."

"You have no idea." His jaw tightens, and he drags me up from the edge of the bed and pulls me into his arms, burying his face in my hair. "I know I keep saying it, but I need to know you believe me when I tell you that I will protect you and Viviana, no matter what it takes."

His words should create a sense of peace and safety, but something won't let me feel that. Something wraps around my chest and squeezes so tightly that it makes it impossible to breathe most of the time.

"But how can you protect me when we don't even know what's going on? We're just sitting here, and I feel like we're waiting for something bad to happen."

Isaac drags his face back and takes mine in his palms. "I've had an uneasy feeling, too, and the mystery of that text message doesn't fucking help, but none of that matters. No matter what we face, I'm going to make sure you two are safe."

"I know you'll try."

He drops his forehead against mine. "I'll do more than try. Your father may have the training and the reputation, but I have something he doesn't."

"Oh yeah? What's that?"

"*You.* I just got you back. I just got my *daughter.* I have my *family*, and there is absolutely no way anything's going to get in the way of that...again."

Again.

The only thing that got in the way the first time was me. I swallow thickly and slip out of his hold to pace the room. "What if it's not that simple? What if..."

He takes a step toward me. "What if what?"

"What if it's *never* safe? What if I'm always running? What if I'm always hiding? I can't..." Tears finally trickle down my cheeks. "I can't keep living like this. It isn't fair to me, and it isn't fair to Viviana. I thought...I tried to escape my parents so many times, begged them to let me live on my own, change my name so it couldn't be traced to them. Let me have a life. But they wouldn't let me go. And maybe they had good reasons not to. They were worried about my mother's business rivals. They were worried about me having a seizure and nobody being there, but I'm an adult." I throw up my hands, the decades of anger at how they've been making me live finally boiling over. "Fuck. I'm almost twenty-six years old, and I feel like I haven't lived. I haven't been outside of that house for longer than a week or two at a time, and only when I'm somewhere with my parents or my guards. Never alone. I've never—"

He closes the distance between us and drags me up against him. "Don't say never. We had our weekend."

I nod, fighting against the sob that wants to slip from my lips. "Yes, we did."

"Do you remember what I told you about my family? How everything was planned? How this is what I *had* to do, that I *had* to come back?"

"Yes."

And I vividly remember the pain in his voice when he talked about it.

"Believe me, Jack, I feel the same fucking way you do. Sometimes, it feels like having Hawke as a last name is a death sentence because it means I'm stuck here in New Orleans. I'm stuck in this job." He shakes his head. "My dad can't do this forever. He's almost sixty years old and going to want to retire at some point if my uncles let him. And the bigger our businesses grow, the more we open, especially if this hotel goes through, we're just going to have more and more work, more and more things to handle, more enemies, in the courtroom and outside of it."

He releases a long, heavy sigh filled with the weight of what's been rested on his shoulders.

"And while Savage and Gabe and Kennedy do everything they can to handle the business side, we are the ones who fight the real battles. My dad and I are the ones in court arguing against assholes trying to encroach on our business. We are the ones fighting with the goddamn zoning board when they try to fuck us. We are the ones paying off people, threatening people, blackmailing people, and doing anything we can to ensure what's best for the business." He pauses for a moment, a faraway look in his eyes. "And there are days when I really question how long I can do it. So, believe me, I fucking get it, Jack. I do. I really fucking do."

I felt it that weekend—that we were kindred souls who really understood each other and had some deep connection based on the expectations and responsibilities we had to endure. And I feel it even more now.

"Is there any way out?"

He closes his eyes and lowers his forehead to mine, then shakes his head gently. "They're my family, Jack. And just like you love your parents and you miss home, no matter how much you might resent it, it still is your home. And this is mine. And these are the people I love more than anything, who I'll do anything for. I could never just walk away from it. Not any more than you could ever really walk away from your parents and start over somewhere as someone else. You could never cut them off, and neither could I."

"Shit." Tears stream down my face like a torrent, my breath catching. "I'm so worried about them."

"I know you are. But try not to think about that. Try to think about the twenty-plus people out there who already love our daughter, who have already accepted her—and you—as part of this family, who want to welcome you, who want to help protect you and make you feel comfortable here. Think about the amazing meal my nana prepared because, let me tell you, she is one good fucking cook."

He pulls back and takes my face in his hands again.

"And think about the fact that you have a man who will dedicate his entire fucking life to you and will burn down the world to protect you and our daughter from anything that could possibly harm you."

"What if it's you?"

His body stiffens, his brow furrowing deeply. "What do you mean?"

"What if you are the thing that could hurt me?"

He considers my question for a moment, his warm eyes searching mine. "Fuck, Jack, I would never hurt you."

"Maybe not intentionally, but this..." I press my hands against his chest and feel his heart thundering against my palm. "The way I always feel when I'm around you...it's intense. It's irrational."

Really, we barely know each other.

Two days five years ago...mostly spent in bed.

And now, two weeks where we've been trapped in this intense situation, emotions running high.

I struggle to find the words I'm looking for to *really* explain it, to explain how I've always felt around him.

This deep ache in my chest, like part of me is missing when he isn't near. This all-consuming need to feel his touch, his kiss, his passion *all the damn time*. The physical pain when I think of the possibility of losing it again. The feeling like I'm drowning every time I look into his eyes.

I curl my fingers against him. "It *hurts,* Isaac, *this* hurts... because it's too much sometimes."

It's just too much.

Isaac tightens his grip on my face, forcing my head up more, ensuring his gaze is locked with mine. "No, Jack." He lowers his mouth to mine and stops just a millimeter away from kissing me. "It isn't too much. It's exactly right."

16

JACK

Isaac slams his mouth to mine, eliminating all ability to respond or to even breathe as his body presses to mine. He walks me backward until my shoulders and spine hit the door, rattling it behind me.

A groan slips from his mouth into mine, his hands angling my face exactly where he wants me in order to devour me completely.

It's precisely what I was just trying to explain to him—the way he *consumes* me. Like a raging inferno tearing through an old house, he eradicates all my ghosts, obliterates and burns away everything haunting me with the heat of his passion.

One look.

One touch.

One kiss.

And I'm a goner for this man.

When we're like this, I can just *feel*. I can just be Jack, who takes what she wants and doesn't care about the consequences. I can let go of the pain of the past and the uncertainty of the future.

I can lose myself swimming in the blue haze of lust staring back at me.

I wrap my hands around his neck, tangling my fingers in the unruly hair at his nape, needing to draw him closer, to feel him completely against me. He grinds his hard cock against my stomach, a little groan rumbling in his chest.

My pussy clenches in anticipation of what's to come, longing to have him inside, needing to feel so filled, so complete.

"No, wait." I jerk my head away from his, my breath coming out in short bursts. "Isaac, we can't do this here. It's your grandmother's house, your father's bedroom."

A lecherous grin curls his perfect lips. "I'm pretty confident my dad has done things much worse in this room."

He kisses me again before I think too much about that possibility and drops one hand to the hem of my shirt. Deft fingers trail over the skin at my stomach, just above the waistband of my pants, making me shudder and jerk back from the featherlight touch.

Christ.

This is so wrong.

And like I told him...it's all too much.

But I can't control myself when we're like this, when he's like this, demanding, intent on taking what he wants and giving me exactly what I need.

This is the same man I met in that bar—the one I knew could give me something I hadn't been able to find before. And he more than did that. Now, he's doing it again. Trying to kiss away my fears, to destroy any reservations I have about what's happening between us, about where our future might lie. And while those still linger, my feelings in this moment are crystal clear.

My clit throbs with the need for friction, for him to touch me, for him to fill me up with something other than this fear and anxiety that have been drowning me since we arrived here, the way only *he* can.

He tugs the waistband of my pants and manages to jerk them down far enough for me to kick off my slides and step out of them. Kissing him, I fumble with his belt to free his cock and take it in my hand to stroke the long, hard, thick length. He groans into my mouth again, the sound making his chest vibrate where it presses to mine.

"Fucking hell, Jack, the way you touch me, the way your body responds to me." He kisses his way across my cheek and brushes his lips against my ear. "You were fucking made for me, Jack, all this, everything. It was fucking fate, or serendipity, whatever the hell you want to call it."

Fate.

There's that word again.

It has floated around in my head since the second I realized who Nolan was—that this can't all be a coincidence. Someone's hand is at play. Whether that be God or fate or some unknown energy at the center of the universe, it brought us together.

It gave us *this* again.

He lifts me easily to wrap my legs around his waist, aligns his cock, and plunges into me in one hard thrust that slams me back against the door, shaking it loudly.

"Oh, God."

"God isn't here, baby. Just me."

He thrusts into me again, hitting exactly the right spot he needs to that will help make me forget what just happened out there with his family, to make me forget the fact that my life and the lives of everyone I care about are currently in danger, to make me forget, for a few moments, why this is so damn complicated and not as simple as what we both want.

One hand grips my hip, holding me steady and helping pin me against the door as he pummels me, slamming into me over and over again, rattling the wood behind me as well as my ability to maintain any sort of focus on all the other things going on around us.

"You and me, Jack, this is it. This is what it was all about." He kisses that spot behind my ear that sends a shudder through me. "When all this is over, I'm going to make sure to give you everything you've ever wanted. I'm going to make you happy."

Make you happy.

Such a simple phrase.

He makes it sound so easy, but nothing about this has been.

I don't even know how to be happy anymore.

But with his cock inside me, filling and stretching me, he's doing a pretty goddamn good job at the moment.

I scratch my nails on the back of his neck as he grinds his pelvis against my clit, trying to give me the friction I need. A warm, white, fuzzy haze starts to encroach on the edges of my vision. Dropping my head back against the door, I gasp and squeeze around him.

"You keep doing that, Jack, and I'm going to come way before you do, and that is not something I will ever fucking do."

I open my eyes. "Then, you better up your game."

He draws his head back, his eyes glowing with amusement and lust. "Is that a challenge?"

The corner of my lips pulls up. "Take it however you want it."

"Oh, Jack, I will take you however I can." He leans forward and nips at my lips, sucking the bottom one between his teeth and biting down hard enough for a little jolt of pain to shoot through me. "And I have so many fucking ways in mind that we haven't had a chance to try yet."

Oh, God.

My entire body pulses at the promise of his words as he continues to thrust into me relentlessly, not giving a damn that someone might come back here and walk in on us or hear us. He doesn't seem to give a shit that twenty-plus members of his family are only ten feet away, that our daughter is right there. In this moment, all he sees is me. And while I want to only see him, that doubt, that fear, that anxiety, creeps up in the back of my mind.

Isaac stills his hips. "Don't do that, Jack."

"Don't do what?"

He takes my face in his palm. "Don't think. Just feel."

With that, he plunges into me again, and I roll my hips to meet each thrust. The steady, low heat burns at my core, starting to spread out into my limbs until it erupts in a cataclysm that sends me jerking on his cock. He grits his teeth and empties himself inside me, the hot rush filling me as I sag against him, still pinned to the door.

Isaac presses a kiss on my neck and then across my cheek to my lips. This one's slow and sensual, any hurry long gone, replaced by a sense of peace we both know won't last.

"Shit."

It's the only word I can think of at this moment.

"I would like to stay here with you forever, Jack, but there are a whole lot of people waiting out there." He brushes his lips over mine and grins. "And I get to sit next to you at that table, knowing my cum is still inside you as you eat."

"Christ..."

My pussy flutters and squeezes around his still-hard cock inside me. "At least let me go to the bathroom and clean up."

He shakes his head. "No, I want to know it's there. I want to know I've been in there trying to get you pregnant again."

"Jesus. You have to stop talking like that."

One of his dark brows rises. "Do I?"

"Yes."

"How come?"

"Because I—"

Heavy footsteps and laughter sound in the hall outside the door, and Isaac pulls back from me, his cock slipping out. I shift my underwear back into place and scramble to find my pants on the floor. He tries to re-buckle his pants, and the door opens.

Stone and Nora stumble in, laughing, his lips on her neck.

Nora's eyes are closed, her head tipped back, but Stone's blue ones meet mine.

"Oh, shit." He jerks away from Nora, and her eyes fly open to land on us. Stone clears his throat uncomfortably as he examines our frazzled states. "Sorry—"

Nora's smirk grows. "Well, it looks like someone else had the same idea."

Yeah.

This isn't awkward at all.

Isaac moves in front me—still pantsless—and buckles his belt, offering his parents a disgusted sound. "Stop acting like teenagers."

His mother's jaw drops incredulously. "Excuse me? Look who's talking."

Another set of footsteps comes down the hall, and Kennedy sticks her head in, her eyes narrowing. "What the hell is going on in here? It's time to eat."

Stone and Nora cast another glance at us and slip from the room, and I swallow thickly, try to rub out the wrinkles from my shirt, and run my hands over my hair. Though, I doubt it will do any good.

I take a step toward the door, but Isaac moves behind me and presses his chest against my back, dragging me to him and nuzzling my ear.

"I'm definitely starving, but it isn't for my grandmother's lasagna. I can't wait to eat your cunt when we get back home, knowing I have been there."

Sweet mother of God.

I have to go sit at dinner with his family after he says that to me...

What kind of fucking torture is this?

ISAAC

IT DOESN'T EVEN TAKE a full two minutes sitting at the table before someone has to open their mouth.

Pope takes a sip of his wine and grins at Jack. "So, Mina, or do you prefer Jack?"

He smirks at me.

She glances between us. "Uh, either is fine."

Pope motions between us with his fork. "Just how did the two of you *meet*?"

The emphasis he puts on the word makes me stiffen, and Jack does the same next to me as her cheeks turn bright red.

Dani elbows him from his left. "Just because your mother isn't here doesn't mean you can be a dick, Pope."

He feigns innocence, his dark eyes widening and his mouth falling open. "What? I'm just curious."

I scowl at him and shove a piece of garlic bread into my mouth. "That probably isn't a good story to tell at the dinner table, cousin."

Or anytime, really.

What happened that weekend is between Jack and me. It isn't anything to share with *anyone*, let alone my nosy family.

Jack clears her throat and shifts uneasily. "Um, we met in Chicago, when he graduated from law school."

That's more than I would have told them, but it might appease the vultures circling for tidbits of juicy details. At least for a little while.

Nana makes a tsking sound from the end of the table where she sits with Viviana to her right, unwilling to let the girl get more than two feet away from her since we've arrived. "Leave the poor girl alone, everyone."

Mom just smiles at me from her place on the other side of Viviana, not bothering to hide her amusement.

"*Everyone?*" Kennedy raises a thin blond brow. "What did I do?"

Astrid and Atlas both nod. "Yeah, what did we do?"

They say it almost in unison, then offer each other an annoyed look since they hate when they end up doing "twin" stuff.

Nana points at everyone around the massive table with a stern look. "You all might not have said anything, but you were thinking about doing it. So, zip it."

Nana has spoken.

And once Antonia Hawke makes a declaration, it's final.

No one would dare defy her—at least not within her earshot.

Coen grins and scans the table, covered with various dishes carefully and lovingly prepared, as well as dozens of glasses and plates, and snorts. "Nana, how are you going to fit everyone at the table anymore?"

Nana waves a dismissive hand. "We'll make it work, dear."

I scowl at his observation. While it isn't a direct reference to Jack and Viviana's appearances in our lives, it's a roundabout way of questioning the two new family members.

The only reason there's room for Viviana and Jack today without issue is that we're missing a few people who have *excused* absences—Luca and Byron, who are still on vacation in Greece, and Saint and Caroline, who snuck away this weekend to Lake Charles to celebrate their anniversary without the Hawke clan. While Jude isn't here, either, he hasn't shown up in two years, so we gave up on his seat a long time ago.

But Alessandra's absence and empty chair next to Angelina draws my eye. "Where's Allie?"

Everyone continues to dig into their food, no one really answering my question. Which suggests no one knows what the hell is going on with our youngest cousin.

"Storm, is she okay? Angelina said she didn't show up at work the other day."

Storm sighs and rolls her eyes, glancing at Landon before she answers. "You know how Allie can be. My guess is she just has a new boyfriend she's spending time with and doesn't want anyone to know about him."

I take a bite of my lasagna and chew a little too aggressively. "Gee, I wonder why, when you've given Jack such a warm reception."

Everybody chuckles even though I wasn't joking, and Savage leans back in his chair slightly, his plate already clean. "This is nothing compared to what Skye did to Dani the first time I brought her to Sunday dinner."

I raise a brow and look at Aunt Skye. "What'd you do?"

She shrugs nonchalantly, casting a quick annoyed look at her sister-in-law. "I was just looking out for Savage."

Dani scowls at her. "You were a total—" She stops herself and glances at Viviana, where she sits next to Nana. "C-U-N-T to me for no reason."

Skye barks out a laugh. "Oh, I had a reason. I thought you were a total gold digger, and I didn't want Savage hurt again."

Everyone chuckles as Dani rolls her eyes and takes a drink of her wine. "Yeah, such a gold digger."

Dani snorts and shakes her head. She has reason to laugh, considering her two Pulitzer Prizes hanging on the wall in her office. While she certainly isn't making the kind of money Uncle Savage does, she's doing just fine on her own as an investigative reporter, and even though she's slowing down and getting close to retiring, something tells me she's never really going to stop writing. She loves the rush too much. Although, I think it gives Uncle Savage a coronary every time she leaves town to sniff out a new story.

"You know"—Dani dangles her wine glass from her fingertips and points to Jack—"I would love to do an interview with you about your parents."

I drop my knife to my plate with a clank. "Oh, hell no. That is not fucking happening."

Jack tenses next to me and peeks my way. "Um, yeah, I don't think that's a good idea."

Dani's brow furrows. "Why not?"

Gabe snorts. "Why not? I'll give you a one-word answer —Cutter."

Dad nods his agreement. "I have to agree with Gabe here. I think it's best that we leave Jack's family out of any future stories. We all know how that went with Luca."

Dani leans back in her chair and takes a sip of her wine. "To be fair, that wasn't my article. It was Caroline's."

Pope gapes at her. "So now you're blaming Mom?"

Dani shrugs. "It was her article, her idea."

Savage shakes his head and holds up his hands. "Let's all just move away from that topic of conversation for the time being, shall we?" He forces a smile. "We have better things to discuss than old troubles, right?"

I sure as fuck hope he's not going to talk about the new ones. The last thing we need to be discussing publicly at this dinner is what's happening with Jack while Viviana is sitting right here.

Somehow, our little girl has managed to stay relatively even-keeled during all this, but it won't last forever. She misses her grandparents and all her things back at their home in Chicago, and no matter how many toys her mother and I buy her, it can't replace them or what she left behind.

I run a hand across Jack's shoulders and lean toward her. "You okay?"

She nods, but her plate is barely touched.

"You don't like it?"

"Oh, no, the food's delicious. I just lost my appetite."

I brush my lips against her ear. "You're going to need to build up your strength for what I have in mind for us later. Plus, when I finally do get you pregnant, you're going to need all that energy to grow my baby."

She gasps slightly, and her cheeks flush as she shifts uncomfortably next to me, glancing at me with reproach for making the comment at the table, though I'm sure worse things have been said here.

Bishop swallows whatever she's eating and turns to Nana. "When do Byron and Luca get back?"

Nana tears her attention away from Viviana for a second. "I think next week, if I remember correctly." She looks toward the empty seat we've reserved for Jude, even though he's never here. "I wish Jude would've come. That boy is always so busy."

She tsks and shakes her head as she takes a bite of her food that's probably now cold. That woman hasn't eaten a hot meal since I've been alive, and I would wager she didn't when her kids were growing up, either. She's always taking care of everyone else and ensuring they have everything they need before she even considers sitting down to have a bite of her own food. And with Viviana here, she has one giant distraction.

Angelina sighs. "Nana, you know we try to get him to come every week. I texted him this morning, but"—she shrugs—"there's only so much we can do."

Even when Allie does come, she can't manage to drag him away from his place, so with her MIA, there wasn't a chance in hell of getting him here.

Nana sighs. "I know, but I think Luca could get him here. He has ways of getting things accomplished."

I practically choke on my wine and look toward her with my eyes narrowed.

Did Nana really just suggest that Luca physically force Jude to come to Sunday dinner? Because I would pay to see that.

Angelina shakes her head. "You all need to cut him some slack. He didn't grow up like this." She waves her hand around the overcrowded table, so long you can't even talk to anybody on the other end of it without shouting. "It isn't easy for him."

Atlas and Astrid both nod, and she toys with her napkin and sets it on her empty plate.

"I agree. Last time I saw him, he was fine—dug in deep on whatever he's working on right now. He just can't handle all this, and I don't blame him."

Neither do I.

It's hard enough for me to handle all of them as family, so I can't imagine what it would be like for someone who went through what he did as a child and then to get tossed into this sea of sharks at age ten.

Bishop finally finishes her plate and pushes it away. "I'm going to have to do an extra hour or two of training tomorrow to work that off. Thank you, Nana."

Nana reaches over and pats her hand. "You're welcome, dear, but you should take a break from all that kung fu nonsense."

Bishop chuckles. "It isn't kung fu, Nana; it's jujitsu."

"Whatever it is, you and Atlas work too hard at that stuff."

"Yeah, yeah, yeah." Atlas' blue eyes harden to ice. "I know. And I should find a real job, right, Nana?"

He pushes away from the table in a huff and storms out of the dining room. Astrid gives everyone a look of reproach and goes after him.

Nana's eyebrows raise. "What did I say?"

Oh, she knows exactly what she said.

The woman might be almost ninety years old, but she's still smart as a whip. She sees everything, and that was a not-so-subtle jab at the profession none of us wanted for Atlas. Not after what happened to the grandfather none of us ever got to meet.

Viviana shovels pasta into her mouth, and Nana reaches over and wipes her face with a napkin.

"Isaac, dear"—she smiles at me—"are you going to be buying a house now?"

I practically choke for the second time today and manage to swallow my bite of lasagna and cough before I can grab a sip of water. "Excuse me?"

She glances from Viviana to Jack to me. "Well, I just assumed you'd buy a house now that you have a family."

Fucking hell.

So much for not stirring up shit at the table, Nana.

"Um, that's to be determined, Nana."

Dad looks to her. "Mom, cut them a little slack. This is all pretty new, and there are other extenuating circumstances."

She tsks and waves a hand. "Extenuating circumstances, my ass. He has a beautiful daughter here and a beautiful woman next to him, and they deserve a beautiful house to go home to instead of that cold, sterile condo."

Savage snorts. "You didn't hate it when I lived there."

She points her fork at him. "You were single when you started living there, and as soon as Kennedy was old enough, you guys moved out of there and got a proper house."

"True..." he nods slowly and looks to me. "She has a point."

I push my plate away and throw up my hands. "Oh, now you're going to pile on, too?"

He grins at me. "What did you expect bringing them here?"

"I know."

I should have known better, but it would've ended up like this no matter when I finally pulled the trigger and threw them into the fray.

Now, I just hope I won't have to pull another one in order to protect what I finally have.

17

JACK

I wake without the normal hard wall of heat behind me and turn onto my back, spreading my hand across Isaac's side of the bed. It hasn't even been a week—a blink of an eye in the grand scheme of things—but already, waking without him, something feels off.

Something is missing, and instinctively, my body rolls to his side, and I bury my face in his pillow. I inhale his masculine scent, which instantly stirs something deep in my core.

The bathroom door opens, and he steps out, buttoning his cufflinks on his pale-blue, striped dress shirt, his black dress slacks hanging sinfully perfectly from his hips. He raises a brow, and now that his mom has removed the stitches from above his eye, the move looks a lot less painful.

"I didn't wake you, did I?"

I shake my head and nestle back down into the warm covers. "No, I just woke up, and you weren't here."

He approaches the bed slowly, looking every bit the powerful attorney heading off to decimate someone in court that I know he is. It shouldn't be legal to look that good this early in the morning. All I want to do is grab him and drag him back into bed with me to continue what we did last night.

Because Isaac fulfilled the promise he made and utterly destroyed me.

In the best damn way.

Everything aches, each muscle and part of my body remembering his touch and craving it again.

He leans over and kisses me, the sharp, minty taste on his tongue tangling with mine. I wrap my arms around his neck and pull him to me, groaning needily against his lips.

His low chuckle vibrates his entire body, and he pulls back slightly. "As much as I would love to fall back into bed with you today and stay here as long as Viviana allows it, I have to go. The zoning meeting is today."

"Oh, shit." I release him and push up onto my elbow. "I forgot about that."

While he's done his best to keep the family business private, the hotel project and problems they've run into became the topic of conversation at dinner once everyone moved on from giving me shit. There are definitely things he's not telling me that none of them would mention in front of Nana, but I understood enough to know the meeting is essential to move forward on the project.

It's the future of the Hawkes—the brand of opulent boutique hotels all over the city and, eventually, the region. This first step has to go flawlessly, or they may never recover from the setback.

The pressure of that fact creates deep worry lines on Isaac's forehead.

I reach up and brush my fingers across the healing cut. "Do you think everything will be okay with the new head of the board?"

After Broussard's resignation press conference last night, it seemed as though Isaac had relaxed slightly, but this morning, that tension has returned, almost like he's anticipating a fight today.

He rises to his full height, disappears into his closet, and comes back, slipping on his suit coat, his jaw locked hard as he tugs down his sleeves slightly. "It should go well. We paid enough for it to."

"Oh, I see."

I settle back into bed, the infinite possibilities of what his words could mean racing through my head.

Did they pay Broussard to resign?

Threaten him?

Pay off his replacement to ensure this goes through?

All the damn above?

None of that was on the menu for discussion at the dinner table, nor would I have expected them to reveal their business dealings openly.

He approaches the bed again, his eyes narrowed on me. "What's that look for?"

"What look?"

"The look you just gave me."

Shit.

I hadn't *meant* to give him a look. "Nothing." I shake my head.

"Bullshit, Jack. We may not have spent a great deal of time together, but I can read you like a fucking book." He sits on the edge of the bed and turns my face to his with a gentle hand on my chin. "What?"

"Is that how you got all this?" I spread my hands out wide. "Your family buying people off, back door deals?"

Anger flashes in his eyes for a moment before he shakes his head to clear it. "No. A lot of hard work built this, and occasionally, some things have to be done that aren't necessarily on the up and up to protect it. But believe me, we've all worked very fucking hard to get where we are."

"I don't doubt that." I've seen how hard he works, how hard everyone in his family does. "It's just..."

"It's just what?"

I release a sigh, trying to gather my thoughts that always seem so jumbled every time I think about the current situation. "You know, I grew up in a house where doors were always closed. My parents were always working on something, talking about something, doing something that they didn't want me to know about."

He runs his fingers through my hair and brushes it back from my face. "I know, and you hated it."

I nod. "I did. I know they thought it was for the best to keep me out of the business. My mother is one of the very few women who've actually succeeded in that role, and they didn't want me to have anything to do with it, not only because of that but because the stress of what goes on could trigger my seizures."

"They're naïve if they thought they could keep you out completely, that you wouldn't hear and see things and figure out what was going on."

"I told you I wanted to get away from it all, that I tried to leave."

"Yes, you did. And you said they wouldn't let you."

"They wouldn't. Every time I'd pack a bag and get ready, they'd intervene. They'd stop me. They'd double the security on me to ensure I couldn't leave the compound. It was a constant battle for even a few hours to myself without the cameras or someone physically watching me. And I hated always being in the dark about what was happening."

"Did you want to be involved? Did you really want to take over your mother's empire and become her heir?"

"No one's ever actually asked me that question before..."

And the answer doesn't come as easily as I thought it would.

I twist my lips. "I don't know. Honestly, I don't. Part of me says that if they had given me that chance, if they had included me in the business when I was old enough to understand, I probably would want it, but they didn't. And instead, I became bitter at them for what they did to me."

"And now you are with us, too? With me?"

The pain in his words stabs at my chest. "If I'm being honest…"

"Of course, I want you to be honest with me, Jack. I always have been with you."

I swallow and look at him, trying to see past that pale Caribbean blue that makes me want to get lost in him. "I feel like if I stay here with you, I would just be trading one version of that situation for another. I'd be going from their world of crime and deception and violence to yours."

"We're not criminals, Jack. It isn't the same thing at all."

"Maybe you don't see it that way, but it's just varying degrees, isn't it? Blackmail is illegal, isn't it? Paying off government officials is illegal, isn't it? Threatening people physically, even if you don't follow through with it, is illegal, isn't it? Don't you do all those things…and worse?"

His body stiffens, and he shifts away from me slightly, the anger tightening his shoulders. "I do it to protect our business, Jack, to protect the people I love. I don't do it because I'm greedy. I don't do it because I want the power. Fuck, I don't even *want* to do it." He pushes up from the bed and runs his hands back through his still-damp hair. "You think this is where I saw myself when I went to law school? You think this is how I wanted to be living my life?" He shakes his head. "I knew what my dad did. I was old enough to understand, but I would much rather be in the courts defending people who need it, doing pro bono work, or working for indigent defendants like the Innocence Project, trying to right wrongful convictions. But that was never an option. My dad and I are the fixers, and now, what I do is scaring you."

I push myself up against the headboard and pull my knees to my chest. "I'm not scared, Isaac. I'm fucking terrified."

"Of me?"

"Of all of this."

"You told me you were going to stay."

"No." I fight back the tears burning in my eyes. "I told you I *wanted* to stay."

"Shit." He squeezes his eyes closed for a moment, then opens them and stalks back to the bed to kiss me deeply, like he's trying to reach down into my soul and calm all the turmoil raging there. "I'm not letting you go again, Jack. No matter what I have to do to prove it to you, this is where you belong, you and Viviana. We'll talk more tonight."

He turns and walks out of the bedroom, his expensive Italian loafers clicking on the floors and down the stairs, each step echoing to me and feeling like it's pushing him further and further away from me, so far I don't know if we'll ever be able to reach each other again.

My words hurt him, even if I needed to say them and he needed to hear them.

If he really wants us here, wants us to stay, he has to understand that I won't allow him to do to me what Mom and Dad have. I want a partner, not a new jailer, who thinks it's what's best for me because he creates enemies who may set their sights on anyone he loves.

ISAAC

SCANNING the members of the Board of Zoning Adjustment at their seats at the front of the room, I continue to fight to push aside what happened with Jack this morning so I can concentrate on getting the damn job done.

We've waited far too long to get to this point to have it derailed by me letting something slip because I'm too busy trying to figure out how to convince her to stay.

I force my focus back on my presentation. "So, as the board can see, the proposed Hawke Enterprises hotel project does not pose any sort of threat to the residents in the neighborhood, nor for the city. Property values will only rise in the area with our establishment opening. Any noise or construction mess created will be minimal, and we'll attempt to have the entire project done in less than a year. Of course, Hawke Enterprises is also prepared to compensate neighbors for any inconvenience it might cause during that time."

Money talks, and when we were selecting potential locations, the people living around the lot were more than happy to accept our terms of compensation in light of the noise, dust, and other things that might annoy them during the process.

I glance behind me at the people sitting in the gallery, then return my focus to the members of the board in front of me.

Dennis LeBlanc leans back slightly in his chair and chews on the end of his pen. With the new head of the zoning commission now firmly in our pockets, this should be easy. But I know better than to assume anything ever will be.

He nods slowly. "I appreciate your presentation, Mr. Hawke, and that you've now addressed some of the concerns my predecessor previously raised to members of the board from some of the local residents in the area. I feel as though we have sufficient information now to make a final vote."

Thank fuck.

"I'd like to speak before you do, Mr. LeBlanc."

Shit.

I whirl around at the familiar voice from behind me and clench my fists at my sides to prevent myself from immediately decking the asshole.

Cass fucking Whitaker...what the hell is he doing here?

I shouldn't even ask myself that question. I know what he's doing here—trying to fuck with us again. He strolls in, briefcase in hand, and inclines his head in greeting to several people in the seats who smile at him.

Fucking hell.

"Members of the board, my name is Cassius Whitaker, and I represent several members of the local community who have concerns they feel have not been adequately addressed by this board or Mr. Hawke."

You've got to be fucking kidding me...

I watch him settle at the other end of the table. "And what concerns are those, Mr. Whitaker?"

He smirks at me. "Though I missed the beginning of Mr. Hawke's presentation, what I didn't hear was any sort of reference to the potential clientele that could be drawn to this establishment."

"Excuse me?" Dennis leans forward slightly, suddenly looking a little flustered with a flush spreading up his neck. He tugs at his collar. "I'm not sure what you're talking about, Mr. Whitaker."

Whitaker spreads out his hands and motions toward me. "We're just going to pretend that the Hawkes don't hawk human flesh." He smirks at me again. "Excuse my play on words. But their family and Hawke Enterprises are well known for their many strip club establishments as well as their connections to organized crime."

Whoa, whoa, whoa.

I was willing to let this go for a moment to uphold the integrity of the meeting, but now, he's crossed a line.

"If I may interject, Mr. LeBlanc...we don't have any connections to organized crime. You'll find that my father and I are both in good standing with the state bar. Ask any of the judges in town, and they'll tell you that we operate in a completely legal manner and are well respected in the community."

Cass sneers at me. "On paper. Let's say we ignore the fact that Luca Abello is one of their major partners. If the Hawkes are referring patrons of their *other* establishments to the hotel, perhaps drawing them to stay there with some sort of packages being offered, who knows what that's going to bring into the neighborhood? This is a major concern."

LeBlanc clears his throat and shifts, glancing at his colleagues on the board. "I know my predecessor raised the same concerns. But frankly, Mr. Whitaker, you have no evidence to support this accusation, nor is there any reason to believe the Hawke Hotel would not be exactly what it appears to be, an upscale boutique hotel that caters to members of the upper echelon who will come to New Orleans to spend money and put it into our economy. It's exactly what this neighborhood needs." He shuffles some papers in front of him. "The zoning is proper for it. There's nothing on paper that gives me reason not to put this up for a vote. And I see no reason why I can't personally vote in favor of it."

"And what about the rest of the board?" Whitaker scans all of them. "Are all of you prepared to sign off on this project, knowing the problems it could create for your constituents?"

They all glance at each other and shift uncomfortably.

And here I thought things were finally resolved once Broussard resigned, but it seems Whitaker isn't going to back off.

This isn't him acting solo. There's no way the neighbors came to him with this concern, randomly sought him out. This is Falco Enterprises coming after us again, after the ploy to pay off Broussard failed. And the fact that there's still a faceless enemy when we already have so many makes me grit my teeth.

Whitaker narrows his eyes on LeBlanc. "And just where is your predecessor? I heard a mysterious family emergency caused him to resign."

LeBlanc moves around some papers and avoids eye contact. "Yes, that's my understanding."

I take a few steps to close the distance between us and lean into Whitaker. "If you really want to go there, I'm more than happy to reveal the photographs I have of you bribing him and to pull his skeletons out of the closet."

He continues to smile for everyone in the room as he leans back toward me. "And I would be more than happy to play the recording I have of the phone call that you made threatening him."

Fuck...

I should have anticipated it, but I didn't think Broussard was smart enough to actually record his phone call.

Wait a minute...he isn't...

"Did you *bug* his phone?"

Whitaker offers a little half-shrug. "I don't reveal how I do business any more than you do, Mr. Hawke."

"Well, you're not going to win on this, and I suggest you tell your clients to back the fuck off because I'm at the end of my rope with them."

"I think you have bigger fish to fry, Mr. Hawke. From what I hear, you've pissed off some very powerful people."

They know.

The words flash in my head. A cold tingle spreads through my arms as everyone in the room continues to watch us and wait for us to continue. "What do you mean?"

He raises a brow. "Well, if you don't know, then you're in a lot more fucking trouble than I thought." Whitaker spreads his hands wide and takes a step away from me. "A vote then?"

LeBlanc nods. "Yes. Yes, a vote."

Whitaker squares his shoulders. "I would let the board know there will be forthcoming lawsuits should this project continue."

Of course, there will be. I would expect nothing less.

I return to my table and wait for the vote.

LeBlanc calls for it, and five hands go up, with two voting against it. "We have a majority, so the plans will be approved. Congratulations, Mr. Hawke. You'll be breaking ground soon."

Fucking right. We will be.

At least one thing is going right with everything else crumbling around us.

I grab my briefcase and stalk out of the room. A reporter tries to shove a microphone and camera in my face, but I push them away and head out the door, down the steps, and out onto the street.

The fresh air helps cool my blood somewhat, but if that asshole keeps coming at me, I'm going to have to do the very things Jack hates so much.

I'm going to have to play dirty.

I stop at the red light and wait for the walk signal to cross to my car parked across the street. My jaw clenched, I reach for my phone to send an update to Dad.

"Beautiful shoes."

The deep, heavily accented voice comes from my left, and I glance over at the man with broad shoulders, thick, wavy brown hair, and dark stubble on his face. His crisply tailored suit hangs off his frame beautifully, and I look down at his shoes to see they match mine exactly.

I smirk. "You have good taste."

He grins at me. "So do you, Mr. Hawke."

I narrow my gaze on his face, trying to place him. "Do I know you?"

He offers a shrug. "It seems we share the same taste in a lot of things—shoes...women..."

Panic seizes my lungs.

"Who are you?"

A black car squeals to a stop in front of us, the back door opens, and he slips inside without answering.

It peels away from the curb as my phone vibrates in my jacket pocket. I reach in and pull it out, glancing down at the text message.

Fucking hell.

18

ISAAC

UNCLE GABE

Get over to the Grind as fast as you can.

S *hit.*
I read the text one more time before I slide into my car, turn it on, throw it into drive, and peel away from the corner on my way to see what the fuck is going on.

Who the hell was that guy on the corner?

Not Satriano.

I've seen his mug in photos while I was researching him, though most of them were older since he keeps himself locked away where he's well protected.

Could it have been him?

Rain pelts the windshield, a steady, cold drizzle that leaves a gloom hanging over the city that matches my mood.

Whatever is going on at the Daily Grind, it's the last thing I want to be dealing with. I need to get home to Jack and Viviana.

Every moment away from them feels like hours. Every second filled with a bone-deep feeling that something bad is coming.

And that man on the corner wasn't just being friendly.

I press the voice control button in the car. "Call Gabe Anderson."

The ringing comes through the speakers, and he picks up almost immediately. "Hey."

"What's going on?"

"I don't know. I just got a text from Angelina saying there's a suspicious-looking man at the Grind, and she doesn't know what to do."

"Shit. I just had a run-in with a *suspicious* man myself outside the zoning meeting. Where are you?"

"Nowhere fucking close. I'm out with Bishop and Saint, looking into some information we received about Broussard. We're trying to determine if he talked or could be behind the text message."

"Hell. Whitaker just showed up at the zoning meeting and said he has a recording of me threatening Broussard."

Gabe releases a litany of curses, his phone cutting in and out like he's somewhere with shit service. "That isn't good."

"No. It isn't. What did you find?"

"Nothing concrete yet. I'll let you know in a few hours. Just get over and see what's going on with Angelina. Let me know if you need me."

"Will do."

But first, I call the security desk at the condo and ensure all is quiet as I speed the few remaining blocks to the normally relatively quiet street where the café sits.

Nothing looks out of place—a few people walking down the sidewalk with umbrellas, a handful of cars parked along the curb...

Still, the hair on the back of my neck stands on end as I pull up the car, slam on the brakes, and throw it into park in front of

Hawke's Daily Grind. I grab my gun from the glove compartment, slide it into my waistband, slip out into the rain, slam the door behind me, and run in.

The bells ring above me, signaling my entrance, and Angelina looks up from behind the counter and inclines her head toward the rear of the shop. Allie clears plates and mugs from a table to my right, and I pause next to her.

"You guys okay?"

She gives a sharp nod and peeks over her shoulder. "He's been here for two hours, and he's just...watching us. He's been drinking espresso, but he hasn't pulled out his phone once. He's not reading the newspaper or a book. He's not doing anything but *watching*. It's just weird..."

Certainly is...

I casually make my way around the corner of the display case until the back corner table comes into view and stops me in my tracks.

Fuck.

Cristiano Roselli sits with his back against the wall, his perfectly tailored suit looking immaculate as he leans back slightly with one ankle crossed over his knee. "Isaac Hawke...I was wondering how long it would take for someone to show up." He checks his watch. "Two hours." Shaking his head, he takes a sip of his coffee. "You might want to consider tightening the security of your various locations, given the rumors I'm hearing..."

I stop on the other side of the table from him and grip the back of the chair. "What the hell do you want, Roselli?"

The fucker has the audacity to feign surprise at the tone of my question and spreads his hands out casually. "Just to have a friendly chat."

"You don't do anything friendly."

He grins at me. "That's true, but I thought it wise we have a conversation, given everything that's happening in the city."

What the hell is he getting at?

He could be referencing any number of things, and I'm not about to volunteer information on anything he might *not* know about.

"I'm not sure what you're talking about, Roselli."

He raises an eyebrow. "You're not?" A heavy sigh slips from his lips. "Let's not play games here, Mr. Hawke. There's no reason to pretend. You've done something to piss off the Satrianos."

I stiffen. "Where the hell did you hear that from?"

Roselli offers a nonchalant shrug. "Did you really think I wouldn't find out?"

That was the hope.

Men like Roselli always seem to have an inside track on what's happening with all the other families, and it's quite possible he has knowledge we're still trying to get.

"What do you know?"

His lips curl slightly. "That your *friend,* Giacomina, had an unfortunate incident that required a little hospital stay..."

The words hit me like Atlas' blows, directly to my chest, forcing the air from my lungs.

"How do you know about that?"

Another grin overtakes his lips. "Did you think the Satrianos would come into my town and not tell me they were here and why?"

Ice floods my veins, making my legs and arms tingle. The man standing next to me on the street flashes through my head. "They're here?"

Another shrug. "Possibly. At the very least, on the way. They made sure to alert us of the little trip so we wouldn't 'get the wrong idea' about it. That's how wars start, Mr. Hawke."

"No." I practically growl at him. "Wars start when people threaten innocent women and children. That's what the Satrianos did. Anything they have coming their way, they've earned."

He offers a half-shrug. "I'm not saying I disagree with you on that. You know that ever since I took over from Luca, I've done my best to keep things civil between your family and my organization out of respect for your connection to Abello. But..."

"But what?"

"But *Luca* has a lot of connections." He leans forward slightly and takes another sip of his coffee. "Ones that are, shall we say, slightly concerning now that the Satrianos are in town. I hope he doesn't have any intention of offering them something to get them to back off your friends, something that he has no right offering."

"They're not here because they're interested in anything in New Orleans other than trying to track down Valentina Marconi's family."

He slowly stirs his espresso. "Are you sure about that? The Satrianos have been around for a very long time. They have a lot of friends in a lot of places, and I've always found it rather odd that they haven't tried a bit harder to expand beyond their current borders."

"You think they'd come all the way over here and not go right back when they're done? They have no reason to stay."

They've shown no interest in expanding beyond Italy other than in making alliances with people like Valentina here in the States. They have their hands full there and a massive territory to control. If they made attempts to take anyone out over here, it wouldn't just cause a major war between factions. It could unsettle what they have already established solidly.

One of his dark brows wings up. "Are you so sure about that? Do you know what started the disagreement between the Satrianos and the Marconis?"

I shake my head.

"You might want to talk with Valentina's daughter and see if she might be able to shed a little bit of light on that."

I narrow my eyes on him. "She doesn't know anything about her family's business. She's not involved."

"Are you sure?"

"Yes, of course I am."

Even as I say the words, uncertainty starts to form in the pit of my stomach.

He climbs to his feet and buttons his suit coat. "Take this as a friendly warning, Mr. Hawke. If the Satrianos start stirring up any sort of trouble for me or my business, I'm holding you and your family accountable."

"We have nothing to do with them. We want them out as much as you do."

"That's all well and good, but you're also the only reason they're here. I warned you they were coming and had hoped you would take the warning and get them out of town quickly."

Holy shit.

It was Roselli?

His mouth sets into a hard line. "I hope not to get wind of Luca rekindling any sort of old friendships."

"I'm telling you, he wouldn't do that. He's out. Has been since the moment he turned things over to you."

"I hope you're right, Mr. Hawke."

He moves to step around me, but I press a hand against his chest—an offense that, were one of his men in here with him, would likely end up with a bullet through my fucking head.

Roselli slowly glances down at it, then back up at me.

I lean in close, so none of the other customers milling about who might be eavesdropping can hear me. "You don't *ever* threaten my family. I don't give a fuck who you are or how much power you have in this city. You do not threaten the Hawkes."

Amusement twists his lips. "Or what?"

"Or I'll make sure what you do to people looks like child's play...and I'll do it with my own fucking hands."

He smirks. "You don't have it in you, son. All bark, no bite. You may do fine in a courtroom, but out on the street, all you are is a pretty face who wears your daddy's name to make you feel tough. You talk with your father and your uncles and let them know what I said. I'll be watching everything very carefully, and I don't want to hear any sort of talk that's going to upset the delicate balance we've established."

"If anything gets unbalanced, it's because of you."

Roselli offers another smirk. Then his gaze darts behind me to Alessandra and Angelina working at the counter. "The women in your family are quite striking, aren't they? Dark beauties like Angelina and Alessandra there and such pretty little blondes in Kennedy and Astrid." The corner of his lips curls up. "You have your work cut out for you, watching all of them and keeping them safe."

He takes a step around me as I clench my hands to keep myself from grabbing my gun and shooting him in the head right here in the damn café. That wouldn't solve our problem and would only create a bigger one.

A few steps away, he pauses in front of the display counter and turns back to me. "I bet your daughter would enjoy one of these sweets. You might want to bring one home for her."

All the blood rushes from my face and freezes in my veins instantly as I watch him walk out slowly, inclining his head toward the girls as he does, acting like he hasn't just threatened everything I love in one fell swoop.

JACK

I DRAW the last line on my sketchpad and examine the scene of the river I've done at least a dozen times since I arrived, but never like this. Something about this time of day is magic—the fingers of light fighting to stay on the horizon and glisten on the water before they vanish completely. Tonight, the storm clouds only accentuate the beauty of the scene.

Capturing it isn't easy, and people looking at this will likely say I failed.

But I want to remember this view—always.

I flip it closed, then set it on the lounge chair on the patio and step up to the railing to take one last look at the river before the rain starts falling again and forces me inside.

Viviana's laughter floats out to me even through the closed door, and I turn and watch her at the table with Astrid, going through some workbooks and flashcards she brought over for her.

Thank God she's here.

She really is great with her—naturally sweet, kind, and soft-spoken.

So different from Atlas.

If I had to try to take over her schooling myself while dealing with my seizure and recovery on top of all the stress, I don't think it would have gone very well.

As it stands now, I'm barely holding myself together. What happened with Isaac this morning still has me rattled. I never intended the discussion to go in that direction, but I couldn't hold it in.

I can't pretend everything is fine when it isn't. I can't act like we're this picture-perfect family when we were forced into this situation by necessity. I can't feign ignorance about what he and his family do in their business and act like it's completely okay with me.

I'm torn between returning to the life Mom and Dad have created for me, one full of guards, locked doors, and secrets, and one here with Isaac, filled with backdoor deals, blackmail, and threats.

Neither is what I wanted for myself or for Viviana.

This situation with Satriano only pushed that reality to the forefront of my brain again. I don't want to keep running, but I don't know if running to Isaac is the answer, either.

Why is everything so hard?

I grab my sketchpad and slide open the door, stepping into the welcome warmth.

"Hello, Mina."

I jerk my head toward the voice near the fireplace.

Savage.

I hadn't even noticed he was here. "Hi. I didn't know you were coming by today."

He nods and offers a tight smile that doesn't quite reach his eyes. "You and I need to have a little chat, and I thought it was best to do it when Isaac wasn't here."

My stomach churns slightly, and my steps falter. "Um, okay."

Savage motions down the hallway. "Let's go back to his office."

"Okay." I stop at the table and kiss Viviana on the head, looking down at the project she's working on.

Astrid smiles at me. "She's doing really well with her numbers. She knows the alphabet forward and backward, and her addition is already better than most of the first-grade-level kids I know."

"Awesome." I rub Vivi's back. "Are you having a good time with Ms. Astrid?"

She bobs her head enthusiastically. "Yeah."

I meet Astrid's gaze. "I need to go talk to your uncle."

She nods, and I slip my sketchpad onto the table and follow Savage down the hallway and into Isaac's office. He enters in front of me and points back toward the door.

"Close that behind you."

Shit.

My hand shakes as I push it closed and turn back to face him. He motions toward the chair next to him, and I take a seat, putting us on the same level.

"What did you need to talk to me about?"

He considers me for a second, his strong jaw set hard and a muscle there ticcing, then scrubs a hand over the light gray and black stubble on his cheek. "I don't really know where to start with this, but I'm sorry about what happened at dinner last night."

"Sorry about what?"

"The Hawkes can be a bit..." He smirks. "Overwhelming."

I chuckle. "Well, there are a lot of you."

"There are, and we've all known each other for a very long time. Everyone kind of gives each other shit and ribs each other, and sometimes, when someone new enters the picture, we forget that it can be a little terrifying to them." Concern darkens his Hawke blue eyes. "You seemed a little spooked by what we said outside before dinner."

"I was."

There's no point in lying to him about it. It seems like all the Hawke men can see right through me.

"I want you to understand something, Mina. Your father entrusted us to watch you and Viviana for a reason, and I'm assuming he has no clue she's Isaac's daughter."

I shake my head and look down at my hands. "No, my parents don't know. Hell, Isaac didn't even know until we got here."

He releases a heavy sigh. "I figured as much, and that's what I wanted to talk to you about."

"What do you mean?"

"When all this is over, when your father takes care of what he needs to with Satriano and he comes back for you, what are you going to do?"

Shit, as if it isn't bad enough having the pressure to answer that question from Isaac, now I have it from his uncle, too.

I swallow back the tears threatening and shake my head. "Honestly, I have no idea."

He pats his hand over mine. "I figured. There's something I want to explain to you, something that you should have picked up on last night, but just in case you didn't, I want to make sure you have the full picture.

"We've had a lot of loss in this family. A lot of good people who didn't deserve it got hurt and worse. The decisions some members of this family made affected others in unanticipated ways." He sighs. "I'm not intentionally being vague. There just really isn't any point getting into all of that. What matters is this —we stayed a family. Once you're in, you're in."

I nod slowly. "I gathered that based on not only what I've seen, but what both Isaac and some of the others have told me. Saint says you guys are like family."

He smiles. "Yes, Saint and Caroline and Byron and Luca are Hawkes, even if they don't share an ounce of our blood, but you and Viviana are different."

"Different?"

He points toward the living room. "That little girl is a Hawke, and that does mean something, just as much as you being a Marconi does. Your father and your mother are going to want you to come home."

As painful as it is to admit it, I nod. "Yes."

"Which means taking that little girl away from Isaac and the family here."

A weight settles on my chest, and I release a heavy breath. "I know, and honestly, I'm just trying not to think about it, not to deal with it until I know what's happening with my dad and my mom. I need to know they're okay before I can think about another calamity."

He offers me a kind, half-smile. "I understand that, but you need to understand that once you're a Hawke, you're always a Hawke. We protect our own. We love them, and we fight for them. You can't expect Isaac to just let you walk away with his daughter."

The way he says the words feels more like a threat than it should, but I know exactly what he's saying.

Isaac *will* go to court and fight me if he has to, and he'll use every resource at his disposal.

He *will* play dirty.

He'll tell the judge who my mother and father are, that going back to Chicago and exposing her to that life is a danger to his daughter, and with the power the Hawkes have here, especially in the court system, he'll win.

"So, you're saying I don't have a choice."

He shakes his head. "No. I'm asking you to consider your choices very carefully. You can't expect him to let you walk away again. I've seen the way he looks at you. I saw how distraught he was when you had your seizure. That man loves you, whether he's said it or not. We Hawke men aren't great with words and can sometimes be"—he clears his throat—"a little controlling and overbearing."

I let out a bitter laugh. "A little?"

Savage offers me a half grin. "But we mean well. We have good hearts, all of us."

I never doubted that for a moment. I knew it the first time I met Isaac, and he's only proved it the longer I'm here.

That was never the problem.

"I...care about Isaac. A lot...I just don't know if being here is what's best for me."

His dark brows rise slowly. "*Care* about him?" A grin pulls at his lips. "Sweetheart, you more than *care* about him. I can see it in the way you look at him as much as when he looks at you."

"But is that enough?"

I don't know why I'm asking Savage this. I barely know the man, but somehow, he feels like the right person to be having this discussion with.

He releases a heavy sigh. "Let me tell you what I've learned about relationships and love in my sixty years on this planet—it's *always* worth it. It's worth working through anger and pain and the things you think make it impossible. It's worth it."

A tear falls down my cheek, and I wipe it and try to smile. "Maybe things will be clearer once this Satriano stuff gets resolved."

"We're going to keep you safe, sweetheart, but you also need to think about the future. You can't just *hope* things work out. You need to *make* them work out. That's the only way I succeeded in this business as much as I have. I *made* things happen for myself. I took what I wanted, and I got it done."

"No matter the cost?"

Something flashes in his eyes, a pain deep inside that clearly bears a story I don't know. "There are costs I wish I didn't have to pay. Things that affected others. The same goes for things that Gabe and Stone and all of us have had to do, but in the end, we all came out stronger. Hawkes always rise."

"What?"

"Hawkes always rise." His broad shoulders rise and fall. "It's kind of our motto."

I grin. "Who came up with that?"

He motions toward a picture hanging on the wall, and I get up out of the chair and move over toward it.

Savage and Danika with Kennedy, Gabe and Skye, Stone and Nora, holding a baby that must be Isaac, and Storm and Landon, standing in front of a building with a sign that reads *The Hawkeye Club III.*

"That was the day we opened THREE."

"Great picture."

He moves over toward me. "It is, but it was a really painful day, a very hard one for Storm."

"Her first husband passed away, right?"

He nods. "And while we were all standing there, looking at THREE as it was about to open for the first time, she turned to Skye, and she said we were going to make it, that things were going to be okay. That Hawkes would always rise. And it's just something that's stuck since then."

"I hope it stays true."

He gives me a sad smile. "Me, too."

19

ISAAC

"Come on. Come on. Pick up."

I swerve around the car in front of me, the tires slipping on the slick road. The light drizzle from earlier today has become a steady deluge that soaks the streets and floods them in certain areas. Dangerous puddles stand at every corner, but I can't slow down—not after what Roselli just said to me.

The moment he stepped out of that door, I had Angelina and Allie close up early and get the hell home, and that's exactly where I need to be.

I jab my foot against the gas pedal even harder and shift gears as I head toward the condo. "Fucking pick up."

The phone rings and rings and rings, but no answer from Gabe.

"What the fuck is he doing? He said to call him." I slam my palm against the steering wheel. "Shit. Shit. Shit."

Whatever he, Bishop, and Saint are doing, they're either

somewhere with shitty phone service, or he's getting his hands dirty. Either way, he's out of commission.

"Fuck."

I hit the end button and dial Savage. Each ring through the speakers of the car ratchets up my anxiety tenfold. Every second poses a greater risk to Jack and Viviana. A greater chance of Satriano finding them and taking them from me forever.

Satriano is here.

The reality slams into me, stealing my breath, and I force myself to try to suck in air. It's the very thing we've been dreading, trying to prevent—he's here for the girls.

Savage finally answers. "Isaac, what's up?"

"They know."

"What?"

"They *know*. The Satrianos know Jack and Viviana are here."

"Fucking hell." He jostles the phone. "Are you sure?"

I swerve around another car in my way, and they blare their horn at me, the driver flipping me off. "Yes, I'm positive. I just had a meeting with our friend Roselli."

"Shit."

"He was at the Daily Grind."

"Are Angelina and Allie okay?"

Relatively speaking.

It scared the shit out of them.

How could it not?

I don't think I've ever seen them so freaked out as when I told them who he was and that they needed to close for the day and get somewhere safe. They aren't part of this world; none of us are, really—save Luca in his former life.

None of us could have expected an all-out mafia war starting with us at the center of it.

"They're fine, but he made it very clear how easy it was for the Satrianos to find Jack and that they alerted him of their intent to *visit* New Orleans."

"How did Satriano find her?"

The light turns yellow in front of me, but instead of slowing down, I swerve around the cars waiting and gun it through the intersection to the blaring protestation of horns. "The hospital."

"Shit." His voice holds the same disbelief I felt when Roselli told me how easy it was for them to track her. "Of all the—"

"As soon as they admitted her, the records went digital, and they clearly had somebody scanning and watching for anything with her name."

"Fuck." Savage snarls and mutters something under his breath about technology. "I didn't even think about that."

"Me either. None of us did."

In that moment, seeing her in the grips of a seizure, all I thought about was getting her *help*. Now that decision could be what takes her from me for good.

Savage releases an angry sigh. "How could we have known she was going to end up in the fucking hospital or that anyone would be watching that?"

"We couldn't." I slam my palm against the steering wheel again. "Shit, shit, shit."

"Did you call Gabe?"

"I just tried, but he isn't picking up."

Savage grunts. "I think they were heading out to the bayou."

"What the fuck for?"

"I'm not sure. He was a little cagey about it. Something to do with Broussard. Did you call your dad?"

"Not yet. I thought you might know how to reach Gabe. He needs to know how bad this is." So much worse than I could have ever imagined. "There was a man outside the zoning meeting today...I think it was Satriano."

"You *think*?"

The man's face flashes before my eyes as I try to concentrate on the road. "He didn't look like the man in the photos I found online, but they were old. He might have changed his appearance. No one has seen him in person in years."

Satriano could be *anyone.*

And that man was making a statement.

Coupled with the information Roselli gave me, it makes it more likely than not that the man at that corner was the one we've been fearing this entire time.

Two cars block my advance, and I peel around them to the left into oncoming traffic. Horns blare at me as I swerve back, narrowly missing a head-on collision, the bright lights practically blinding me.

"What the fuck are you doing, Isaac?"

"Trying to get back to the condo."

"I just left there maybe half an hour ago."

A tiny bit of relief floods my chest at knowing they were safe so recently. "Who's there?"

"Jack, Viviana, and Astrid, but I think they were finishing up their lessons. Skye mentioned maybe heading over there to bake some cookies, so she might be there by now. I told Atlas to keep an eye on them once I left so they weren't alone, but I don't know if he's over there yet."

"Call him and get him over there now if he isn't."

"They'll be okay." Savage's calm, authoritative voice comes through the line, but it can't calm the feeling that something bad is about to happen. "No one can get up there."

"Yeah, and we thought no one could find them here, either."

I end the call with anger directed at everyone, especially myself.

How could I not have seen this coming?

Why did I leave them today?

This damn zoning meeting shouldn't have taken priority over the girls. Nothing should. Yet I argued with Jack and walked away...

Guilt claws at my gut, threatening to tear me apart from the inside.

I race around the corner, the back end of the car skidding out wildly behind me. "Fuck. Fuck. Fuck. Fuck."

Struggling to regain control, I grip the wheel tighter, as if it will somehow make it easier to control the vehicle and my emotions.

The last person I expected to see at the Grind was Roselli, but now, he's been dragged into this and is making threats because the Satrianos have. Whatever the fuck Jack's mother did to piss them off is potentially going to start a war in New Orleans because of something that did or didn't happen in fucking Chicago.

And Jack's in the middle of it all.

Maybe she was right.

Maybe there is no escaping it. Maybe this is what her and Vivi's lives are going to be forever. Maybe it can never change.

Always running.

Always hiding.

Always wondering who will come after them next.

Fuck.

And Roselli's words ring in my ears...

You might want to talk with Valentina's daughter and see if she might be able to shed a little bit of light on that.

I always assumed she didn't know anything about her mother's issue with Satriano. The way they kept her in the dark about the business, it didn't make any sense that they would let her in on something that might start a war.

But maybe I was wrong...

Bright lights flash in the rearview, almost blinding me, and an SUV advances on me fast. It rides up almost against my bumper, revving its engine, audible even over my own and the rain pounding against the car and windshield.

"What the fuck?"

I glance down at my speedometer. I'm going seventy when no one else should be with the roads like this.

And that isn't a fucking cop.

I take the next right, the tires slipping on the slick pavement again, and almost slam into the back of another car. Narrowly avoiding it, I veer into oncoming traffic. The bright lights in front of me are almost blinding, but I veer back into my lane, the chorus of honks echoing in my ears.

The SUV doesn't even bother maneuvering around the car I just made it past and clips it from behind, sending it spinning off into the oncoming traffic and clearing the path to me.

There isn't any question now—whoever is behind that wheel is coming after me and coming after me hard.

The Rosellis?

The Satrianos?

If I go back to the condo, I'll lead them right to the girls.

"Fuck."

Instead of turning right toward home, I crank on the wheel and go left at the next intersection, blowing through a stop light on red. Three cars slam into each other behind me, and the SUV swerves around them and continues its pursuit.

I make it halfway to Mom and Dad's house with the SUV hot on my trail before another red light stops me with a solid line of cars blocking the way and heavy oncoming traffic filling all the other lanes.

"Shit."

I slow down, and the SUV barrels toward me from behind. The only thing that's going to stop it is slamming straight into the back of my car.

No fucking way I'm going down like this.

I crank the wheel to the right and drive up over the curb, across the sidewalk, and down the next street. The SUV follows easily, speeding up on the slick streets.

The metal guardrail on the curve up ahead shimmers wet,

reflecting back my headlights, and I slow down to make the left turn, but the SUV clips the back of the car. The tires skid out from behind me, and the car slams into the protective railing that's supposed to keep it on the road.

It gives way easily, and I careen to the right, flipping through the air onto the embankment leading down to the Mississippi.

JACK

FLOUR SPRAYS out from the large mixing bowl all over the counter and puffs up into the air violently, making me cough. Viviana continues to whisk, giggling more and more the bigger mess she makes, her laughter filling the high ceilings.

While the sound is music to my ears, given the tension permeating everything recently, I reach out and wrap my hand around hers to stop the madness. "A little more gently, Vivi. We don't want to destroy the kitchen completely."

Skye chuckles next to me, where she scoops from a bowl of already-completed dough and puts the cookies on the baking sheet. "Let her do it."

"Why?"

She points to the flour all over the counter and various other ingredient bottles strewn around. "Because Isaac's going to have to get used to having his kitchen destroyed. Don't you think?"

Heat floods my cheeks.

It's the second reference someone from the family has made to us living with Isaac permanently. Coupled with the comment about the house from Nana at Sunday dinner, they clearly expect us to stay.

I help Viviana stir more slowly this time. "Yes, having a four-year-old can certainly be messy. And I'm not sure he's ready for the full force of it."

She barks out a laugh and rolls her eye, inclining her head toward her son. "Try having two of them at the same time."

"Oh, come on," Atlas yells from the living room, where he's sprawled on the couch, watching a hockey game. "We weren't *that* bad."

Skye glowers at him even though he doesn't turn around. "Yes. You *were*. *You* in particular. At least your sister had the decency to try to clean up after herself. You didn't give a shit and treated me like your maid."

He snorts and shakes his head. "Yeah. Well, we all know how fucking perfect Astrid is."

I wince slightly and inch closer to Skye. "Do they have some sort of sibling rivalry I don't know about?"

Astrid constantly hangs out at his place, and they've always been very loving with each other when I've seen them together. I never would have thought there was any sort of tension there.

She smirks at me. "They're twins. What do you think?"

Fair enough.

Growing up as an only child, I never got to experience any of that, and part of me wonders if I missed out on something great or something horrible.

"I guess I can see that. Having to share everything—even a birthday."

"It doesn't help that Atlas takes every possible opportunity to defy his father and me."

"Really?"

She nods and dumps the last of the ingredients into the bowl Viviana's working on now that it's well-mixed. "Good job, Viv. Keep stirring."

I peek at Atlas to ensure he can't hear us now discussing him. "He seems pretty laid back and even-keeled to me."

Skye shakes her head. "That isn't the problem. Considering he bashes people's faces in for a living, he's actually pretty relaxed. But there's a family history with boxing that makes my mother very nervous about him doing it. He doesn't want to work in the family business, which"—she holds up a hand—"I'm not saying he has to. Really, we try to let our kids build their own lives, but the opportunities he could have with the family…"

"Doesn't Astrid work for the school district, though?"

"Oh, no, she went to college and got her teaching degree, but she actually works for Hawke Enterprises. She's an educational liaison."

"What the hell is that?"

She chuckles. "Well, it's kind of a made-up position. You know how"—she glances at Viviana—"we have a certain type of club?"

I nod. "Yeah."

Hard to forget…

"Well, a lot of the girls only have high school educations. Some of them don't even have that. So, she works with them to get their GEDs and helps them enroll in college. Tutors them if they need it."

"Really? And you guys offer this to your employees?"

She shrugs almost nonchalantly and turns to put the tray of cookies into the oven before pulling out an empty one to start filling. "You have to understand my brother and husband. They think of our girls like their little sisters, and they want what's best for them. If they can help them succeed, they will."

"Yet they'll let them dance and get naked for money?"

She snorts and shakes her head. "Danika used to call them pussy peddlers."

I bark out a laugh at the term that bounced around in my head, too, when I first heard I was coming to stay with the Hawkes, and Viviana looks up at me with her brows furrowed.

"What's so funny, Mommy?"

I wave her off and try to get her re-interested in using the spoon to make balls of dough. "Nothing, baby." Inching back toward Skye, I nudge her. "I mean, they kind of are, aren't they?"

She shrugs. "They are, but not the way most people see them. They take care of the girls just like their family, the same way they do us. They encourage women to take control of their own lives on their own terms. If a woman wants to dance for money for herself or her kids, more power to them. But they also want people to have the opportunity to do more...if they want it. And they'll always help anyone in trouble."

Everything she said seems to fall in line with what I know about this family. "I've definitely seen the protectiveness."

"The Hawke men are great guys. They'll do anything for the people they love. And they'll be just about anything you want them to be to make you happy...except submissive."

"Oh yeah." I chuckle. "I got that."

Skye spoons on more cookies with Viviana's help. "They like to be in control, and when they're not, they completely lose their minds. This whole situation with you and Viviana must be driving Isaac mad."

Releasing a heavy sigh, I lean my hip against the counter. "You have no idea."

The longer it goes on, the more I see it, but knowing there's nothing I can do to make it any better guts me.

"But he's treating you well?" She turns toward me, hand tightening around the spoon. "Because if he isn't, so help me, God—"

I press a hand to her shoulder. "No, he's incredible. That isn't the problem."

"But there *is* a problem?"

Glancing at Viviana, I nudge Skye to the other corner of the kitchen. "I'm worried about what's going to happen when my dad and mom show up here to get us. It could get messy for everyone."

"Including you?"

"Especially me."

She pats my shoulder. "Honey, if the Hawkes know one thing,

it's messy. You should have seen the shit that went down when I hooked up with Gabe."

"People weren't happy about it?"

Skye issues a sardonic laugh. "You could say that. We had a long battle to get to where we are today."

"But you guys have been married for a long time, haven't you?"

She snorts. "Oh, we're not married."

"Excuse me?"

"Gabe and I aren't really the marrying type, but we've been together for thirty years, so I don't think either of us is going anywhere."

I grin at her. "It would appear not."

She winks at me. "He would never leave me. He enjoys my cookies way too much."

Is that a sexual joke, or does she really mean these cookies?

Hopefully, it's the latter since thinking about Isaac's aunt and uncle getting busy is almost as bad as seeing his parents about to back at Nana's house.

"Don't worry too much, Mina. Everything will work out. I have faith in that."

Skye moves back over to the counter and steps behind Viviana to help her make more evenly sized cookies. I lean against the counter and watch them, trying to just enjoy a relaxed, fun moment for once.

But it's impossible.

Having faith is hard when I've constantly hit a wall trying to get what I want out of life. I want to believe there's hope for the future, that there's a way everyone wins in the end.

I want to...but an energy fills the air—like a storm is coming, one that's going to envelop all of us, one I can't escape or run from.

The Satrianos...

Dad...

Isaac...

My feelings are all twisted up in the blustering winds, mixing with the force of the driving rain falling outside. All of it threatens to drown me. And the longer I'm here, the more time the storm has to brew.

20

ISAAC

Smoke billows from the engine compartment and into my face through the shattered windshield. I try to inhale a breath but only get more acrid air filling my lungs that makes me cough. Pain radiates from my side and engulfs my head.

Fuck.

Everything hurts, each tiny movement enough to make my stomach turn and send the world around me spinning even though the car has finally come to rest.

I try to move, but my seatbelt restrains me, keeping me in the seat and in the direct path of the thick smoke and rain pouring into the mangled car. The smell of gasoline hits my nose, and I gag and tug uselessly at the seatbelt.

Gotta get out of here.

Agony shoots through my ribcage with every minuscule movement, and I push down the airbag and try to blink against the darkness. A single headlight shining straight ahead offers the only illumination, showing nothing but the craggy rocks the car ended up on.

Shit, I went off the road.

Rain continues to cascade through the windshield, even harder than before, cutting the smoke somewhat.

Images flash before me.

Leaving the café.

The rain.

An SUV behind me.

A chase.

The curve and guardrail.

There was somebody behind me, and now, I'm a sitting duck.

I wrestle with the seatbelt, gritting my teeth against the pain it causes, and manage to get it unbuckled. The tiniest bit of pressure releases from my chest, but when I try to throw open the driver's side door, it won't budge.

"Fuck."

The fall must have crunched the frame badly enough to lock it in place. I examine the passenger side, muster up all the strength I have, and scramble over it. Each tiny shift of my body is enough to make me almost pass out, but I somehow get my fingers into the handle and pull, then throw it open and stumble out onto a hill dropping down toward the water.

Hell.

If the car hadn't rolled and stopped here, I would've ended up in the goddamn Mississippi.

I cough again, my throat burning from the smoke and the smell of gasoline in the air.

Headlights flash above near the broken guardrail, and tires squeal to a stop. It could be a good Samaritan stopping to ensure I'm okay after the crash, but I can't take that chance—not with what I know could be out there. Whoever knocked me off the road could have come back to make sure they finished the job.

I reach for my gun, but it isn't tucked into my waistband

anymore. It must have fallen out when I climbed over the center console.

Fuck.

Those men chasing me will be packing, and they aren't going to hesitate to fire. I lunge back into the vehicle and search in the darkness, frantically running my hand around in the floorboard until I find it.

The weight of it in my hand offers a modicum of security, but good aim is the only thing that can save me now.

Ducking behind the side of the car and watching the road through the cracked glass, I try to keep myself protected as much as possible. Doors open and slam, and mumbled voices reach me, but over the driving rain and the sound of the engine still trying to run, I can't make out what they're saying.

I go to grab my phone from my jacket pocket, but it's empty.

Shit.

It was probably in the center console when I crashed, which means, there's no way for me to call for help. I listen for the sound of sirens responding to the crash, but only the rain pelting the crunched metal and the straining whine of the engine fill my ears.

I'm on my own...

Two large shadows appear in the headlights at the top of the road and stare down at the wreckage. I stay crouched behind the car, looking through the cracked window as they start to make their way down the hill.

Fuck, fuck, fuck.

At this point, it doesn't matter who it is. Their ill intent was made clear the second they started chasing me and reiterated when they pushed me off the road.

I rack the gun and wait, peeking over my shoulder as they approach. When they're five feet from the wreckage, I check again and see them both pull out their weapons.

Goddammit, this isn't what I wanted to be doing today, or any day for that matter.

I wait for a second and listen to the crunch of their shoes along the rocks as they move closer. If I wait any longer, the only thing I have for cover will be in the way of my clean shot.

One thing Uncle Gabe taught me was to take the most make-able shot, so I can't stay here any longer.

I aim the best I can through the driving rain with a shaky hand and fire two shots into the man on the left, then turn toward the second, who dives around the hood for cover.

Shit.

I drop down and peek under the frame, but the fucker's smart enough to sit against the wheel well, just like I am, for some form of protection.

"You can't win this, *Mr. Hawke.*" The voice rings out in the night, sending a chill through my soaked clothes.

Maybe not, but I can sure fucking try.

I aim under the wreckage again and fire two shots to the left of the tire, and he jerks away from them to the side, far enough for me to send a bullet straight into his right leg.

He roars out in pain, then pushes to his feet and rounds the front of the car, firing. Bullets slam into the open door, one grazing my arm.

I unleash my last few rounds at him, and one strikes his chest. He stumbles back and drops his weapon, then tumbles down the hill, rolling violently until I hear the splash in the water.

Jesus...did that really just happen?

My entire body trembles, my hand shaking so violently that I can barely hold the gun. I sit back against the frame and try to breathe, but my chest keeps tightening, sucking in air getting harder and harder.

Fuck, I have to get out of here.

They're going to have friends who'll come looking for them. These guys were professionals on a mission sent by someone whose focus was getting rid of me or capturing me to try to use me.

My bet is on Satriano.

Roselli tried to prevent a war by warning us about what was coming. He has no reason to come after me now, but Satriano... that's another story.

I struggle to my feet and make my way around the back of the car. My toe catches on a large rock, and I stagger forward, catching myself with a hand on the trunk. The body of the first man I shot remains sprawled out on the hill, soaked by the rain, blood washing away from the body across the rocks.

The faint light offered by the headlights of the vehicle on the road illuminates his face, but it doesn't offer me any hint of his identity.

I start my climb up. Agony roars through me with every step and pull of every muscle, but I manage to drag myself back up onto the wet blacktop. Rain pours down, an almost solid sheet of water that chills me to the bone.

But my body doesn't want to move.

I slide down to my knees and take several breaths, trying to make sense of what just went down. Their SUV sits directly in front of me, and I glance up and down the street. No other vehicles approach—yet—but I don't have much time before someone comes along, sees the accident, and calls the cops.

Move, Isaac.

My body doesn't want to respond, sheer exhaustion mixing with the pain in my ribs and head. I reach up and touch my temple, and my fingers come away bloody—the cut over my eye reopened by the crash.

Get up, Isaac.

I climb to my feet, pull open the passenger side door, and dig into the glove compartment to hopefully find something. It takes a few seconds of blinking to get my eyes to focus on the words on the page.

Fucking rental car company...

But it's something.

Gabe and Saint should be able to use the information on it to track who rented the vehicle and point the finger in the direction of the men I need to go after. And if Roselli was right and Satriano is here, then he's within striking distance, but so am I.

I grab the paperwork and shove it into the back of my pants, then set off down the road toward Mom and Dad's house. Only a mile separates me from safety, but making it there is far from guaranteed.

Blood trickles down my cheek, mixing with the falling rain, and I press my hand to my side where my ribs are likely broken. Each step sends pain radiating through my body, and my vision continues to go in and out of focus as I stumble down the road, away from the crash and the two bodies.

Mom should have what she needs to treat me at home. There isn't any time to go to the hospital, and even if there were, they would just call the police immediately and I'd end up in cuffs.

I may end up there anyway, but not right now.

Getting to the girls and making sure they're safe is more important than explaining what just went down to the authorities. I'll deal with the fallout of my actions later. More bodies may have to drop before Viviana and Jack are truly out of danger, and if I have to be the one to do it, so be it.

Whoever this was isn't just playing around.

Whatever deadly game started is about to end, and I'm not about to let the girls get caught in the crossfire.

JACK

"Shouldn't Isaac be home by now?" I glance at the door again, but there still isn't any sign of him. Darkness fell outside hours

ago, and he was supposed to be home right after the zoning meeting. "Shouldn't the zoning meeting have been done before five?"

Now that Viviana is asleep, his absence is even more notice-
able. Even with Atlas staying, the condo feels cold and empty, and
I shiver and wrap my arms around myself against the chill.

Atlas glances at his watch again but avoids making eye
contact with me. "Yeah, I'm sure he'll be home soon."

A muscle in his jaw tics, and he keeps his focus on the after-
game report, his knee bouncing up and down wildly like it has
been the last half an hour.

I lean closer to him. "What aren't you telling me?"

"Huh?"

"What's going on? Is something wrong?"

He shakes his head. "Don't worry about it. He'll explain when
he gets here."

"Don't worry about it?" I push up from the couch and pace
behind it. "Easy for you to say. You obviously know what the fuck
is going on while I'm being kept in the dark."

"It's not that. It's just..."

"What?"

He sighs and pushes to his feet, rubbing the back of his neck,
making his massive, tattooed arms bulge. "He wasn't exactly sure
what was going on or if he was going to be able to come back here
when he spoke with Uncle Savage. He made it to his parents'
house, and his mom is treating him—"

"Treating him? Jesus Christ, is he okay?"

Atlas winces. "I think so."

"You *think* so? What the hell kind of an answer is that?"

He looks ready to respond, but the door opens behind me,
and I whirl to face it.

Isaac walks gingerly through in sweatpants and a T-shirt he
definitely didn't wear to the zoning meeting and with a
bandage over his eye that was already ripped apart once by
Atlas. Other bruises are starting to form along his cheek and

temple, and he has one hand pressed to the left side of his ribcage.

I rush over to him, stopping short of throwing myself at him so I can examine his injuries. "Jesus Christ, what happened to you?"

Stone enters behind him, followed closely by Gabe. Both wear stern looks and walk with a set to their shoulders I've only ever seen on Dad's men when they're mounting up to go out on a mission I'm not supposed to know about.

"What the hell is going on?"

Isaac closes the few steps between us and drags me into his arms, then winces.

"Oh, my God. Are you okay?"

He nods. "Yes, just a little beaten up."

"By what? What the hell happened?"

He sighs and glances at his father and uncle, then looks down the hallway toward the bedroom. "Is she asleep?"

I nod. "Yeah."

"Good. I don't want her hearing any of this. I don't want to scare her."

"Shit, that bad?"

He gives a harsh nod, and I wrap my arm around him and help him to the couch, but instead of sitting, he slips from my hold and moves over to the bar to pour himself a drink, which he tosses back immediately.

"I already filled them in." He nods to his dad and uncle. "But you two need to know." He turns back to Atlas and me. "Angelina contacted us earlier today, said there was a strange man at the café who wasn't leaving. He gave her a weird vibe, so I went to check it out because Gabe was busy dealing with other family business and had Saint and Bishop with him."

"Okay." Atlas' gaze darts between Isaac and the other two men. "Who was it?"

Isaac's jaw hardens. "Roselli."

I freeze. "What did he want?"

"To let me know that he knew you were here, and so do the Satrianos."

My heart climbs into my throat, my entire body going numb. "What? But how is that possible?"

The blue of Isaac's eyes darkens to an almost midnight. "The hospital records."

"Oh, God." I clutch at my chest where my heart thunders against my ribcage. "They were monitoring them?"

Stone nods. "They must have had some sort of software scanning for your name coming up in police reports, at hospitals, anything they could access."

"So, when I had the seizure and had to get admitted..."

His lips press into a firm line. "The Satrianos found you, along with the Rosellis, and I don't even want to think about why *they* were looking for you."

"Are they friendly with the Satrianos? They wouldn't have been helping them, right? Aren't they rivals?"

Gabe rocks his head from side to side. "That's more complicated."

"Maybe I can explain."

The unfamiliar voice has me turning back toward the door I hadn't even noticed had opened again.

But I instantly recognize the man standing just inside—Luca Abello.

Wearing perfectly pressed black dress pants and a crisp black button-down shirt, he approaches and holds out his hand to me. "I'm sorry we're meeting like this. I'm Luca."

I slide my hand into his much larger one, and the warmth of it quickly replaces the chill running through me. This man controlled all of New Orleans and has a reputation that matches Mom's, but he walked away from it all. "I know who you are."

The corner of his mouth quirks up. "I see you have your mother's beauty."

"I didn't know you knew her."

He grins. "I know everyone in the business. I was a friend of your grandfather's. I'm sorry you never got a chance to meet him. He was a great man."

"Thank you."

Luca releases my clammy palm, wanders over to the bar, and squeezes Isaac's shoulder. He winces but pours a drink and hands it to Luca.

Scotch in hand, Luca leans against one of the leather chairs. "The relationship between the Rosellis and the Satrianos is complicated, and I fear it just got more complicated because of what's going on with you and your mother."

"I still don't understand what *is* going on. What the hell did she do that the Satrianos are so pissed off about?"

Isaac drums his fingers on the side of his glass. "I was going to ask you the same thing. Roselli suggested you would know what started all this."

What?

"How the hell would I know? My parents don't tell me anything."

Luca glances between Stone, Gabe, and Isaac before he settles his gaze on me. "Satriano wanted you to marry him."

"Excuse me?" I take a step toward him. "I must have misheard you."

He shakes his head and takes a sip of his drink. "I wish you did. His wife passed away several years ago, and he wanted to cement the relationship between your mother and his crew, likely because he had been feeling her drift away from him recently. She's always been very reluctant to get involved with certain aspects of the business, and he felt that tying your families together would make that change, ensure she was cooperative in all respects."

"But...my mother would never do that."

Luca nods slowly. "Exactly. So, by requesting it, he was

putting her in an impossible position. Either she says yes and offers you to him on a fucking platter and ends up forced into a position where she might have to follow orders she doesn't want to, or she says no and creates an enemy, giving him a reason to take her out."

"Oh, my God."

Isaac slams back another drink, then approaches and wraps his arms around me. His entire body trembles violently, his skin cool and clammy.

"So, what the hell happened to you? Roselli?"

He pulls back and looks down at me. "I'm not sure. Somebody chased me. I was trying to go to my parents' house. I didn't want to lead them back here in case they didn't know where you were, but they forced my car off the road, and they shot at me. I killed two of them, but we aren't entirely sure whose men they are."

"It isn't good either way."

He shakes his head. "No, it isn't. And the police are going to come knocking soon. They'll find my car, the bodies, the bullet casings. I have to go in and talk to them, and they might lock me up for a while until things get sorted out."

"Lock you up for a while?" Panic seizes my entire body. "Are you fucking serious?"

They can't do that. He was only defending himself. Doing what he needed to in order to survive an attack by deadly men.

He takes my face between his palms and tilts my head up toward him, brushing his thumbs over my cheeks. "If they take me, if I'm not here, they'll protect you. They'll make sure you and Viviana are safe."

"But what about *you*? You're going to be a sitting target in lockup. They have people everywhere."

"I know, but I do, too. And I can take care of myself."

"Jesus Christ, Isaac." Tears stream down my face. "What the hell is happening?"

He pulls me against him, and I bury my face in his chest,

releasing a sob that seems to tear through the air. Isaac holds me tightly for a few minutes, letting me cry until I finally force myself to drag my head back up.

Gabe approaches us and rubs his hand on my back. "I'm sorry you're in the middle of all this. You don't deserve it. Your mother doesn't, either."

Luca takes a last drink and sets down his empty glass. "And this is complicating things between the Rosellis and the Satrianos. Roselli knows that if Satriano married you, it would give him a foothold in the states. Now that it's not happening, Satriano can take out your mother and take that place all the same—it may actually be better for him. That's a threat to Roselli that your mother never was. Your family has never been ambitious that way. She's never expanded beyond Chicago, but Satriano is another story."

"Why is this happening?"

Isaac kisses my forehead. "I'm so sorry, Jack."

"And we still haven't heard from my mom or dad?"

Gabe shakes his head. "No, I'm sorry. Getting information from our usual sources has been...difficult. We know there was an explosion, and we think it was your father, but we don't know what happened."

Isaac turns to his uncle. "What about what you were doing in the bayou earlier?"

The bayou?

What the hell is he talking about?

Gabe sighs and glances to Stone and Luca before settling his gaze on Isaac. "We had been tracking Broussard's phone. Monitoring his activities. We got a ping in the bayou and went to check it out—found him with a damn hole in his head."

Isaac scowls. "Self-inflicted?"

Gabe offers a shrug. "At least made to look that way, though I don't necessarily buy it. Too convenient, don't you think?"

Stone nods. "I sure do. That ping pulled you away from the

city when both Roselli and Satriano made pretty big statements. One of them is likely behind it."

My brain can't process what's going on, all their words coalescing into a jumble of incomprehensible sounds. "So...what the hell do we do now?"

Stone leans against the fireplace, stoic concern furrowing his brow though he's remained silent. "We wait and see how things fall out and who gets caught in it."

Gabe's phone rings, and he grabs it from his pocket and answers. "Yeah?" He frowns, then focuses his gaze on Isaac. "I'll tell him."

Isaac raises his re-stitched brow, now swollen and red. "What?"

He shoves his phone back into his pocket. "That was Saint. He's downstairs in the lobby, and the police just showed up looking for you."

"Shit."

I launch myself at Isaac, wrapping my arms around him probably too tightly. "Don't go."

He kisses the side of my neck and nuzzles into me. "I have to, Jack. But I promise, I'll be back."

Isaac pulls away from me and walks to the door, Gabe and his father hot on his heels. He opens it and turns back. "Tell Viviana I love her."

They all step out, and the door closes with a deafening *click* that seems to reverberate around the room—like it's sealing his fate.

21

ISAAC

Detective Reed steps into the interview room and casually slides into the chair across from me at the shitty, rickety metal table, dropping a file folder onto the shiny, scratched surface. He offers me a not-unkind smile and spreads out his hands. "Well, this is an interesting change for you, Mr. Hawke."

I lean back slightly in the uncomfortable plastic chair to release some of the pressure sitting forward puts on my ribs, but I still have to bite back a wince. The ACE bandages wrapped around them don't do much to help with the pain, but little would at this point.

His shrewd gaze assesses me carefully, from the cut over my eye, down my face, and over the clothes I borrowed from Dad when I finally made it to their house. "I'm used to seeing you in a fancy, expensive suit. Not dressed like you just came from the gym and looking like you had your ass kicked."

Offering him a slight shrug, I grin. "I have a lot of different looks."

He chuckles. "I'm hoping one doesn't include an orange jumpsuit in your future." Reaching into his pocket, he shakes his head. "Now, you know I have to read you your rights."

I smirk. "You have the right to remain silent. Anything you say can and will be used against you in a court of law. You have the right to an attorney. If you cannot afford one, one will be appointed to represent you. Do you understand these rights as they've been read to you? With these rights in mind, do you wish to speak to me?"

With the number of times I've heard them during law school, it would be impossible for me *not* to have the little *Miranda* card memorized.

Reed grins at me. "That makes it a lot easier."

"It sure does."

And I'll do anything to move this along quickly. After everything that happened tonight, having to say goodbye to Jack and walk out of the condo, not knowing when I would be back, almost killed me.

"I assume you want to wait until your father gets here."

I shake my head. "I sent him home when he wanted to follow me here to the station."

His graying eyebrow rises. "Really?"

"I don't need him."

Reed offers a sigh. "I wouldn't be so sure about that, Mr. Hawke." He flips open the file in front of him. "You're willing to talk to me about what happened?"

I shrug. "Why wouldn't I? I don't have anything to hide."

"I'm just surprised you didn't sit here and say 'lawyer.'"

I smirk. "What's that they say? Never act as your own lawyer. Well, I'm not taking that advice. I need to get home as soon as possible, and the only way to do that is to talk to you. And like I said, I have nothing to hide."

He leans back slightly and props his hands in the back of his head. "Okay, so fill me in. From the looks of it, you murdered two men tonight."

Cutting right to the chase.

The man doesn't beat around the bush, and I can certainly appreciate that. Any tactics he tried to use on me wouldn't work anyway—a fact he's likely more than aware of.

I nod slowly. "Yes, I did. But it was justifiable homicide done in self-defense."

Reed assesses me for a few moments, his wise gaze again roving over my appearance. "So *you* say…"

He has to question anything I tell him, delve deeper, push me harder. If he didn't, he wouldn't be doing his job. And Derek Reed is very good at his job. He wouldn't have made lead detective in the NOPD or be sitting across from me right now.

I drum my fingers on the table. "Do you have IDs on the two men?"

If they did, they would know what I was up against, and none of this would even be in question.

He shakes his head. "Not yet. Not anybody we recognized right away."

"Because they aren't from here."

"Oh, yeah? Where are they from?"

"Likely Italy."

Leaning forward, he grabs his pen and twirls it in his fingers. "And what are they doing in New Orleans?"

"Trying to get to my girlfriend and my daughter?"

The word "girlfriend" feels wrong coming out of my mouth when describing Jack, but I don't have a fucking clue *what* we are right now.

He narrows his eyes on me. "Your daughter?"

I bob my head. "I was visited by Roselli earlier today. He warned me that a family called Satriano was coming to town, if not already here, looking for Giacomina and Viviana."

"And just why would they be after them?"

Here's the punch line.

"Because Giacomina is Valentina Marconi's daughter."

He lets out a high-pitch whistle. "Well, well, well. You've gotten in deep with some very dangerous people, haven't you, Mr. Hawke?"

I shake my head, shifting again to try to relieve the pressure on my ribs. "They haven't done anything wrong and are complete innocents in this."

"So *you* say."

"They came here to hide out from the Satrianos, and when I left Roselli, an SUV chased me and ran me off the road. When I got out, two men with guns came down the hill at me. I had to fire, or they would've killed me."

He drops his pen and flips through several crime scene pictures.

I lean forward slightly to try to see them but instantly regret the movement when the sharp bite of pain radiates through me. "Surprised you have those already."

His dark eyes flick up to me. "I asked for the crime scene tech to send what they had right away. I'm sure they're still there, scouring everything."

"I bet." I motion toward the file. "And you can see from the photos that they fired at me. Look at the holes in the door, in the hood."

He nods slowly. "So, let's just say I buy your story."

"Is there any reason not to?"

A sardonic grin slowly spreads across his lips. "You Hawkes have a complicated history with organized crime, don't you?"

"You could say that. Though it was long before my time."

He rests his elbows on the table again. "I was just starting on the force when your dad was working for Dominic Abello as his private lawyer."

"That was a long time ago." I grin at him. "You must be getting close to retirement."

Reed chuckles. "My wife would like that, but I'm not quite ready to hang up the shield yet. I would miss out on all this fun."

"Yeah, today was real fun for me."

He closes the folder. "You know I have to pass this along to the DA."

"I know." I glance at the door he left partially cracked, likely in an effort to get me to feel more relaxed. "Am I free to go in the meantime? Or are you going to make me sit here for two days while he contemplates whether he's going to issue any charges or not? Because we both know he won't."

"You were big supporters during his campaign, weren't you?"

I don't bother to fight the grin. "He was the best candidate, and he sure loves the prime rib at The Hawke's Nest on Friday nights."

Reed smirks and releases a heavy sigh, sitting back again. "If what you're telling me is true, this is only the beginning of what could be a very bloody war here in town."

"You're right about that."

"Where's the gun you used?"

"My parents' house, and I'll gladly turn it over for you for testing so you can compare it to all the bullets littered around that scene." I gingerly get to my feet with a wince. "But let's be honest, there aren't going to be any charges. There isn't going to be a trial. The DA doesn't want to touch this with a ten-foot pole and get between the Hawkes and someone like the Satrianos."

"How does Roselli factor into all this?"

I pause at the door. "He was just trying to protect his territory from anybody who might decide to step into it uninvited."

Reed considers my words for a moment. "So, what you're saying is we need to increase the men on the streets until these Satrianos leave?"

"It would be a good idea." I turn the handle and step out but turn back to him. "And Detective?"

He leans back in his chair and raises his brows at me. "What?"

"You know where to find me. I'm not going anywhere."

"I know you're not. And that's the only reason I'm letting you walk out of here."

Sometimes being a Hawke does pay off...

JACK

MY KNEE BOUNCES ENDLESSLY.

Up and down.

Up and down.

Up and down.

On repeat.

Just like it has the last several hours since Isaac walked out that door to meet the police waiting for him downstairs.

Each breath I take feels like it won't fill my lungs, panic gripping my chest in its tight clutches and squeezing so hard that it hurts. I rub at it aimlessly, staring into the crackling fire that doesn't offer any warmth against the chill that consumes me.

What if they charge him?

Isaac might go to prison for the rest of his life for something that happened because of *me*, because I came here and brought all this into his carefully controlled world.

The eerie silence overwhelming the condo since Viviana went to bed and I sent Atlas home only makes it worse, like I'm trapped inside a tomb in one of the beautiful old cemeteries here in town, buried alive and just waiting for the air to run out.

I push myself up and pace in front of the fire again, unable to sit still, unable to do *anything* but wonder about what's happening to Isaac.

Where are you?

Something rattles the doorknob, it turns, and someone eases

the door open slowly. Isaac steps in and closes it carefully behind him before throwing the lock into place.

"Oh, thank God you're home." I rush over to him and wrap my arms around him, squeezing him tightly and pressing my body to his. "I was so worried."

He winces and stiffens, slipping his hand between us to push against his side.

"Shit, I'm sorry."

The fact that he's still hurting, that he almost died in that crash only hours ago, had disappeared from my mind the moment I saw him. All I wanted was to be in his arms and never leave. Now, seeing the anguish on his face, I try to pull away, but he tugs me against him even harder and buries his face in my hair, inhaling deeply.

"You should have had Atlas tell me you were on your way back."

"My dad picked me up when I was done at the station and dropped me off." He lifts his head and scans the condo. "They left you alone?"

"I sent Atlas home. He's just across the hall, and I didn't need him here."

He takes my face between his palms. "Yes, you do. I need to know there's somebody here with you all the time, especially after what happened tonight."

He almost died.

He had to *kill* two men to protect himself...

And us.

Tears burn in my eyes, and I can't manage to control them or keep my lips from trembling. "They're going to keep coming for me, aren't they?"

"I don't know, babe." He tightens his grip on my face. "But it doesn't fucking matter if they do because I'm going to kill them before they can again."

I jerk back, free from his hold. "No."

"What?" His dark brows knit together, pulling the fresh stitches over the left one. "What do you mean, *no*?"

"You can't." I shake my head, trying to stamp down the panic threatening to overtake me. "If you go after him, if you kill him, you *will* go to prison."

He steps forward and takes my face between his hands again, brushing his thumb across my cheek. "It doesn't matter if you're safe."

"It does matter. What the hell are we supposed to—"

"Mommy?"

Shit.

Viviana appears at the end of the hallway in her *Frozen* nightgown, clutching a teddy bear, and stares at us. Her gaze darts to Isaac's face. "Daddy, are you okay?"

He's a fucking mess.

Cut over his eye.

Dried blood still marring his temple and cheek.

His father's sweatpants and T-shirt hanging off a body that's clearly broken with his hand braced against his ribs.

I slip from his arms and make my way over to Viviana.

Isaac follows and squats in front of her, clearly trying not to show her how much it hurts to do it, and brushes her wild hair back from her face. "I'm sorry. Did I wake you up, kiddo?"

She rubs at her eyes. "I heard something. What happened?" Her gaze narrows on the cut on his face. "Are you okay?"

He offers her a half-smile. "I'm fine, kiddo."

Her bottom lip starts to tremble, just like mine.

Oh, hell.

Through everything that's happened the last few weeks— fleeing from Chicago, being torn away from her grandparents and everything she knows—she's maintained her easy-going demeanor. She keeps her emotions contained, assessing everything carefully and only reacting when she feels she has a grasp on the situation.

But this is too much.

A tear trickles from her cheek. "But you're bleeding."

"Not anymore, honey."

Isaac scoops her up with a groan and settles her against his chest. She wraps her legs around him, and he winces and grits his teeth together as she clings to his neck and buries her face against his chest.

He turns back to me. "Let's go to bed."

I move to step past him down the hallway to take Viviana back to her room, but he grabs my arm and squeezes my bicep gently.

"No." He nods up toward his bedroom and tugs my arm to get me to follow him. "My room. I don't want either of you out of my sight."

I flip off the fireplace as we pass it, and we make our way up the stairs slowly and into the bedroom. I don't even bother turning on the lights, just follow him straight for the bed and watch him set Viviana down, letting her crawl to the center of it.

Isaac keeps his gaze locked on his daughter, his breaths coming hard and short, and I slip into bed and wait for him to do the same.

Viviana immediately rolls toward him and clings to him, and he slides his arm around her and tugs her close while I settle in on the other side, cocooning her between us.

"You don't have to worry about Daddy, Viviana." He trails his fingers through her hair. "I'm going to be okay. I'm always going to be here to protect you."

His promise makes me lift my head and meet his gaze. He can't possibly keep that promise, not with everything that's going on, not with all the uncertainty, but he means it all the same.

He kisses the top of Viviana's head, then reaches over and brushes his fingers along my cheek. "I mean it, Jack. I'll do anything I have to."

"I know you will. That's what scares me the most."

I settle back down on the pillow, and he lies in bed with us, staring up at the ceiling, likely replaying the events of the last few weeks in a constant loop in his head the same way I have been.

God, has it really only been a few weeks since I saw him in his dad's office? Since it felt like my life flipped on its axis and started spinning backward, since literally, everything changed?

Even a month ago, I never would've thought it was possible that I would be here with Isaac again, but now with his arms wrapped around Viviana and me, I can't imagine life being any different.

Memories creep into my head of Mom and Dad and Viviana, of the way she smiles when she's with them, the joy they bring to her life back home.

Because it *is* home.

No matter how many times I tried to run from it, from *them*. It's the only home I've ever known, the only place I've ever felt safe and loved.

Until now...

This moment.

Acid crawls up my throat at the thought of having to leave, and I swallow it back and kiss Viviana again as she settles into the rhythmic breathing of sleep, cuddled against Isaac.

This is a man who likely never even held a child before, and he's had fatherhood thrust on him in the most chaotic of ways. Yet, already, Viviana knows he's her father, accepts it, and I can see the love he has for her. I believe every single word he says about what he's willing to do for her...and me.

But I don't know if it's enough.

Satriano is going to keep coming. He wants me, wants a bargaining chip to draw Mom out and force her to act, and he doesn't seem the type to stop or give up.

Isaac drags his fingers through my hair, and I shift to throw my leg over his, snuggling as close as I can with Viviana between us.

That man expected Mom to just hand me over like a piece of meat, like fucking chattel, something to be traded, a fucking commodity. She was set up to fail, to give Satriano an excuse to come here and take her out, to step in in Chicago and take everything the Marconis built there for the last century as his own.

And he doesn't care who he hurts, not me, not Viviana, not any of the Hawkes who are just trying to protect us.

Isaac's body finally relaxes slightly into the mattress, and I try to do the same, all the stress of the day draining any remaining adrenaline from my body until I'm so bone-tired I can't keep my eyes open anymore.

They drift closed, and the rhythmic breathing of Viviana and Isaac fills my ears until I finally allow myself to be pulled under into the darkness.

22

ISAAC

As much as I hated having to get out of bed and leave the girls there this morning, after everything that happened yesterday, I needed a fucking shower. I craved this hot water cascading over my sore muscles and washing away the grime and dried blood and events I'd rather forget. Yet despite the relief it's offering, every time I lift my arm to wash my hair or scrub my body, pain radiates through my rib cage.

Of course, there's nothing they can do for cracked ribs, so I just have to grit my teeth and bear it.

I turn off the water, grab a towel, wrap it around my waist, and wipe away the condensation on the mirror to check out the true damage I haven't even had a chance to look at.

The swollen, red cut over my eye looks even worse than it did when Atlas broke it open. The stitches Mom had to put in make it look gnarlier than it actually feels, and the bruises along my cheek are darkening from where the airbag must have hit me.

Thank fuck for that, or I probably would be dead.

I let my gaze drift down over my chest to my ribs, where purple bruises are already starting to form.

That's going to hurt for a long fucking time.

But everything that happened is worth it if it meant taking out two of the fuckers who are threatening my girls.

I step into the bedroom and peek over at the bed, but they're still buried under the covers. So, I slip into the closet and pull on a pair of sweatpants and a T-shirt—not without a few grumbled curse words at the pain it causes—and step back out to make my way over to them.

Jack lies with her back to me, arms spread across the center of the bed where Viviana slept last night.

Where the hell is Viviana?

I scan the room, then reach out and squeeze Jack's arm, shaking her gently. "Jack."

Her eyes flutter open and struggle to focus on me. She blinks rapidly a few times. "What?"

"Where's Viviana?"

She stretches, arching her back slightly and putting her hand over her mouth as she yawns and scans around the bed. "Um, I don't know. You didn't see her?"

I shake my head and run a hand back through my damp hair. "I was in the shower and just came out."

Jack collapses back onto the mattress, still groggy, eyes red. "She must have gone downstairs to get something to eat or juice or something. Wasn't Saint supposed to come over this morning? She loves his pancakes."

I grin at her. "Yeah, she does. So do I. He makes a pretty fucking good pancake. Go back to sleep. I'm going to go look for her and get some of those pancakes myself."

"Okay." She rolls back over and snuggles down into the bed.

I drop a kiss to her cheek before I pad out of the room, pull the door closed behind me, and step onto the small landing that overlooks the living room.

The empty living room.

And empty dining area.

Where the hell is everybody?

I hustle down the stairs and into the kitchen, not without a wince or two, but it's pristine, exactly the way it was the last time I was in here—with a plate of cookies under cling wrap in the center of the counter.

"What the fuck?"

My heart skips a beat, then starts beating faster, and I flatten my hand to my side and jog down the hallway to the guest room. "Viviana?"

Her name echoes down the hallway, and I push open the cracked door to her bedroom.

"Vivi, are you in here?"

Nothing.

I race to the bed and throw back the covers just to make sure she didn't come down here to sleep in her own bed, then check the bathroom and the closet.

"Where the fuck is she?"

Trying to tamp my panic, I rush down the hallway and up the stairs to throw open my bedroom door. "Jack, wake up."

"What?" She jolts upright. "What's wrong?"

"Viviana's gone."

She rubs at her eyes. "What? What do you mean, she's gone?"

"She isn't *here*."

Her eyes widen. "Oh, my God."

I rush over to the end table to grab my phone, but it isn't there. "Shit, my phone was in the car. I don't have it."

And Jack doesn't have one, either.

Fuck.

"I already checked her room downstairs. Check the rest of the condo. I'm going to Atlas' so he can call everybody and we can figure out where the fuck she is."

"Okay..."

She scrambles off the bed as I hustle back down the stairs, race through the condo, throw open the door, and launch myself across the hall to Atlas' door. I pound on it, then try the handle, which opens easily.

"Atlas!" I scream his name as I stumble in. "Atlas. You here?"

"What the fuck?" Muttered curses come from the second floor, and his bedroom door opens. He steps out onto the landing in nothing but a sheet wrapped around his waist and looks down at me, rubbing at his eyes. "What the fuck, man? It's early."

"Is Viviana over here?"

His eyes narrow on me. "What? No. Why the hell would she be? Is she missing?"

I nod. "I can't find her at my place."

"When's the last time you saw her?"

"She was in my bed with Jack and me before I took my shower this morning. So, twenty minutes, thirty, at the most."

"Fuck."

I tug open the door and glance back at him. "Call everybody. I'm going down to the lobby to review the security footage. Make sure nobody got in here while we were sleeping or something."

"You know that's impossible."

"I know…"

But she's not here, and there has to be an explanation.

I run out of his condo to the elevator, slamming my finger against the call button a million times as if that's going to make it come any faster.

Where the hell is she?

It's impossible for anyone to get up here unless they know the code, and only the family has it. We have security in the lobby—extra security, given everything that happened yesterday.

There's no way.

There's no fucking way anyone got up here.

The elevator finally dings. I step into it and press the button for the ground floor, then pace inside the car, my bare feet slapping on the metal. I pinch the back of my neck, my heart caught my throat.

Where the fuck is she?

It feels like it takes an hour to reach the ground floor. When the door dings, I rush out and skid to a stop immediately.

A man stands in the center of the lobby in a black suit, Viviana next to him, holding his hand and staring up at him with a smile on her face.

"Viviana, come here." I step forward. "Come to Daddy."

I motion for her to come toward me, but the man scoops her up and holds her at his hip, a grin spreading across his lips.

"You have a beautiful daughter, Isaac." He reaches up and brushes some of her dark hair away from her face. "Imagine my surprise when I came in and the elevator opened to this perfect *principessa* waiting inside it."

"What?"

Viviana turns and looks at me, her wide blue eyes full of fear that she's in trouble for doing something wrong. "I'm sorry, Daddy. I wanted to come see Saint."

Holy shit...

She must have been watching us put the code in the elevator all this time and memorized it. I take a step forward and another, then scan to my left at two sets of legs sticking out from behind the security desk and a pool of blood starting to trickle out from underneath the bodies.

The man glances over there and offers a half-shrug. "I'm not sure if one of them is Saint, but either way, they're going to need one." He chuckles at his own joke and bounces Viviana. "You'll figure out why that's funny when you're older, *principessa*."

I fist my hands at my sides. "Give her back."

He smirks. "Well, I wouldn't have much leverage if I did that, would I, Mr. Hawke?"

"Who the hell are you?"

Not Satriano.

This was the man standing next to me on the sidewalk yesterday.

Fuck.

His eyes drift down to my bare feet, then back up. "A different look today than the last time we saw each other, Mr. Hawke. But I think you can guess who I work for. My employer will be very happy to meet Ms. Viviana here."

He tickles her chest playfully, and she giggles, completely unaware of what's really going on.

I take a step forward, and he retreats toward the doors where two of his men stand, weapons at their side but ready to use them at any second's notice.

"I'm not letting you leave here with her."

He raises a dark brow. "Yeah, how are you going to fucking stop me?"

JACK

I PACE INSIDE THE ELEVATOR, chewing on my bottom lip and watching the numbers slowly drop.

Not fast enough.

Come on.

Come on.

Come on.

Atlas said Isaac came down to check the security cameras, and there *has* to be something on them. Some sort of explanation for where Vivi could have gone.

She has to be here somewhere.

She has to.

There isn't any way someone got into the condo. Isaac or I would have heard something, and I doubt anyone could even get to the floor. I glance at the number panel where the code has to be entered. The security here is ironclad.

So, where the hell is she?

I try to take calming breaths, my body beginning to heat and my vision starting to blur around the edges.

No.

Don't panic.

The elevator dings, and the doors slide open. Angry voices hit my ears before I run out into the lobby and jolt to a stop behind Isaac, where he's frozen in place.

It takes a second for my brain to process everything in front of me.

"Oh, my God."

A sinister looking stranger stands in the lobby, holding Viviana close to him, with two armed men near the double glass lobby doors.

Who the hell is that?

I rush forward toward them, but Isaac lashes out his arm across my chest and stops me.

"Don't." He practically growls the word between clenched teeth. "Don't."

"But Isaac—"

He whips his head to the side and locks gazes with me. The usually calming sea of blue rages like a tempest of fury and panic. He tips his head toward the security counter.

Blood pools from behind it, two sets of feet sticking out —unmoving.

I gasp and slap my hand over my mouth as tears start to form.

What the hell is going on?

I scan the lobby again and see exactly why he held me back. The two men near the door with guns ready don't seem like the type who are going to let me interfere with whatever the fuck is going on, and the moment I moved forward, they pointed their weapons straight at us.

Whoever these people are, they're here with a purpose. They're precisely what we've been running from. Our worst nightmare come true.

Satriano found us.

And somehow, Viviana ended up in the arms of one of his goons.

The man smiles. "And you must be the famous Giacomina, or did I hear you go by Jack now?"

Fucking hell, how does he know that?

Likely the same way they knew we were here in New Orleans in the first place.

The hospital...

If they spoke with any of the nurses who helped me, they could have revealed what Isaac called me.

It's the *only* way he could have such personal information.

He offers a sinister grin and bounces Viviana. "Here's what's going to happen. I'm going to take Viviana, and you're going to let me if you want her unharmed. And when your mother resurfaces and turns herself over to my employer"—he shrugs nonchalantly—"you'll have your daughter back."

"Fuck you." Isaac hisses the words and takes another step forward, undeterred by the men lifting their guns. "I'm not letting you take her."

Me either.

Viviana will *not* become a victim of this world I was born into. She will not suffer because of the blood in her veins the way I have. That little girl deserves everything Isaac and the Hawkes can give her—love, protection, a place where she isn't getting dragged into wars that aren't hers for the rest of her life.

But Satriano's man seems undeterred by Isaac's words. "There's no way you can stop me, Mr. Hawke. Things were set in motion by others long before you got involved, and this is how it ends. *Il gran finale.*"

Never.

I move forward next to Isaac and shake my head. "No, it isn't. Take *me*."

"What?" Isaac whips his head my way, his mouth agape. "No."

The anguish in his eyes and pain in the single word slice like a blade through my chest, but I force myself to step away from the man who holds my heart and toward the one who holds our daughter. "I'm sorry, Isaac, but I have to." I turn to Vivi's captor. "Take me. Leave Viviana with her father."

The man narrows his eyes on me, so dark they're almost black, like his soul must be for him to be able to drag an innocent four-year-old into this. "What sort of game are you playing?"

"No game." I shake my head, holding up my hands. "Your boss wanted to marry me, right? That's what all this is about." I spread my palms out wide. "Well, I'll do it."

"No." Isaac's scream echoes through the lobby off all the metal and tile and glass, deafening to my ears, the most anguished sound I've ever heard. "Over my dead fucking body!"

Vivi's captor smirks. "That can be arranged, Mr. Hawke, if that's what you really want."

I can't react to the way Isaac's distress wrenches my heart in two. I can't let myself think about what marrying a man like Satriano means. I can't let myself imagine what it would be like to walk down the aisle in a white dress with Isaac waiting at the altar instead of one of Mom's enemies.

Not if I want to keep advancing toward what I have to do.

I swallow through my tears, trying to keep my voice level so I won't scare Viviana. "I'll marry him willingly. I won't fight him on it. Just let her go."

The man's evil grin returns. "I think my boss would be quite pleased with this offer, but it doesn't resolve the problem of your mother and your father."

No, it doesn't.

When they learn what I've done, they're going to burn down all of Calabria or anywhere else Satriano tries to hide.

"I'll deal with them." *Or at least try.* "I'll explain the situation." *Try to reason with them.* "I'll get them on board." *And maybe Hell will freeze over.* "They won't be a problem for you anymore." *Problem isn't a big enough word.* "Just let Viviana go."

Please!

Isaac issues a low, primal growl, like a feral animal sending a warning. "There's no fucking way in hell I'm letting you do this, Jack."

He storms toward me, but one of the men with the guns rushes forward and levels it on him. Right at his chest. Only inches away.

Isaac skids to a stop and holds up his hands.

The man who seems to be in charge of our fates looks from me to Viviana and back to me. "This seems like a reasonable offer, and if my boss is anything, it's reasonable."

He closes the few feet between us and hands Viviana to me. She wraps her arms around my neck, clinging to me as I clutch her impossibly close.

Running my hand over her hair, I kiss her cheek. "Are you okay, baby?"

She nods, casting an uncertain look toward the man who was holding her. "Mommy, who is that?"

I force a smile as a tear trickles from my eye. "A friend. I have to go with him, but I'll see you soon. You're going to stay with Daddy."

"No." Isaac moves forward again, but the goon with a gun gives him a look that stops him in his tracks.

"It'll be okay, sweetheart." I try to memorize her sweet face, suddenly feeling like there's a real chance I'll never see it again. "I'll see you soon. Be good for your daddy."

I press a kiss to her forehead, then turn and walk over to Isaac to hand her off. He takes her from me, but before I can step away, he grips my upper arm, digging his fingers into my flesh painfully.

"I'm not letting you do this." His eyes fill with angry tears. "You're not marrying that monster, and you're not going with them as a damn hostage. You could have another seizure."

The tears fall in earnest now as emotion clogs my throat. I try to swallow through it as I look into the eyes of the only person who's ever made me believe a real life is out there somewhere, that happiness can exist even in the worst of circumstances.

"I have to, Isaac. It's the only way this ends. Take care of her."

I jerk free of his hold and step backward until I reach Satriano's henchman. He grabs my arm roughly and drags me toward the door.

"It's been a pleasure doing business with you, Mr. Hawke." He grins over his shoulder and winks. "But don't expect an invitation to the wedding."

He ushers me outside, his two men following closely behind while keeping their weapons trained on Isaac.

Isaac rushes toward the building entrance as the man forces me into an SUV waiting at the curb. He shoves me in across the smooth leather and slides in next to me, yanking the door closed behind him.

I wince at the sound, like the final nail being hammered into my coffin.

Through the tinted glass, I watch Isaac tug open the glass door and run out onto the street after us, barefoot, with Viviana in his arms.

We peel away from the curb, and for the second time in my life, I watch Isaac Hawke disappear from view, knowing I'll never see him again.

23

ISAAC

The vehicle flies down the street and turns the corner before I even have a chance to suck in a breath. My entire body feels numb, like I'm not standing here, staring at the last spot I could see the SUV before it disappeared from view, like none of the last few minutes really happened at all and I'm stuck in some nightmare.

Viviana's frantic sob ringing in my ears finally breaks me from whatever trance I'm in. "Mommy, come back!"

I squeeze her to me. Her tiny body shakes violently with her tears and anguish, and I rush back toward the door, jerking it open to the lobby that now holds so many awful memories.

Shit.

I can't let her see the blood or bodies.

I tug her head down against my neck to ensure she won't be subjected to that and rush toward the elevator, where I jam my finger into the button. There isn't any time to waste. If I don't get after Jack quickly, I'll lose her for good.

That isn't happening...

Over and over again, I try to repeat it in my head.

You'll get her back.

You'll get her back.

You have *to get her back...*

The elevator finally arrives, and the doors slide open. Atlas starts to rush out but jerks to a stop when he sees me, his observant gaze taking in our states of distress and shock.

I hand Viviana to him. "Go to Atlas."

He scoops her up and holds her against his bare chest as she sobs. "What happened?"

"Satriano's men had her." I swallow back the bile climbing up my throat at what they might have done with her had I not come down in time, had Jack not sacrificed herself. "He-he just took Jack."

Atlas's eyes widen. "What? Where was security?"

I give him a look that answers the question because I won't say the words in front of Viviana or voice the fact that one of them could very well be Saint. "Get her upstairs. I'm going to go check the men."

"I already called everyone." He rubs his tattooed hand on Vivi's back, trying to comfort her while processing everything I'm throwing at him. "They're on their way here."

I give him a sharp nod and let the doors close to bring them back up to safety, then hustle back behind the counter, my stomach roiling at what I know I'm going to see there.

The blood pool continues to spread out across the pale Italian marble, an ominous warning of what's no longer just coming for us but already here. This isn't just a threat anymore; it's an act of war.

My hands shake, and I brace one against the counter and hold my breath as I step around it toward the bodies.

"Shit."

I gag and cover my mouth to keep myself from retching. Anthony and Thadius stare up at me with wide, dead eyes. Both of them are long gone, gaping wounds in their chests, with their weapons still safely encased in their holsters at their hips.

Those fuckers didn't even give them a chance to defend themselves.

"Fuck."

There isn't anything I can do for them now, but it isn't too late to save Jack from whatever that monster has planned for her.

Tires squeal and brakes sound outside the building, and I rush toward the front doors and fling them open to Gabe and Dad climbing out of their cars at the curb. A white SUV comes to a stop behind them, and Saint lumbers out. All of them hustle in, scanning the street for anyone who might be watching us.

Dad ensures the door is closed behind him before he scans my face. "What the fuck is going on? Atlas said Viviana is missing."

I shake my head, trying to suck in a breath and calm my racing heart so I can relay the information to them. "I have her. She's fine. But they took Jack."

Gabe glowers at me. "*Who* took Jack?"

Who? Who was it?

I don't even know his name, but he has her now.

"One of Satriano's men."

"Fuck." Dad pulls out his phone and starts dialing. "I have to let Savage know what's going on."

Gabe scans the lobby, narrowing his eyes on the pool of blood trailing around the edge of the counter.

I clamp my eyes closed, trying to eliminate what I just saw from my head, but all it does is engrain that image even more. "They're dead."

Saint winces. "I was supposed to be here this morning. I was running late..."

I reach out and squeeze the big man's arm. "It wasn't your fault. There's nothing you could have done. You probably would've ended up dead just like them."

"Shit." Gabe looks out the floor-to-ceiling windows, scanning up and down the street. "Which way did they go?"

"North in a black Mercedes SUV." I try to visualize the vehicle again. "I couldn't get a license plate and didn't see anything else identifying."

Gabe pulls out his phone and dials someone. "I'm going to have my guy at the DOT start checking traffic cameras, see if we can track it."

"Fuck." I scrub my hands over my face and try to get control of my breathing. If I don't, my heart will burst straight out of my chest. "We have to get to her. We have to find her fast. This stress…it could cause another seizure."

Saint sends off a text message, likely to Bishop and the rest of his crew, with the information we do have. "Do you think they'll hurt her?"

I look up at him, the words sitting like acid on my tongue. "She agreed to marry Satriano."

His heavy, dark brows fly up. "What?"

"She agreed to marry him so he'd turn Viviana back over to me." Just saying it makes me want to retch again, and I flatten my hand over my stomach to try to control it. "Who the fuck knows how long we have before they actually do it."

Gabe covers his phone for a second so whoever he's on with won't hear him. "They'll need a marriage license if they want it to be legal."

I shake my head. "They might not even do it here. He might throw her on a plane and bring her back to Italy."

"Fuck." Saint dials someone on his phone. "I'm calling all my contacts at the airports within a hundred miles. We'll ground any private jets."

The room starts to spin, and I stagger backward and lean against the counter, my breaths coming shorter and harder. "What if we're too late? What if—"

Dad squeezes my shoulder. "Breathe. It'll be okay. We'll find her."

"What if we don't?" I double over, my ass planted against the counter, the only thing keeping me from falling face-first onto the marble. "What if she has a seizure and they don't know what to do? What if—"

"You can't think like that." He squats in front of me until his eyes meet mine. "We'll find her."

"And I'll rip out Satriano's jugular with my own bare fucking hands." I squeeze my fists together until my nails bite into my palms. "That motherfucker..."

Saint finishes his call and examines the bodies again. "Is Viviana okay?"

Fuck.

She must be losing her mind by now. At only four, she can't possibly understand everything that happened, but she's observant enough to feel the tension and know her mother leaving wasn't a good thing.

"Viviana...I need to go back up."

Dad helps me stand again. "I'll go with you. Gabe and Saint can take care of this." He motions toward the bodies. "We can't get the police involved."

"I know."

Fortunately—or maybe unfortunately—Gabe is all too familiar with what it takes to clean up this type of a mess, and Saint is no stranger to helping do the dirty work.

I scan the massacre one more time. As long as no one heard the shots and no one else in the building comes down before they get it cleaned up, we should be okay. "It's still early; early enough that the other building residents shouldn't be up. But just in case, once I get back up, shut down the elevators and send an alert to all the residents telling them they'll have to use the stairwell. That will feed them out the back door instead of into the lobby."

Saint nods. "Got it taken care of."

I stumble to the elevator and press the call button, leaning my forehead against the wall as I try to make sense of everything that just happened.

Dad wraps his arm around my shoulders and squeezes. "We'll get her back. He's not going to be able to leave town with her."

I turn my head to look at him. "Even if he's stuck here, that doesn't mean she's safe. Who knows what that bastard will do to her?"

His jaw tightens. "She's a strong woman, Isaac. She can handle herself."

I slam my palm against the wall. "I know she can. But she can't control the seizures, and if he lays one fucking finger on her, so help me God..."

"I know, son. Believe me, I fucking know."

The elevator arrives. We hustle in, and I punch in the numbers to take us upstairs. "We need to change the elevator code. Viviana knows it."

"Fuck." Dad's brow furrows. "Is that how she got down here?"

I nod. "She was looking for Saint."

He shakes his head. "We can't tell him that. He'll just feel guilty about it."

"I know."

Saint wears his heart on his sleeve, and he doesn't like failing at anything. He takes everything as a personal failure, and he will let it eat away at him until it destroys him.

I lean back against the wall, close my eyes, and try to inhale several deep breaths, but all I get with each one is Jack's scent still lingering in the elevator car from when she came down.

"Fuck." The vise tightens around my chest as we climb. "How the hell did this happen?"

The doors open again, and I rush out of the hallway and into my condo. Atlas sits on the couch, Viviana still clutched in his arms, her face buried against his neck as he rubs her back.

Her head jerks up at the sound of the door opening, tears streaming down her face. "Daddy, where's Mommy?"

Fucking hell.

I thought I understood what pain was, believed I had suffered enough over the years to know how to process it and feel and move through it, but Viviana's words tear me apart in a way that makes it clear I haven't had a fucking clue what real pain is.

The sharp ache in my ribcage, the cut over my eye, the damn wound where the bullet grazed my arm, none of it matters when I'm looking at Vivi's tears.

I rush over to her, and Atlas stands to pass her off to me. She throws her arms around my neck, and I clutch her to me, probably too tightly, but it isn't enough for me to feel like she's safe.

"Your mommy's coming back, sweetheart. Soon. I promise."

Atlas' eyes meet mine, and I see the same fury building in them that I do right before he goes into the ring with an opponent. Only this time, it's stronger, harder, far more intense, because this isn't just a fight for his own life; it's a fight for Jack's.

Dad paces the other side of the room, phone to his ear, calling in every fucking favor he can and talking to anyone he can think of who might be of assistance.

I rub my hand over Vivi's back. "Get Astrid over here to sit with her."

Atlas nods, pulls out his phone, and sends off a text. It buzzes almost immediately with a reply. "She'll be here in fifteen minutes."

"Good."

I want to stay here with Viviana, want to never let her leave my arms again.

But I can't.

I have to go find Jack and get her back...

No matter what it takes.

JACK

THE QUIET, terrifyingly disinterested man, who just threatened to take Viviana, sat next to me in that car, silently staring out the window like he hadn't just destroyed my entire life, now leads me into the living room of a stunning Creole townhouse.

It's the kind of home I would have loved to explore while here in New Orleans—stately, ornate, full of vibrant color and history —but all I can see right now is the man sitting on the sofa who offers a dark grin.

Leonardo Satriano...

All of this is because of *this* man.

His lust for power has brought us to this moment.

"*Benvenuta*, Giacomina, I'm so happy you're finally here, *carina.*"

He slowly rises to his feet, adjusting his navy suit over lean muscle. The lightly graying hair at his temples suggests his age, but Satriano clearly keeps himself in shape for a man almost fifteen years older than me. He approaches slowly, his heated gaze raking over me in a way that makes me want to gag.

"I have to say, I was surprised to get the text message from Emilio indicating you had agreed to the arrangement I tried to make with your mother."

Agreed to?

This man is delusional.

Totally crazy.

It's no wonder Mom didn't want to work with him. The bits and pieces of information I've overheard over the years about the Satrianos painted a violent picture, and seeing him in person, I can understand how people might be easily drawn into his web.

But I can see him clearly, can see beyond the fancy suit, the debonair air he puts on. I can *see* the monster inside, the one who orders entire families to be killed without batting a dark eye.

I sneer at him and fold my arms over my chest. "I didn't have any choice, did I?" I glare at the man next to me. "He was going to take my daughter."

Satriano turns to Emilio with a half-smirk. "He wouldn't have harmed the *bambina*. We were just trying to send a message to your mother."

A message...

He says it so cavalierly, as if taking a four-year-old from her mother's arms and threatening to kill her is fair game in his world and top on his list of tactics.

"I got it loud and clear, which is why I am here willingly. Leave my daughter alone, leave the Hawkes alone, and I'll do whatever you want."

A low chuckle sounds in his chest, and he reaches up to run his fingers through my hair affectionately. I shrink away from the touch, and a shudder rolls through me at the heat in his gaze.

"Whatever I want, huh?" He leans in and brushes his lips against my ear. "I want more than just your compliance, Giacomina. I want everything your mother has, too."

And there it is...

The motive we all knew was behind all of this.

Satriano isn't content to be a god in Calabria anymore. He wants more. He wants the territory the Marconis have held in Chicago for almost a hundred years. And he's willing to do anything to possess it.

I try not to flinch away from him. If I have to marry this man to keep everyone safe, I'll have to learn to pretend. "I'll talk to her and my father, assure them this is my choice, and I'll tell them they need to back off. They'll listen to me."

He pulls back with his dark brows raised. "You really believe that? That it'll be so easy?" He tsks and shakes his head. "My experience with your mother and father has always been that nothing is easy with them."

"That's true." I nod slowly, unable to hold back the jab. "And my father rarely fails. Though I heard he may have missed you at your compound recently."

Satriano smirks. "Ah yes, the explosion designed to take me out." A humorless grin spreads across his face, darkening his eyes and making him truly look as evil as I know him to be. "Too bad I had already left to make my way over here. All he managed to do was anger me and injure a few people who remained on the premises." He grins. "Nothing life-threatening, though."

Dammit.

And knowing he failed is going to eat away at Dad and make him want to come at Satriano even harder. There's nothing I can say that will stop him. He's a machine once he's on a mission, and Satriano was already on the top of his hit list *before* he took Viviana or I agreed to this joke of a marriage.

Satriano is right—they're not going to just back down because I tell them to.

Still, I have to buy some time, do something to help them figure out how to end this without anyone I love getting hurt, and if it means marrying him...I swallow thickly...or anything that entails, I'll do it to protect the family. To protect Viviana.

"Tell me you'll leave them all alone if I do this."

He reaches up and grips my chin, staring directly into my eyes with his hard, almost onyx ones. "If they stay out of my way and comply, they won't be harmed."

That isn't much of a promise, but it's likely all I'm going to get from this man.

"Now, I had planned on taking you back to Italy so we could have a proper wedding ceremony at my estate. But"—he shrugs slightly—"I've already received a call from my pilot about an issue at the airport. My guess is it's the Hawkes intervening."

Hope blossoms in my chest, warming my heart and making me twitch in his grasp. "They're going to come for me."

"You better hope they don't. But even if they can find you, by the time they do, you and I will already be wed. So even if they try to stop me, it'll be too late. Things will be set in motion that can't be stopped. Your mother's empire will belong to me the moment we say *I do*."

A cold sense of dread settles over me. Something about the way he said it. "You're going to kill her anyway, aren't you?"

He smirks. "I told you I won't, if they don't get in our way."

They will.

There's no fucking question they will.

He knows it as well as I do.

Shit.

I glance at Emilio, still standing next to me, the one who so coldly killed the security guards at the condo building and easily snatched a small child to use as a bargaining chip without remorse.

Satriano glides his thumb over my cheek. "Don't look so nervous, Giacomina. I promise I'll treat you well as long as you give me what I want."

Another shudder rolls through me at the promise in his words, my entire body revolting at the idea of him touching me. "What is it you want?"

"*All* of you." He leans in slightly, stopping with his lips just over mine. "I need an unquestionable heir who carries both our bloodlines. Several, actually, just to be safe." He winks. "In our line of business, things tend to happen to those in power."

Something flickers in the back of my head, an old memory, something I overheard Mom and Dad talking about years ago. "Right, you had a brother, didn't you? Older...who was killed ten years ago."

He nods slowly. "It was...*unfortunate*, but it did open the way for me to step up into the leadership."

The suggestion hangs there that he may have had something to do with his brother's death, that there's more to the story, but I'm not feeling bold enough at the moment to ask for clarification or make any accusations. I wouldn't put it past this man to kill his own flesh and blood in order to capture an empire as large and lucrative as the one the Satrianos control.

"We'll make beautiful children, Giacomina. And they'll have anything in the world that they could ever want. A beautiful mother. A father who buys them anything and everything their hearts could desire, who provides and gives protection. They'll live in a gorgeous villa and have a life most people could only dream of."

He makes it sound so pleasant, but it isn't much different from how I grew up—trapped in a prison by the people who love me in order to protect me. Still, I force a smile.

"That does sound lovely."

If I'm going to have to do this, if I'm going to have to marry this man and make him happy to ensure everyone's safety, then I better get used to lying and putting on my game face.

His slow grin raises goosebumps on my skin, and he leans in and finally kisses me. Slow and sensually, a kiss designed to try to seduce me when all it does is make me want to vomit in my mouth.

He pulls away with warmth flickering in his eyes. "I'm so pleased you feel that way and that there's no animosity over how this has gone down." He takes my face in his palm, his hand cold, so unlike the way Isaac's is when he touches me, and I have to fight back a sob that threatens to escape my throat. "You're going to be such a beautiful bride, Giacomina. I can't wait to see you in the dress I've already picked out."

Wait...what?

"You've already picked out a dress?"

"I told you this would happen fast, *carina*. We'll be wed by the end of the day."

Terror grips me, the icy dread wrapping around my spine and threatening to make my legs buckle out from underneath me.

There isn't any time.

No time for the Hawkes to find me.

No time for Mother and Father to intervene to try to stop this.

I have to marry Satriano.

If I don't, everyone will be in danger, more danger than they already are.

He will still try to take them out, still try to rid the world of anyone who could potentially try to intervene on my behalf. My only chance is to get word to them to leave it be, that I'm okay, and pray they realize it's the only way to keep Viviana safe.

It's too bad it will never work.

Isaac will come for me.

Dad will.

Even Mom will get her hands dirty to save her own.

I force another smile that he returns.

His fingers brush over my left hand, the pad of his thumb stopping over my empty ring finger. "By the end of the day, you'll be Mrs. Satriano."

And my life will be over.

24

JACK

The small white church seems to tower above me, foreboding with the darkening sky behind it. A metal plaque on the right side identifies it as *St. Mary's Catholic Church,* but all it will ever be to me is the place where I gave away my life.

Looking up at it from inside the limo feels like staring my future in the face but having no way to escape it. Even if I wanted to run, I couldn't in this massive white princess gown and stilettos.

It's all wrong.

The wrong dress. The wrong shoes. The wrong church. The wrong man.

Tears stream down my cheeks, likely smearing all the mascara the woman who got me dressed spent so much time ensuring was perfect.

This is it.

This is the moment I have dreaded my entire adult life— when being a Marconi finally bites me in the damn ass. Mom and

Dad tried to keep this life from touching me, but it still managed to wrap its dirty fingers around me and drag me down to the depths of Hell.

Satriano's man, Emilio, opens the door and extends a hand to me to help me out of the limo and onto the sidewalk. A light drizzle starts to fall, and I scan up and down the sidewalk for any sign of Isaac or anyone else who might be able to stop this.

Please...

An unvoiced and unheard plea to no one.

The entire area around us is quiet, almost as if everyone can sense something very bad is about to go down inside this quaint, old building, and they don't want to be anywhere near it when it does.

I take a step toward the church, and the inscription above the double doors stops me in my tracks. *HIC DOMUS DEI EST ET PORTA COELI...*

Here is the house of God and the gate of Heaven...

More like Hell...

Emilio opens the heavy old door adorned with sunburst crosses and ushers me inside with a firm hand at my back, ensuring I'm well aware that there isn't anywhere to go, nowhere to run.

He may only be one man, but he showed exactly who he is and what he's capable of doing in Satriano's name when he tried to take Viviana.

There isn't any point in fighting this anymore.

My fate waits for me at the altar, dressed in a perfectly tailored tuxedo, an uncomfortable-looking priest standing next to him, anticipating my walk down the aisle.

The woman who got me prepared for today stands to the left of the altar, apparently meant to act as my bridesmaid or perhaps just a witness to the ceremony. She barely said a word the entire time she did my hair and makeup, and now, she only offers a sad smile because she knows.

She *knows* I don't want to be doing this, but she won't say a word or do anything to stop it.

Why would she?

Why would anyone?

The priest has to know with the way he looks at me with such concern and casts furtive glances toward Satriano.

Everyone here knows this is a sham, but it will happen all the same.

Emilio offers me his arm with a smile, as if escorting me down the aisle to marry a man I despise is a joyous duty and not akin to holding a gun to my head.

Each step I take, my legs quiver more, until halfway down the short row of pews, they begin to shake so badly they feel like they'll give out from under me.

Keep it together.

If I don't, something much worse than what's about to happen here is going to take place, and I can't risk that.

I *won't* risk that.

Isaac said he would protect Viviana and me at any cost, but it's my time to pay that price. I have to give up Viviana and him. It's the only option.

I could never subject her to this kind of life, and I could never take her from Isaac. It's time for him to have her, to love her the way I know he can, and protect her so this world doesn't touch her. It's the least I can do for her and for him—to ensure they're both safe.

The look the man at the altar is giving me assures me I won't be.

His reputation is well-earned, and I'm turning myself over to him. If I fight him for even a moment, it could hurt everyone else. So, I'll give in, let him do with me what he will.

Right now, that means fighting every fiber of my being that's telling me to break out of Emilio's hold and run back down the aisle, out onto the street, and beg for help.

Instead, I take step after determined step until I'm finally standing in front of him, before the priest and God, and the man who will be my husband...the wrong man.

The tears continue to fall, but I reach up and swipe them away.

I don't want him to see me break. I don't want him to know how this is utterly destroying me. I can't let him see what it's doing to me because he will exploit it. He will take every sign of weakness, anything he can use to his advantage.

If I'm going to have to spend my life with this man, he's only going to see one side of me—the one that *doesn't* break.

Satriano steps forward and pulls my hands into his. "You look stunning, *carina*." He reaches up and brushes a finger across the low V-neck showing my breasts. "A vision of virginity in white." With a grin, he leans forward slightly and eyes the priest. "But we both know you're no virgin."

I cringe as he leans away, desperate to pull my hand out of his, but I leave it there, waiting for this all to be over. Maybe once it's done, once it's all legal, once he takes me back to wherever it is we're going, maybe I can start trying to figure out a way to live with it, with my new reality.

The priest raises his hand. "Are we prepared to proceed?"

Satriano turns to him. "Yes, *Padre*. We are."

The priest gives me an uncomfortable look that tells me he doesn't want to be here doing this any more than I do and clears his throat. "We are gathered here today to join Leonardo Satriano and Giacomina Jackson-Marconi in holy matrimony, under the eyes of God and in this holy space."

Satriano waves his hand. "Let's just cut to the chase, *Padre*." He spreads his hand wide to the empty church. "We don't have to put on a show for anyone."

Our officiant winces and nods. "Leonardo, do you take this woman to be your lawfully wedded wife, to have and to hold, to cherish in sickness and in health, 'til death do you part?"

"I do."

"And do you, Giacomina, take this man to be your lawfully wedded husband, to have and to hold, to cherish in sickness and in health, 'til death do you part?"

I try to speak, but nothing comes out, the words lodged in my throat. My gaze darts between Satriano and the priest. "I-I-I d-d-do."

"Then, by the power vested in me, by his Holy Father and the state of Louisiana, I now—"

The double doors at the rear of the church open before he can utter another word, and bullets fly toward the altar.

One strikes Satriano in the arm, and he dives on top of me, knocking me backward, down against the marble floor. My head falls back and hits it with a sharp crack, sending stars dancing across my eyes and pain radiating through me.

Bullets tear into the wooden pew across from us, where Satriano's man, Emilio, returns fire.

Who is it? What the hell is going on?

Satriano pushes up off me and peers over the top of the pew. His lips curl into a sinister snarl. He grips my upper arm painfully and drags me across the floor as I kick and scream and try to pull out of his hold. "They think they can try to stop this. They don't know who the fuck they're dealing with."

He pulls out a gun and returns fire, dragging me toward a side door, past the cowering woman who helped me dress for this charade. Bullets ricochet near him, and he kicks the door with his foot.

The smell of the rain that had just started to fall and the cooler air slams into me as he forces me out the side entrance, and a deafening, close shot rings out.

ISAAC

MY WELL-PLACED shot hits Satriano's shoulder, and his gun falls from his hand onto the cobblestone path. He cries out and lunges for it, still dragging Jack behind him, blood trickling down his arm from being hit inside.

Jack's gaze meets mine, and she kicks him in the back and jerks out of his hold. The second she's free and jumps away from him, I unload four more shots into his chest. He crumples to the ground, coughing and sputtering up blood. His body twitches as he tries to press his hand over one of the wounds.

I race over to him as he reaches out his good hand for the weapon only a foot away, but I press my boot onto his palm, crushing it under my weight as I stare down at the man who both brought Jack back to me and was about to take her away again.

"You really thought you could get away with it, you piece of shit?"

I grind my boot down on his hand, and he cries out as additional shots sound behind me in the church. Jack sits only a few feet away on the ground, her chest heaving, tears streaming down her face, and blood splattered across the once-white dress.

"I guess no one warned you, Satriano. You never fuck with the Hawkes."

I raise the gun and fire a single shot through the center of his forehead.

He sags completely—finally, no longer a threat. But staring down at his lifeless body doesn't ease my pain.

Only one thing will.

I lift my foot from his hand and turn toward Jack.

She stares blankly ahead, her eyes unfocused, body rigid.

Fuck.

All the stress...

Almost losing Vivi...

Being taken by Satriano's man...

Forced into this wedding...

The gunfire...

It's triggered another seizure.

I rush to her and drop to my knees against the hard ground, ignoring the jolt of pain it sends through my legs. "Jack..."

She grabs my arm and shakes her head, her body tense and her eyes still locked on nothing—unfocused. "I-I...it-it's okay. Focal...focal...seizure..."

Oh, thank God...

I scoop her into my arms, and after a few agonizing moments, she throws hers around my neck, sobbing, tightening her grip on me, and muttering something I can't quite make out.

It could have been so much worse.

All of this could have ended so badly.

If we hadn't found her in time...

If she had another bad seizure...

I drag my head back and take her face between my palms, kissing her deeply to stop her from going completely into shock. It silences her long enough for her body to stop trembling slightly. I pull my lips away and her tear-soaked eyes finally focus on me.

"You're okay, Jack."

"Viviana..." Jack blinks rapidly a few times, like she's still trying to process everything and work through the lingering effects of the focal seizure. "She's okay?"

I nod. "She's with Astrid."

"Oh, thank God."

She throws her arm around me again and hugs me tighter than I ever have been before, like she's terrified that if she lets up even slightly, I might float away into the darkening sky.

The rain starts to fall harder, but we don't budge as she continues to sob against me.

"You shouldn't have come, Isaac. You could have gotten hurt."

"There was no way in fucking hell I was letting you marry that bastard. I'd rather die than let that happen."

She pulls back slightly. "How did you find us?"

I offer her a half grin. "We have a lot of friends in town. We blocked the airports so he couldn't leave with you. But I knew he'd try to get this bogus ceremony done, and done legally, so that he'd have more to hold against your parents. I called some friends in the clerk's office until I found the one who issued the marriage license to him."

"But how did you find the church?"

I lean in and press my forehead against hers. "We know the priest. He actually married my parents. We started calling the churches—"

"Oh, my God."

"If we had been five minutes later..."

"No"—she shakes her head and kisses me frantically—"don't think that way."

Movement behind me makes me turn toward the church, and Cutter walks through the door, his sunglasses in place despite the dark, dreary day.

"Dad?" Jack frees herself from my hold and races to her father, practically throwing herself at him.

He catches her and holds her to him, burying his face against her neck. "I'm so sorry, *tesoro*, that any of this happened."

"How are you here? When did you—"

He pulls back as I climb to my feet and join them. "After I failed to take out Satriano in Italy, I went to regroup with your mother, and then, we learned Satriano was here. We got back stateside as quickly as we could. We landed only twenty minutes after Satriano took you."

"Mom's here?"

He gives a quick nod and tips his head backward. "Inside."

She rushes in and leaves me alone with Cutter, who pulls off his glasses and levels me with his one blue eye and dead white one. "Now that my girls are safe, I think you and I need to have a chat."

I knew it was coming, that I put it off as long as I could. With

Jack missing, I was able to postpone the difficult conversation we needed to have when he first arrived in town, but now it's time for all of our skeletons to be laid out. "Viviana—"

"Is your daughter." He scowls. "I know."

"What?"

He considers me for a moment. "I've known the Hawkes for a long time, Isaac. She was always a beautiful child, striking blue eyes and dark features. But I never put two and two together. There was no reason to think you ever met Mina...until we landed here, until I saw the way she reacted to you in your father's office."

"You knew before you even left?"

He gives me a sharp nod. "If anything, it made me more confident about leaving them here, that they were in the right place with the people who would protect them."

Holy shit.

"I didn't know about her, who Jack really was. If I had, I would've..."

Done anything...

His jaw tightens. "I figured as much. The Hawkes don't seem like the type to abandon their children or the women they care about." He motions back into the church. "If today's events are any indication..."

"I'd do anything for them, Cutter. I would've burned down this entire city if I had to."

"You and me both." He starts to walk back into the church, but I grab his arm. He slowly lowers his gaze to look at it, then looks back up at me.

I've barely survived the last few days, and what I'm about to do might be signing my own death warrant. Still, I have to say it.

"They're not going back to Chicago with you. I can't lose them again."

His jaw hardens. "That's not your decision to make. It's hers."

We step into the church and find Jack seated next to Valentina Marconi in one of the pews, arms wrapped around her, sobbing.

"After all of this"—Cutter glances my way—"it might be better if we take her somewhere for a while."

The thought of that happening feels like knives stabbing into my gut.

"But this isn't the time or place to argue about it. She's safe for the moment, and so is Viviana."

Gabe, Dad, Saint, and Bishop move around the church, each of them on their phones making the calls necessary to get this cleaned up before the police find out what went down.

I may have gotten away with what happened last night because I defended my own life, but the cold-blooded murder of a man like Satriano, and in a church, no less, isn't something that's going to slide.

Cutter must sense my unease because he rests a hand on my shoulder. "If there's any blowback from this, let it come to her mother and me. We did it. We leave the Hawkes out of it. Do you understand?"

I give him a sharp nod. "I do, but they're my family, too. I can't let you take all that heat."

"Hopefully, there won't be much. Satriano wasn't exactly well-loved by his men. Most despised him." He looks over at the body of Emilio lying against the altar. "With his right hand gone and a few we took out in Italy, I'm not sure what was left of his core group. Anyone who remains is going to need time to rebuild. We have eyes and ears on everything over there, so we'll be ready if anyone comes again."

"So will I."

Jack finally pulls away from her mother and swipes at her tears. Cutter and I approach, and Valentina climbs to her feet, looking every bit the powerful donne she is—her long dark hair cascading over her shoulders and a perfectly pressed suit complemented by her spiked heels.

She steps forward and offers me her hand. "Isaac, welcome to the family."

I slip my hand into hers and shake it, and she pulls me toward her and leans in, pushing up on her tiptoes to reach my ear.

"But if you ever hurt my girls, I will make what we did here today look like child's play. Do you understand me?"

I swallow thickly and nod as I pull back and smile at her. "We're in complete agreement there."

She smiles and pats me on the arm. "That's good news. Now..." She scans the church. "I'm going to go light a few prayer candles, then I want to go see my *bambina*."

That's all I want, too.

To hold my girls.

To feel them and know they're okay.

I make my way over to Jack and pull her up from the pew, tugging her against me again. "Let's go home."

She nods and lets me scoop her up and carry her out of the church. It isn't the way I anticipated holding her in a wedding dress. Definitely not one splattered with blood and not one she wore for another man. But there's time to fix that. It just won't be today.

It didn't slip my notice that she didn't question what I meant when I said *home*.

We still haven't finalized any of those plans, haven't figured out how any of this is going to work, but with her parents behind me and Hawkes around us, we won't have much time to figure it out.

Everyone is going to want answers.

And I need them, too.

JACK

Gunfire rings in my ears, a memory of the not-so-distant past turning into a present nightmare, and I jerk awake in the dark room, reaching out across the bed for Viviana and Isaac while my heart thunders in my chest.

All I find are still-warm sheets against my palm.

I push myself all the way up and start to slip out of bed when the door opens. Isaac sneaks in, closing it behind him softly.

"Where were you? Where's Viviana?"

He jerks toward me, eyes narrowed on me. "I thought you were asleep?"

"I just woke up…"

There isn't any point in telling him about the nightmare. The way he's looking at me, he can already tell something's wrong.

His concerned gaze locks on mine as he approaches the bed. "Are you okay?"

Such a loaded question.

Am I okay?

The last few weeks have been a whirlwind filled with secrets, revelations, pain, and confusion. But looking at Isaac, I can't ignore all the good things, too.

I found him. *We* found him.

Viviana has her father, and I have "Nolan" after years of wondering about the man who has never left my mind.

He slides in next to me, burying his face against my chest and tugging me up to him. I relax against his warm skin and release a sigh, true contentment filling me and allowing me to let go of the lingering bad vibes and haunting memories from my nightmare, even though my heart doesn't want to stop hammering against my ribcage.

"Where is Vivi?"

Isaac slowly drags his fingertips along my arm. "She woke up and wanted to sleep with Grandma and Grandpa, so I brought her down to the guest room so she could be with them."

"They're okay with her staying there?"

He snorts and nods, brushing his lips to my forehead. "They're more than okay with it."

I release a heavy breath. "Okay..."

Whatever she needs to be comfortable, to feel safe.

She can have anything she wants right now. There will be time for limiting Isaac's desire to give in to her constantly. With all the changes and trauma she's endured the last few days, I wouldn't deny her anything, either.

He tilts my chin up and locks his gaze on mine. "Are you sure you're okay? Your heart is racing."

I shake my head, running my fingers through his hair. "I don't know. Should I not be? Is there something wrong with me that I'm not still a blubbering mess?"

Isaac brushes his thumb across my bottom lip. "What happened was pretty traumatic. It would be for anyone. But there's nothing wrong with you, Jack. Far from it. You're the most incredible, strong woman I've ever met. What you did..."

Darkness clouds his eyes, like a tempest passing over

normally smooth waters, and he stares at me, looking deep into my soul, past all the walls I've tried to keep up and all the reasons I hold on to that this won't work.

"It was stupid and reckless..." Anger tightens his jaw, but it vanishes just as quickly. "And it was also the bravest thing I've ever seen."

"I couldn't let them take her."

He shakes his head, squeezing my chin harder. "You really think I would have allowed that to happen? I don't care if I had to kill all three of them with my bare hands while riddled with fucking bullets...I would have figured out a way to stop them before they took Vivi."

"I know...that's why I had to go. I couldn't let you get hurt. I couldn't bear the thought of anything happening to you because you were trying to protect us."

"Jesus, Jack..." He drags me up across him and kisses me softly, his lips moving over mine almost reverently, like he's worshipping at an altar and saying a prayer. "Don't ever do anything like that again. If anything had happened to you..." He squeezes his eyes closed and inhales a heavy breath. "I couldn't lose you again. I can't. I won't survive it."

I'm not sure I could survive losing him, either.

But so much has happened.

So many things that could keep us apart.

"Are you sure everything is okay?" I shake my head, fighting the tears threatening to fall. "The police are going to come looking for you again. I couldn't watch you get arrested and go to prison for protecting us—"

He seizes my face in his palms. "I'm not going anywhere. We got everything cleaned up at the church. Like I said, we know Father Martino personally, and he's not going to be reporting anything to anyone. We canvased the neighborhood, and it appears no one was out on the street close enough to hear the gunfire. Those old church walls muffle quite a bit."

"What about all the damage done inside?"

"It's going to be closed for a while for"—he makes air quotes —"*renovations*, and we'll pay for anything that needs to be fixed. It'll be good as new."

"Will it, though? Will you?" I squeeze my eyes closed. "You killed people in the house of God."

He captures my face in his warm hands again, tipping it up to him. "And what was I supposed to do? Let that bastard force you into marrying him? Let him touch you? Let him turn you into a pawn in his game with your mother?"

I shake my head. "No, I get it. I know why you had to do it. I just..."

"I know, Jack."

He presses his lips to mine softly, and I lean into it, absorbing him and the feeling of peaceful contentment that settles over me every time we're like this together. Almost as if he can sense what I need, he rolls me onto my back and shifts his body over mine, the weight of it pressing me down into the mattress and cocooning me in his strength.

Still, the closeness can't dispel the unease twisting me up inside. "Did my parents say anything to you about what's going to happen tomorrow?"

Isaac winces slightly and drops his head down against my chest. "Your dad wants to take you somewhere." He shrugs. "I don't know where. Away until things cool down a bit."

"And then?"

"I don't know." He lifts his head and shakes it. "I assume he'll want you back in Chicago."

That's a pretty safe assumption, given everything.

I press my palm against his stubbled cheek, grazing my fingers over the stitched cut above his eye. "You won't move there, though, right?"

He shakes his head. "I can't. You've seen what it's like here, everything constantly going on with the businesses and the family. We have people who want us to fail, people who want to ride on our coattails and steal what we have made. And now..." His gaze hardens slightly. "We may have made a new enemy if there's anyone in Satriano's crew who comes looking for him."

I shudder and close my eyes. "I don't even want to think about that."

Isaac shifts up and presses his lips to mine again, his hand trailing over my exposed thigh. "Then let me help you forget."

Groaning, I shift my body against his, instantly heated at the promise of his words.

It feels wrong to want this, to want *him* after everything that happened today, but the adrenaline still coursing through my veins only makes me want it more, makes me want *him* more.

I wrap my left leg around his hip and press my heel into his ass, urging him closer. His hard cock nestles between us, and he pulls away, gasping slightly.

"You're sure?"

Nodding, I drag his face back down to mine, brushing my lips against his. "Yes, Isaac. I need this. I need you."

He issues a low, approving growl. "Good, because I need to be inside you almost as much as I need to breathe right now."

Those words send a flutter of butterflies through my stomach, and I arch into his touch as his hand slips between my legs to cup me there.

His lips feather over my neck. "Every time we're together like this, Jack, it's like that first night—when I just fucking knew. When I knew I had to have you. When I knew I had to have you *forever*. When I knew one night wasn't enough, that two weren't. A lifetime won't be."

I crane my neck back, granting him better access as he kisses his way up to my ear and sucks the lobe between his teeth.

"I need this, Jack. I need you...always."

"*Anche io ho bisognio di te, Isaac. Stai a casa.*"

He freezes for a second, then a small grin plays at the corner of his lips as he slips my thong to the side and glides a finger into me.

"Oh, God." I clench around him, my body begging for more. "Please..."

He groans in my ear. "Already wet for me." His warm breath flutters against my heated skin. "You know, I dream about what you taste like. About how your cunt feels around my cock. How your nails feel scoring down my back." He presses his lips to that spot just behind my ear. "The little noises you make when I fuck you echo in my mind twenty-four hours a day. Even after I've come inside you, I still dream about doing it again and again."

His words only heighten my need and build the tension in my primed body. "Please." I dig my nails into his bare shoulders as he slowly drags his finger in and out of me, curling it slightly to hit that perfect spot. I rock my head from side to side. "No, not tonight. I can't handle it if you—"

He captures my words with a kiss and shifts his hand to grind his palm against my clit. "How about something else, baby? How about I give you something that will make what I did to you in that hotel and on the steps seem like nothing?"

Nothing?

Making me come like a rushing waterfall can never be nothing, and I don't know if I can handle anything that intense right now.

"Jack, let me make you come harder than you ever have. Let me destroy what you thought pleasure felt like."

I nod frantically, thrashing against his ministrations, unable to fight the need and allowing it to overcome my fear. "Okay."

Isaac knows how to work my body, how to ensure I get everything I need even when I don't know I need it. And right now, I need to just *feel*. I need to do exactly what he told me to that weekend we spent together—to let go of all the shit, of all the turmoil, just *be* and enjoy what he can offer me.

He smiles against my lips and pulls back, shifting onto his

heels as he continues to work me over with his fingers, gliding his thumb across my clit and rolling it expertly there.

"Fuck." I force my eyes open and see he's pushed down the waistband of his silk pajama pants to free his cock and strokes it with his left hand as he works me over. "What are you going to do?"

A slow grin spreads across his face, and he pulls his hand from inside me and smacks my thigh. "On your stomach."

Oh, God...

My entire body quivers as he moves back and pulls off his pants, then climbs back onto the bed and drags my thong down and off my body, tossing it onto the floor. His fingers toy at the hem of his T-shirt I slept in, and he drags it up and off, letting it fall to the floor with his pants.

Isaac leans over me, pressing his hard, lean muscle against me, his warm breath fluttering in my ear. He takes his palm and tilts my head to the side until our eyes meet. "You know I would never hurt you, right?"

I give a sharp nod. "Yes."

"Good." He slips his left hand between my legs, and his finger is back into my pussy, slowly pumping in and out, then he glides the moisture up and around my ass.

I jerk away from the touch, clenching my cheeks around his hand, and he grins against my cheek.

"Trust me, Jack. I won't hurt you. Relax."

Relax.

It feels like I haven't been able to relax for years. Constantly fighting—against my life, against Mom and Dad, against the enemies always lurking. Constantly wanting—freedom and the man whose name I didn't even know. Constantly dreaming—for things I knew I could never have.

But now I'm here in Isaac's bed, in his arms, finally *safe*.

I release a heavy breath, desperately trying to let go of everything I've been holding in, all the pain and anguish and longing, and watch him out of the corner of my eye with my face against the pillow and my chest pressed to the mattress.

He grinds his hard cock between my thighs, and his fingers work their magic between my legs, slowly probing the tip of one into the place no man has gone before.

Instantly, I clench around him, but he kisses his way to my ear and whispers, "Relax. Let go of everything, all the pain of the past and everything that's happened. Let go."

I thought I had, but it's still there, on the periphery, trying to break in and seize my ability to enjoy this.

Relax.

Let go of everything...

I sink into his words, letting myself become jello on the mattress, and he finally slips his finger inside me a little farther. Instinctively, I squeeze around him, and he groans.

"You do that around my cock, Jack, and I'm going to come in three fucking seconds."

"Good," I whisper the word, but his deep chuckle lets me know he heard me as he shifts back off me and reaches for the nightstand.

He tugs open a drawer and pulls out something. A second later, the cool liquid splashes against my ass, and I jerk away from it. But he slowly begins working it in, allowing his finger to slide even deeper into my ass.

Fuck.

I've heard people who swear this feels incredible, that it's nothing like anyone says it is, but I didn't believe them.

Until now.

Now that Isaac is here, touching me like this, my head's spinning. Heat spreads through my entire body, searing across my skin, out through my limbs. Everywhere.

He pulls his finger from inside me and brushes the smooth head of his cock there. "I promise this will feel good, Jack. Unlike anything you've ever experienced."

Everything with Isaac has been like nothing I've ever experienced.

The joy.

The pain.

The need.

He grips my hip and lifts me up and back, then uses his knees to push my legs out farther, spreading me open to him.

His lips press between my shoulder blades, and he kisses his way down my spine, then realigns himself and nudges the head of his cock against where he wants to be.

"*Ho aspettato per tanto tempo per sentierti dire que mi vuoi. Dimi que sono la tua casa.*"

ISAAC

JACK STIFFENS UNDER ME, her entire body going still as she cranes her neck to lock her gaze with mine again. "What did you just say?"

"I said, *ho aspettato per tanto tempo per sentierti dire que mi vuoi. Dimi que sono la tua casa.*" I kiss her cheek. "I've waited a long time for you to admit you need me. To tell me *I* am your home."

Her amber eyes widen. "You speak Italian?"

I grin at her and lean down, brushing my lips across hers. "I sure do, Jack. Luca and my Nana taught me. I understood every single word you've muttered under your breath at me whenever we've been like this. The things you're too afraid to say to me in English." I prod her with the head of my cock. "And I know what you just said to me—that this is your home now, that *I* am." I lean down and feather my lips against her ear. "And you are mine, *mia amata.*"

She always was—from the moment our eyes met in that bar five years ago.

Time and thousands of miles may have separated us, but she was always there. Haunting me with her beautiful eyes, her passionate touch, the way she seemed to understand me then and see exactly who I was when I wasn't even sure myself.

Jack has been my dream woman my entire life, even before I knew her. People don't normally find that. Not everyone gets *this*.

And I won't let it go.

Ever.

"Did you hear me, *mia amata*. You're *mine*."

Jack issues a little mewl, and I slip inside her slowly, gritting my teeth against the tight resistance her body offers, taking the one thing no one else ever has.

Staking my claim.

Sweet fuck.

She clamps down on the head of my cock, and instantly, my balls seize up, wanting to unload in her. That warm tingle starts at the base of my spine, and I clench my jaw and suck in several long, slow breaths, trying to wrangle my control.

When it comes to Jack, I never seem to have any.

I certainly didn't that weekend.

It was supposed to be one night. A quick, hot fuck with a beautiful woman to celebrate graduation before I came home. It wasn't supposed to mean anything.

How quickly that changed...

This woman owned my soul the moment I got inside her.

She always will.

I bend to lay my body fully against hers, kissing across her shoulders and along her neck to her ear, savoring the taste of her warm skin. "You do that again, and I'm coming, Jack. And I'm not ready for this to be over—not for me and certainly not for you."

This is the moment to give her everything—all of me while I take all of her.

I need her to come harder than she ever has in her life, need her to experience what it's like to have an out-of-body experience, to let go *completely* of everything that holds her back.

The things she clings to no matter how hard she might fight them.

Animosity toward her parents...

Her desire for a life away from who she is...

Guilt over how she left me that day five years ago...

Pain of knowing that decision kept my daughter from me for so long...

All these things weigh down on her like a ten-thousand-pound weight sitting on her shoulders.

And I need her to forget.

I need her to just *be* so that when we wake in the morning, she'll know what she has to do, that she and Viviana are part of me, that we're a family, that they're Hawkes now, and that we belong together.

Because we do.

We always have.

I ease into her more, slowly going deeper and deeper as she groans and clutches at the sheets. Each tiny movement I make earns me a strangled groan or mewl. I reach under her with my right hand and find her clit, slowly rolling my fingers across it as I push even more.

"Oh, God..." Her eyes roll up, her arousal coating my fingers.

"Relax, *mia amata*." I pull back slightly and slide back in, a little deeper this time. "This is mine." Again. "*You* are mine."

I finally push into her all the way, and her mouth falls open on a silent gasp as I roll my fingers across her clit even faster. Her body vibrates against mine, her knees barely holding her up. I slowly withdraw my cock, then ease into her again, starting an impossibly slow rhythm that makes me grit my teeth to prevent me from coming immediately.

Watching Jack come is like seeing a beautiful masterpiece

painted in real time, and I can already feel it building in her, her body tensing, coiling, getting ready to explode.

I thrust two fingers into her cunt and thumb her clit as I continue to slide in and out of her. She issues a low, long groan, her hips rolling to meet mine.

Fuck, she's beautiful like this...

Completely immersed in the moment...

Completely at my mercy...

I have to fight every fiber of my being that begs me to drive into her hard, but that isn't what this is about. It's about what *she* needs, what she deserves more than anything.

Release.

And she's so close that my hand at her core and cock in her ass are the only things keeping her upright.

Her breaths come out in hot, heavy pants, like she's gasping for air while grasping for her control over everything she has none over.

"Let go, *mia amata*. Let go!"

She finally comes, her entire body stilling before it twitches and undulates under me, her hips slamming back into mine as I continue to push into her and drag her orgasm out with my fingers. Her cunt clasps around them, a rush of her own release pouring out while she squeezes my cock with her ass. It's enough to make me lose control finally, and I empty myself into her in hot spurts before I collapse on top of her and roll to the side, dragging her with me.

I pant against the back of her neck, and her chest heaves in her attempt to catch her breath. My heart slams against my ribs, the rapid tattoo matching the frantic way I always feel around her.

This is it.

What I always wanted and never had with anyone else.

A desperate, frenzied need for only her.

The feeling that this woman alone is *everything*.

This is *it.*

She is *it.*

I graze my lips across the damp skin on her neck, kissing and licking and enjoying the feel of her in my arms, her body cocooning my cock.

Silence settles around us, only our labored breathing interrupting the perfect moment. I could lie like this forever, with Jack in my arms, doing absolutely nothing but feeling her body against mine, and I would be completely content with life.

I reach up and grab her chin, nudging it sideways toward me until I can see her face. "Are you okay?"

She lets out a heavy breath and nods. "I don't think *okay* covers it."

Grinning, I kiss her cheek, then let her head back down onto the pillow. She groans and snuggles into it, and I press my lips to her shoulder and squeeze her probably too tightly.

"Were you ever going to tell me you speak Italian?"

I chuckle in the darkness and shake my head. "I hadn't planned on it. It was much funnier listening to you without you knowing I could understand every word."

"Kind of deceptive."

"So was you saying things in Italian so I wouldn't understand you."

"True."

I reach up and tweak her nipple, making her jerk. "You can't pull one over on me, Jack."

"Sorry, Counselor. I forget how easily you can see through bullshit."

I grin against her skin. "I do, which is how I know everything going on in your head is bullshit."

Jack stills. "What do you mean?"

The last thing I want to do is ruin this moment, but this conversation has been a long time coming, and after almost losing her today, I'm not about to go another second without settling the things we need to.

"I saw your sketchbook, Jack."

She stiffens. "You did?"

I nuzzle the back of her neck. "I did. And I saw the sketch you did of me...that morning."

"That morning fucking broke me, Isaac." She shakes her head, releasing a heavy breath. "I can't imagine what it did to you."

"It did break me, and watching you do it again today destroyed me. But having you here like this, knowing you're safe and protected, and *mine*, has put me back together. You and Viviana are all I ever need. And I'll do anything, give you anything, to make you happy. This is it for me, Jack. You are." I turn her head back toward me again. "You wouldn't have drawn that. You wouldn't have thought about me every time you touched yourself. You wouldn't have dreamed about me if you didn't feel exactly the same way I did that weekend—and now."

Tears shimmer in her eyes. "We barely know each other, Isaac."

"We know enough."

"What about my parents? Chicago? Vivi's entire life is there, everything she's ever known."

"We were both terrified of what your parents were going to say, of what they were going to do when they found out Viviana was my daughter, but they seemed almost happy about it. I've proven to them that I can protect you, that I can keep you safe, that the Hawkes will."

Her amber eyes glint in the moonlight.

"You're a Hawke now. You've been one since the moment I saw you in that bar five fucking years ago. You were mine then, and you're mine now. And you're not leaving New Orleans. We can visit your parents, and they can come down here, but this is where you two belong, and you all know it. Vivi's life may have started in Chicago, but it's here now."

For a brief moment, Jack watches me like she isn't sure she agrees with my words. A rock settles in my stomach, wondering if I've misjudged all of this, gotten it all wrong.

She reaches back and runs her palm along my cheek. The corner of her lip twitches, and she finally smiles. "I know. And after today, after almost losing you for good, I could never walk away from you again." Her bottom lip trembles, and a tiny sob slips out. "I-I did what I had to, to protect Vivi and you, but I never would have survived that. I couldn't have."

"I know, Jack." I press my lips to hers and try to absorb some of her pain. "And I'm so fucking sorry it came down to that. You never should have been put in that position. It won't happen again. I promise—"

"Don't." She shakes her head. "Don't promise there won't be more threats. That our lives won't always be tangled with the Marconis. I can't control who my parents are any more than you can, and I can't run from it. I think all *this* has proven that hiding never works. Even if we left here, even if we changed our names and tried to find some new city, a place where no one knew who we were, we would always be watching, always be waiting, always be a potential target." She shrugs slightly. "Secrets always come out, right? I never thought I would see Nolan again, never thought Vivi would ever have her father, but life found a way. So don't promise me anything but that you'll always be here."

The harsh reality of her words grates at my heart. She's right. No one will ever be able to promise her something can't happen in the future, that another enemy won't threaten her or Vivi simply because she's a Marconi. Not any more than I can always protect all the Hawkes from those who would see us fail.

All I can do is try.

"Fuck, Jack. Of course, I will. I'm not going anywhere."

She gives me a sad smile. "Good. Me either."

"And Vivi isn't allowed to leave the condo again until she's at least thirty..."

Jack barks out a laugh, the sound light and true. "You know you can't always control everything, right?"

I growl. "I can fucking try. She's my daughter—"

"And you can't always give her what she wants, either." Jack offers a reproachful look. "She has to learn she can't have everything."

This seems like a debate we'll be having for the rest of our lives.

Jack got four long years with Vivi, and I have to make up for all the lost time any way I can.

"But you *can* have everything, both of you. I'll give it to you."

"You're going to spoil her rotten."

I kiss her lips deeply, sliding my tongue along hers and groaning into her mouth. "I'm going to spoil *both* of you rotten. It's my new full-time job. Fuck Hawke Law. This is now what I live for."

Whatever this is between Jack and me...

Fate.

Serendipity.

Whatever you want to call it...

We were meant to meet that night, and we were meant to be brought back together like this. The years of pain and separation were always so this could happen exactly how it did, exactly the way it was supposed to so that we can be in this moment and appreciate it.

I could dwell on all the time I missed with Jack and Vivi, let myself wallow in the guilt of it all, but that would cloud the time we do have together. And we now have all the time in the world.

"I love you, Jack."

She reaches back and brushes her hand over my face. "I love you too, Isaac, and I believe you."

I grin at her. "Good. Because if you didn't, I wouldn't be able to let you leave this room until I'd convinced you."

Her laughter fills the quiet air. "I don't think I could survive whatever you have planned for that."

"Probably not, but we could still do it if you want to."

I grind my hips against hers again, my cock hardening again deep inside her ass. She clenches around me, and I groan into her ear.

Her giggle makes my heart skip a beat. "That sounds like a good idea to me."

"You're never leaving me again, Jack."

She shakes her head. "I wouldn't dare. Not when I know how ruthless you can be."

EPILOGUE
THREE MONTHS LATER

JACK

A light breeze blows down the street, bringing with it the smells of the water and food cooking at The Hawke's Nest just a few doors down. My stomach growls at the familiar scent of the juicy steaks that have become one of my favorites, even though I just ate.

Pope ambles over and slides into the chair next to me at one of the small tables out on the sidewalk in front of Hawke's Daily Grind, glancing over to where Isaac and Viviana play with Astrid and Kennedy at the table on the other side of the door.

He holds up a hand with a half-smirk on his face. "Now, I know I'm only a *human* doctor, so maybe I'm mistaken." He points at the girls. "But that appears to be a cat on a leash, not a dog."

I laugh and look over to Viviana just as she scoops up Fluffy and cuddles her close. Nodding, I take a sip of my water and sigh. "Yep, that's Fluffy."

The newest member of the family, who is already being

spoiled just as badly as Vivi has been the last few months. That cat has more toys than I did as a child.

"Fluffy?" He nods slowly, narrowing his bourbon eyes. "I feel like there's a story there."

I smirk at him as Isaac glances over toward us. "The story is, her father lets her have anything she wants."

Pope's forehead wrinkles. "I thought Isaac is allergic to cats?"

"He is. He's getting allergy shots now."

Because he's completely insane.

Goes to get a dog and comes back with a cat because "Vivi really wanted it."

Pope barks out a laugh and slams his palm on the table, making me jump slightly. "God, he's such a fucking pussy pushover, isn't he?"

I can't fight my grin. "When it comes to her, he definitely is."

Isaac walks over with his hands on his hips, eyes narrowed. "Why do I get the feeling you two are talking about me?"

Pope smirks. "Maybe because we were."

Isaac leans over and presses a kiss to the top of my head, then reaches down and rubs my expanding belly. "You doing okay? Is it too hot out here?"

The late spring sun beats down on us, and I tilt my face up to it. "Are you kidding? This weather's beautiful. This time of year in Chicago, there could still be a freak storm that would dump snow on us."

His lips twitch into a grin. "So...not regretting your decision to stay?"

I shake my head and stare up at him. "Not one bit."

Surprisingly.

For so long, I thought staying here with Isaac would be like moving from one prison to another. That it wouldn't change anything. That I'd still feel restricted and confined and like my life was being controlled by someone else. But it's been the freest I've ever felt.

Isaac's controlling and possessive nature might aggravate me at times, but I know his heart. I understand where it's coming from. He lost me twice, had to watch me sacrifice myself, not knowing if he would ever see me again. After all that, he has every right to be worried, but he also understands I need my space, my freedom—things I never had living under the Marconi roof.

And even if he *insists* someone is always with me when I go out, these people have become my family, too, my *friends*. It isn't like dragging one of Dad's goons along.

I could never regret this life.

Being with Isaac.

Watching him bond with Viviana.

Having the family I never thought could exist.

Pope watches Viviana play with Fluffy and Astrid. "So, Jack tells me you have a cat."

Isaac scowls and takes the seat next to me and across from Pope. "I tried to get a dog, but—"

Pope chuckles. "But the princess always gets what she wants, right?"

Isaac gives Pope a knowing grin. "You'll understand when you have kids."

His "cousin" barks out a laugh and pushes away from the table, holding up his hands in surrender. "Who said I want kids? I'm too busy for that, even if I did."

Isaac motions toward the inside of the café where the rest of the family gathers. "Tell that to my mom. She did medical school while she was pregnant with me and while I was a newborn, and all of her internship and specialty training while I was a toddler and young child."

Pope grips the back of the chair. "Your mom is kind of Wonder Woman. Also, she had your dad to help."

One of Isaac's dark brows rises. "Well, if you have a child, I would presume there would be a woman to help you."

"Again, no kids on the agenda for me."

Isaac smirks and rolls his eyes at Pope's easy dismissal. "Whatever."

With his dashing good looks, I have no doubt Pope likely has a line of women a mile long just waiting for a date with him, and he's amazing with Vivi—a real natural despite his apparent rejection of fatherhood.

I motion to Isaac. "He probably thought the same thing until I showed up with Vivi."

Isaac swats my shoulder playfully, and Pope ambles back into the café with a peek back at Vivi, her cat, and his cousins.

I let out a heavy sigh and watch everyone through the glass. "It seems like we picked the perfect day to make the announcement."

He reaches over and rests his hand on my stomach again. "Well, you're starting to show. If we hadn't said something, they would've figured it out soon enough."

True.

It would have been impossible to hide it much longer.

I wave at his mom, who smiles at me through the glass. "I'm pretty sure your mom knew already."

"Probably."

"And I think Atlas did, too. He walked in on me puking in the kitchen once while I was trying to cook dinner."

Isaac snorts and shakes his head. "I told you, it's my job to help you with that."

"Oh, he didn't help." I shake my head. "He just hightailed it out of there as quickly as he could, as if he walked in on something that terrified the fuck out of him."

"I'm sure it did."

Leaning back in his chair, Isaac rests his head in his hands and inhales deeply, scanning the street up and down. He may appear relaxed to anyone else, but the tension in his shoulder and jaw screams the reality—he will *never* relax.

He will always be watching, waiting for anything that might come along that could harm us, always ready to defend us or anyone else in the family who might be a target.

I follow his line of vision to the open business space almost directly across the street. "You guys own most of the street, don't you?"

He nods. "Yeah, Luca and Byron bought those six lots." He points across the street to the first six. "And my dad owns the ones on this side with Storm down to the end of the block."

"Why is that one empty? It seems like an ideal location for something."

I'd always wondered why no one ever did anything with it. It would make a great art gallery space...

Isaac releases a sigh. "Luca and Byron gave it to Jude so he could open a bookstore and operate it while he lived upstairs..."

Movement in one of the windows above the open, empty space catches my eye, and Luca appears. He sees us watching and gives me a quick wave.

I wave back. "Do you think Jude's going to come down? Everyone else is here."

"Doubtful." Isaac returns his attention to me. "He hasn't come to a family event in so long that I'm starting to forget what he looks like."

No shit.

I haven't even met him, only waved when I've been at the café and happened to see him in the window. The annoyance in his voice tugs at my heart. "Allie said he's just really busy trying to finish his book."

"He's always busy trying to finish a book. He never stops writing and always uses it as an excuse to avoid all of us and do nothing with the supposed bookstore he wanted to open so badly."

I shrug. "Maybe it's true. You know how creative people can

be. It might be hard for him to walk away from it when he is in the moment."

Isaac leans in and brushes his lips against my ear. "Kind of like it's hard to leave the bed when I'm in there with you, *mia amata*."

Heat floods my core, and I shift slightly on the chair to relieve the pressure there. "Yeah, kind of like that." I rub my stomach. "It's what got us Viviana and this little nugget."

ISAAC

SITTING IN THE WARM SUN, the smells of the café, the sounds of the Hawke family laughing inside, and the crisp, fresh spring air all around us, any number of eyes watching us might not be the ideal place to say something like that to Jack, but she's never been more beautiful.

Pregnancy just does something to her...

It does something to *me*.

Her skin glows, her smile more radiant, her body fuller and even more luscious.

I can't keep my hands or mouth off her.

Despite my constant anxiety over her and the baby, I can't remember a time I've ever been happier. For once, everything feels like it's exactly how it should be—like all is *right* with the world. Even Falco Enterprises and Whitaker have seemed to lay off the last few months, giving me a much-needed break from fighting on multiple fronts. Soon, we'll break ground on Hawke Hotel, and our future will be now.

It makes my spine tingle with that uneasy feeling that something is coming again.

I rub Jack's arm. "You're sure you're feeling okay."

She rolls her eyes and huffs. "Yes, I'm *fine*. You know both the neurologist and my OBGYN said I'm perfectly healthy and that the adjustment in meds means the baby is as safe as possible, too. You have to stop worrying so much."

As if that's possible.

I'd be a nervous wreck with her pregnant even without the complication of her epilepsy, but knowing we're doing everything we can to ensure they're both healthy and constantly monitoring her and the baby gives me a modicum of relief.

"Daddy! Daddy, look!"

I glance over my shoulder and find Viviana on her knees, holding Fluffy's front paws and making the poor thing dance like a circus bear. "Oh, honey, I don't think she likes that."

Vivi's little brow furrows. "Yes, she does, look."

Shockingly, the kitten seems unperturbed, and Astrid and Kennedy both laugh where they sit at the table next to Viviana on the sidewalk.

Kennedy shrugs. "I don't know. She seems to like it, Isaac."

"Do you like it when your dad makes you dance in front of the media and bend over backward to handle things for him?"

The way she complains about it sometimes, I know Savage pushes her to her limits.

She narrows her eyes on me. "Good point." Kennedy turns her attention to Vivi. "Let's not harass the cat, kiddo."

Astrid rolls her eyes and waves me off. "Oh, go fawn over your pregnant girlfriend some more."

I grin at her. "Thank you. I will."

That's my absolute favorite activity. It's probably excessive, really, but I can't stand having her more than a few feet away from me. She has to practically shove me out the door to work every day. But it's probably what has ensured our relationship hasn't failed. If I were with her twenty-four-seven, she's already told me it would be suffocating.

I turn back to Jack and find her staring through the windows at the rest of the family, a faraway look in her eyes. "You, okay?"

She nods. "Yeah." She offers a sad smile. "I guess I just kind of miss my parents."

"We did invite them."

"Yeah, I know. But things are happening that they're not telling me."

I reach out and pull her hands into mine, squeezing them gently. "I know you don't like being kept in the dark, but sometimes, it *is* for your own good. They won't even tell *me* what's happening until they know more."

Gabe and Skye sit at a table near the front window with Atlas and Bishop, playing a heated game of Scrabble. "You think Gabe knows?"

If Cutter's going to tell anyone anything about what's happening in the fallout over the last three months, it's going to be Gabe. But he hasn't come clean with me if he does know anything.

"I'm not sure. You know if I get anything out of him, I'll share it with you."

She scowls at me. "No, you won't."

"Okay, maybe I won't, but—"

"Yeah, that's what I thought."

I bring her hands to my mouth and brush my lips over her knuckles. "But I'm just trying to keep you safe. You, and our son, and Viviana."

She pulls a hand away and rests it on her stomach, her eyes suddenly widening.

My breath catches in my chest. "What? What's wrong? Is it the baby?"

A grin spreads across her face, and she nods, grabs my hand, and tugs it down to her stomach. "He's kicking."

"What? Isn't it too early for—"

A slight thump hits against my palm.

Holy shit.

Our son moving inside her...

Tears burn my eyes, and I struggle to swallow through the emotion clogging my throat. "Oh, my God."

She reaches up and takes my face in her palm. "It's really real now, huh?"

I nod, slowly rubbing her belly as he continues to kick occasionally. "It is really real now. I'm just so happy I have a chance to be here this time."

Jack leans forward and rests her forehead against mine. "You're going to be the most amazing father to him, just like you are to Viviana."

I shake my head. "I'm not so sure. I don't know how to do the baby thing. Fuck, I barely figured out the four-year-old thing."

She chuckles and pulls back, grinning at me, then motions into the café. "You have a lot of support, and everyone's super excited to have another Hawke baby."

I nod. "I know, but still...I'm going to fuck up a lot of things."

"You *definitely* are, but that's okay. I sure as hell did. And Viviana turned out okay."

I drag her off her chair and onto my lap, burying my face against her neck. "You did an amazing job with her. I couldn't imagine trying to raise a child with Cutter around. Not to mention your mother."

A shudder she must feel rolls through me.

She laughs and wraps her arms around my neck. "She isn't that bad."

I raise a brow at her. "Are you kidding? Your mother's fucking terrifying. People say your dad is the one to watch out for, but it's definitely Valentina."

"Well, she didn't get her position by being a docile pussycat, did she?"

"No, she certainly didn't."

The door opens across the street, and Luca steps out, checking both directions before he hustles across the street toward us, wearing dress slacks and a blue button-down shirt and looking every bit the mafia don he used to be. "Hey, guys. Sorry I'm late."

I smile up at him. "No problem. Where's Byron? I thought he was coming with you?"

He runs a hand through his salt and pepper hair. "He had to take care of something at the club but said he'll be over in a few minutes."

I motion up to the condo. "Any chance your son is coming down?"

Luca's smile fades as he looks back to the window. Jude appears, his blond hair flopping over his face as he stares down at us, arms crossed over his chest.

"He's busy."

I snort. "Yeah, he looks really busy."

Luca gives me a reproachful look. "You really need to go easier on him. He's been through a lot."

"We all have, and yet...we're all here as a family celebrating."

His eyebrows shoot up. "What are we celebrating?"

I move my hand away from Jack's belly and point to it. "Our son."

A giant grin spreads across his face. He reaches forward, shakes my hand, then plants a kiss on Jack's cheek. "*Congratulazioni, mamma. Sono così felice per te.*"

She smiles at him. "*Grazie.*"

A roar of laughter comes from inside the café, and Luca glances up.

"I'm going to go in and say hi to everybody." He opens the door, the bell ringing above him, then turns back. "If you two need anything, you know all you need to do is ask."

Coming from him, that offer really means something. He may be happily retired from the "life," but Roselli was right— Luca has a lot of friends and connections. People who can make things happen. Though, I plan to stay as far away from any of them as possible. I don't want to risk unraveling the "peace" we have back with Roselli since we eliminated Satriano.

Viviana races over with Fluffy in her arms. "Mommy, Daddy, I think Fluffy's hungry."

I narrow my eyes on the aptly named fluffy white ball of fur. "Why do you say that?"

"Because she just tried to bite my hand."

I bark out a laugh. "Maybe she bit your hand because you were trying to make her dance with you."

Vivi scowls again, and I pull her up onto her mom's lap—content to have both of my girls settled on mine.

"I don't think so, Daddy."

"Okay, sweetie. We'll make sure she's not hungry." I lean in and brush my lips against Jack's ears. "But I am. I know exactly what I want to eat when we get home."

Her mouth falls open, and she turns to look at me and glances down at Viviana and back up. "That silver tongue of yours, Counselor...it's going to get you into a lot of trouble."

It already has.

But I wouldn't trade this type of trouble for anything in the world.

Being a Hawke comes with a million complications and expectations that can weigh you down and suffocate you, but it also brings something immeasurable—love.

JUDE

SOMETIMES, I hate being a Hawke...

Want more Isaac and Jack?

Click here to grab an exclusive bonus epilogue!
Ruthless Hawke bonus epilogue: https://BookHip.com/QCARRZH

Did you miss where it all began? Grab *Night Hawke*, the free prequel featuring Isaac and Jack: *books2read.com/NightHawke*

Get the next book in The Hawke Family Second Generation Series!

Jude and Angelina's story in *Reticent Hawke* here: books2read. com/ReticentHawke

NOTE FROM THE AUTHOR

Thank you for reading Isaac and Jack's story. This book has been a long time coming and brings together so many threads. Not only is Isaac the first in the second generation of the Hawke Family, but Giacomina is also the start of the second generation of my Inland Seas Series and Deadliest Sin Series (two interconnecting series that take place in Chicago).

Cutter and Valentina's story can be found in *Rogue Wave*, the second book in The Inland Seas Series about modern pirates who work for the Chicago mob. (However, I do recommend starting with book one in the series, *Squall Line*, so you don't miss any important backstory). Their story continues in the other Inland Seas books and in The Deadliest Sin Series (that has overlapping plots and timelines).

From the moment Isaac was born in the original Hawke Series and Giacomina was born in The Deadliest Sin Series, I knew I wanted these two worlds to cross, and that they'd be perfect for each other.

I also knew I wanted Giacomina to have epilepsy.

Millions of people live with epilepsy and other types of

seizure disorders, and many are treated differently because of their conditions.

Obviously, Jack's parents had *other* reasons to fear for her safety beside her medical condition, but the way they tried to prevent her from living her life out of fear was never anything Jack agreed with. She wasn't going to let her epilepsy stop her from having what she wanted—freedom, a real life with school, friends, a relationship. That's what leads her to Isaac aka "Nolan" in the prequel *Night Hawke* (free and available now) and sets up the story here in *Ruthless Hawke*.

After speaking with several friends who have epilepsy and learning details of their experiences, I knew I wanted Jack to be the kind of woman who never lets it get in her way and won't stop living. There is no "one" experience with epilepsy, and I've done my best through extensive research and discussions with friends about their personal experiences to show Jack's journey in a positive way, while also staying realistic.

I hope you loved this story as much as I do.

Gwyn

ACKNOWLEDGMENTS

Thank you to everyone who helped bring the second generation of my favorite family to life! Christy, Renee, Stephie, and Caoimhe - I could never do it without you!

A special thanks to Sarah Shannon and Megan Jones for sharing their personal experiences and beta reading Ruthless Hawke to help make sure it shines!

I am so excited to be back in the Hawke world.

ABOUT THE AUTHOR

Gwyn McNamee is an attorney, writer, wife, and mother (to one human baby and two fur babies). Originally from the Midwest, Gwyn relocated to her husband's home town of Las Vegas in 2015 and is enjoying her respite from the cold and snow. Gwyn has been writing down her crazy stories and ideas for years and finally decided to share them with the world. She loves to write stories with a bit of suspense and action mingled with romance and heat.

When she isn't either writing or voraciously devouring any books she can get her hands on, Gwyn is busy adding to her tattoo collection, golfing, and stirring up trouble with her perfect mix of sweetness and sarcasm (usually while wearing heels).

Gwyn loves to hear from her readers. Here is where you can find her:

Website: http://www.gwynmcnamee.com/

Facebook: https://www.facebook.com/AuthorGwynMcNamee/

FB Reader Group: https://www.facebook.com/groups/1667380963540655/

Newsletter: www.gwynmcnamee.com/newsletter

Twitter: https://twitter.com/GwynMcNamee

Instagram: https://www.instagram.com/gwynmcnamee

Bookbub: https://www.bookbub.com/authors/gwynmcnamee

OTHER WORKS BY GWYN MCNAMEE

Billionaires of New Orleans:

The Hawke Family Series

Savage Collision (The Hawke Family - Book One)

He's everything she didn't know she wanted. She's everything he thought he could never have.

The last thing I expect when I walk into The Hawkeye Club is to fall head over heels in lust. It's supposed to be a rescue mission. I have to get my baby sister off the pole, into some clothes, and out of the grasp of the pussy peddler who somehow manipulated her into stripping. But the moment I see Savage Hawke and verbally spar with him, my ability to remain rational flies out the window and my libido takes center stage. I've never wanted a relationship—my time is better spent focusing on taking down the scum running this city—but what I want and what I need are apparently two different things.

Danika Eriksson storms into my office in her high heels and on her high horse. Her holier-than-thou attitude and accusations should offend me, but instead, I can't get her out of my head or my heart. Her incomparable drive, take-no prisoners attitude, and blatant honesty captivate me and hold me prisoner. I should steer clear, but my self-preservation instinct is apparently dead—which is exactly what our relationship will be once she knows everything. It's only a matter of time.

The truth doesn't always set you free. Sometimes, it just royally screws you.

AVAILABLE AT ALL RETAILERS:

Tortured Skye (The Hawke Family - Book Two)
She's always been off-limits. He's always just out of reach.

Falling in love with Gabe Anderson was as easy as breathing. Fighting my feelings for my brother's best friend was agonizingly hard. I never imagined giving in to my desire for him would cause such a destructive ripple effect. That kiss was my grasp at a lifeline—something, anything to hold me steady in my crumbling life. Now, I have to suffer with the fallout while trying to convince him it's all worth the consequences.

Guilt overwhelms me—over what I've done, the lives I've taken, and more than anything, over my feelings for Skye Hawke. Craving my best friend's little sister is insanely self-destructive. It never should have happened, but since the moment she kissed me, I haven't been able to get her out of my mind. If I take what I want, I risk losing everything. If I don't, I'll lose her and a piece of myself. The raging storm threatening to rain down on the city is nothing compared to the one that will come from my decision.

Love can be torture, but sometimes, love is the only thing that can save you.
AVAILABLE AT ALL RETAILERS:
Books2read.com/Tortured-Skye

Stone Sober (The Hawke Family - Book Three)
She's innocent and sweet. He's dark and depraved.

Stone Hawke is precisely the kind of man women are warned about—handsome, intelligent, arrogant, and intricately entangled with some dangerous people. I should stay away, but he manages to strip my soul bare with just a look and dominates my thoughts. Bad decisions are in my past. My life is (mostly) on track, even if it is no longer the one to medical school. I can't allow myself to cave to the fierce pull and ardent attraction I feel toward the youngest Hawke.

Nora Eriksson is off-limits, and not just because she's my brother's employee and sister-in-law. Despite the fact she's stripping at The Hawkeye Club, she has an innocent and pure heart. Normally, the only thing that appeals to me about innocence is the opportunity to taint it. But not when it comes to Nora. I can't expose her to the filth permeating my life. There are too many things I can't control, things completely out of my hands. She doesn't deserve any of it, but the power she holds over me is stronger than any addiction.

The hardest battles we fight are often with ourselves, but only through defeating our own demons can we find true peace.

AVAILABLE AT ALL RETAILERS:

books2read.com/StoneSober

Building Storm (The Hawke Family - Book Four)

She hasn't been living. He's looking for a way to forget it all.

My life went up in flames. All I'm left with is my daughter and ashes. The simple act of breathing is so excruciating, there are days I wish I could stop altogether. So I have no business being at the party, and I definitely shouldn't be in the arms of the handsome stranger. When his lips meet mine, he breathes life into me for the first time since the day the inferno disintegrated my world. But loving again isn't in the cards, and there are even greater dangers to face than trying to keep Landon McCabe out of my heart.

Running is my only option. I have to get away from Chicago and the betrayal that shattered my world. I need a new life-one without attachments. The vibrancy of New Orleans convinces me it's possible to start over. Yet in all the excitement of a new city, it's Storm Hawke's dark, sad beauty that draws me in. She isn't looking for love, and we both need a hot, sweaty release without feelings getting involved. But even the best laid plans fail, and life can leave you burned.

Love can build, and love can destroy. But in the end, love is what raises you from the ashes.

AVAILABLE AT ALL RETAILERS:

books2read.com/BuildingStorm

Tainted Saint (The Hawke Family - Book Five)

He's searching for absolution. She wants her happily ever after.

Solomon Clarke goes by Saint, though he's anything but. After lusting for him from afar, the masquerade party affords me the anonymity to pursue that attraction without worrying about the fall-out of hooking-up with the bouncer from the Hawkeye Club. From the second he lays his eyes and hands on me, I'm helpless to resist him. Even burying myself in a dangerous investigation can't erase the memory of our combustible connection and one night together. The only problem... he has no idea who I am.

Caroline Brooks thinks I don't see her watching me, the way her eyes rake over me with appreciation. But I've noticed, and the party is the perfect opportunity to unleash the desire I've kept reined in for so damn long. It also sets off a series of events no one sees coming. Events that leave those I love hurting because of my failures. While the guilt eats away at my soul, Caroline continues to weigh on my heart. That woman may be the death of me, but oh, what a way to go.

Life isn't always clean, and sometimes, it takes a saint to do the dirty work.

AVAILABLE AT ALL RETAILERS:

books2read.com/TaintedSaint

Steele Resolve (The Hawke Family - Book Six)

For one man, power is king. For the other, loyalty reigns.

Mob boss Luca "Steele" Abello isn't just dangerous—he's lethal. A master manipulator, liar, and user, no one should trust a word that comes out of his mouth. Yet, I can't get him out of my head. The time we spent together before I knew his true identity is seared into my brain. His touch. His voice. They haunt my every waking hour and occupy my dreams. So does my guilt. I'm literally sleeping with the enemy and betraying the only family I've ever had. When I come clean, it will be the end of me.

Byron Harris is a distraction I can't afford. I never should have let it go beyond that first night, but I couldn't stay away. Even when I learned who he was, when the *only* option was to end things, I kept going back, risking his life and mine to continue our indiscretion. The truth of what I am could get us both killed, but being with the man who's such an integral part of the Hawke family is even more terrifying. The only people I've ever cared about are on opposing sides, and I'm the rift that could end their friendship forever.

Love is a battlefield isn't just a saying. For some, it's a reality.

AVAILABLE AT ALL RETAILERS:

books2read.com/SteeleResolve

You can find information on the rest of Gwyn's books on her website:

www.gwynmcnamee.com

www.ingramcontent.com/pod-product-compliance
Lightning Source LLC
Chambersburg PA
CBHW072023020726
47501CB00006B/1934